Knight in Highland Armor

Highland Dynasty Series ~ Book One

by

Amy Jarecki

Rapture Books

Copyright © 2015, Amy Jarecki

Jarecki, Amy
Knight in Highland Armor

ISBN: 978-1502390295
First Release: January, 2015

Book Cover Design by: Kim Killion

To Maria McIntyre.

Chapter One

Dunstaffnage Castle, Firth of Lorn, Scotland, 29ᵗʰ August, 1455

The cries of the motherless baby shrieked through the passageway and filled his chamber. Seated at the round table beside an immense hearth, Colin cradled his head in his hands. He could do nothing to stop his newborn son's cries. Yes, he, the feared Black Knight of Rome, had also been powerless to prevent Jonet's death. He'd now lost two wives. The first to the sweat, and last night, his dearest Jonet's lifeblood drained into the mattress while baby Duncan suckled at her breast.

The relentless high-pitched screams gnawed at Colin's insides. He'd stood beside his wife while her face turned from rosy to blue. It happened so fast, the midwife had little time to react. Colin had barreled through the stone corridors, shouting orders. He'd sent for the physician, though by the time the black-robed man arrived, Jonet had passed.

Colin hated his weakness. His heart stuck in his throat. His eyes burned with unshed tears. Why did death follow him like a shadow? He'd seen more than his fill. A Knight of the Order of St. John, a Hospitaller, Colin had seen unimaginable brutality and death in his seven and twenty years. The war against the enemies of Christendom had earned him the reputation of Black Colin, a knight feared throughout the Holy Land and beyond.

He combed his fingers through his hair. A dark cloud of despair filled his insides. Jonet was his beloved. Beautiful, with luscious raven hair and a winsome smile, she embodied his ideal of femininity.

He bit his fist and forced back his urge to weep. He had not shed a tear since the age of seven. By God, he would not show weakness now, not even while sitting alone in his dimly lit chamber.

Colin's gaze dropped to the missive lying open on the table. He steadied his hand, picked it up, and reread the critical request delivered this morn.

…Your brothers continue to fight in your absence. Since Constantinople fell to the Turks, the infidel Muslims have increased their efforts, raiding Rhodes and surrounding islands. Though I understand your duty to your family following the death of your father, the esteemed and venerated Lord of Argyll, we desperately need your leadership and your army forthwith.

I fear our stronghold at Rhodes and indeed our Order will fall if we cannot marshal our efforts and drive our enemies out of Christendom once and for all.

I respectfully appeal for your return to Rome for a third term, for once a Knight Hospitaller, you are bound to the Order for life.

Dutifully, your brother in Christ,

Jacques de Milly, Grand Master, The Order of St. John

Colin slapped the missive onto the table and shoved back his chair. The crying intensified. He stood and paced, clenching his fists. So many things demanded his attention. He'd executed not a one with a modicum of success. After the death of his father, his first priority was to see his nephew, the new Lord Argyll, established in his lofty role. Until order on that side of the family was restored, he'd overseen the obedience of the crofters who paid rents. Fortunately, with England embroiled in civil war, threats to the Campbell dynasty were minimal— merely feuding clans and marauding outlaws.

The crying stopped. Thank God. At last he could think clearly. Wallowing in his own self-pity would serve no one, and most certainly would not hasten his voyage back to Rome. His nephew had assumed his role of Lord Argyll with little resistance. At least that significant hurdle had been surmounted.

A light tap disturbed his misery.

Colin faced the heavy oak door. "Come in."

Effie, the woman who'd nursed him as a babe, now in charge of Duncan's care, entered and curtseyed. "The wet nurse has arrived, m'lord."

"I assumed the same, given the sudden quiet."

Sadness filled her eyes. "He's a strong lad."

He scratched the two days of stubble peppering his face. "Aye, if his lungs are any indication, he'll become a feared knight of Christendom."

"Following in his father's footsteps, no doubt."

Colin forced a smile, though the ache in his heart made the effort near impossible.

Since the death of his ma, his old nursemaid had played the part of a mother figure, though his reliance on her advice had waned considerably after his marriage to Jonet and tours of duty for Rome. Effie stepped further into the room. "You look troubled, m'lord."

Hot ire flared up the back of his neck. What did she expect, a man hewn of iron? He met her concerned gaze and inhaled. Of course, Effie meant well. "I've received a missive from Rome requesting another crusade."

"No." Effie clasped her hands to her chest. "Duncan needs you…"

"My son needs a mother," Colin snapped. "A bairn has no place in a knight's arms."

Effie steepled her fingers to her lips. "Have you a woman in mind? And what about your castle? The curtain wall has only begun to take shape now that you've returned. Someone must manage the project and complete the keep."

Colin fisted his hips. "I do not need you to inform me of my responsibilities."

She bowed her head obsequiously. "Yes, m'lord." Then, casting aside her deference, she eyed him like she did when he was a lad. "Merely thinking of your comfort, Colin."

He threw up his hands. "The master mason can oversee."

"In my opinion, that man has not proved his skill in managing the labor."

"Did I ask your opinion?"

Effie didn't bother to bow this time. "M'lord." She held up her palms. "These hands washed your noble arse. I do believe that fact has given me the right to look after you in adulthood, especially since there is no other living elder to do so."

Colin ground his teeth and rolled his gaze to the ornate relief on the ceiling.

Effie moved in and placed a hand on his forearm. She'd made the gesture countless times before, but it soothed him directly. He blinked and thought of his mother. He longed for the touch of another human being after a sleepless night wallowing in the sorrow of his plight. He shook his self-pitying thoughts from his head. "I will not shirk my responsibilities before I go. I shall pen a missive to the grand master explaining I will be detained. Then I'll ask the king for assistance in finding a mother for Duncan." He cupped Effie's weathered face in his palm. "Does that meet with your approval, matron?"

"Yes, if you must go at all. My stars, Colin, you've already served in two crusades. Surely the Hospitallers can find a replacement."

"Aye, but I have experience. A man who's faced battle before is worth ten who have not."

After Effie took her leave, he resumed his seat at the table. Penning the missive to Jacques de Milly was easy. The missive to the king, however, took a great deal more thought. Colin would prefer to find his own match, but this time, the woman would not be for him. Colin wanted nothing more to do with the fairer sex. Aside from his duty to procreate, he could not allow his heart to care for a woman as it had for Jonet *and* Mariot before her. Loving a woman carried great risk. They were frail creatures, and losing one brought more pain than losing a whole contingent of men on the battlefield.

He dipped his quill into the black ink.

Most honorable and revered King James II,

I desire to open this correspondence by expressing my gratitude with your grant of lands following my meager role in quelling the Douglas uprising. The generosity of Your Royal Highness extends beyond anything I could have expected or hoped for.

It is with a heavy heart that I must request assistance from your apostolic majesty. Word of my beloved Jonet's death may have already reached Your Highness. Most unfortunately, my infant son has been left without a mother. As you are aware, the Order of St. John is in dire need of my services in the war for Christendom, though I cannot in good conscience return to Rome without a mother for my heir.

Therefore, I must prevail upon you and your most noble Queen to assist me in finding a suitable stepmother for my son. Having

been abroad a great deal, together with my duties in support of
Scotland, I am left with no prospects for marriage.
I remain your most humble servant in Christ,
Colin Campbell, Lord of Glenorchy

Resting the quill in the silver stand, he sanded the parchment to dry the ink and then reread the missive. Colin hoped his mention of the Douglas uprising wasn't too presumptuous, though it would remind the king of the value of his services. He folded the missive and held a red wax wafer to the candle's flame. After dripping a substantial glob, he sealed it with his ring—the crest of Glenorchy.

Indeed, Colin's role in the uprising had been anything but meager. That mattered not. He needed a wife, and he needed her posthaste. His letter clearly established the fact he wanted a mother for Duncan more than a woman with whom he would share a bed. Colin shuddered. He would have nothing to do with a wife. Not now. Not ever again.

Chapter Two

Dunalasdair Castle, Loch Rannoch, 16ᵗʰ September, 1455

Margaret was in her father's solar recording figures in his book of accounts when the approach of hoof beats roused her from calculating a list of sums. Margaret rarely erred when it came to numbers, a point of fact long overlooked by her father, Lord Robertson, Chieftain and Baron of Struan—until the day she glanced over his shoulder, calculated the math in her head and recited the figures flawlessly.

Ever since, she'd been placed in charge of checking the factor's figures. A necessary responsibility that ensured no one ever cheated her father.

By the racket clamoring from below, there were more than a few horses approaching. Margaret rested her quill in the ornate wooden holder and dashed to the window. A crisp breeze blew in off the deep blue waters of Loch Rannoch. Margaret preferred natural light, and would endure a mild chill to have it. Only in the dead of winter did she pull the thick furs over the castle windows.

Gazing to the courtyard below, Margaret's heart skipped a beat. It wasn't often the king's men paid the stronghold of Dunalasdair a visit. No mistaking it, these men wore red tunics with the bright yellow lion rampant over their armor. Something important was afoot.

She craned her neck and leaned further out the narrow window. Mounted on large warhorses, the soldiers appeared incredibly virile. Unfortunate their helms completely covered their faces from her viewpoint. She'd like to glimpse a handsome new face.

Father marched down the courtyard steps and accepted a missive from the leader. Margaret prayed it contained good news.

Perhaps Father would invite the soldiers in for refreshment before they made their return journey. Mayhap they would even stay the night. Surely there would be music in the great hall, and with so many men, it would be necessary to dance with each one to ensure no guest was omitted from the festivities. Margaret clapped with excitement.

The one thing she enjoyed more than helping her father with the estate's affairs was dancing. Would the king's men prefer country or court dances? Most likely the slower court dances would be to their taste, though Margaret's favorite was lively country dancing. She'd been to court not too long ago, where she learned the latest grand dances. They were very stately, of course—and somewhat seductive. She turned from the window and pictured an imaginary courtier—Lord Forbes, the man she'd met at court and with whom, she suspected, her father was secretly negotiating the terms of her betrothal. At two and twenty, the time for her to wed was nigh.

When the dashing and most imaginary Lord Forbes asked her to dance, she fanned herself. "Me? Why yes." Craning her neck to meet his gaze, she feigned an appropriate giggle. "I'd love to."

Margaret curtseyed and envisioned him leading her to the line of dancers. She performed the steps, swinging as if her partner had locked her elbow, her skirts swishing along his powerful calves, neatly wrapped with woolen hose. Margaret adored the new style of men's doublets, so short, a fashionably dressed man's hose provided much to be admired—right up to his well-muscled behind.

Margaret chuckled at her errant thoughts and continued her dance, spinning across the solar. Oh how mortified her mother would be to know she so admired the opposite sex. Of course, she had very little experience with them, aside from constant needling by her older brothers, and the occasional morning spent watching the guard spar in the courtyard.

Margaret's brown locks swished against her back when she gaily skipped toward her imaginary Lord Forbes.

The solar door opened.

With a cringe, she stopped midstride. "Father." The pitch of her voice shot up. "I didn't expect…"

He held up a folded piece of parchment. "I've a missive from the king."

Heat burned her cheeks. She didn't care for her father to catch her in a pantomime daydream. "Aye. I saw his men. Are you required at court?"

He cleared his throat and looked not to Margaret, but at the missive in his hand. "Of sorts. Please retire to your chamber. I've sent for your mother. I must speak to her at once."

Margaret stepped toward him. "Whatever is the matter?"

"Do as I say." He pointed to the door. "We shall attend you shortly."

Margaret bowed her head and offered a clipped curtsey. "Very well."

She hurried up the winding stairwell and down the passageway to her chamber. Once inside, she raced to the window. The soldiers below were accepting food from

Cook. She slinked away, her shoulders drooped. Obviously they wouldn't be staying.

What had father meant by *of sorts*? Were they going to court or not? Where would the king be this time? Edinburgh Castle, Holyrood, Stirling Palace, Linlithgow?

A stone dropped to the pit of Margaret's stomach. Was Scotland at war? Surely Da hadn't been called into service. At seven and fifty, Lord Struan had already carried the torch for Scotland, and on numerous occasions.

Margaret paced, her mind rife with concern. The king must know Da was too old to wield a sword. A turn on the battlefield would kill him for certain. Surely her brothers would be able to stand in his place...but then perhaps the king needed Lord Struan as a dignitary. Perhaps Da was required abroad as an ambassador.

By the time Margaret heard the rap on her door, she'd convinced herself Father would be Scotland's Ambassador to France, and she'd find her husband in the wonderfully scandalous and delightfully stylish French court.

She grinned broadly when her parents entered. They maintained their serious countenances, though Margaret refused to see it as a bad sign when they did not return her smile. Her parents often refrained from displaying their emotion—a tactic she'd practiced on her brothers without much success.

"The news from the king concerned *you*, Margaret." Da was unusually somber.

Surprised King James would pay her two thoughts, Margaret's breath caught. "Me?"

Mother's wimple billowed as she stepped in and took Margaret's hand. "We must set to work at once."

Margaret gaped at her father over Ma's shoulder. "My presence at court has been requested?"

Da cleared his throat. "The king has asked for your hand in marriage."

"*My* hand?" Tears stung her eyes. "Is our queen dead?"

Father held up his palms and shook them. "No, no. The king has requested you marry one of the noblemen."

"A nobleman?" She glanced between her parents. "'Tis not Lord Forbes, is it?"

"No, my dear." Ma frowned at Da. That couldn't be a good sign. "Oh, just out with it, Robert."

"Very well." Father cleared his throat. "You shall wed Colin Campbell, Lord of Glenorchy, and venerated Knight of the Order of St. John."

Margaret stared at her father. She forgot to blink, and her mouth must also have been hanging open, because her tongue went dry. "You mean to say I am betrothed to *Black Colin*? The Black Colin of Rome? Famed Black Colin who crushed the Douglases?"

Da tugged on his beard like he did when attempting to come up with a suitable reply. "Aye, but you're forgetting he fights the enemies of Christendom. Without men like he, our God would not reign supreme."

Margaret doubted the news of the Douglas demise had yet to reach any part of Scotland. "Without men like he, we'd be sleeping soundly at night."

Da held up a finger. "Lord Douglas threatened the king."

Margaret crossed her arms. "Lord Douglas was murdered by the king, and you know it."

"Stop." Mother stepped in and grasped Margaret's shoulders. "We cannot renege on a royal order. You *will* travel to Stirling Palace and marry Lord Campbell. He's recently lost his wife and needs a mother for his infant son. You shall swallow your pride and perform your duty for Scotland *and* Christendom."

"I shall become a stepmother?" Of course, Margaret wanted to marry, but no young woman in her right mind wanted to marry a complete stranger who'd already—and recently—fathered a child.

Da painted on one of his feigned smiles. "I've met Campbell. He's not as bad as his reputation might suggest."

Margaret was in no way convinced. *Black Colin?* Would he beat her and keep her locked in a tower with iron branks holding her tongue?

Mother gestured toward Margaret's collection of trunks. "I've already sent for Master Tailor. There's scarcely enough time. We leave in a sennight."

Margaret watched her parents take their leave. Questions swarmed in her head. *Black Colin? Is he grey with age? Why on earth would the king choose me out of all the eligible women in Scotland? Does he despise me? But then, the king would see this as an honor. The king has been most kind to the Lord of Glenorchy.*

Margaret dropped onto the bed, completely numb. Her life was about to end.

Chapter Three

Kilchurn Building Site, 30th September, 1455.

A half-day's ride from Dunstaffnage, Colin walked beside his nephew, Lord Argyll. Both men shared the same name, thus Lord Glenorchy preferred to use the younger man's title. When his brother died, Colin had fostered Argyll until the lad attained his majority of one and twenty. He looked upon his nephew, only five years his younger, with pride. The lad's impressive height matched his own. Inheriting his brother's dark hair, he'd grown into a powerful and fearsome lord.

Neither man had broken their fast as they stood shoulder to shoulder in their quilted doublets and watched the mist rise from the depths of Loch Awe.

Colin inhaled the crisp autumn air. "I shall never tire of this site."

"'Tis peaceful." Argyll glanced over his shoulder at the newly completed curtain wall. "Do you ever think you'll be finished?"

"Bloody oath, I will be. I've no business maintaining my household at Dunstaffnage." Colin spread his arms wide. "Not when I am lord over these magnificent lands. Besides, every nobleman needs a castle." A muscle above his eye twitched. "If matters would ever quiet down."

Since Jonet's death, getting out of bed each morning had become a chore.

"Honestly, I'm surprised your mason hasn't moved along faster. How long has it been since you commissioned him?"

"I was fighting for Rome—we both were when my father made the appointment."

"Four years, then?"

Colin shrugged. "Near enough."

Argyll arched a single brow. "Four years and only the curtain wall finished? What are you paying him?"

"Too much." The mist now hung above the loch and refused to budge, just like the grey stone walls that surrounded...nothing. Colin growled. "'Tis time to reestablish Mr. Elliot's priorities."

Speaking of the master mason, Tom Elliot marched their way, tools swinging from a sturdy leather belt. "Lord Glenorchy." He bowed and nodded to Argyll. "M'lord. When did you arrive?"

"Last eve, of course." Colin fisted his hips. He never traveled without a contingent of men. Surely Elliot would have heard them arrive, the horses clomping into the wooden stable he used on his infrequent trips to Glen Orchy. "I must express my concern at your lack of progress on my tower house. How is a man to direct the affairs of his lands if he has no castle from which to do so?"

Elliot flushed red above his scraggly brown beard. "Forgive me, m'lord. But the labor situation has been most disagreeable."

"Labor? With people starving in Scotland's cities, you mean to tell me you cannot find a decent hand?"

"No, m'lord. With every step forward, we take a step back—sometimes we arise in the morning to see our work vandalized."

The back of Colin's neck burned. "Vandals? And why am I only hearing of this now?"

"I've sent repeated missives, m'lord."

Colin grimaced. The situation became direr with Elliot's every word. Not a single missive had reached him. "And who *are* these vandals?"

Elliot's eyes darted around the site. He stepped closer. "The MacGregors, m'lord."

Ballocks. Colin thought he'd appeased the squatting clan, paying them off years ago. For the love of God, they'd even sworn fealty to him. "Have you hanged anyone—made an example of a slippery cur?"

"No, m'lord. No one has been caught in the act. I think they're all conspiring between themselves." Elliot shook his head. "Besides, they believe these lands belong to them."

Argyll crossed his arms. "The king would differ with that. These are chartered Campbell lands."

Colin held up a palm to silence his nephew. There would be no question of his rightful ownership. "All rebellious actions must cease immediately. Elliot, in appointing you master mason, you have my seal of approval to deal with any lawlessness with a firm hand." Colin shook his finger under the mason's nose. "I will increase the guard at once. However, if I do not see progress by my next visit, I'll have no choice but to seek out another, more enterprising mason. I want my keep completed within the year."

"But sir, winter's near upon us."

"And I expect you work through the winter."

"'Tis madness. Do you want the mortar to crack? I was just about to say we need to start mudding up the walls in preparation for the freeze. One cannot build with frozen ground and mortar. Your castle will crumble to the ground."

Colin ground his back molars. Must everything be difficult? "It is your responsibility to see the castle is completed within the year—two at most—without structural issues. I will see to it you have the men and materials you need to take the project to completion. You, sir, will work day and night come spring if necessary."

Mr. Elliot's lips formed a thin line. If Colin had another option, he'd fire the mason on the spot, but skilled stonemasons were scarce in the Highlands.

Horses approached at a rapid trot.

"King's men," Argyll said.

Colin didn't miss the relief that crossed Tom Elliot's face. Yes, the approach of soldiers was a distraction, but Colin would not forget his threats. He grasped Tom's arm and squeezed. "You shall continue building until All Hallows Day. I *will* see marked progress, or you shall not return to Kilchurn come spring."

With a nod, Elliot tugged his arm away and headed toward his laborers.

The king's man-at-arms dismounted and marched up to Colin with purpose. "Lord Campbell?"

"Aye?" Colin and Argyll said simultaneously.

The soldier's flustered gaze darted between them. "Black Colin of Rome?"

It wasn't always a bad thing to have an unsavory reputation. At the very least, it commanded respect. Colin dipped his head. "'Tis I."

The man reached inside his cloak. "I've a missive from the king."

Colin accepted the folded velum and ran his thumb under the seal.

"What is it?" Argyll asked before Colin had a chance to read the first word.

Colin shot him a sharp glare and focused on the scrolling penmanship. He thought he'd be relieved when he read the news a match had been made. But Colin's palms perspired. He'd tried to push aside the fact he had asked for a flesh-and-blood woman to move in and share his home—mostly to raise his son. He arched his brow and met Argyll's inquisitive stare. "Do you know of Lord Struan's daughter, Margaret Robinson?"

Argyll, at two and twenty, was still unmarried. Perhaps he'd seen the lass at court. But his nephew shook his head. "I cannot say I've met her, though Lord Struan is a good man."

"Aye, that he is."

"Has the king made a match, then?"

Colin folded the missive and slipped it into the leather pouch on his belt. "Our sovereign has found a stepmother for Duncan. We must away to Stirling. I'll need to spirit her back to Dunstaffnage before I leave for Rome."

Argyll didn't budge. "Wait a moment. You're planning to wed a woman you haven't met because Duncan needs a mother? You're not the type of man to accept simply *anyone*."

"How do you suggest I proceed, given the urgent message from the grand master? I've no desire to marry, but my son must be raised as a proper nobleman—and only another member of the nobility will suit."

Colin hated it when Argyll studied him with wide eyes, as if he hadn't uttered a sensible word. "And what do you assume will be Miss Margaret's reaction to your pragmatic solution for Duncan's upbringing?"

Colin shoved his nephew in the shoulder. "Love, cherish and *obey*. Remember that when you marry. *Obey* is the most important word in the whole ceremony."

"But it's in Latin."

"Aye—however, it carries no less meaning."

***

Margaret had only been to Stirling Palace once, and that had been a joyous occasion. Only a year ago, she'd met Lord Forbes at the baptism of the king's third child, Alexander Stewart. Though their introduction had been brief, she'd found Forbes handsome. But her hopes had been dashed for good. Before they departed Loch Rannoch, Father informed the backstabbing lord was betrothed to an English woman.

No white knight would come to her rescue.

Along the two-day journey south, she became ill—that was what she told herself. First, she considered running away, racing her mare into the forest and hiding—*amongst the outlaws?* Not the most practical idea she'd come up with.

She'd pleaded with her parents until they could hear no more. The further the procession rode from Loch Rannoch, the more she grew short of breath. At one point she actually swooned. The cadence of the hooves on the stony trail tolled the knell of doom. With nothing to do but sit her horse and stare boldly ahead as if she were Joan of Arc, she rode in a state of paralyzed abandon.

Perhaps the Black Knight desired a stalwart woman who was willing to meet her fate head-on.

Late afternoon on the second day of their journey, in the distance, the palace loomed atop a cliff, presiding over the countryside like a volcano ready to erupt. Margaret's palms slipped on her reins. She hated being out of control of things that concerned her. *I swear on everything that's holy, I'll never be used as a pawn again.*

Though her father led the procession at a steady walk, they arrived at the colossal palace far too quickly.

Shod hooves clambered over the timber bridge. Approaching the central triplet gatehouse, Margaret's mouth grew dry. Capped with crenelated wall-walks and tall, conical roofs with a drum tower at each corner, there would be no escape. The chains of the portcullis bellowed and creaked as the heavy gate rose to welcome them through the great arch emblazoned with the lion rampant of royalty.

Trumpets announced their arrival in the courtyard. Before she could dismount, a swarm of servants surrounded them. A groom held her horse and another placed a mounting block beside her mare and offered his hand.

A chambermaid grasped her other elbow. "This way, m'lady. We're all agog with the wedding. The queen has appointed you with the finest chamber in the White Tower."

"Thank you," Margaret mumbled, allowing the maid to pull her through the bustling courtyard into a dimly lit, whitewashed square tower. Her feet moved, but she felt as if she were floating. All that lay ahead was a bad dream. Certainly, she must wake soon.

***

At least they'd allowed Margaret the evening to become accustomed to her surroundings. The only word to describe her chamber was ornate. The ceiling frieze alone must have cost a fortune. A deep forest green, embossed with gold leaf, the opulence numbed her mind. Rich tapestries of purple, green and burgundy shrouded the walls, each one woven with gold thread.

She'd slept in a four-poster bed with purple velvet curtains. Unfortunately, she couldn't enjoy the luxury. In all honesty, this room stifled her breathing like the wooden slats sewn into her new gowns.

Ever since the king's men had visited Dunalasdair Castle, Mother hadn't stopped preparing for the fast-approaching wedding. The morning's doting had driven Margaret to the brink of insanity. She could handle no more of her mother's endless prattle. Did Ma not understand how nervous she was, how utterly devastated her world had become?

Dressmakers and their assistants filled her chamber, and even now, they sat in every available chair, embroidering and stitching seams with the finest silk thread, all of which must be completed by the morrow.

The tension in the room crept over Margaret's skin and attacked her shoulders, clamping them like a vise. Trepidation of marrying the Black Knight worsened, if that was possible. Every time she closed her eyes, she imagined a grizzly old man snarling at her with yellow teeth and an unkempt beard.

She needed fresh air. "Mother, I should like to visit the fair below the palace grounds. Did you see all the tents? I imagine there are a great many wares on display."

Mother looked up from inspecting a worker's embroidery. "How can you think of traipsing through a muddy fete at a time like this?"

"And why ever not?" Margaret pulled away from the tailor, crossed to the window and drew the furs aside. She craned her neck for a chance to spy the activity. *I need a moment of respite even if I go alone.* "Please, Ma, come with me, just for a little while. I cannot stand being poked and measured for another moment. Master Tailor has it in hand."

The man's bony fingers stopped stitching for a moment. He glanced to Margaret with a thankful smile turning up the corners of his mouth.

It appeared she wasn't the only soul in the room who needed relief. One more minute in this stifling chamber, being prodded, poked and pinned was more than she could bear.

Mother wrung her hands. "I don't know. I should really…"

Margaret grabbed Ma's arm and tugged. "Come. I'll go mad if I remain inside—Black Colin won't want to marry a lunatic. Mayhap you'll find a suitable fur to replace your winter cloak. *Pleeeease*."

Mother smoothed her hands over her white wimple and reached for a woolen mantle. "Very well—but only a quick walk around the grounds, and then straight back. I think 'tis best to keep you hidden from the nosy nobility. Let their eyes behold your beauty on the morrow."

Margaret snatched her green velvet cloak and slipped the hood over her head. She cared not if she was covered—she was escaping this chamber and all the worrisome thoughts that had her innards twisted in knots.

Margaret looped her arm through her mother's as they paraded out Stirling Palace's fortified north gate, with two of her father's guardsmen following at a respectful distance. The throng below hummed. White tents flapped in the breeze with a mass of colorfully costumed nobles and not-so-colorfully dressed commoners. They moved in a web of activity, accompanied by minstrels playing lutes and wooden flutes. Smells of humanity burned her nostrils—how invigorating it was to be out of doors. Everywhere Margaret looked, something was for sale—pigs, fruit and food to her right. Bright textiles, leathers, knives and everything imaginable ahead and to her left.

When she spied a bowl full of red apples, her mouth watered. She hastened to the display. "The fruit looks delicious."

A dirty-faced vendor with brown teeth grinned at her. "Fancy a peck of apples, m'lady?"

"Perhaps." Margaret mulled over the assortment of pears, dates and nutmeats. A young tot peeked out from behind the vendor's cart. His blue eyes sparkled from beneath a layer of dirt. The child's hair was matted, his cheeks sunken. Why, he appeared half starved. Margaret's heart squeezed. She smiled at the child and snapped her gaze to the vendor. "I'd like a half-dozen each, apples, pears and dates, if you please."

The man's grin spread to his ears. "Aye, m'lady. Have ye a basket?"

Margaret bit her lip and glanced back to her mother. In her haste to leave, she hadn't thought to bring one. "Have you a basket for sale? It appears I've left mine behind."

"Honestly," Lady Struan groused in Margaret's ear.

The vendor held up a gnarled finger. "I've just the thing, but I'll have to charge ye a penny."

Mother gasped. "Thievery."

Margaret held up a hand. "'Tis only fair. I should have thought to bring mine."

The man filled the rickety old basket and held it out. "Four pennies, m'lady."

She dug in her leather purse that hung from a cord on her belt, and handed him the coins. "Thank you, sir." Margaret shifted her gaze to the laddie and plucked the largest apple. "This one's for you."

A huge grin lit up the child's face. "Ta." His darling little voice peeped when he accepted the gift with both hands.

Mother grasped her elbow and led her into the throng. "How could you allow that man to take advantage of you so?"

Margaret twisted her arm away. "I did no such thing. Did you see the half-starved child hiding behind the barrow?"

Mother frowned.

"I was simply buying the lad enough food to last through winter. Had I a mind to barter, I would have paid no more than one and a half."

"Thank heavens someone else will be providing your allotment in the future. It pains me to see coin tossed away with such frivolity."

Margaret tightened her grip on the basket handle. She loved her mother dearly, but the woman thought charity was giving alms at Eastertide and that was the end of it. She'd seen plenty of hardship, collecting rents from the estate's crofters. A master with figures, Margaret knew full well her father could support a number of starving commoners without feeling the slightest pinch to his coffers.

Mother led her toward a tent filled with textiles. "Cloth from the east is more worth your coin, my dear."

Margaret sighed. She'd spent the past week up to her eyeballs in cloth, standing for hours on end while the tailor pinned and snipped an entire new wardrobe. Dutifully crossing the grassy aisle, Margaret followed her mother's lead. A juggler caught her attention. Dressed in bright yellow and red with a pointed hat, he tossed three balls high in the air.

A midget, clad in matching costume, held up another ball. "One more, master?"

"Toss it up."

The little man threw it in and the juggler miraculously added it to the pattern of colorful flying balls. Margaret slid the basket over her wrist and clapped her hands. She rarely got to see jesters and players near Loch Rannoch. The juggler's balls spun in a tantalizing circle that appeared to blend into one ring.

Margaret reached into her purse to pluck a farthing when horse hooves pummeled the ground. Looking up, she scarcely had the chance to dash aside. Two riders thundered through the fete at a brisk canter. She tripped over her gown. The fruit flung from her basket as the horses sped past. Margaret crashed into something sturdy and hard. Her hands whipped around it, saving herself from falling. Her hood flew from her head and dropped to her back.

It wasn't until a pair of massive arms encircled her that she realized she'd fallen into a man—a very large, very strong man. She inhaled. The heady and exotic fragrance of cloves laced with a hint of ginger and male toyed with her insides. Struggling to drag her feet beneath her, Margaret made the mistake of grasping him tighter. His back muscles bulged beneath his quilted doublet. Her heart fluttered.

"Forgive me," she uttered breathlessly.

His enormous hands held her shoulders firmly and helped her gain her balance. "Are you all right, m'lady?"

Flustered, Margaret pushed away and smoothed her fingers over the white ribbon encircling her crown. She brushed her fingers down the length of her exposed tresses, cascading over her shoulder to her waist. First, her gaze leveled on his red tunic, with a white cross emblazoned on the center of his very broad chest. Then her eyes drifted to his face, framed by dun-colored curls. Beneath his cap, they shone like silk in the sun, and she wanted to reach up and touch them to see if his hair was actually as soft as it looked.

Dark brown, wide-set eyes gazed upon her with a glint of humor. They were so friendly, her tension immediately eased. His features were undeniably masculine; his bold nose slightly bent toward full lips that grinned, revealing a row of healthy white teeth.

"I…I am unscathed, thank you." Margaret inhaled a stuttered breath and hoped to heaven she wasn't blushing. "Please forgive me."

"There is nothing to forgive. Those lads had no business riding through the fair at full tilt. I shall have a firm word with them."

"I'm sure they are long gone..." Margaret peered up at his feathered ermine cap—a fur only worn by Scottish barons like her father. "...m'lord." She stepped back, taking in the whole picture. She'd seen the square white cross on his tunic somewhere before—it definitely identified him as a knight, though she could not place the order. Unusually tall, he had to be at least eighteen hands—six feet was enormous, especially compared to her five. He wore a stylish doublet of black beneath the sleeveless tunic. His woolen hose were also black, and they clung to his thighs like a second skin. His muscles bulged when he stepped toward her with fashionably pointed shoes.

Mmm. 'Tis said clothes maketh the man.

He bent down and retrieved her basket. "I believe this is yours."

"Thank you." Margaret spotted apples and pears scattered everywhere. "But I'm afraid the fruit I've purchased is ruined."

He frowned and stroked his bold chin. "Most unfortunate. Please allow me to replace it."

"That should not be necessary. I only wished to help a poor man feed his family."

"Most charitable of you, m'lady." He offered a polite bow. "If you no longer require my assistance, I shall be on my way."

"Very well. Should I fall again, I shall simply find another gallant knight to keep me from dousing myself in the mud."

"A lucky man indeed to rescue a lady as bonny as you." He bowed again and tapped his fingers to his hat. "Good day, m'lady."

Margaret swooned, watching him walk away. Broad shoulders supported by a sturdy waist. To her delight, the knight's doublet was short enough to give her a peek at his muscular buttocks. With a sigh, she smacked her lips while the crowd swallowed up the magnificent warrior's form. If only her betrothed could be half as handsome.

"Margaret," Mother called from across the aisle. "Come, I have something to show you."

This time, she looked for racing horses before she set out. God forbid she fall into another knight. And heaven help her. On the morrow, she'd have to look upon such magnificent specimens with disinterested eyes. How on earth would she do that?

Chapter Four

Stirling Palace, 7ᵗʰ October, 1455

Returning from the stables, Colin found Argyll on his way to the castle. "Have you seen her?"

The younger man shook his head. "Nay. I could only come up with a sentry who confirmed she'd arrived with her parents. I'll wager they're keeping her hidden."

"Blast." Though Colin fully intended to go through with the wedding, he would have preferred a report on Margaret's looks from a disinterested party. Nonetheless, on the morrow, he would wed a plain woman who undoubtedly had matronly, child-bearing hips. Duncan would love a mother be her comely or nay.

Argyll regarded Colin's casual dress. "Will you be attending the feast in the great hall?"

"I'd prefer to take my meal in my rooms. Though it would be acceptable for *you* to make acquaintance with Margaret Robinson, I fear it would be awkward to meet her the night before our wedding."

"Aye." Argyll slapped his back. "Her feet might grow cold and she could request a reprieve."

Colin cringed. "That too—at least I shan't give her the opportunity."

A pair of giggling lassies walked past, batting their eyelashes. A muscle in Colin's jaw twitched. Beautiful women seemed to be everywhere at Stirling. He wanted none of it. Soon he'd head home to Kilchurn with his portly wife, and all the sweet-fragranced lasses who flitted their wares around court would be left to their own tantalizing devices.

Argyll headed in the direction of the giggles. "I'll see you on the morrow, then?"

"On the morrow."

***

The following morning, Margaret stood in the center of her chamber holding her arms out to her sides. She'd been in that position so long, she could have sworn the tailor hung two stone weights from her wrists. From the glimpses she could steal in the looking glass across the room, the gown was everything her mother had hoped it would be.

But to Margaret, it was like being outfitted in chains to be paraded in front of the gentry.

The overdress, made of red velvet, had gold thread woven in a pattern that reminded her of icy snowflakes. Fashioned in a V with narrow strips of sealskin, the collar tapered down to the high waistline, also cinched with sealskin. White silk gathered like lace between the gaping V covering her breasts—at least, for the most part. Following the latest fashion, wooden slats had been sewn into the tight bodice. Margaret found them incredibly uncomfortable and stifling, though they made her waist appear a tad smaller.

While she stood being trussed like a peacock, a chambermaid braided her long tresses. She rolled them on each side and secured them with a caul atop Margaret's ears, where they would form a part of her headdress. Mother had ordered a double hennin in the same fabric as her gown, covered with a sheer red-tinted veil. Margaret eyed the hat on the sideboard. It was a garish headpiece, embellished with gold cording and reinforced on the inside with wire. Margaret would have preferred a simple veil or French hood, but Mother would be disappointed if she said otherwise. Besides, what did it matter? Perhaps Black Colin liked outlandish hennins.

Margaret shuddered. God save her, she had no recourse. This day she would walk across the courtyard and marry a notorious knight in the Chapel of Michael the Archangel.

"May I please lower my arms?" she asked.

The tailor stepped back and examined his handiwork. "Slowly."

"The way you talk, I'll never be able to move." Margaret held her breath and let her arms drift to her sides. "Mayhap we'll have to conduct the ceremony here, where I can stand in this spot."

Mother stepped beside him and examined the fashionably long sleeves that extended past Margaret's fingertips. "She needs to have full movement, of course."

"Indeed. I first wanted to ensure all the seams and tacks are secure." He tugged at the shoulders and waistline. "Yes. Miss Margaret, you can dance to your heart's content this eve."

After Margaret's headpiece was in place, her eyebrows plucked, her face powdered, cheeks made rosy with soft ochre and lips reddened to the color of her gown, Mother clapped her hands. "Leave us."

Margaret regarded her reflection while the chamber emptied. She hardly recognized herself. Her new husband would be marrying Miss Margaret Robinson, courtier imposter. She looked like a painting one would find hanging over a fireplace mantel. If only she could impersonate a portrait, she wouldn't be forced to proceed with marrying the most feared knight in all Christendom.

Mother shut the door and turned. She smiled, holding something in her hands. "I cannot believe this time has come so quickly." She held out a bold necklace with a crystal the shape of a small egg. It rested in a setting of silver decorated with four pieces of red coral alternating with four silver balls. "This charmstone is part of your dowry."

Margaret ran her fingers over the garish thing. "My, 'tis enormous."

"With no male heir, this was passed to me. It has been in our family for countless centuries, and is said to bring good fortune to all who wear it. Those who drink water into which it has been dipped will also be protected by its charms." Mother held it up. "Wearing this today will bring good tidings to your marriage."

"Och." Margaret fingered the large stone. "'Tis too precious to give to the likes of me."

"No. I daresay its shine is far diminished by my daughter's radiance." Mother moved behind and fastened the heavy silver chain. "You have learned well, and I've no doubt you will be a fine matron of your keep."

The matron of a keep? That's what I always wanted, isn't it? Margaret sucked in a ragged breath. "Thank you."

"Few women have attained your level of education—men as well. Though the ability to read and write and calculate sums is admirable, do not allow your skills to intimidate your husband."

Margaret turned and faced her. "Are you saying I should play dumb?"

Mother ran her fingers across the charmstone. "Not at all. I'm only suggesting you pay heed to your husband's wishes."

"Do you think he'll not want my assistance?"

"On the contrary—I think he will encourage it, just as your father has. But you can be opinionated as well as industrious. All I'm saying is to think about how your words might affect him before you express yourself." She chuckled. "Men may appear tough on the outside, but inside they wound easily."

"Honestly?" Margaret mulled over her mother's words. "I wonder if a man like Black Colin has a sensitive side." She seriously doubted that.

Mother pursed her lips. "You must stop referring to him so. His reputation comes from the battlefield, where one must be ruthless or face certain death. You're well aware he's one of the king's most loyal subjects."

Margaret sighed. This conversation had taken on many faces over the past sennight, but always ended by putting her betrothed on a pedestal. No one seemed to care about the trepidation dampening her skin like a clammy cloth.

Mother stepped closer, as if she had a secret the walls mustn't hear. "Before I leave, there is one more thing we must discuss."

Margaret met her mother's gaze. The woman's eyes softened, almost appeared compassionate.

"Are you aware of what will be required of you this night?"

Heat flared up Margaret's cheeks. "He'll come to my bedchamber?" She could but whisper.

"Aye, and as his wife, you must submit."

This, too, had Margaret's insides twisted in a knot. Worse, discussing it with her mother seemed so...unnatural. "Will he hurt me?" She wasn't sure if she'd actually spoken the words aloud.

But mother offered a consoling pat on the shoulder. "Most likely he will try to be gentle—however, the first time always hurts a little."

Margaret groaned and buried her face in her palms. She'd been to weddings before—come the morrow, her virtue would be on the bed linens for all to examine. Nausea churned her stomach. "This all seems nightmarish. If only I could have been matched with Lord Forbes."

Mother's pat turned into a firm grasp. "Colin Campbell is ten times the man, and his holdings of land and cattle are far greater. The king's appointment is an honor, young lady, and when you walk out the door, you will hold your head high and rise to it."

The ice returned to Mother's steely stare. Margaret nodded and cast her gaze to the floor. Yes, she would go through with this marriage, because if she refused, she'd be acting against the wishes of the king, her parents and at least half the powerful nobility in Scotland. She would meet the infamous Colin Campbell, but she would have her wishes met as well. After all, she was the daughter of a powerful baron. She brought with her a dowry that rivaled any other woman in the land—including the heavy charmstone necklace chilling her skin. Yes, she would perform her duty as a wife, but in return, her expectations of respect and freedom to manage a keep had best be met. *Is that too much to ask? Most certainly not.*

Mother stepped back and smiled. "You look as beautiful as a picture. I'll let the priest know you're ready, and send in your father."

Once alone, Margaret turned full circle. She'd been wrapped up like a package, scarcely able to take a deep breath. Normally she had an appreciation for new gowns and fine things, but today she most certainly resembled a stuffed pheasant, dressed to adorn the king's table.

Margaret wrung her hands and stared at the door. So many unanswered questions filed through her head. Would baby Duncan be at the wedding? Would he instantly be thrust into her arms? Though equipped to run a keep, as the youngest, she had no experience with bairns. Surely Colin had a nursemaid for the lad, else he would not have survived.

She studied her reflection in the mirror. "Lady Campbell." Her new title didn't sound all that bad. "Lady Margaret of Glenorchy." She liked that even better. How Colin received a barony, as the third son of the Lord of Lochaw, had her muddled. The Campbell family must be very powerful indeed, as was their reputation.

A rap rattled the door. Her heart raced with her jolt. It creaked open. Her father's smiling face peeked inside. "Are you ready, sweetheart?"

Margaret spread her hands to her sides. "If there's no other way."

"I'm sure the circumstances are preventing a bride's normal excitement—though many women are thus wed." He smoothed his fingers across her cheek. "Everything will be fine."

"Will it?" If only her wits would stop jumping across her skin.

He smiled with a knowing confidence. "Aye, and if you have reason for concern, send me a missive and I shall meet with Lord Campbell myself."

She inhaled as deeply as her bodice would allow. "Thank you. I cannot say how much your words give my mind peace."

He offered his elbow. "I may be giving you away in marriage, but you will always be my daughter."

Upon her father's arm, she crossed the courtyard while a chambermaid carried her heavy velvet train.

When they arrived at the chapel door, Margaret remembered nothing about passing through the inner bailey. She wouldn't have been able to tell someone what time of day it was, if the wind was blowing, if it was cloudy or raining—or if she'd stepped in a pile of horse manure, for that matter.

Wiggling her toes in her slippers; her feet were dry. Stealing a glance behind her, she exhaled. The cobblestones had recently been cleaned of debris.

She gripped her father's arm tighter when two pages opened the heavy double doors. Much warmer than the outside air, the Chapel of Michael the Archangel was packed shoulder to shoulder with people, all watching her cross the threshold. Rays of light streamed in from the stained-glass windows that lined the far wall.

With the change in light, Margaret couldn't focus. Blindly, she leaned on Father's arm while he escorted her through the throng. Too crowded—the sickly odors of humanity mixed with heady perfumed oils turned her stomach. Clammy heat prickled her skin. She looked back. People swallowed the path to the door. Margaret had nowhere to run.

Her heels clicked the floorboards, loud as a blaring trumpet. Courtiers parted, her train skimmed the wood as she walked. *That's right, the maid was instructed to drop it once I stepped across the threshold.*

Finery surrounded her. Every guest clad in rich velvets and silks, adorned with sparkling rubies and garish jewelry. She scanned the faces ahead and gasped. Father was leading her straight up to the king and queen's thrones, set high upon a dais at the rear of the chapel.

Margaret glanced toward the altar, straining for a peek at Lord Glenorchy, but the crowd blocked her view. Upon the platform, they stopped before the royal thrones. She curtseyed deeply, and Father bowed.

The royal couple were dressed in rich gold velvet, adorned with red silk and ermine collars. The queen wore a gold embroidered hennin, more garish than the one atop Margaret's head. The regal woman smiled with brightly rouged lips.

With giant rings on his fingers, the king raised his hands and gave her an approving nod. What else would he do? Take one look at her and decide his earlier judgment had been ill conceived? Margaret almost wished he had.

"Let the wedding begin," King James boomed in a deep, authoritative voice.

When she turned, Margaret saw him. She couldn't make out his face beneath his helm, but a tall, broad-shouldered warrior stood beside the priest. Lord Colin Campbell waited at the far end of the chapel. An enormous, looming presence, he wore a coat of blackened ceremonial armor with a red cloak attached at his shoulders. If she weren't terrified, and if this man weren't about to marry her sight unseen, she might admire the craftsmanship.

'Tis said armor maketh the warrior.

Father tugged Margaret's arm, and they continued down the center of the parting crowd under the scrutiny of all eyes. As they neared, Margaret stared at Lord Glenorchy's breastplate. It was emblazoned with a square cross—the same one she'd seen on the knight's tunic at the fete yesterday.

She risked a glance at his face.

Gasp.

He was staring at her with a stunned expression. Her stomach turned inside out. It was the same dun-haired, brown-eyed knight from the market. *Oh, praises, he's not a toothless, grey-haired miser.* Goodness, at the fete he'd been so agreeable, so pleasant. How could the man standing beside the priest be Black Colin of Rome?

They strolled past her beaming mother, and Father stopped. Margaret craned her neck and regarded the man who in the coming minutes would become her husband.

His shocked expression had been replaced with a cool gaze, his lips thinning. Did she displease him?

If she could dive behind her mother's skirts, she would. *Holy Mary, Mother of God, help me.*

Father took her right hand and placed it in the knight's palm. Fingers covered with cold iron gauntlets closed around hers. He gave her a clipped nod, and they turned to face the priest. Margaret tried to watch Colin out the corner of her eye, but her vision was blocked by her veil. There was certainly no emotion flowing from his icy finger armor.

The priest, clad in long black robes, chanted the ceremony in Latin. Trembling, Margaret closed her eyes and tried to concentrate on the foreign words. Over and over her mind replayed their brief encounter. She'd admired him. Was it a sign? Would he be kind? Would he accept her with all her flaws, including her opinionated comments that constantly irritated her mother?

The priest stopped and nodded to Lord Glenorchy— Colin. His right hand had no gauntlets, only a black leather glove. A man standing next to him handed him the ring. Colin turned to her, his face incredibly handsome, yet unreadable. He slid the band over her finger. Margaret only had enough time to glance at the stone—a sapphire set in silver—then he leaned forward and kissed her forehead.

Chapter Five

Stirling Palace 8ᵗʰ October, 1455

Colin couldn't bring himself to look at Margaret through the entire ceremony. Yesterday, if he'd known the king had chosen the lass with the penetrating green eyes, he would have called off the wedding at once. Colin thought he'd been clear, requested a matronly woman who could tend Duncan's needs. A widow would have suited well. But this woman was fresh as a raspberry on the vine, ready to be plucked—right up to her expertly rouged lips.

Her gown was exquisite. Of course, he'd expect no less from Lord Struan's daughter. Any woman would present a vision wrapped in red velvet—lips drawn into the shape of Cupid's bow. But did she have to look at him like that? Her jade-green eyes were so intense, he swore she could expose his darkest secrets. Oh no, he mustn't encourage her to look upon him at all.

He'd meant it when he vowed not to allow himself heartfelt yearnings for any woman. He would not give his heart again, no matter if she did have eyebrows arched over almond-shaped eyes the color of moss. He could not allow her to tempt him. He would resist silken skin and hair the color of polished autumn chestnuts. Colin would have none of it. He'd perform his duty as a husband and involve his heart no more.

Demonstrating his resolve right there in front of God and the high priest, he kissed her forehead. No lovesick mouth-kissing for him.

The crowd mumbled their approval. At once, he swiftly escorted her out the door and into the great hall. The tables were arranged around the perimeter of the room, the center later to be filled with dancers. Colin walked at a steady pace, expecting her to keep up regardless of her folds upon folds of heavy velvet skirts. He led her to the dais and pulled out a chair, gesturing for her to be seated. "My lady."

Margaret's gaze met his for an instant. His gut clenched—merely an attack of jitters, similar to the queasiness a man feels before going into battle. She glanced to the green upholstered seat and bit her lip, as if she needed to contemplate what to do. "Are we not to remain standing until the king and queen make their entrance?"

Colin didn't care to be second-guessed by anyone—though she was probably right. He peered through the tapestry-lined hall—guests were pouring in, though no one had yet taken a seat. Before he could reply, trumpets on the balcony blared the announcement of the royal couple's advance.

He offered Margaret a thin-lipped nod, and they stood until the king and queen made their way to the dais, with Lord and Lady Struan following closely behind. Margaret grasped the edges of her skirts and curtseyed while Colin bowed, hovering over her silken white shoulder. Damn her succulent smell. Colin licked his lips. By God, with what fragrance did the woman use to bathe? He'd have to make a point of insisting on something more practical and less feminine. He absolutely could not tolerate her distracting him every time she came within an arm's length of his person.

Of course, he wouldn't have to worry about *that* once he returned to Rome.

The royal party sat in their respective thrones, and Colin again gestured to the chair. Margaret smiled. "Thank you, m'lord."

King James caught his eye. "I must say, the queen offered up quite a suitable solution to satisfy your need for a wife."

Queen Mary raised her goblet. "I spied Lady Margaret at court, and her father was all too eager to tell me of her skills with the factor's books and her ability to run a keep."

"True, my dear," the king said. "She has the utmost qualifications to manage whilst Lord Glenorchy is in Rome."

Margaret gaped at him. "You're off to Rome?"

Colin reached for the ewer of wine and filled her goblet. "We have a great many things to discuss." He poured for himself. "You have talent with figures?"

Her gaze slid from the top of his head to the seat of his chair. "Among other things."

Colin shifted uncomfortably. "What about children?"

She bit her bottom lip—blast her coyness. "Absolutely no experience whatsoever."

Groaning, Colin raised his goblet and guzzled. What in God's name? He may have not mentioned a "matron" in his missive, but he'd made it clear he needed a mother for Duncan. His infant son was the only reason he'd gone through with this madness—of course, it didn't seem like madness when he penned the missive, but presently, he feared he'd lost his mind. "You *are* aware the king arranged this marriage because I need a mother for my son?"

Margaret lifted her goblet and sipped daintily. "Aye. 'Tis about the only thing in this whole affair that has been made clear." She leaned in, blasting him with her damnable perfume. "But no one made mention that I'd be performing the task *without* his father."

Colin needed another drink—but something stronger than wine. Evidently the woman was skilled with her tongue as well as her quill.

Trenchers laden with food arrived. Colin removed the gauntlets from his left hand and pulled off his gloves. Lord and Lady Struan smiled approvingly, out of earshot at the far end of the table.

Margaret's gaze roved over him again, making him bloody uncomfortable. "Your armor is magnificent. Why did you wear your gauntlets only on one hand?"

He tugged at his collar plate. "I needed dexterity to handle your ring."

Margaret held her hand up to the candlelight. Colin had brought the sapphire back from the Holy Land, planning to give it to Jonet one day. But now another woman examined it in a silver setting.

"'Tis a magnificent wedding gift. Thank you."

He sighed when he caught sincere appreciation in her eyes. "You're welcome."

With no whisky in sight, Colin poured himself another goblet of wine then held up a trencher. Margaret selected a slice of lamb with her eating knife. She averted her eyes and focused on her food. He let out a deep breath and sipped his wine. He usually didn't feel awkward around women. After all, this was his third marriage. He should be relieved the ceremony was over and on the morrow they could begin the journey back to Dunstaffnage.

Eating, Margaret watched him out of the corner of her eye. He should say something to her, but damned if he could think of a thing. If he complimented her, she might just like him, and he wasn't sure he wanted that. He looked to the vaulted ceiling. *Bloody hell.* Of course he wanted her to like him. Their interactions might be more palatable if she didn't hate him, at least. But he would tolerate no nagging.

Colin reached for the bread. Simultaneously, Margaret did as well. Their naked fingers brushed. Colin's skin tingled and the hair at the back of his hand stood on end. With a gasp, she snatched her fingers away and nodded to the loaf. "You first, m'lord."

He raised his brows. She was nervous. He broke the bread and offered her a piece. "Allow me."

"Thank you."

Again the silence created a void between them. Roaring in his ears, the crowd's hum picked up, and the king's laughter rolled from the center of the table. Colin hadn't paid a lick of attention to the royal party. He rubbed his fingers against the hem of his velvet doublet to quash the damned tingling. Colin never tingled. He was a knight, for Christ's sake.

He popped a piece of bread in his mouth and washed it down with wine. The festivities couldn't end soon enough. He needed the solace of his chamber, where he could think. Margaret glanced at him and smiled. His lips turned up. *Damnation.* He shouldn't have smiled in return.

Margaret rested her eating knife on the table. "I thought we might talk a bit before…" Her eyes trailed away.

Ah. The wedding night. She would be nervous about that. Colin didn't even want to think about it. "Talking is not necessary."

She arched a perfectly shaped eyebrow. "Oh? And how else do you suggest we come to know one another?"

"Time, m'lady."

Margaret's gaze drifted. Colin couldn't read her—though he didn't want to. He didn't want to know what her pretty head was thinking, or her opinion of him. He wanted this night to be over.

The musicians on the balcony increased in volume.

Margaret clapped. "Do you dance, m'lord?"

Colin's stomach muscles clenched. "Not really." He prayed he could make it through the evening without dancing with the lass.

Margaret's face fell, and she folded her hands in her lap.

King James rapped his fist on the table. "We shall see the wedding couple in the first dance."

The entire hall erupted in polite applause. *Blast the king.* Pushing back his chair, Colin stood and bowed. "M'lady."

Margaret grasped his hand, and he led her down the steps and to the center of hall. Her hands were soft and ever so much smaller than his. Her palms perspired—so did his, and Colin wished he'd thought to put his gloves back on. The doeskin would provide the slightest distance.

No other couples joined them. *Fye.*

One of the musicians called for a volta. Colin assumed his position, roiling on his insides. Must they choose the most provocative dance known to modern man? Could they not have settled for a circle dance where he'd merely have to swing this woman by her elbow and look pleasant?

Margaret stood opposite him and curtseyed. A sultry drum started a sensuous rhythm. Her intelligent gaze didn't leave his face. She studied him as if memorizing a map. The flute began. Margaret sprang to life, her chin held high, expertly executing the steps. Together they danced. Her skirts brushed the back of Colin's legs, the part not protected by armor—it almost tickled.

She ran toward him for the lift, not once blinking her deep pools of green. Colin had no recourse but to grasp her waist and raise her up, twirling her across the floor. In the recesses of his mind, the crowd's applause registered.

Slowly, he lowered her toward the floor as the dance demanded. Her sweet fragrance, more sultry than a field of wildflowers in summer's heat, wafted over him. Colin sucked in a ragged breath, tried to step away, but she matched his pace. Hand in hand they danced until the music ended with Margaret in a deep curtsey.

Again the crowd applauded—louder this time.

Smiling, she placed her palm in the crook of his elbow. "I say, you dance quite well for a man who was expecting to spend the evening draining the ewer of wine."

Ruing her sharp tongue, Colin clenched his jaw and led her back to the dais without a word. Perhaps he'd been heavy-handed with the ewer, but that was none of her concern.

Resuming their seats, he wanted nothing more than to take a stroll along the palace battlements to clear his head.

Fortunately, half the gentlemen in the hall sought to dance with his new bride. Colin switched to ale, rather than whisky. Becoming dead drunk would not help him later when he needed his wits to perform his duty, though inebriation would be a welcomed state. He reclined in his chair and kept to himself. The room aflutter with jovial laughing and clapping, he chose to refrain from joining in. He would not easily forget Jonet, the quiet woman who'd been his partner for the past six years. A complete stranger could not step in and replace his lost love, nor did he care for an outspoken, comely lass to try.

It was far easier on his heavy heart to have Margaret off dancing, enjoying herself where he could not touch her, or smell her, or talk to her. He did, however, watch the lady from behind his goblet, akin to watching quarry when hunting.

She moved with uncanny grace and laughed like she had not a care. Colin recalled the days when he laughed with such abandon. But war and death had robbed him of his ability to chuckle from his gut like an inexperienced lad. Margaret was made for the dance floor. She executed every step with grace, and Colin imagined she practiced in her father's keep for hours to become so adept.

Her gaze shot to his and connected before he lowered his lashes and stared into his ale. He couldn't allow his young wife to cause irrational stirrings. Her eyes had affected him at the fete. Yes, the color was unusual, but more so, her expression had grasped his attention. Intelligence lurked behind those pools of green. Have mercy, her small nose suited her face and her lightly moistened, plump lips had practically begged him to kiss them. He must guard himself. It was a warrior's duty to understand his weakness and devise ways to protect and strengthen against it.

"And what say you, Glenorchy?" The king's voice cut through his thoughts. "She is a lovely bride."

Colin straightened in his chair. "Aye. I hope she will be a suitable stepmother for my heir."

"You are aware she can read and write. She will be an excellent tutor for Duncan's early years," the queen added.

Colin dipped his chin respectfully. "Then I agree. Lady Margaret is the perfect choice. I could not have found a more suitable replacement for Jonet if I had searched for years myself." Except she could be five year' older, a stone heavier and great deal less comely.

The queen offered a pleased smile and then turned her attention toward the other side of the table. Colin took a healthy swig of ale, content to once again be left alone with his grief.

***

Margaret stood in the center of her chamber while two maids removed the heavy gown. Colin had walked her to the door and excused himself, saying he must attend to a few things. Her new husband had been nothing but polite. Though he lacked the glint of humor she'd noticed at the fete. His dark brown eyes also held a sadness she hadn't noticed the day prior. Was he dissatisfied with her? Did he not find her attractive? The tension in her shoulders might actually ease a wee bit if she'd sensed he approved of his new bride.

She thought she'd danced well, but he hadn't even smiled at her from across the room—just leered behind his tankard of ale.

That he'd left her outside her chamber was a relief. Perhaps he wouldn't return and give her a chance to come to know him before…before.

She pushed the heels of her hands into her eyes. She couldn't even think about it.

Surely they both were nervous. Yes, Colin had been married formerly, but she doubted he'd not met his previous brides prior to the ceremony. Had he? She might ask him if the opportunity presented itself—if she would ever in her lifetime feel comfortable around him. Heaven's stars, from the stern way he glared at her, Margaret feared she'd apprised poorly on all accounts.

The maid lifted the hennin from her head. Margaret smoothed her hands over her braids.

"Sit on the stool so I can brush out yer tresses, m'lady."

Divested of the heavy gown, Margaret sat wearing only her linen shift. Once again she felt like herself—no wooden slats binding her ribs, no ridiculous wired hennin pinching her head. The soft brush running through her hair soothed her concerns away. Margaret closed her eyes and let the maid work until her tresses had been brushed to a luminous sheen.

"Shall I turn down the bed, m'lady?"

Her tension raced back tenfold and Margaret's shoulders stiffened. "That will be fine." She tried to keep her voice even.

All too soon, the chambermaids took their leave. Margaret still perched on the stool. Alone. Would Colin come to her? Having feigned sleep the night before, her eyelids were heavy. Perhaps he would consummate the marriage some other time? But what about the old hens on the morrow? Her virtue must show on the linens. Shuddering, Margaret rose and blew out all the candles except the one on the bedside table.

After she splashed her face in the basin, rubbed her teeth with mint leaves and rinsed, she climbed between the crisp linens and stared at the velvet canopy above her bed. She was married. Lady Margaret of Glenorchy.

Her fingers clenched the bedclothes and tugged them under her chin.

Chapter Six

Stirling Palace, 8ᵗʰ October, 1455

As if in a stupor, Colin stared at his ceremonial armor resting on the settee. He wore it only on special occasions. The suit had cost him more than his battle armor, yet it wouldn't provide much protection in a fight. He'd now worn the suit in three weddings and to his father's funeral. He hated the blasted thing and hoped never to wear it again.

He groaned. His thoughts served only to delay his *obligation.*

His squire had long since left. Wearing a linen shirt and woolen hose, he paced. Though he'd never admit it to a soul, the roiling in his gut was nerves. The one thing he must lawfully do was consummate this marriage. Until he performed his duty, Margaret would have every right to attest their vows had not been satisfactorily carried out. No doubt the queen's women would examine the linens in the morning. If he did not perform his duty this night, he would bring scrutiny upon his house, and in no way would he allow such a social misstep.

It must be done.

Jonet, forgive me. You must know I'm doing this for our son. One day we shall meet again and I'll rest beside you through eternity.

Colin had only fathered two sons in eight total years of marriage. One had survived. Yes, Duncan was a healthy bairn showing promise for a long life, but it was Colin's duty to ensure there was issue upon his death. If, God forbid, Duncan did not survive him, there must be another child ready to step into the barony. The survival of the Glenorchy line depended on it.

He pushed out his chamber. He would perform the necessary deed and return to his rooms. Easy enough. Wedded twice before, he was more experienced than most men on their wedding night. She'd be nervous— he'd put her at ease and then carry out his duty quickly.

Somehow he arrived at Margaret's door much faster than he'd anticipated. He clenched his stomach muscles and knocked.

"Lord Colin?" Her voice resounded through the door. The soft Highland lilt caressed his skin, sending a wave of gooseflesh up his arms. Colin frowned. *Bed her and take your leave.*

He creaked open the door. Margaret lay on the bed, a single candle illuminating waves of brunette locks, her face glowing, pure. A cannonball sank to the pit of Colin's stomach. Six years ago Jonet awaited him, nervous as a finch, eyes round. Except Jonet had greeted him with a smile rather than lips pursed into a bow. But circumstances had been different then.

Margaret pulled the bedclothes tighter under her chin. "M…my lord. I thought you mightn't come."

He stepped inside and closed the door. Her chamber unfamiliar, a peat fire glowed in the hearth. He grasped the latch and squeezed. No. Colin was a warrior, damnation. A warrior never turned his back on his responsibilities.

He clenched his fists and strode toward the bed. "We've a task to perform." His voice was gruffer than he'd intended.

"A task?" Her knuckles turned white. "I-is that what you call it?"

Determined, he grasped the hem of his shirt.

She held the bedclothes firm. "M'lord," she squeaked, skittish as a willow warbler's call. "Would it be too much to ask if we could chat for a bit? Mayhap it will calm these…my awful jitters."

Colin released his hands and looked at her face. Her eyes pleaded. He'd seen that look many times on the battlefield—the complete, unadulterated terror of a young novice. He sat on the edge of her bed and combed his fingers through his hair. *I am not a beast.* "Very well."

Her fingers relaxed their grip, and she sat up. "The king mentioned you're returning to Rome?"

Colin kept his head turned away, though he could see her out the corner of his eye. "I didn't want to burden you, but aye. I have been summoned by the Grand Master of the Order of St. John."

"I see." She smoothed a hand across the comforter. "And when will you set sail?"

"Soon. There are things which need my attention first."

"Such as?"

"You ask a great many questions."

"Apologies—'tis just there's so much I do not know about you."

Her gaze bored into his back with the force of a stonemason's chisel, yet he could not turn and face her. Too fresh, Jonet's death still blackened his heart—this first night all too familiar. If only he could have waited…

"When will I meet Duncan?"

The corner of his mouth turned up. "He's with his nursemaid—the same woman who nursed me as a bairn."

Margaret audibly sighed. "'Tis good he is well cared for."

"Aye. He's a strong lad with powerful lungs."

"I'm sure he's the image of his father."

He was the image of Jonet—at least in coloring. Colin again clenched his fists. He needed to his *chore* over with.

Clearing his throat, he faced her. God, he could lose himself in those green eyes. He might indulge her allure during sex—it did make it easier for him to perform his duty without using his hand to coax an erection. He leaned forward and placed his lips on her forehead. *Sugared lavender.* Her scent alone made his cock lengthen. Thank God. He would have been mortified if his manhood hadn't come to perform.

If only Margaret weren't a virgin, what he was about to do might be pleasant for her…the king should have found him a widow, blast it all.

He lowered his lips to her ear. "The queen's ladies will be here in the morning to attest consummation of our marriage."

She slipped lower beneath the bedclothes. "A-aye, my mother said as much."

So she knew something about what was to come. Good. He could do this quickly and be gone.

***

Margaret relaxed a little, lulled by the deep tenor of his voice more than his words. Still, her heart pounded in her chest. If it wouldn't have been incredibly improper, she would have pulled the bedclothes over her head and asked him to leave. The mere thought of allowing a near stranger to touch her intimately chilled her to the core. Thank heavens he'd agreed to chat for a bit.

While they spoke, Colin kept his face averted. What did he have to be nervous about? He'd been married before. And when he turned to face her, she'd caught a glimpse of that same spark from the fair—the one that had spun her insides upside down. Then he covered it with a guarded frown, similar to the one he'd worn during the feast, as if he wanted to keep distance between them.

Next, he touched his lips to her forehead. Margaret grew more confused than ever. The gesture didn't seem impassioned. A wee groan escaped his throat and sent her insides aflutter, but he hadn't kissed her like a husband kisses a wife.

He reached for the bedclothes and dragged them from her grasp. "I'll try not to hurt you."

She swallowed. Her heart pummeled her chest.

He slipped off his pointed leather shoes and crawled into the bed beside her. Without a word, he nuzzled into her neck and placed a heavy hand on her abdomen. Never in her life had a man touched her so. Margaret's breathing stuttered.

Slowly, he slid his palm up and covered her breast. His hand, weighty yet gentle, kneaded her tingling flesh. Margaret closed her eyes and tried to imagine dancing— anything but his fingers plying her flesh. She stiffened and gritted her teeth.

"Ye smell good enough to eat." His voice turned buttery along with his Highland lilt.

She glanced at his face. Colin's eyes were closed, his lips parted. A hard column of flesh jutted into her hip. He slipped his hand around her waist and pulled her close as he rubbed himself against her. A deep moan rumbled in his chest. Margaret watched him as if she were outside her body.

He'd yet to kiss her on the lips. In all of her imaginings, the first step to lovemaking was a mouth-to-mouth kiss. She'd seen couples—even her parents—share a tender kiss, but Colin seemed to be growing impassioned without the need for her to do anything at all.

He skimmed his hand down the length of her body and stopped just below her belly button. Margaret couldn't breathe. Colin grasped her shift and began to tug it up.

Ice shot through her veins. She bolted upright. "Wha...what are you doing?"

Colin's eyes opened. He rose up on his elbow. "Are you afraid, lass?"

"No...yes. Aren't you supposed to kiss me first?"

He moved his hand to her stomach. "Aye, but I did kiss you."

"On the lips?"

A muscle in Colin's jaw twitched with his deep inhale. "Very well." He lowered his gaze to her lips and inched toward her.

Margaret planted her hands on the mattress and shoved her back against the headboard, turning her chin aside. *Kiss me now? This is more like being examined by a rheumy-eyed physician.*

Colin stopped, his gaze dark. "Changed your mind, did you?" He grabbed her shift and yanked it up. Before she could twist away, he pushed his knees between her legs. "Since neither one of us is feeling amorous this night, I'll make this fast."

Margaret squirmed, but he pinned her with his body. He ran kisses along her neck. "I'm kissing you Margaret. Is this what you want?"

She whimpered against her tingling flesh. His thick column pressed between her legs, sending her world into a maelstrom of fire as he rocked himself. "Feel my cock against your womanhood. A man gets hard when he's ready to breed with a woman."

Cock? She'd never heard that word before, but there was no question what it was. It sounded exciting, yet terrifying at the same time. A tight heat spread deep inside. Margaret clutched his shoulders and closed her eyes. His arms were huge—his muscles bulged as he held himself above her, pinning her in place, but not crushing her.

"'Tis my duty to sew my seed in your womb."

Her breath stuttered. She couldn't talk. He was so much more powerful than she. A fluttering heat spread through her sacred place. She wanted him, but didn't. She wanted something more—more kisses, more caresses, something to make her feel comforted or cherished.

His hips insistently rocked, rubbing the thick column against her mons. She closed her eyes and tried to match his shockingly wanton motion.

"There, lass, give in to it." His voice softened, ever so *intimate*.

He slid his hand between her legs. Rough fingers brushed across her, bringing a spasm of tight heat she never knew she could experience without being burned. A rough pad touched an incredibly sensitive spot, turning her insides molten. Margaret gasped.

"Aye, lass." He slid his finger down further and slipped inside.

Margaret couldn't move. She stared at his face in awe. In one moment, he made her feel more passion than she'd ever dreamed possible. Oh yes, the swirling of his finger inside her sent shivers coursing through her entire body. In and out, he stroked her slowly.

"Ye are tight, lass, but wet." His smooth voice cooed as if plucking the bass strings of a harp.

Her lips parted with her stuttered inhale.

Slick with her moisture, Colin's finger again moved to the sensitive spot he'd first touched. Lord, yes. She tilted her hips, craving more, her body aching for him to rub faster.

All too soon, he moved to his knees and tugged down his hose. Margaret tensed. Never in her life had she considered a man could be so enormous when mating. He planned to put that thing—that *cock*—inside her? She tried to shift her hips away, but he covered her with his weight again—this time not as gently.

His cock jutted between her legs, rubbed against her, flesh to flesh. The heat in her loins spiked. Slipping his hand between them, he grasped himself and pressed into the place that had become slick with her own moisture.

His eyes turned dark. "This might hurt a bit, but I'll try to be gentle."

With a rumbling groan, he pushed—entered her. Her insides stretched, then with one more shove, she tore. Lord help her, it stung. Margaret clenched her teeth, digging her fingernails into his back. He pulled it out and slid back in. Her eyes flashed open. *Again?* She shuddered with the torturous rip of her flesh.

"Forgive me," he grunted. "'Twill be over soon, lass."

Colin fisted the bedclothes and pushed harder. A cry caught in Margaret's throat. A shot of pain burned as he slid deeper inside, stretching her beyond her limits. Colin's mouth was next to her ear. His breathing sped. He slid out and in, over and over. The pain grated as if his manhood was shredding her insides.

Margaret struggled to move out from under him, but the more she stirred, the faster he thrust. A grunt caught in his throat. His entire body went rigid, then he roared and held himself deep within her. His manhood pulsated inside.

He'd planted his seed.

Gradually, Colin relaxed atop her and his breathing returned to normal. Margaret inadvertently moved her hips. His cock rubbed across her exposed flesh. Something inside demanded more. She rocked her hips just as he had done. Ah, yes, that did feel good, now he wasn't filling her so tightly. A picture of his exposed manhood appeared in her mind. Alas, she understood.

But Colin withdrew from her and sat on his haunches. Before she could say a word, he pulled up his braies and covered himself. Margaret sat against the headboard and curled her legs under her shift. She tried to look him in the eye, but his gaze trailed to the bloody streak on the linens. Her virtue. Gone.

"We'll be leaving on the morrow."

Was that it? No kissing? No spending time in each other's arms? Colin slipped into his shoes and walked to the door. Margaret was tongue-tied. He pushed into the hallway without so much as a goodnight.

Her blood rushed beneath her skin. Her husband had performed his duty and left. An empty chasm filled her chest. Overwhelmed with an urge to cleanse herself, Margaret threw her feet over the side of the bed and stood. She gaped at linens—her ugly virtue staining blood red for all to admire on the morrow.

As she walked to the basin, her womanhood ached— sore from being invaded by *him*. Heaven help her, how many times would she have to endure his stringent coupling?

She stripped off her shift and dipped a linen cloth into the water. She started with her face, smoothed it under her arms, across her breasts—everywhere his hands had been. Finally, with a shaking hand, she wiped the cloth between her legs. It stung. She wrung the linen in the basin, leaching her blood and his seed.

Black Colin was everything his name suggested—just like a spider. He tantalized his prey with an enticing display, but when they fell into his web, he showed no mercy. Chilled, Margaret ran a drying cloth over her moist skin and tugged her shift back over her head.

When she pulled the bedclothes to her chin, she closed her eyes to a positive thought. He'd be headed back to Rome soon.

Chapter Seven

Stirling Palace, 9ᵗʰ October, 1455

Margaret's eyes snapped open after someone pulled the furs away from the window and blinded her with a ray of light. She wasn't one to sleep past dawn, but trepidation over last night's activities kept her awake into the wee hours.

Chambermaids filled the room.

A young lass placed a tray on the small table beside the hearth. "'Tis time to break your fast, m'lady."

Margaret stretched. "I'd prefer to sleep a bit longer."

An older woman shook out Margaret's traveling gown. "You are to eat and attend him in the courtyard. Lord Glenorchy's orders."

Already ordering me about, is he? The heartless cur.

No sooner did Margaret rise than the linens were stripped from her bed and whisked out the door—for examination, no doubt. *At least the queen will be pleased.*

Margaret spooned stewed dates over her porridge and ate while the chambermaids bustled about. "I'm surprised Lord Glenorchy wants to depart so soon. He was up quite late."

The lasses chuckled, as if they knew what he'd been up to. Of course they knew. Margaret's cheeks burned. Her deflowering obviously provided a great deal of amusement for the queen's chambermaids. Had she been at Dunalasdair Castle, she would have quashed their giggles with a sharp rebuttal. Unfortunately, she didn't have the energy this morning. Refusing to allow her shoulders to slump, Margaret finished her porridge and took her time dressing.

Mother entered, smiling broadly. "And how is my wedded daughter this morn?"

Margaret held her bodice against her ribs while a maid tied the laces. "Good morning, Mother." She chose to avoid the question.

With a furrowed brow, Mother studied her. "I take it all did not go smoothly last eve?"

"Not at all." Margaret groaned. She did not want to have this conversation with anyone, let alone her mother.

Lady Struan grasped her hand. "Things will improve, I can attest to that."

"He's an ogre."

Mother bit her bottom lip. "Give him a chance. He'll come good. The first year's always the most difficult."

"Now you choose to tell me?"

A guard appeared at the door. "Is Lady Glenorchy ready? The lord awaits."

The maid secured Margaret's hair beneath a French hood. With her cloak over her shoulders, Margaret kissed her mother. "Pray for me."

Eyes moist, Mother caressed her cheek. "Go with God. Everything will be fine. You shall see."

The guard accompanied her to the courtyard, where Colin waited at the head of a well-armed contingent, two score of men, wearing red tunics with a white cross over their hauberks. In the center of the procession, men were securing a wagon laden with her trunks.

Lord Colin, clad in a coat of blackened armor with the visor raised over his helm, watched her descend the steps.

He could have smiled, though he squinted against the sun and frowned, as if her tardiness had caused him undue inconvenience. Margaret watched him through downcast eyelids. Perched atop an impressive black warhorse, he certainly played the part of a black knight. In her mind there was absolutely no question as to who he was or what he stood for. *Heartlessness.*

The guard led her to a mare near the rear of the procession and helped her mount. Margaret thanked him and hooked her knee over the lower pommel of the sidesaddle. She smoothed her skirts and gathered her reins, cuing her horse to follow the procession at a trot. After last night's *ramming*, the hard leather saddle was none too comfortable.

Margaret clenched her teeth against the pain and glanced behind her. Six guards took up the rear. They looked more like they were riding into battle than across the countryside. Yes, outlaws were everywhere, but who in their right mind would take on half Lord Glenorchy's numbers—or could afford to? His entourage was a blatant display of wealth, for certain.

She grumbled under her breath. Flaunting one's wealth could bring more danger than if they traveled with a dozen well-trained soldiers, as her father did.

When the sun moved higher in the sky, indicating late morning, a knight clad much the same as Colin circled back and rode in beside her. "How are you faring, m'lady?"

"Did Lord Glenorchy send you back here to inquire as to my health—sir…?"

The man smiled. Though dark hair peeked from beneath his helm, there was a resemblance between he and her scoundrel of a husband. "Forgive me. I am Lord Colin Campbell of Argyll."

Margaret gaped. "You mean there are two of you?"

He rolled his hand and bowed his head. "My uncle calls me Argyll to keep it simple."

"Colin is your uncle? You look as if you could be brothers."

He smiled easily—Colin's smile, but friendlier. "That we do. He's only five years my senior."

This man was the same age as she. "I see."

"Lord Glenorchy might seem a bit gruff at first..."

"I'll say."

Argyll chuckled. "But there's no one better—no other man on this earth to whom I would trust my life. I was his squire until I reached my majority."

"How unfortunate for you." Margaret bit her lip. Had she just let her pent-up anger slip past her lips? She'd best hold her tongue, especially when speaking to a relative of her—*that man.*

"He's had his share of strife. His first wife died of the sweat. She lost two bairns in childbirth. I suspect you know the rest."

Margaret covered her mouth with her gloved hand. Colin's lot had been difficult, to say the least, but that still did not assuage his boorishness toward her. She opted to change the subject. "How long will it take us to travel to Loch Awe?"

"Two nights and a bit. Uncle Colin plans to stop and check on the progress of his keep before we proceed on to Dunstaffnage."

"Dunstaffnage? All the way to the coast? But I thought Lord Glenorchy's major holdings were at Loch Awe."

"They are, but baby Duncan resides at Dunstaffnage until the work on Kilchurn Castle is complete." Argyll smoothed the reins through his fingers. "Has Colin not told you?"

Margaret shifted in her uncomfortable saddle. "I daresay he hasn't mentioned much to me at all." They were heading to Dunstaffnage? What could she expect at that archaic castle? Would she have a free rein to manage the keep's affairs, or would Colin frown upon a woman with a mind for figures? He might very well opt to lock her in a tower with his colicky infant. The more she considered it, the more she convinced herself she'd be locked away. A man like her husband would not appreciate her unique talents.

The blackguard hadn't come to collect her himself, hadn't bothered to dismount and show her courtesy when she arrived in the courtyard, and now he rode at the front of his men as if she didn't exist.

Colin's arrogance surpassed all imagination. Riding at the head of the guard where he'd be the first attacked if they were ambushed? He'd be killed for certain—not that his death would affect her in any way.

***

Argyll rode in beside Colin as they approached the inn at Callander. Lord Glenorchy had made arrangements for his retinue ahead of time, but that did nothing to allay the churning in his gut.

Colin glared at his nephew. "Enjoy riding beside my wife *all day*, did you?"

"Och, are you jealous?" Argyll gathered his reins. "Someone needed to make the lady feel welcome." He batted the air with his hand. "Bah. Leaving her alone at the rear of the guard like she's your prisoner? Honestly, uncle, your new cloak of indifference does not become you."

"I…"

Argyll clicked his spurs and galloped ahead.

Colin growled through his teeth. He probably should have said something to Margaret when they stopped for their nooning rather than practice sparring with his guard. But he always sparred to enliven his muscles during a long journey, and he vowed he would act no differently because the woman rode with them.

He didn't care if Margaret held him in contempt. The hole in his heart still bled. How could any man recover from grief in a month? If only he could have borne Jonet's pain and died in her place. Allowing his heart to harbor any feelings for Margaret was akin to betraying Jonet's memory.

Colin slapped his reins against his steed's shoulder and led the procession to the stables at the back of the inn.

He bit the inside of his cheek. He detested his behavior last eve. Though Margaret had lain on the bed and submitted to his advances, it still didn't feel right. Taking a virgin wife like she was a village whore? He would kill any man for committing such an offense. His self-loathing escalated to new heights, first because of Jonet's death, and now because he couldn't find it in his heart to give Margaret due respect—tenderness, even.

Though he had a responsibility to procreate, he could not visit her bed again. He vowed he'd not again tread on her honor. She was a highborn lady and he would protect her as member of his house. She would raise his son, and for that Colin must be grateful.

After dismounting, he strode straight to Margaret's mare. She'd already slipped her leg off the upper pommel of her sidesaddle and braced for a side dismount. Doubtless she had performed the maneuver on her own several times, but no wife of his would be left to dismount unassisted.

Colin reached up and clamped his hands on her waist. "Allow me." Her midriff was pliable and warm to the touch. On their own volition, his fingers kneaded her flesh, a faint recollection sparked. Their coupling last eve hadn't been entirely unpleasant.

White lines formed around her pursed lips. "I am quite capable."

Ignoring her, he lifted. She was so light—far more petite than Jonet had been. He nearly lost her over his shoulder. With a grunt, he steadied himself and recovered, lightly placing Margaret on her feet.

"Thank you, *my lord*," she clipped. The sarcasm in her voice did not go unnoticed. She despised him for certain.

"I apologize if I was a wee bit heavy-handed." Colin didn't release his grip right away, befuddled that encircling her tiny waist, his fingertips touched. Beneath the folds of her gown, and most likely due to his own pigheadedness, last eve he hadn't realized how small Margaret actually was. He could have broken the lass, climbing on top of her and having his way. Colin's gut roiled. He deserved her cool indifference.

Margaret cleared her throat and eyed him with not a glimmer of amusement. In fact, she looked rather angry. "I can manage from here."

He snapped his hands away. What in God's name was he doing standing there like a dim-witted pup? Mayhap it was best for her to be upset with him—at least for now. He cleared his throat. "I've arranged for you to have your own room this eve."

"How fortunate. Please have my meal sent up. I should prefer to eat alone." With that, she turned on her heel. Chin held high, she strode into the inn.

Colin watched her. That blasted scent of sugared lavender trailing in her wake nearly made his knees weaken—nearly, though he stood firm. This *match* was going to be far more difficult than he'd imagined, especially if she kept challenging him with those green eyes. Christ almighty, they pierced through him as if she could see through to his soul.

***

Margaret sat in an uncomfortable wooden chair and worked on embroidering a skullcap for baby Duncan while the merriment below stairs rumbled up through the floorboards. Mother had suggested starting the ornate bonnet shortly after the king's missive announcing her marriage had been received. Embroidery was a dreary way to pass the time, though Margaret enjoyed seeing the end results of her work.

This task, however, seemed more a chore of duty rather than a labor of love. She shifted in the chair, her bottom unholy sore from performing her *wifely obligation* and then riding all day. She prayed Colin would leave her alone and allow her some time to heal before he came to her again. Margaret shuddered as the voices rose with muffled laughter. She hoped he'd fall into his cups this night and never wake.

Tying off a stitch, she released a heavy sigh.

In all honesty, she would prefer to be down in the inn with the men listening to their merriment and music. Though she wouldn't dance with Colin. Making a French knot, Margaret paused and gazed into the log fire. Her husband said he didn't care to dance. Were her days of carefree dancing over? Her heart sank. Dancing was the exercise she enjoyed above everything else. Would he take that away from her?

Margaret's mind drifted to the day's events. She'd be a mite more comfortable with her lot if Colin had been open and discussed their destination before setting out. She hated being treated like chattel. He seemed not to care for her in the slightest, at least until they'd arrived at the inn.

Heaven's stars, she'd nearly died when Colin marched up to her by the stables. She'd already braced herself for a dismount. Her husband had ignored her the entire day— why would she expect him to attend her once they arrived at the inn? She practically jumped out of her skin when he wrapped his big hands around her waist. He lifted her with such force that at first she thought the brute would throw her over his shoulder. But he placed her on her feet as if she were as fragile as a dove.

Then her heart had fluttered, as if she actually thought the man handsome. Well, of course she'd already determined he was pleasing to the eye before they'd been properly introduced. But nothing about Colin Campbell fit the list of attributes she desired in a husband...the first being love, followed by respect, a good sense of humor, and most especially, a fine appreciation for *dancing*.

Blast him and blast his brutish ways. She wrung her hands. In no way would she allow him to take away everything she in which she found delight.

Merciful madness, before she'd met Colin, she'd enjoyed watching men spar. But when they stopped for their nooning, he'd blatantly tried to impress her by fighting two at once—whilst stealing glances her way. *His arrogance defies all reason.*

A light tap resounded at the door. Margaret bristled and said nothing. The matron had already brought her tray, winking and carrying on as if Margaret was a happy bride.

The door cracked open. "Lady Margaret? Is everything all right?"

Must his voice be so deep? Colin's sound rumbled within her and she clapped her hand to her chest to quell it. "Y-yes. All is fine."

Without her invitation, Colin stepped inside and closed the door, wearing his arming doublet and thick woolen chausses.

"No coat of arms?" She bit her lip. Would he punish her for such a remark?

His brows drew together. "There's little chance of attack here. I frequent this inn often on trips to court." Thankfully treating her jibe as an innocent question, he watched her out of the corner of his eye while he took a seat on the opposite side of the hearth and stretched out his legs, crossing them at the ankles.

She stared at him for a moment—a man reclining in her chamber—a complete stranger, in all honesty. Black Colin, enforcer of the laws of Christendom. Her husband. Margaret lowered her eyes and whipped a few stitches, willing her hands to steady.

Very aware of the bed sitting across the room, she tried to think of anything she could say to prevent him from coaxing her there. "Why must you return to Rome?"

He didn't answer straight away, creating an uncomfortable pause that made Margaret's brow perspire. "The grand master sent me a dire request. I received it on the eve of Jon...er...Duncan's birth." His gaze darted to the fire, pained like he'd been stabbed in the arm with a dagger.

The same night his wife passed. Margaret contemplated his profile—bold, angular, deadly, yet sad. *He must have loved her very much.* "Have you *any* idea when you shall take your leave?"

He rubbed his hand over his jaw. "I must first ensure the building of my keep is set to rights and see you settled at Dunstaffnage with Duncan."

"Dunstaffnage—the king's lands? Why not Glenorchy lands?"

"The tower house is not yet finished. My family has governed Dunstaffnage since the time of Bruce."

"But building the castle needs supervision, does it not? I am quite able—"

"A building site is no place for a lady and a bairn. I spent a great deal of time at Dunstaffnage as a lad. It is well fortified and far away from clan feuds and the threat of outlaws. You will be safe there."

"Kilchurn is unsafe?" *Circumstances grow worse by the moment.*

He adjusted in his seat. "'Tis not yet fortified as Dunstaffnage is…and there is some unrest with the crofters which I need to address. But mark me, it will be every bit as impenetrable as Dunstaffnage by the time it's ready for you and Duncan to reside there."

So he did intend to put her in a tower and forget about her while he sailed for Rome. Margaret heeded her mother's words and chose to tread lightly. "You are aware I managed a great many affairs for my father."

"I'm sure you did quite well at it, too." He leaned forward. "From the safe confines of your father's keep."

"But—"

"I'll not discuss it. Your duty is the care of our son, and I'll see to it you both are protected within well-fortified walls."

Margaret pursed her lips. Aye, she'd lived in a castle, but she'd worked hard to earn the respect of her father's men, as well as the crofters who paid rent to till his lands. She could be a help to Colin if he was to leave the country for an undetermined period of time. She surveyed his presumptuous stature from head to toe. The Lord of Glenorchy didn't appear a man who'd bend to a lady's word. She must prove herself. She prayed an opportunity would present itself soon.

He stood and stretched. The heady scent of pure male washed over her. His arms alone bulged with muscles she'd never dreamed existed in a man. Margaret's heart hammered in her chest. She glanced back at the bed. Her palms perspired so, the needle dropped to the floor.

His gaze met hers for an instant—the deadly one that turned her blood to ice. Margaret could scarcely breathe. If he tried to lay a hand on her, she'd tell him how much the saddle had hurt all day because of the previous night's boorishness. He stepped toward her. Reflexively she clutched her fists under her chin.

He frowned, his brown eyes turning black. "You should sleep," he said gruffly. "We leave at first light."

Margaret watched him walk toward the door—broad shoulders, tapering to firm hips, supported by legs as solid as oak. *At the fete I wondered how I would look upon such a magnificent masculine form with disinterested eyes. Now I know.*

Once he left, she hurried across the floor and turned the lock. Thank heavens he hadn't mounted another *attack*.

Chapter Eight

The Highlands, 10ᵗʰ October, 1455

The next day, the retinue continued on, slogging through miserable wind and spitting rain. Before dark, Colin led the procession into a clearing surrounded by tall birch and evergreens. Fortunately, the rain had stopped, though the ground was soggy. Colin dismounted and strode toward Margaret's place behind the wagon, his black cloak slung across his armored shoulder. "Build a fire, men—if you can find anything dry enough to burn."

He sent out a hunting party and had the campsite bustling with activity before he reached Margaret's mare. "Apologies for the weather, m'lady." He grasped her waist, lowering her to the ground like she weighed nothing.

She tried to laugh, but it came out like a snort. "As if you could do anything about the rain." She was still angry with him.

He inclined his head toward the wagon. "I shall make you a dry bed for the night. I'll not see you lying in the muck with the men."

Shivering, Margaret studied the muddy ground, strewn with thick patches of moss. She wished they all could sleep in the wagon. The ground would be comfortable for no man. "Thank you."

In his heavy armor, Colin easily leapt into the back of the wagon and started moving things to the sides and stacking her trunks in the nose, creating a gap in the center. "I'll lay down a plaid for you after supper." He held up his finger, his eyes popping wide as if he'd had an idea. "I've just the thing to ensure you stay dry."

Margaret wrung her hands. "There's no need to go to any trouble."

"For a woman?" He marched to his horse and untied his saddlebag. "There's nothing but trouble."

Her hands dropped. Things between them might be a wee bit easier if he *liked* her. But no, he considered her a burden—one more yoke to add to his list of responsibilities.

Colin turned and flashed a sheepish smile. "I see I've failed at my attempt at making a joke."

She crossed her arms. "I must admit, I've some difficulty understanding your humor."

He unfolded an oblong piece of oiled leather. "I purchased this doeskin at the Stirling fete for a pair of shoes. I'll secure it over the wagon so you'll stay dry if the rain should start up again."

"How kind."

Colin used his dagger to make holes in the corners of the hide. "I'm not a complete ogre."

"Oh no?"

Margaret thought he'd be angry at her terse remark, but he glanced up with hurt in his eyes—a look that tied her stomach in knots. She busied herself looking for dry kindling. Why on earth would he *not* want her to think him an ogre? He'd behaved as one. Was he trying to make it up to her by fashioning a bed in the back of a rickety old wagon? He'd need to come up with something a fair bit more chivalrous than that.

Margaret kneeled, reached under a thick conifer and found dry twigs. She deposited them in the center of the site and took on the task of stacking stones in a circle for the fire. Chilled to the bone, she imagined they all needed warmth.

Men stopped by, carrying armfuls of wood and dropped them into a growing pile before setting out for more. Each one grinned in his own way, showing their appreciation of her willingness to help.

Colin hailed his squire. "Maxwell, come help me remove my armor."

Margaret pretended not to notice when he slid his cloak from his sturdy form. But her insides shivered in concert with her skin. Why couldn't he be reed thin or chubby, or anything but a rock-solid warrior? The man was so utterly distracting. *But he doesn't like me.*

She shook her head. Earlier, she'd spotted a satchel of char cloth and flax tow in the back of the wagon. She collected it with a flint and striking iron.

Maxwell already had Colin's leg irons removed. The redheaded lad had been trained well. Margaret gaped. *God's teeth, Lord Glenorchy needs to keep his body covered more than a woman ought. His form is scandalous.*

Colin turned his head, and Margaret continued to the fire pit before he could catch her staring. On her knees, she placed the swatch of char cloth in the center of the pit and struck the flint to the iron. A spark immediately took flame, and she quickly piled it with quick-burning flax tow. She picked up a handful of twigs while blowing on the tiny flame. The flax ignited and she carefully added a twig, and then more, stacking them to allow air to the flame so not to snuff it.

"Margaret."

The back of her neck prickled. Colin stood directly behind her. She chose not to turn, picked up a thicker branch and placed it on the growing flame. "Aye?"

"No wife of mine will dirty her hands when there's a host of men about who can start a fire." Before she had a chance to respond, he beckoned a pair of soldiers. "William, Fionn. Stoke the fire and fashion a spit whilst you're at it." Colin stepped beside her and offered his hand. "Are you chilled?"

She looked at his callused palm—*as callused as his heart*. "Not only cold, but damp as well." Margaret stood without his assistance.

Persisting, he placed his hand in the small of her back. "I'll fetch you a saddle blanket to sit upon whilst the fire warms you."

She nodded, wishing he'd leave her alone. His sudden interest in her welfare was disconcerting. The blackguard made it difficult for her to maintain a deep level of hostility when he tried to be nice. And now that his armor had been removed, every muscle bulged under his tight-fitting woolens. Must he walk around the clearing in nothing but chausses and a short arming doublet? Yes, Margaret would have appreciated watching a man of his physical stature attend her, but not Black Colin. She would not succumb to his physical allure—he'd made it clear he had no amorous feelings for her. She turned away, willing him to wrap himself in his cloak to keep her eyes from straying over every inch of his muscular physique. No man should be thus endowed.

Colin placed a saddle blanket on the ground and retrieved his cloak from the wagon. "Allow me, m'lady."

She gasped when he gently wrapped it around *her* shoulders. Tugging the fur-lined garment across her body, she stepped away. "You need your cloak. There's a chill this eve."

He slapped a hand through the air. "Bah. I'm toasty dry. I've been swathed in iron all day. I need a cool breeze to enliven my limbs."

Margaret sat. Colin had no intention of covering up. The scent of spice and rugged warrior washed over her. She brushed her nose across the cloak's soft fur and closed her eyes, inhaling. Curses. Why couldn't he smell like a swine's bog?

The blaze had grown into a bonfire by the time Argyll and his hunting crew crashed through the wood with a red deer suspended from a pole.

Slapping the men on their shoulders, Colin grinned. "Well done. We shall fill our bellies this night and sleep soundly."

Argyll smiled at Margaret. "Hugh felled the beast with a single arrow."

She looked at the archer admiringly. "Then Hugh shall have the first cut."

Comfortable under Colin's cloak, Margaret watched the men interact with each other, joking, taking turns spinning the carcass on the spit. They all stole glances her way, observing her with curiosity. She didn't mind. She was assessing them as well—who had the sharpest wit, who was tallest, who carried pikes or swords or bows. Colin had amassed an impressive army. She suspected these were the men who followed him to Rome and back, and from their bantering, they'd been together for a long time.

As darkness crept over them, the air grew heady with the smell of roasting meat. Her stomach rumbled—she could taste the juicy venison already.

Colin opted to recline on his saddle across the fire. Margaret swallowed against the thickening in her throat. *Why would he do that? Did he not ask the king to find him a wife?* And now he had married her, he acted in the most peculiar ways, first catering to her comfort and then staying as far away from her as he could without removing himself from his company of men. A chill cut through the cloak.

Lord Argyll took a seat beside his uncle and flashed a lopsided grin at her. His twisted face formed an unspoken apology, followed by a quirk, as if he also didn't understand why Colin had chosen that particular spot.

"Have you dried from the rain, m'lady?" Maxwell, the young squire, asked. At least he'd been bold enough to sit alongside her.

"Aye. All except my toes."

"Where do you hail from?" another asked.

"My father is Lord Struan. His lands include Loch Rannoch, west of Pitlochry."

"Is it nice there?" All eyes stared at her.

"'Tis a lovely Highland loch. Probably not much different to Loch Awe."

A big fellow laughed. "Except Dunalasdair is a fine keep, unlike Kilchurn, which will never be complete if the grand master keeps hailing Lord Colin to Rome."

Colin shot him a stern glare. "She'll be done within the year."

The men laughed, and Colin spread his palms toward Argyll. The younger man shrugged. "Don't look at me. I questioned the same only a fortnight ago."

"Do you miss your family?" Maxwell asked.

Margaret looked directly at Colin to ensure he was listening. "Yes. Very much. They were most kind and loving."

"Do you have any siblings?" The boy was full of questions.

She narrowed her gaze. "Two elder brothers who would protect me with their lives."

Colin shifted as if a rock prodded his backside.

Maxwell picked up a stick and poked the fire. "What sorts of things do you enjoy?"

"Music, but most of all, I love to *dance*." Margaret glared at Colin across the flame. "I could dance for hours every night."

Lord Glenorchy frowned. "Is that blasted meat cooked?"

The man at the spit leaned over the fire for a closer look. "Not yet, m'lord."

"Can you make it?" Maxwell asked.

Margaret knitted her brows. "Whatever do you mean?"

"Make music? Do you play an instrument or sing?"

She chuckled. "Aye. I play the lute and sing a little. I daresay I wouldn't be a Highland lassie if I didn't."

"Can you play for us?" the big man asked.

Margaret cast her gaze to the wagon. "I'm afraid my lute is in my trunks."

Argyll jabbed Colin in the ribs. "Go fetch it for her, uncle. It will be a pleasant diversion to staring at all these ugly faces across the fire." He bowed his head toward Margaret. "Excepting you, m'lady."

"Och, come, m'lord," the soldiers chorused.

"Wheesht, you're all carrying on like a flock of hens." Colin stood and eyed Margaret with his fists on his hips. "You'll need to point out where it is. I'm not digging through all those trunks for naught."

***

Colin let out a deep breath and trudged toward the wagon. He chose to sit across the fire from Margaret, thinking it a good idea to put distance between them. He'd not considered what the firelight would do to illuminate her porcelain skin, or how charming she'd look when interacting with the men. He wanted to bark at them, tell the lot to keep their mouths shut and ignore the lass. Aye, that would put him in good favor with his men. He pressed the heel of his hand against his temple.

He was behaving like an arse.

The lady came up behind him, making the hair at his nape stand on end. Those hypnotic green eyes bored into his back. Colin swiped his hand across his neck to quash his damnable tingling, and climbed into the wagon. He examined her assortment of trunks. "Which one is it?" he barked.

"The big one on the bottom."

Of course it couldn't be in one of the light little trunks that was easy to access. He had to untie his makeshift tent and move just about every piece of luggage aside to reach it, mussing his earlier work to make her a suitable place to sleep.

He'd run around like a lovesick newlywed seeing to her needs. He was such a complete and utter muttonhead. His gut was wound tight. He shoved a mid-sized trunk aside. After Colin finally cleared the path to Margaret's mammoth trunk, he yanked open the hasp and threw back the lid a bit more vigorously than he ought.

The lute wasn't on top. "I don't see it here." He slid his hand down the sides. Nothing.

The wagon jostled and Colin turned around. Margaret had deftly climbed up unassisted, standing inches from his nose. *Sugared lavender.* His damned knees practically wobbled.

She cleared her throat. "If I might pass, I'll retrieve it."

Colin glanced behind her. There was no place to move. "Uh." He shuffled sideways. "Perhaps if we turn together we can switch places."

She nodded, and stepped toward him, looking up with those huge almond-shaped eyes. In the dim light all he could see was the whites of her eyes and the outline of her oval face, but her fragrance gripped him like a vise. He scooted his feet as she moved. Something jabbed him in the back. His body squashed against hers. Soft, pliable breasts rubbed his chest. Colin tried to arch his hips back, but his manhood crushed against her. Her warm breath caressed his skin. Colin's groin turned to fire.

She tipped up her chin. He could see the green of her eyes now. Rimmed by gold flecks, they glowed, reflecting the firelight. Colin's tongue tapped his upper teeth and he sucked in a sharp breath. Placing his hands on her shoulders, he drew her even closer, overwhelmed by an urge to kiss her. He crooked his neck, his heart pounding.

With a gasp, Margaret averted her head. Colin's lips nearly collided with her cheek, but she shoved her way past him and faced her trunk.

A cold breeze quashed his inner flame to embers. *Christ, what in God's name was that about? She's a vixen sent to torment me.*

Margaret slid her hand deep into the trunk. "I packed it in the middle of my gowns to keep it from breaking."

Colin clenched his fists. He should have stepped aside as soon as he got the trunk free. What had come over him? He was no adolescent lad sneaking from the campfire to steal a kiss. He'd better shove a stopper in his flask, for obviously the whisky had made his unmentionables turn to lusty fire.

Jumping down, he offered his hand. Her slender fingers met his rough pads. Her hands were fine-boned and soft—even smaller than…

Damnation.

Once on the ground, Margaret raised her chin and headed back to the campfire, leaving him standing there, cursing under his breath like a tinker. He shook his head. Bloody hell, he had enough to worry about.

Before he resumed his seat beside Argyll, Margaret strummed a chord. The conversation stopped. She looked up and surveyed the expectant faces with a polite smile. Then her fingers struck the strings. A rich, airy tune danced upon the breeze, as if a butterfly were flitting round the circle.

Every eye focused upon her, every mouth open. Sitting, Colin watched her, transfixed. He'd never even heard a minstrel play with such precision or clarity. His heart leapt with every strum, and then her eyes met his across the flame. Her face appeared enchanted, as if he were dreaming. His feet itched with the urge to stand, walk around the fire and claim her.

For an instant, she lowered her lids. Colin gasped. Then her voice sailed to him with the breeze. Clear as a crystal bell, her tune caressed his skin and made gooseflesh stand proud. He never wanted the song to end. She raised her lids and met his eyes again. Endless emotion filled those eyes, and he wondered what life experiences a sheltered lord's daughter could have endured to make them so expressive. She glanced aside, and suddenly he knew.

He'd violated her.

Bile burned the back of Colin's throat. He had performed his duty as a husband. But the excuse didn't matter. What he'd done was wrong. Colin stared at the ground before him. He couldn't look at her now, not when she thought so little of him.

But why should I care what Margaret thinks? God help me, I need this journey to be over.

With a final strum, the music hung in the air for a moment, until silence spread across the clearing like a black-robed villain. Argyll led the applause. All the men chimed in, laughing, clapping—a couple even wiped their eyes.

With lead in his gut, Colin forced himself to glance up. Margaret had turned her attention to Maxwell, who showered her with unabashed praise.

God help him. Colin had not married a stepmother for Duncan. He'd married a woman—a stranger, layered with a great many talents he'd yet to uncover. Part of him would rather leave them hidden—yet his gut squeezed with an unwelcome yearning to discover them all.

He should not have wed so soon after Jonet's death.

"The venison's ready," called the man by the spit.

Thank the good Lord for food. Colin had probably lost his wits due to hunger.

Chapter Nine

The Highlands, 10ᵗʰ October, 1455

After Lady Margaret excused herself for the night, Argyll leaned toward Colin's ear. "You're not going to allow your wife to sleep alone?"

Colin shrugged. "She'll be fine in the wagon."

"Will she?" Argyll elbowed him. "Have you noticed the way the men have been looking at her?"

Of course he'd noticed—could have planted his fist in every single face. Nonetheless, he trusted his men. "Mind your tongue."

"You're a fool when it comes to women."

"Wheesht. Put a stopper in your gob." Colin stood. He'd best set the wagon to rights and ensure Margaret had the privacy she needed to—well, to take care of her *female needs*.

She emerged from behind a bush, smoothing out her skirts. "M'lord?"

Colin hopped back into the wagon. "I'll rearrange these things again." He spied her instrument resting on the floorboards. "Shall I place your lute back in your trunk?"

"Please."

He shoved things into order, doubled his plaid over and laid it down. He then affixed the oiled deerskin over the top like he'd done before. "It's nay a four-poster bed, but should be comfortable enough for the night."

"I'm sure it shall be fine." She removed his cloak from her shoulders. "Thank you for lending this to me. I'm dry now."

He hopped down and grasped it. Margaret rubbed her outer arms.

Away from the fire, it was bloody cold—even felt like they might see an unseasonal snow. "Have you anything warmer?"

She pulled her woolen mantle around her body. "This one serves me well."

Colin growled and looked toward the heavens. Thick clouds loomed overhead. He'd lost his mind, going against his better judgment. "Come, climb into the wagon. I'll keep you warm."

"'Tis very kind, but I assure you it is unnecessary."

He grasped her waist and plunked her arse onto the wagon. "I'll not hear another word about it." He flicked his wrist. "Climb under the tarpaulin and lie on your side."

She stared. "But—"

"Do it, I say. I'll not touch you—you have my word."

Her lips formed a line and she gave him a single nod before she crawled under his makeshift shelter. In her wake, she left behind a fragrance that made his head swim. Colin reached inside the leather purse at his hip and pulled out a flask. Mayhap he needed one more tot of whisky before he climbed beside the lady and kept himself celibate for the night—especially when she smelled so bloody intoxicating.

He pulled the stopper off with his teeth and tossed back a healthy swig. The liquid warmed him as it slid down his gullet. He coughed. "Are you set, Lady Margaret?"

"Aye." There was a tremor in her voice.

The whisky did nothing to allay the guilt clamping his gut. He climbed into the wagon. Damn it, he owed an apology to no one. Everything would be back to normal as soon as they reached Dunstaffnage. He could manage anything for a couple of days, especially a woman.

He pulled himself alongside her, trying not to touch his body to hers. He preferred to lie on his back, but his shoulders were too wide. He rolled to his side, mirroring her. There was nowhere for his arm to rest—he tried to slip it between them, but shoved Margaret in the back. "Sorry."

"'Tis all right."

Och, must she sound so bonny?

He huffed and peered over her shoulder. "I'll have to drape my arm across you."

"Must you?"

"'Tis just an arm, lass."

Gingerly, he slid it over her waist and let out a breath. She did too.

Colin tried to keep his nose away from her hair, but gave up, resigning himself to an eve surrounded by her scent. He'd likely be awake all night thinking of brutal battles—anything to keep his cock from jutting into her buttocks. He closed his eyes and pictured Jonet—lovely raven hair, pale blue eyes—nothing like Margaret, with her green eyes and voice that could lull a man into bonded servitude.

Margaret's breathing took on the slow cadence of sleep. She seemed so tiny, frail beneath his arm.

Something in his chest tightened, made his mind go completely blank. He tried to remember his lost love, but when he closed his lids, green eyes stared back.

***

Margaret opened her eyes and resisted the urge to bolt upright. Colin's heavy arm tugged her tighter to his body. His deep bass voice moaned, sending a rumble through her chest. He shifted his hips against her.

Heaven's stars—rigid as the hilt of a sword, his maleness ground between her buttocks. A spike of heat shot amid her hips. Her unwanted reaction galled her to no end. Margaret clamped her thighs together to stanch it. *My traitorous urges must cease.*

Holding still as a statue, she lifted her head high enough to peer out the bottom of the wagon. Predawn, a violet hue shrouded the forest. Was that snow beyond her feet? Beneath the tarpaulin and Colin's fur-lined cloak, she was warm, especially her backside. Colin's body emitted more heat than a hearth. *At least the Black Knight is good for something.*

A bird called. Not long and the camp would stir to life. Margaret inhaled a shallow breath and dared not move, lest he wake and try *that* again. God forbid, how could anyone do something so indecent with the men nearby? Even though Colin vowed he would not, she didn't trust him. Margaret would slip out of the wagon this minute, if it weren't for his arm clutching her flush against his incredibly warm body. Her every muscle rigid, she prayed he would wake and release his torturous grasp.

Violet turned to cobalt. More birds. Footsteps broke twigs alongside the wagon. Water splashed the ground with a hiss. Someone grunted. More footsteps. "Good morrow, Maxwell—turning the snow yellow, I see."

"Bloody oath, nearly froze me cods off. This weather is preposterous." The young man didn't sound quite as polite as he had last eve.

Colin sputtered. He sat up so quickly, he tore the tarpaulin from its ties. Margaret gagged on a mouthful of snow. Coughing, she brushed the icy fluff away. In an instant, she'd gone from toasty warm to completely freezing, snow biting into her cheeks.

Colin scrubbed his hands over his face then glared at her as if she'd tried to accost *him*.

"Good morrow?" Margaret leaned away.

He slapped his chest and coughed. "Good morrow. You should have awakened me sooner."

She bit the inside of her cheek, drew her feet beneath her and stood. "If you'll excuse me, I must attend my needs."

"Wait a moment." Colin shook like a dog. "I shall stand guard."

She balled her fists, trying to conjure a suitable retort. Was it necessary for him to hover?

He cast his gaze to the sky. "Not to worry. I'll turn my back."

Margaret glanced around at the men bustling about, coming from the forest, adjusting…themselves. Having Colin stand guard was her best option.

True to his word, he kept his back turned to her. She made quick work of her business and slipped passed him. "Thank you."

Colin grunted and stepped behind a clump of broom himself. "Maxwell, load the wagon," he bellowed from the trees. After, he proceeded to traipse around the around the campsite like an ogre. "Quickly, men, gulp down your oatcakes. We'll be in Glen Orchy before nightfall…fresh straw and a warm stable will be better than this miserable, wet white stuff."

Margaret had to agree with him there. Most of the men only had a single woolen plaid draped over their shoulders for the night. They all must have been as miserable as wet puppies.

Colin gave her a leg up, and she inched her bum into the saddle. Her soreness had eased. "May I ride beside you and Argyll, m'lord?"

He gave her a slap on the knee. "Nay. You're safer behind the wagon. We've got to pass through the trail at Loch na Bì. 'Tis the most notorious place for outlaws."

She took up her reins. "Then I suggest you ride where you'll not place yourself in harm's way."

He chuckled and leaned toward her. "Now what kind of knight would I be if I cowered behind my men?" His dark eyes teased her, and Margaret's miserable heart fluttered against her chest. He could irritate her with his arrogance, truly.

The crossing through the forest at Loch na Bì was uneventful, aside from the narrow, muddy trail bogging the wagon. The men had to help push and drive the oxen, using long branches to hoist up the wheels. Perhaps Colin had conjured his story about the area being fraught with outlaws just to keep her away from him. *Likely.* This entire trip had done nothing to allay her trepidation about the Black Knight. Though he may have shown her a thread of courtesy now and again, ignoring and keeping her behind the wagon demonstrated a complete lack of regard.

Once back in formation, she'd had enough. If she didn't assert her position as Lady Glenorchy now, Colin would most likely lock her in a wing of Dunstaffnage with his miserable son and forget she ever existed.

She picked up her reins and leaned forward. With a tap of her heel and riding crop, she gave her mare the cue to canter. At least her horse had some spirit—snorting through huge nostrils, easily overtaking the procession. Margaret slowed beside Argyll's right. Colin, thank heavens, was on his nephew's left.

He craned his armored neck toward her. "Margaret, 'tis not safe for you to ride at the front of the march."

"Nor is it for you, m'lord, but you do it regardless." She could have stuck her tongue out and made an ugly face, though she didn't dare.

He returned his gaze to the path ahead. "Argyll, take Lady Glenorchy back to the rear."

Margaret sidestepped her mare outside Argyll's reach. "I will not ride alone, and I will not be tucked away behind a rickety old wagon that blocks the scenery."

"Honestly, uncle," Argyll said. "We're nearly there."

Margaret flashed the younger man a "thank you" smile.

Choosing to see Colin's lack of response as acceptance, she lowered her reins and relaxed her seat. The rush of water filled her ears. "What river is this?"

Argyll looked to Colin, but when her husband didn't respond, he shrugged. "The River Orchy—I've caught many a fish in her rapids."

"Sounds like fun sport." Margaret stole an anxious glance at the Black Knight. "I'm looking forward to seeing the progress on Kilchurn."

Colin pulled his steed ahead. "Aye, and it had better be substantial," he groused. His stallion broke into a full-out gallop.

Defeated yet again, Margaret arched a brow toward Argyll. "He appears decidedly grouchy this day."

"Vandals have been preventing the building from making headway. Colin increased the guard right before he left for Stirling."

"Does he have any idea who the culprits are?" *Vandals? 'Tis a wonder he's afraid to have me supervise the building effort.*

"The master mason thinks it's the MacGregors."

Margaret patted her mare's sorrel neck. Could she help? "What do you think?"

"Colin needs to dig to the bottom of the problem before he starts storming around like a mad bull. The MacGregors of Glen Orchy pledged fealty to him."

"Hmm. Not something any self-respecting Highlander would take lightly."

Argyll eyed her. "Exactly."

"Does Colin feel the same?"

"Colin keeps his feelings to himself, though he's as familiar with the Highland code of honor as any man." Argyll turned to her, his face stern. "His reputation was well earned. There's no man more skilled on the battlefield than your husband. He took Jonet's death rather hard. Her body hadn't even been laid to rest when he received the missive from Rome requesting another term in the Crusades."

Margaret watched Colin's form grow smaller in the distance. Argyll could help answer some of her questions. Colin did indeed have grave issues that needed his attention before he set sail. "Do you think it wise for him to leave for the Holy Land straight away? Surely the grand master will understand he must put his house in order."

"Aye, but Colin believes it's his duty to save the world."

Margaret flicked her reins. "What of saving his family?"

Argyll bowed his head. "That, m'lady, is something you must take up with him."

When the River Orchy opened to an estuary, Margaret gasped. Ahead, the mist hovered over the loch, just as she'd often seen on Loch Rannoch, but the scene was even more magnificent than her home. To the west, majestic mountains loomed, shrouded in mist. Ahead, a verdant pasture with shaggy red cattle stretched along a tract of land that extended at least a mile, splitting the deep blue water.

Near the far end, men pushed barrows and chiseled stone. The immense curtain wall appeared so new, it could have been built yesterday. It bore not a trace of moss or ivy. Above it, Margaret imagined a great tower house with rounded turrets at each corner. From that vantage point, she'd be able to see the entire length of the loch and watch the mist rise. Kilchurn had the potential to be one of the greatest architectural works in Scotland. She could picture it.

Margaret might be wed to an archangel of war, but she could lose herself in this place. A castle of grandeur and great possibilities, she would preside as lady of the keep with pride, and Colin Campbell would not deny her—especially if he was in Rome.

Ahead, Colin sat on his steed deep in thought. Argyll and Margaret rode in beside him. "I'll never grow tired of beholding the view when the trees part," Colin said, as if speaking to himself.

Margaret sighed. "'Tis magnificent. Every bit as stunning as Stirling Palace."

Colin inclined his head to the west. "We'll stay the night in the cottage. Wait here whilst I speak to the master mason."

Margaret followed his gaze. A stone cottage with a large stable sat in the center of a fenced yard. Behind it, several more cottages speckled up the hillside. A wave of color caught her eye. A group of women held up their skirts, stomping on their washing along the river edge.

Margaret watched Colin ride away with Argyll. *My heavens, how long am I expected to sit here?* She dismounted and handed her reins to Maxwell. "I'll be visiting with the ladies."

He blinked twice, looking like a pompous toad. "The crofter's wives?"

"And why ever not?"

Maxwell's shoulder ticked up. "It just doesn't seem proper, m'lady."

She rolled her eyes. "Hogwash."

Margaret strolled over to the five women and waved. "Hello."

All but one ignored her—the others exchanging glances between themselves. The one had thick legs and a round face. She didn't smile, rather gave Margaret a guarded once-over. "Ye come to help us?"

"Now that's the best idea I've heard today." She sat upon a boulder and removed her shoes and hose. "How is the water?"

"Bloody cold." Round Face had a gruff voice.

Margaret smiled—at least someone responded to her query, the first step in making new friends. "We had a sprinkling of snow on the trail last night."

Another looked up. "Where did ye come from?"

"My husband and I are traveling from Stirling, but I hail from Loch Rannoch."

"Your husband? And who might that be?" Round Face asked.

All five women stopped and looked at her.

Margaret glanced over her shoulder and then gave them her most devious grin, waggling her eyebrows. "King James matched me with Black Colin." She hiked up her skirts and waded into the ice-cold rushing water, made louder by absolutely silent voices.

Then they all spoke at once.

"How dreadful."

"Ye ken he just lost his wife…"

"…and he has a wee bairn."

"And he intends to return to Rome for another crusade."

Margaret grabbed a plaid from a basket perched upon the rocks and doused it in the water. "Aye, and yet my parents insisted it was a good match." She sighed loudly. "After all, who can go against the king's orders? It was my duty to marry him."

The women exchanged oohs and ahs.

"You must be very brave indeed."

"Indeed."

"Indeed."

Margaret stomped the plaid, making a show of her washing skills—she'd learned them from her nursemaid. Washing clothes with her skirts wrapped up around her knees had been great sport for a child of nine. "Aye, he's a fearsome lord."

"Is he?" They all gaped at her with interested, wide eyes.

Margaret nodded, knitting her brows with affected concern. "He's worried about building the keep. Said there have been reports of vandals."

"Aye." The round-faced woman put a fist on her hip. Stout, she looked like she could flatten a Highland wrestler with a solid punch. "And Master Elliot is blaming it on our men."

"Oh?" Margaret stopped stomping. "'Tis a disgrace. Why do you think he's doing that?"

One lassie turned her back. "He's a lazy bastard," she mumbled so quietly, Margaret had no doubt the words weren't meant for her ears.

She tried not to gape at the young woman's vulgar tongue. "Have you any idea who's causing the damage?"

"Nay," another said. "Lord Colin increased the guard."

She squished the plaid between her freezing toes. "Have there been problems since?"

Round Face shook her head. "Not with vandals."

Five heads again shook in unison.

"But we dunna want our men blamed…"

"There never is enough sand…"

"Or stone…"

"I'm worried about food for winter…"

Margaret clasped her hands to her cheeks. "My, it does seem the whole venture is befuddled."

"We'd like to see the keep finished. It would bring us all peace of mind."

Margaret wrung out the plaid and tossed it into the "clean" basket. "Are you all MacGregor women?"

"Aye, and Campbells," they chorused.

She fisted her hips. "Your men pay fealty to Lord Glenorchy?"

"Aye. We're guardians of this land and proud of it." Round Face clearly was the leader of the group.

Margaret met her gaze. "But why are you afraid there'll not be enough food come winter?"

"Black Colin, er, Lord Glenorchy's factor—"

"Wheesht," the young one silenced.

Margaret stood straight. Her next words must be spoken with utmost care, else she'd lose their trust—and a chance to uncover the pillager. "I assure you, your reply will be held in confidence. If you suspect anything, anything at all, I must be made aware." She placed a hand over her heart. "I vow not a one of you will suffer consequences for speaking out. All suspicions will be discreetly explored."

Lips pursed, they all gave stern nods to the leader. "The man is a cheat. If ye ask me, he's behind the vandalism. He's responsible for the lack of supplies, for certain."

Hmm. Now she was getting somewhere. "And who is Lord Glenorchy's factor?"

"Walter MacCorkodale." The woman pointed to the hills. "His clan owns a wee parcel of land west of here."

Margaret followed the gesture then glanced toward the unfinished castle. Colin was riding toward them rapidly.

"Thank you." She stepped out of the river and picked up her shoes as Colin rode within earshot. "'Tis been ever so enlightening chatting with you ladies. I do hope we can spend some time together again. I'm sure there shall be many feasts once the keep has been completed."

Each one smiled warmly.

Frowning, Colin appeared as if he could skewer her with his mammoth sword when he cantered up, leading her mare. "I asked you to stay with the guard."

"Apologies, my lord." She winked over her shoulder. "I thought it would be pleasant to meet the women who support your men."

Grumbling under his breath, he hopped down and helped her mount. She felt rather empowered by her slight disregard of his orders. Evidently, she was growing impervious to his blackguard glares. Besides, they would be staying at the cottage for the night. He had absolutely no reason to hurry her.

***

Colin's jaw twitched. He opened the door to the cottage and stood aside to allow Margaret to pass. She waltzed inside, completely oblivious to his dark mood. He removed his cloak and draped it on a peg. "I use this cottage for hunting. It isn't much, but better than sleeping in the stable."

She turned full circle, unpinning her cloak and handing it to him. "'Tis quaint."

Stark was a better choice of words. A hearth with cooking utensils, a wooden table with four mismatched chairs, a worn settee and an eight-point stag's head on the wall. The only other room was the bedchamber. Her heels clicked the floorboards while she walked across and opened the door. The chamber wasn't much fancier—a hearth, a large bed, a round table and two chairs.

Colin allowed her to explore whilst he set to building the fire. Margaret was certainly the jauntiest, most outspoken wife he'd ever had. His gut twisted. He didn't care if it were a trifle—she'd disobeyed him. He wouldn't tolerate disobedience in his men, and he wouldn't stand for it with her either. Ever since they left Stirling, she'd jabbed at him with little twists of phrase, and then she rode out of formation and joined him at the front of the retinue. He never should have allowed it.

The thing that had his insides twisted the most was her blatant disregard for a direct order. He told her to remain in her saddle. How difficult was it to follow one simple instruction? If there had been a threat nearby, he never would have been able to protect her.

Margaret's footsteps lightly tapped around him. "Only one bedchamber, m'lord?" Her voice, not so self-assured, had a tremor.

"Aye." Honestly, he hadn't thought about the sleeping arrangements, and right now he didn't want to.

He struck the flint against the char. A flame leapt to life and he stacked twigs around it. Once the fire could be left alone, he faced her with his hands on his hips. "The next time I ask you to do something, I'll expect you to be mindful of my request."

She mirrored his pose, her small fists on feisty, disrespectful hips. "Why shouldn't I speak to the local women? They're our kin, no?"

"No…I mean, aye." Leave it to her to steer him away from the subject at hand. "Dammit, woman. Your safety is my concern. How can I protect you if you're off hiking up your skirts, washing with the commoners?"

Margaret's eyebrows pinched together. "I was in danger?"

Blast her inquisition. "Nay, but you could have been. When I give an order, I expect it to be followed."

"So you desire me to obey your every word without question?" She curtseyed. "Oh gallant knight."

"Bloody hell." He pushed past her and stared up at the stag's head. "You make it sound as if I am some sort of tyrant."

"Are you not?"

"Of course I am not." He dragged his fingers through his hair. "I've a great many things to oversee, and—"

The door opened, and a servant walked in with a tray. "Your supper, m'lord."

Colin pointed to the table. "Leave it." His blood coursed hot beneath his skin until the servant took his leave. Colin grabbed his cloak from the peg. "Eat. I shall bed down in the stable tonight, since my presence is so maddening for you."

He flung open the door. "I trust your person can manage to remain within the cottage for the night?" He didn't wait for her response and slammed the door.

Colin marched across the yard to the stables. Marrying Margaret Robinson was the worst idea he'd ever had. He never should have gone through with the ceremony. The absolute last thing he needed was a headstrong wife. Blast her. If things didn't improve when they reached Dunstaffnage, he'd have no recourse but to consider an annulment on the grounds of personal incompatibility.

He pushed inside the stable and tossed his gear beside Maxwell.

The lad sat up. "Is everything all right, m'lord?"

"Aye, everything is bloody wonderful." He kicked the straw into a pile.

"Where is Lady Margaret?"

"In the cottage, where else?"

"So…er…why are you here?" At eighteen, the young squire also could use a lesson in curbing his tongue.

"That's none of your concern."

Maxwell reclined against the wall. "She's pretty."

Colin gave him a stern glare—a warning to keep his mouth shut.

The lad spread his palms apologetically. "I mean, your wife, it's not bad to notice…um…you're a lucky man…er…lord."

Colin plopped down on his mound of hay. "Wheesht, would you shut your gob?"

Maxwell hung his head. "Sorry."

Colin grumbled under his breath. He pulled his cloak across his shoulders and reclined. Just over three sennights and the Kilchurn walls would be mudded up. He needed to remain behind work with the master mason, but doing so was out of the question. Margaret already thought him a rogue. Sending her ahead to Dunstaffnage, though tempting, would be heartless. Besides, he could not allow her to arrive at the castle alone and have Effie thrust Duncan into her arms. The least chivalric of all knights would accompany his wife to ensure his family was settled and comfortable.

He groaned. Traveling there and back would only keep him away for two more days. It was the right thing to do.

Colin closed his eyes on a sigh. Things with Margaret would settle soon and he could tend to his affairs. He rolled to his side. Last night he'd rested in the same position and nuzzled into Margaret's silken hair. Warmth spread throughout his chest. He could bury his nose in that woman's tresses for an eternity.

His eyes flashed open. *No, I could not and must not.* He slapped his hand to his head. This morning he'd awaken with the most painful erection he'd ever had in his life. That bloody woman was the cause. If she hadn't been sleeping beside him, he would have had frozen cods like the rest of his men, and his embarrassing, unholy cock wouldn't have taken so long to ease.

He shifted uncomfortably. It was best for him to sleep in the stable, away from her and that bonny smell. Mercifully, she'd have her own chamber at the castle and could leave him to his miserable mourning. He'd cool down his heated Campbell urges and set his mind on rejoining the crusade.

Chapter Ten

The Highlands, 11th October, 1455

As expected, Margaret rode behind the wagon on this last leg of their journey to Dunstaffnage. Colin had been such an insufferable tyrant last eve, he'd given her no time to discuss her findings. However, in all honesty, she needed to decide how to broach the subject before she told him the women thought his factor corrupt. The idea of conversing with him on such a delicate matter filled her with trepidation. Colin was nowhere near as approachable as her father had been. Would the Black Knight explode in a rage? Last night he'd shown her a sampling of his temper. She had little doubt he could fire off a roar like a line of battlement cannons.

She cringed. At least Mother would be pleased at her restraint. She'd been tempted to follow him outside and tell him exactly what she thought of his overbearing concern for safety and top it off by slamming him with the fact his factor was considered a cheat.

But then, Colin had most likely employed Walter MacCorkodale for a very long time. Her word against a trusted servant would be grave, and at this stage, Lord Glenorchy would probably side with the swindler. Factors were learned and respected men, but could become corrupt if not held accountable—she'd learned that through her father's experience. With Colin's frequent absences and trips abroad, she imagined Walter MacCorkodale had been given too much freedom with his quill, among other things. Margaret would like to meet the man and assess his character for herself. Perhaps she'd gain an opportunity soon.

She chuckled at her antics from the prior day. The Campbell and MacGregor women were of strong Highland stock. Though initially they were guarded, they'd opened up as soon as Margaret started working beside them. The years she'd spent employed by her father had helped her develop a keen respect for crofters. Every soul in the clan was important and deserved both charity and respect. This core value provided the foundation of Margaret's principles. One with which she would never part.

She had no reason to doubt the validity of washerwomen's concerns—especially the fact the MacGregor men were innocent and worked well beside the Campbell clan, and everyone wanted to see the castle completed quickly.

Perhaps Colin had spent the evening speaking to the men, since he'd stayed the night someplace other than the cottage bedchamber. Thank all holiness for that small boon. She'd be content if he stayed away from her bedchamber for the rest of their days.

It was afternoon when she gathered her wits and cued her mare for a canter. Her palms instantly started to perspire when she joined Lord Glenorchy and Lord Argyll at the front of the procession.

Colin arched his brow under his helm. "Lady Margaret." He said nothing to urge her back to the rear.

"M'lord." She smoothed a hand over her skirts. "Were you able to speak to the MacGregors about the vandalism?"

"Heaven's stars, woman." He gave her a stern frown. "You'd best leave these things to me."

"Aye, Colin?" By his wide-eyed response, she'd caught him off guard, using his familiar name with a hint of sarcasm. Though her insides quaked, his reaction served to encourage her to press him. "And to whom shall I leave things after you set sail with no possible way of contacting you for months?"

A muscle in his jaw twitched. "I've said I will not head for Rome before I've got things set to rights."

Och aye, whilst I'm locked away with a wee bairn in some archaic castle? "I see, and affairs will stay in a perfect state of 'right' throughout the duration of your crusade?"

Argyll leaned forward in his saddle. "She has a point."

Colin ran his fingers under his helm. "I assure you, m'lady, all will be in place before I take my leave. The only thing you will need to concern yourself with is Duncan's education and birthing a bairn yourself."

Margaret pulled on her reins. Rolling heat crept up her face. Argyll let out a boisterous laugh.

And she'd thought him a more agreeable character than Colin? *Wonderful.* She'd spent the entire morning gathering her wits, only to be met with a snarl and laughter. Turning her mare, she headed back to the solitude of her "place" behind the wagon. Who needed to ride beside a bombastic, pigheaded husband and his nephew?

Birthing the Black Knight's bairn? So he does intend to continue marital relations. Heaven help me.

She'd almost made it to the wagon when Colin's gauntleted hand reached for her reins. "We're nearly there, Lady Margaret. Come, you'll enjoy the view far more from the lead."

She sat fully erect with a challenging glare. "Are you not afraid outlaws will charge out of the wood and spring upon us?"

"Not this close to Dunstaffnage, lest the fools are out to have their throats cut." He chuckled. "The Campbells have been keepers of this land since Robert the Bruce united Scotland." He inhaled deeply. "Nary a soul in these parts would ride against me and my men."

She turned her mare back around. "Would you would prefer to call this home?"

"Nay. Though we govern, this is the king's land. Innis Chonnell has always been the Campbell keep, now owned by my nephew." A faraway glint shimmered in Colin's eye. "Kilchurn will soon be finished. It will exceed the grandeur of Dunstaffnage, and when it is complete, I shall build a castle even more imposing on Argyll's new holdings in Inverary. The Campbell name shall be feared throughout Scotland."

"I daresay it already is," Margaret mumbled under her breath, steering her mare beside Argyll.

He nodded agreeably. "You do dream on a lofty scale, uncle."

"And why should I not? We are lords of this land." Colin shook his gauntleted finger. "Never forget that."

They rode past a lovely chapel nestled in the wood. Through the trees, a well-worn path led to an outer gatehouse, fortified by stone bailey walls, not unlike her family's keep on Loch Rannoch. Smoke billowing from chimneys, the castle walls loomed atop a solid-rock outcrop. The natural stone, tall as the surrounding trees, projected from the grassy landscape.

They entered a narrow-walled pathway leading to the inner gate. The dark grey curtain stretched high to the heavens. *Much taller than Dunalasdair.* As they rounded the corner, the donjon tower emerged above the walls, with defensive arrow slits strategically placed all the way up to the crenelated top.

"I can see why Robert the Bruce desired a stronghold fortified such as this." Margaret shifted her gaze to the west. "Is the cove an outlet to the sea?"

Colin pointed. "Aye, the castle sits on the point where Loch Etive meets the Firth of Lorn."

"I should like to walk atop the wall and see it."

"Perhaps after you meet our son."

Margaret would have been content if Colin had smiled when he spoke it. But his voice held a monotonous tone, as if he couldn't care less what occupied her time outside of her duties as stepmother.

What have I done to earn his disdain? This whole charade would be much easier to bear if we could be on friendlier terms. My mother and father always spoke to each other candidly. That is all I ask.

Everything turned to blackness when they rode beneath the inner gate's dank portcullis. Margaret tensed. Would this be her prison? She wasn't met with the welcomed feeling of open air and majestic mountains like she'd been in Glen Orchy. True, Dunstaffnage was surrounded by trees and water. She couldn't put her finger on it, but this castle sent chills to her bones. No wonder Colin was driven to build upon his lands. Whether he liked it or not, she would do everything in her power to see to the completion of the tower house. Kilchurn would be her home too, God willing.

***

Relieved to have arrived at Dunstaffnage, Colin could now deposit Margaret in her rooms and move on with his affairs. The dusting of snow they'd had on the trail was a stern reminder winter wasn't far off. If he didn't set sail for Rome soon, he'd be forced to delay his journey until spring. He doubted Jacques de Milly would want to wait.

War didn't stop in the Holy Land like it did during winter in the north.

After dismounting in the courtyard, he ushered Margaret into the keep. "We'll stop at the nursery first. I'm sure you're anxious to see Duncan."

"Indeed."

Fortunately, she didn't argue with him on that point. If the trip was any indication, Lady Margaret was a strong-willed woman—perhaps too much so.

Leading her up the winding tower stairs, his back tingled, sensing her eyes assessing him. Did she appreciate what she saw? Not that he should care. Did she like him at all? He shouldn't care about that either.

Finally, they crested the steps and he led her through the upper passageway and opened the door. The nursery resounded with a healthy wail. Effie's gaze snapped up. She held Duncan in her arms, but Colin's son would not be consoled. The bairn's wee voice struck a chord deep in the black recesses of his heart. Frozen in place for an instant, he wanted to turn tail and run.

The nursemaid stood. "M'lord."

Blinking, he forced himself to cross the room and kiss her cheek. "Effie, please allow me to introduce Lady Margaret."

"'Tis my pleasure." Margaret beamed. Her eyes dropped to Duncan, still holding forth with wee gasps between breaths. "My, he has healthy lungs."

Effie held the babe out to Colin. He had no choice but to cradle him. His black heart swelled with the return of too many raw memories. The bairn cried louder. *Must be my cold armor.*

"I cannot believe I've only been gone a fortnight and he's already changed." Colin pressed his lips against Duncan's forehead. He smelled of sweetness only babies possessed. Closing his eyes, Colin offered a desperate and silent prayer that this child would live well into adulthood.

He held crying bairn out to Margaret. "Meet your stepson."

She cradled him in her arms with a nervous chuckle. The babe immediately quieted. Colin's mouth went dry. To see his bairn take an instant liking to Margaret was bittersweet. He berated himself. Yes, he wanted, *needed* her to form a bond, but seeing her holding Duncan with Jonet's grave still warm made sanity flee. The room spun.

Margaret seemed not to notice the sweat beading Colin's brow. "Such a warm little bundle. Is he eating well?"

"Aye, the wet nurse is never far away." Effie nodded approvingly. "He likes ye."

Margaret's cheeks took on a glow. "How fortunate he has a breast from which to suckle."

Colin needed air. He pinched the bridge of his nose. If only Jonet could have been the one to feed the bairn.

Margaret stepped toward him while gently rocking Duncan. "Are you well, m'lord?"

"Perfectly fine." He tried to smile. "Thrilled to be here at last."

Margaret eyed him as if she weren't convinced— strong-willed and too perceptive for her own good.

Effie reached for Duncan. "You must be exhausted from your journey."

Rubbing her hip, Margaret nodded. "Happy to be out of the saddle."

"I'll put Duncan down then will show you to your chamber."

Colin bowed. "Thank you, matron. I've things to attend." He turned to Margaret. "Try to rest m'lady. We'll have a small meal in the great hall this eve."

Margaret curtseyed and Colin took his leave. He couldn't remove himself from the nursery fast enough.

Marching to his chamber, a maelstrom of twisted emotions coursed through him. Though he was thrilled to see Duncan, the sight of his bairn brought back his misery full force. Jonet had decorated the nursery. Everywhere he looked there was something that reminded him of her. She'd embroidered the bedclothes, even the gown Duncan wore had been embroidered by the woman he'd once adored.

Maxwell met Colin in his rooms and began the process of removing his armor. Colin's gaze shot to his immense four-poster bed. Duncan had been conceived in that very spot. It had been the eve of the Yuletide Feast, he was sure of it.

Jonet had high color in her cheeks that eve—and it wasn't only caused by the mulled wine. Colin guessed she was fertile when they'd supped and she'd lulled him with half-cast eyes.

"Will there be anything else, m'lord?"

Colin blinked. "Pardon?"

"Can I be of further service?" Maxwell asked.

He smoothed his hands over his arms. His mind had been so full of memories, he'd no idea the squire had already removed his entire coat of armor. "No, lad. You're free to go."

Colin sat in his overstuffed chair and rubbed his face. In the past month, his entire life had been sifted through a thresher. Though surrounded by people, he'd never felt so lonely. He pressed the heels of his hands into his eyes. Margaret's face flooded his thoughts. First at the fete, when they hadn't yet been introduced, she was as happy and lively as a kitten. He could have gathered her in his arms and danced a jig.

He lowered his hands and chuckled. *I could be a miserably hopeless romantic if I let down my guard.*

She'd looked as lovely as a painting when she gazed at him and studied his face during the wedding. He inhaled, remembering how much her scent had affected him that first night—and after.

His gut clenched. He cast a sorrowful gaze toward the bed. He should not be thinking of Margaret. Colin crossed the room and grasped one of the pillows Jonet had embroidered. He held it to his face, but only dust filled his nose. He smashed the damnable thing between his palms.

Why did this have to happen to him? Why was he standing in his chamber feeling wretched, hating himself? Men often lost wives to childbirth and were forced to wed another. He'd done nothing but his duty as a father and as Lord of Glenorchy. Christ, he'd even vowed not to allow Margaret into his heart.

He threw the pillow across the room and stormed out the door. Elliot had three short sennights to work on Kilchurn. Blast. Colin needed to supervise the work himself—ensure every effort was put forth before they started mudding.

Without his armor weighing him down, he dashed up the tower stairs like he was flying. Stepping out into the crisp autumn breeze, he inhaled deeply. Moored in the protective waters of Loch Etive, his fleet of sea galleys rocked with the waves. The largest had a tall mast and eighteen oars. Fast and seaworthy, he'd had her fitted with the latest Portuguese cannon when he was in Rome. No other galley in the Highlands could best her.

The warship beckoned. Once he set sail, he'd leave his affairs behind, fill his nostrils with salty air and enjoy the cruise to the Holy Land. Though when he arrived, it would be a different matter. He didn't care for killing, but he'd become exceptionally good at it.

He strolled around the wall walk, greeting sentries along the way. With the wind in his face, his heavy heart lightened somewhat. Arriving at the donjon, he turned and retraced his steps, all the way around and through the west tower.

The Campbells had been caretakers of this castle for over two hundred years. Though Dunstaffnage had been through many sieges, his family always prevailed. The Campbells had faithfully been powerful supporters of the king and Scotland. And now, as a third son, he'd first become a knight and then earned his own title as Lord of Glenorchy—so much more than a third son could wish for. He wanted his castle at Kilchurn completed so badly he could taste it.

Jonet's death had dealt him a calamitous blow. He could not allow his grief to claim his wits. Colin would rise above his melancholy and build a feared dynasty that would remain strong throughout the centuries. Duncan would live. He knew it in the depths of his bowels, and the lad's healthy cries only stood to cement Colin's conviction.

Once he'd made it back around to the donjon, Colin rested his elbows on the wall and stared out over the Firth of Lorn. He didn't want to go inside. This was the first time he'd truly relaxed since—well, he couldn't recall the last time he'd been at ease.

Up there on the wall-walk, tension melted from his shoulders. It had been the same when he was a lad—a quiet walk with the wind in his face, gazing out over the idyllic Highland scenery.

The sunset filled the western sky with brilliant orange. He could watch the changing sky for hours, but his duties awaited and soon supper would be served.

Heaving a heavy sigh, he whipped around and collided with Lady Margaret.

His breath caught in his throat. Every muscle in Colin's body seized to stop his forward progress. So small, the lady tottered and nearly fell through a crenel notch. Colin gripped her hands and steadied her. "Bloody oath, what were you doing sneaking up on me like that?"

Margaret jerked her arms away and rubbed her wrists. "I wasn't sneaking. I stepped outside and you practically barged over the top of me." She wore a cloak fastened around her shoulders, her chestnut locks uncovered. A breeze swept them up in a shimmering flutter of silk.

He glared at her, not about to allow himself to admire her blasted uncovered hair. God's teeth, his heart had practically leapt out of his chest when she'd nearly fallen to her death. "I just lost one wife. I'm not certain I'm ready to lose another quite yet."

"That's good to know." She sidled past him, looking at the view. "Forcing me to ride behind the wagon, I'd begun to wonder."

Must she continually challenge him? "You were safer at the rear."

She turned, a flash of anger narrowing her green eyes. But her face stopped him dead. He leaned closer. The sun made her eyes look iridescent, like the green water in the shallows. It was unholy to have eyes so vibrant.

She opened her mouth as if she were going to speak, but released a breath and turned, sweeping her gaze across the Firth of Lorn. The waves glimmered with a kaleidoscope of sunlit colors. "Your son is a beautiful bairn."

He bowed his head. "Thank you."

"Effie reported he's sleeping well."

Against his better judgment, he leaned against the wall. Oh how he craved idle conversation. "'Tis good to hear."

"Aye." Margaret slipped her bottom into a crenel notch and folded her hands. Obviously, the thought of a lethal fall to the stony outcropping below hadn't crossed her mind. "She said about all he'll do for the next several months is eat and sleep, and...you know."

Colin chuckled. "Of course."

She sat silent for a moment, staring out over the water. The sun had nearly lost its light. "This is a beautiful view. I've never been to the west before."

"I'm glad you like it. Jon...er...I like it up here as well."

Margaret frowned. She'd already proved her intelligence, and his reference to Jonet hadn't gone unnoticed. Fortunately, Margaret didn't utter a word. She set out along the walk, running her fingers atop the stone wall.

Colin followed. His hand itched to take hers, but he clenched his fists against his ridiculous notion. A breeze stirred and picked up her hair, making it sail. A lock brushed his nose. Filled with her scent, Colin reached up and watched while the silken tresses tickled his fingers. Mindlessly, he toyed with her hair as they strolled in comfortable silence.

Margaret stopped.

Colin nearly walked over the top of her. God, he was touched in the head, losing his mind over her bloody hair.

The sky turned cobalt, highlighting a strip of white clouds above. "I don't believe I'll ever tire of watching the sun set." Her soft voice chimed on the breeze.

Together they stood and watched the western sky succumb to the last hint of orange sunlight and fade into deep shade of violet. Margaret's profile looked flawless in the dim light. Porcelain skin, shaded with dark blue. She was too lovely for him—too beautiful for any man with a stone heart.

When blackness fell, the sentries lit the battlement torches. Margaret faced him. "I'd best prepare for supper, m'lord."

Colin's gaze dipped to her eyes, then to her moist lips. He inclined his head. Her breath caught and she raised her chin ever so slightly. Her warmth drew him nearer. His need for comfort twisted around his heart. Ever so gently, he brushed his lips over hers. He smoothed his hand to her silken nape and tasted the skin from her dainty jaw line all the way down her slender neck.

When his lips met wool, she stepped away from his grasp, her eyes dazed. "A-are you w-well, my lord?"

Blinking, he jerked up his head. "God's teeth, forgive me."

Self-loathing blasted wider the gaping hole in his heart. Colin absolutely did *not* just permit her to snare him with her allure. Ballocks, he still might choose to annul this marriage. Thank God she'd said something to snap him from his trance. And what the hell was he apologizing for? Was he not allowed a moment's respite?

He gestured toward the donjon entrance. "Go on ahead. I shall attend you shortly," he clipped.

Once the echo of her footsteps faded, Colin balled his fists. Why did she have to come up and destroy his peaceful solitude? Margaret's presence twisted his gut in knots. He didn't *want* to like her. Perhaps a good long turn in the Holy Land was what he needed to set his troubled mind to rights.

He descended the stairs. At the first turn he stopped. It would be best if Margaret was with child when he set sail. If he were to die in battle, he'd at least have one more son who bore his name.

Heaven help him, he couldn't visit her in the lady's bedchamber. The memories there were rawer than those in his own suite of rooms. No. He should stand beside his decision to stay away from Lady Margaret. Besides, with luck, she may already be with child.

***

Margaret paced in her chamber, tapping her fingers to her lips. For a fleeting moment, she'd sensed a connection with Colin, but of course she had to say something and destroy it. Her knees had wobbled when he'd touched his lips to hers. She'd wanted more, but confusion clouded her mind. Standing beside him and watching the sun set had been so peaceful, like they were beginning to form a bond. Yet further intimacy terrified her.

After, when he'd apologized, she'd become even more confused.

Oh heavens, what was she to do? She needed someone in whom she could confide. Was it normal for a new bride to fear her husband's touch? Groaning, she glanced into the looking glass and straightened her veil before she headed to the great hall.

Late for the evening meal, Margaret pattered up to the dais. Lord Argyll stood and held the chair for her. "Thank you," she said.

He bowed stiffly. "A pleasure, m'lady."

Margaret batted the air with a hand. "You must call me Margaret. We are peers."

He took the seat at the head of the table, and everyone else in the enormous hall followed suit. "Very well."

Margaret took a moment to study the décor. Long wooden tables sat in the center of the floor, filled with Campbells who supported the community—mostly dressed in muted plaids. The walls were adorned with regal tapestries, and behind her, an enormous yellow flag embroidered with the red lion rampant signified the royal charter of this keep. Indeed, the Campbells lived up to their reputation of being King James's right hand.

She lifted the ewer of ale and poured for him. "And what shall I call you?"

"I suppose Argyll will suit. I haven't been called Colin by anyone in so long, I doubt I'd respond to the name."

"That is funny." She filled her own tankard.

A servant placed a trencher of food on the table. Argyll held it up for her. "And where is your husband this eve?"

Margaret scanned the great hall. It was filled with people, but she did not see Colin. "I've no idea." Honestly, she was happy to converse with Argyll without Lord Glenorchy frowning over everything.

Argyll broke off a piece of bread. "Perhaps he's dining in his solar. He's got a great many matters to attend—and the trip to Stirling set him back a bit."

"Did it now?" Margaret eyed him. "I'm sorry to have been such a bother."

He rolled his eyes to the bold, arched ceiling rafters. "Of course, you could never be a bother to anyone."

"Tell that to Lord Glenorchy," she mumbled into her tankard before drowning her comment with a healthy swig. Things between them would be so much more palatable if he at least liked her. Kissing and then apologizing as if a man should never kiss his wife? What on earth was the Black Knight thinking?

"Ah, Margaret," Argyll said. "As I said before, he's a good man. He needs time, is all."

A bit surprised Argyll had heard her comment, she sighed. Colin's nephew may very well be the only soul to whom she could bemoan her woes. "He might need time, but he doesn't seem to need me."

"He does—more than you know." The lord patted her shoulder. "He's just too proud to admit it."

"Well, he'll certainly need *someone* to handle his affairs after he sails for Rome."

"Very true." Argyll shoved a knife of lamb into his mouth. "His father, rest his soul, handled things in his stead during Colin's last crusade."

"I'm quite capable, if he would only realize it."

"I have no doubt."

She desperately needed a change of subject. "I'm looking forward to seeing Kilchurn finished—and on schedule."

Argyll arched a single brow. "Aye? Then you can start on my castle in Inverary next."

"One thing at a time." She chuckled. "And what about you, Argyll? Have you a woman in mind to marry?"

"No one in particular as of yet." He raised his tankard. "Eventually I want to marry, but I'm off to court at first light on the morrow. I'm to assume my appointed position of master of the king's household."

"Oh dear, that does sound tedious. Though you will have an opportunity to meet every available courtier in Scotland."

Argyll laughed. "I like the way you think, Auntie."

"Pardon me?" She whacked his shoulder. "We are both two and twenty. I'll hear no 'aunties' from the likes of you."

He raised his tankard. "Apologies in the grandest order."

She tapped her cup to his with a clank of pewter. "Accepted. Though I must say I shall miss you. I could use an ally around here."

"Never you mind. In time, Colin will become your greatest advocate. I have no doubt."

"I wish I could be as confident as you." Margaret also wished Argyll might have married her rather than Colin. Though the younger man wasn't quite as handsome, he was far more amiable. Colin treated her like chattel. *Curses to his knee-wobbling kisses… You will be stepmother to my son or be damned with you.*

She touched her fingers to her lips as if she'd spoken the vulgar words aloud. Never in her life had she uttered the word damn…or even thought it. She hadn't known Colin Campbell for long, but he surely was bringing out deep-seated angst she didn't care for in the slightest.

A shiver slithered up her spine. She'd been thinking about it since he'd shooed her off the wall-walk. Why had he apologized? *Does he hate me?* She crossed her arms and rubbed the outside of her shoulders.

That was it.

Colin thought her unsightly and dull. Her throat closed. Once Argyll left for court, she'd have no allies here at all.

Chapter Eleven

Dunstaffnage Castle, 12ᵗʰ October, 1455

Margaret broke her fast in her chamber. Colin didn't come down for supper last eve, nor had he made any appearance. He obviously wanted distance, obviously detested being in her presence. She couldn't decide if his detachment or his disdain hurt more. She dabbed the corner of her mouth with a cloth. Definitely his silent rejection caused a knot in her stomach to clamp so taut, she couldn't eat.

Margaret loathed Dunstaffnage. Her chamber reeked of another woman. It wasn't at all like the rooms she'd stayed in at the palace. There was a personality to it—winsome, with ivory linen bed coverings embroidered with garlands of colorful flowers. In fact, the upholstery of the very chair she sat upon had the same floral pattern. Yet another reason to see the tower house at Kilchurn finished soon. Living in the shadow of a dead woman, Margaret would have no hope of surpassing Jonet's legacy. She'd never met Colin's former wife—how on earth could she be expected to fit the mold?

She wandered down the passage and entered the nursery. Effie smiled from the rocking chair. The matron seemed to never leave Duncan's side.

"Where do you sleep?" Margaret asked.

Cradling Duncan in one arm, Effie pointed to a side door. "In the nursemaid's quarters."

"That explains why you're with the lad hour upon hour."

"Aye, but I don't mind. I was born to care for children."

Margaret tapped the cradle and watched it rock. "Do you have any children of your own?"

"One son, a bit older than Lord Glenorchy. They played together when they were lads."

Margaret walked around the tidy nursery, filled with toys with which Colin could once have played. "How nice you were able to keep him with you while you were working. What does he do now?"

"Lord Campbell was kind enough to give him a trade. He manages the stables."

"And your husband?"

Effie smoothed her hand over Duncan's head. "He passed."

"I'm sorry."

"No need. It was ever so long ago."

Wringing her hands, Margaret moved to the window. Colin was mounted with his entourage of men. With a gasp, she glared down at the courtyard. Oh no, she could never mistake his physique when clad in armor. His shoulders were as wide as his warhorse's rump. "Do you know where Lord Colin is off to this morning?"

"Back to Kilchurn."

Margaret crossed her arms and clutched them tight against her ribs. How did Effie know Colin was returning to Kilchurn, when he hadn't mentioned a word to her? "He told you?"

"Aye, stopped in to see Duncan at dawn."

That confirms it. He cannot stand the sight of me. Margaret kept her back turned. Her lack of relations with her husband was none of Effie's concern.

The old woman set the babe in his cradle and came up behind her. "He's a good man, Colin."

"Is he?" She would not speak ill of him to a servant.

"He's suffering from a bout of melancholy. He took Jonet's death very hard."

Margaret continued to watch from the window. Colin led his men out the inner gate. "I'm sure his loss must have been devastating." *If his attitude toward me is any indication, I'm positive he's wallowing in misery.* But Margaret's throat tightened. That he was hurting, she had no doubt, nor did she have any clue as to how to ease his pain—or hers.

"I've known Lord Colin since the day he was born. He can hide naught from me." Effie grasped the window furs. "The lord is still in mourning. I can see it in his eyes."

"Perhaps that's why he can show me no…" Margaret silenced herself. She mustn't have this conversation with Effie. She tapped her hand to her chest. "His former wife was nice, was she not?"

"Aye, caring and lovely. Perhaps not as beautiful as you, but she had an endearing air about her."

Margaret's stomach twisted. "I gathered as much—the endearing part especially." The entourage gone, she turned and regarded the old nursemaid. Effie had a kindly, careworn face. "The mistress's chamber reflects the same."

"Ah. You will have to see that changed."

"I'd prefer to be in Glen Orchy, overseeing the completion of the castle. There I'll ensure every chamber decorated to my taste."

Effie placed a hand on her shoulder. "You do have ambition. It will serve Colin well."

The woman's light touch consoled and Margaret welcomed it. "If he'll only allow me the freedom to do so."

"Give him time, m'lady. He'll come around."

"Aye." Margaret grimaced. "Mayhap not before he goes on another crusade and gets himself killed."

Effie pulled her into a soft embrace, smelling of warm bread. "Lord Colin will not perish in battle. He is far too skilled with a sword."

***

Left alone for an indeterminate amount of time, Margaret took it upon herself to explore the castle. Besides, it was more interesting to discover passages and secrets without a nosy guide. Colin's chamber was beside hers, joined by an internal door. Had she known, she would have pushed a table across it. But it mattered not— he hadn't come to her, and from his cool distance, she thought it a good possibility he might never do so again.

She opened the door to his chamber and stepped inside. A warning tickled the back of her neck as if she were trespassing. Margaret bravely took another step. Perhaps she could learn more about the man she'd married. He slept upon an enormous bed with thick maple headboard and posts. His comforter and canopy were red—*bold colors for a bold knight*. A threadbare, red plaid rug rested in front of the hearth. Though clean, it needed replacing. A round table with two padded chairs were off to the side—he undoubtedly read missives there, at least when he wasn't in his solar.

She sat in one of his chairs and her toes skimmed the floor. A man as tall as Colin might find the seat comfortable, but Margaret preferred her feet to be flush with the floor. The fire in the hearth had burned to embers, and she shivered. Nothing in his chamber welcomed her.

Exploring further, she learned their apartments were not the "lords'" rooms, however. Argyll and the king occasioned an entire "royal" suite of rooms on the floor below.

She found Colin's solar on the second floor, across from Argyll's. The kitchens, bustling with activity, were immense, just like Dunalasdair. However, the cavernous catacombs of cellars with vaulted ceilings seemed to go on forever. As with most Scottish castles, as she'd noted the night before, the great hall was vast, and the kitchen catered not only to the lord's family, but to the large number of clansmen and women who served the Campbells.

Margaret had yet to visit the stables to see if the mare she'd ridden from Stirling was stalled or turned out to pasture. She hoped to find her. Mayhap she'd ride to the chapel and offer up prayers that one day her husband might actually find her alluring or useful and treat her with kindness—not necessarily in that order.

Making her way past the gatehouse, hushed male voices came from the window above, the tone angry. Margaret stopped.

"What do you mean, he left this morning? He only arrived yesterday. Besides, my ploy will only be successful if he is here. The bastard's supposed to be swivving his new wench."

Margaret clapped a hand over her mouth to mute her gasp.

"I'm not responsible for the bloody Black Knight's agenda."

Silence—aside from Margaret's racing heartbeat.

She held her breath, afraid to hear another word. Yet moving now might alert these men of her presence. And who were they, so full of self-importance?

"I had a bit of fun planned for the morrow."

"Oh?"

"Aye, something that would damn the MacGregors once and for all."

The deep voice emitted an evil chuckle. "I do like your tenacity, Walter."

Walter? He must be Colin's factor—the very man the MacGregor women warned about. Margaret's heart thrummed louder.

"Och, I must call it off."

"Reorganize for another time, aye?"

Parchment rustled. "Mayhap make a change. There's a shipment of sand en route. We can strike there." Footsteps clapped floorboards. "I must away," intoned the faceless Walter.

Margaret's hands shook. She darted toward the donjon. With any luck, Walter wouldn't notice her, though her nape prickled. She placed her hand on the latch and glanced over her shoulder. A shortish man with dark hair and a cropped beard glared at her from across the courtyard then disappeared into the stables.

That is he, I'm sure of it. Margaret slipped inside and pressed her back against the door, calming her breath. She must warn Colin straight away.

Whom could she trust to accompany her? Argyll was already gone—left at first light. Walter had spoken openly with the other man in the gatehouse. How many others were in his confidence, swindling Lord Campbell? She couldn't chance setting out alone, not for a day's ride. That would be madness.

Margaret raced up the stairs and collected a few necessities in a satchel. She snatched her dagger from the drawer and slid it into her belt. She'd start in the stable. Surely a young lad with a pitchfork could make a recommendation. She doubted a man like Walter would pay mind to a common hand.

***

Mevan, a burly guard, rode beside her, grumbling all the while. "I still think we should've waited until the morrow to set out. As sure as I breathe, it will be dark afore we reach Glen Orchy." His thick black beard sprouted in all directions, making his helm appear too small for his head.

"Not by much. Especially if we remain at a steady trot."

He shook his head. "Och, Lord Colin will have me hide for this."

Margaret clamped her reins. "Lord Colin would have your hide if you refused to escort me."

"Aye? Then why the secrecy? You should tell me what's afoot."

"I will as soon as my husband can vouch for your trustworthiness." True, the stable boy had recommended Mevan as the strongest and most loyal to the Campbell Clan, but she would take no chances. She was not unfamiliar with men like Walter MacCorkodale. They could worm their way through a man's armor with the most unexpected twists.

He tapped his heels into his warhorse's barrel. "I'm the master-at-arms, is that not enough?"

"Apologies, but nay. At this stage, I've no idea whom I can trust."

Mevan mumbled something that sounded like a curse. Margaret chose not to ask him to repeat it. In all honesty, she liked the big guardsman. At first, he'd been adamant Margaret remain at the castle while he delivered a missive on her behalf. But she couldn't put a written note in anyone's hands. When she'd ridden out the gate, he'd followed, armed to the teeth. Once they arrived at Kilchurn, she'd ask Colin to appoint him to guard her permanently—providing he was free of skullduggery.

She chuckled under her breath. Mevan reminded Margaret of her brother, Robert. They both were stocky, with full beards and blue eyes. Hopefully, she could make a friend of him—in time—if he ever forgave her present, yet necessary secrecy.

"Are you married?" she asked.

"Aye."

"Children?"

"Two. A boy, age five, and a girl, age two."

"You must be very proud."

His eyes twinkled when he glanced her way. "I am, m'lady."

"I shall ensure you are rewarded for coming to my aid. Surely I pulled you away from a great many responsibilities." It never hurt to give due recognition, and the more Margaret considered it, the more she believed him to be innocent.

"Thank you, m'lady." A hint of surprise in his voice, Mevan's posture relaxed. "Me wife will be much obliged."

They stopped once to rest their horses. Fortunately, Mevan carried a parcel of oatcakes and a skin of ale tied to his saddle.

Margaret's legs were stiff. They'd been riding much harder than the procession from Stirling. She stretched her arms forward and reached her fingers to her toes. "I didn't think about food, but I'm hungry."

"I tie a parcel of food to my saddle every morn. It comes in of use more often than not. Most days I patrol the grounds with the guard. You caught me before we were about to ride."

"'Tis a good thing I did. I wouldn't want to be out here alone."

He handed her two oatcakes slathered with butter. "You would have set out on your own?"

"Aye." Her mouth watered when she bit into the crunchy cake, creamy butter smoothing across her tongue.

Mevan offered her the skin of ale. "Whatever news you have for Lord Glenorchy must be grave."

"It is indeed." She tipped it back and took a healthy swig. None too ladylike, but what did one do without a cup?

"Then we'd best not dally."

They rode though late afternoon. When the air turned cold, Margaret shivered and pulled her cloak tight around her shoulders. The autumn day had been chilly, and now the clouds rolled in. It most definitely smelled like rain.

With the heavy covering gathered above them, darkness fell early. They continued along the vaguely familiar, narrow path. Shadows in the trees made Margaret uneasy, as if someone or something stalked them.

A shadow lurked on their flank.

She could have sworn she saw something move, though when she peered through the dim forest, there was nothing at all. She patted her face to pull herself together. It had been a long day, and there was a fair distance yet to travel.

Her heart leapt when Mevan drew his sword in one hissing motion. He held a finger to his lips and inclined his head toward the bend ahead. "Just a precaution," he whispered.

Margaret ran her fingers across the hilt of her dagger. If anything went awry, it was her last defense. With two older brothers, she knew how to use it. God forbid she'd ever need to.

Mevan slowed his horse to a walk. Margaret followed his lead. Slowly, they rounded the stony outcropping. All was quiet—not even the call of a bird filled the air. Margaret grimaced, her eyes wide, each breath whistling in her ears. Her skin crawled as if alive with spiders.

Ahead, a twig snapped.

Margaret's mouth grew dry with her gasp.

Blood-curdling roars erupted from the trees. Every muscle in her body clamped taut. Ice shot through her blood. Three men with swords and poleaxes barreled toward them, though it sounded like more.

"Run!" Mevan yelled, reining his horse around to face the attackers.

Margaret slammed her riding crop against her mare's rump and leaned forward. "Go, go, go!" Slapping her crop in a steady beat, the mare raced into a gallop. The young horse caught wind of Margaret's fear and sprinted faster than Margaret had ever ridden in her life.

The wind picked up her veil, snatching it from her head. Her gut clenched as hoof beats pummeled the earth behind her. She glanced over her shoulder. A hooded man with a cloth tied across his mouth gained on her.

Blast her sidesaddle. In no way could she outrun a man with her legs aside. She rounded the next bend. He'd nearly overtaken her. Margaret slapped her crop and kicked with all her strength. The mare beneath her snorted in a steady, terrifyingly fast rhythm.

The outlaw pulled alongside. Eyes wild, he reached for her reins. With all her strength, Margaret slapped his hands with her crop. Her mare pulled ahead. The brute closed the distance. He reached again. Margaret slapped. His other hand came across and grabbed the crop.

Oh God, save me.

He pulled on her reins. Margaret kicked and leaned out over her mare's head, demanding more speed. Her stomach flew to her throat.

Skimming the top of her hair, a thick branch flew past.

The man's fingers released her reins.

Thud.

Margaret didn't turn around. She'd heard it. Caught by the branch, the dastard had been thrown from his mount. She slapped her hand to urge her horse to continue the frantic pace. They barreled ahead until white foam leached from the mare's neck. Margaret pulled on the reins and ran her fingers along the horse's mane. "There, there, lass. We can ease up a bit." She'd said it more for her own sake than the horse's. She glanced back. No one else followed her, at least not yet.

What had become of Mevan? The brave warrior had been outnumbered.

She couldn't turn back now. It would be madness. She must ride for help—swiftly send a party to Mevan's aid. The problem? Darkness had spread its eerie blanket over her. Rain spewed from the rumbling clouds.

Ahead she made out a narrow path, but recognized nothing.

Chapter Twelve

Kilchurn Building Site, 12ᵗʰ October, 1455

Colin sat in front of the hearth, sipping a tot of whisky. The muffled rain drove into the thatched roof, and the sloppy drips from the eaves slapped the ground outside the cottage window. It had been a long day, but the stone for the tower house foundation had been started at long last. They needed more supplies before they could continue. Finishing the foundation was all he could hope for until they'd be forced to mud up the freshly laid mortar for winter.

The whisky slid down his throat with a fiery bite and warmed his insides. It was nice to spend some time away from Margaret and focus his mind on things in need of his attention. She distracted him like no woman he'd ever met. Now he'd delivered her to Dunstaffnage, her time would be occupied with Duncan's care. With them tucked away within the fortress walls, Colin would have no need to worry about their safety.

Rapid footsteps clapped the soggy ground. The door flew open and Maxwell burst inside. "M'lord, come quickly. 'Tis Lady Margaret."

Colin sprang from his seat. "What the…" His words were spoken in vain as Maxwell dashed away.

The whisky in Colin's belly roiled. *What the bloody hell is Margaret doing here?* Colin hurried through the cottage and out into the pelting rain.

Guards followed her from the stables. She strode toward him with purpose. "I must speak to Lord Glenorchy at once."

Colin dashed up to his errant wife and grasped her elbow. "Why the blazes are you here, woman?" He waved a dismissive hand at his men and led her into the cottage, slamming the door behind.

Margaret stood in the center of the room, pools of water forming around the bottom of her cloak, shivering like a maple leaf in the wind. "My lord…"

He paced in a circle around her. "If you were a child, I'd bend you over my knee. What are you doing out alone? In the dark. In. The. Rain?"

"I…"

He stopped at her side and glared at her profile. He couldn't shout at her when looking in her eyes. "Why are you not with my son?"

She faced him. "He…"

Colin fisted his hips. "Do you realize you could have been killed?"

Margaret stamped her foot. "If you would allow me to speak…"

Narrowing his eyes against her gaze, he leaned forward. "You should not be here…"

She actually snarled. A flash of rage emblazoned her face. Before he could think, she landed a jarring slap across his jaw.

Dazed, Colin stumbled backward. "What the devil?" Never before had he wanted to strike a woman, but she'd pushed him to the ragged edge.

She marched into him, red rims around her eyes. "You may hate me, but I am your wife and I *will* have your respect." She jammed her finger into his sternum. "I should stand aside and watch you fall into ruin. But I will not." Her teeth chattered, but she jutted her face up to his, her full lips red from the chill. "Because I care."

If his chest weren't burning with the need to hit something, he'd crush her into his embrace and stifle her pouty mouth with a heated kiss. Colin forced his lips to curl into a sneer. He drew in a deep breath, willing his anger to simmer below the surface. "This had best be good."

She gestured to the hearth. "If you would sit, I'd prefer to stand by the fire."

With a nod, Colin humored her, at least for the moment.

She removed her cloak, draped it over the table and stood with her back to the fire. God save him, her gown clung to her like skin. Even her nipples stood proud beneath the wet wool. "I overheard a man named Walter explain how he's planning to ambush your next load of sand."

Colin crossed his legs against his untimely surge of desire. She must be mistaken. "Walter?"

Margaret held up her palm, her chest heaving from exertion. "But first, I must vindicate myself. I am not daft enough to leave the castle alone. My guard, Mevan, faced an attack by outlaws and bade me to run. He's back there on the trail." She clenched her fists to her mouth. "I know not if he's alive or dead. Your men are now preparing to go after him."

Colin stood and averted his gaze from the wet cloth clinging to her breasts. "I must go as well."

"Must you? Can the guard not handle this on your behalf?"

"I cannot sit idle when my wife and sentry have been assaulted." He most especially couldn't remain behind in the small cottage with her heaving breasts.

"Very well, but before you leave, allow me to explain." Margaret rubbed her hands and held them to the fire—the view of her backside more alluring than her front. "I wanted to tell you what I learned from the MacGregor women, but didn't gain the chance before you left me alone at Dunstaffnage."

"I didn't—"

She faced him and sliced a hand through the air. "It doesn't matter now. The MacGregor men are innocent."

Blast her wet dress. It befuddled his mind at a most inconvenient time. He rubbed his eyes, forcing himself to focus on her words. "How do you know this?"

"Remember when I spoke to the women at the river?"

"Aye."

"They told me a great many things. The MacGregors want to see the castle completed as much as you do. They've been trying to discover the plunderer—thought it was Walter MacCorkodale, but had no proof."

Colin crossed his arms and shook his head, refusing to look her way. "He has been my trusted factor for years."

"Has he?"

Her defiance was maddening. How dare she question him—dripping wet, attacking every sensible bone in his body? "I have no idea what I would have done without his services whilst I was on crusade."

"Good men can turn to evil."

Lady Margaret's tongue could use restraint as well. "Are you asking me to change my opinion of a trusted servant because you overheard a conversation? Are you certain? Was it he who attacked you?"

"I ken what I heard, but I know not who set upon us. I counted three men. There could have been more. They wore hoods and masks."

Colin dropped his arms. This was the first real lead he'd had to expose the vandals. "Then I will withhold judgment until I know for certain."

"I would do the same if I were in your place." Margaret grasped his elbow. Tingles skittered all the way up to the top of his head. "I would like to attend Mevan's wounds. I feel responsible."

Colin pulled away and strapped on his sword. "I believe you've done enough. I'll appoint a retinue to accompany you to Dunstaffnage in the morning."

Shoving his helm onto his head, he stormed off to the stables. He couldn't spend another moment with Margaret standing in the same room in her wet gown. She may as well have been completely naked. He must act quickly, yet all he could think about was taking his dirk, cutting off her clothing and taking her to the bed—or the floor. That was much closer.

The MacGregor men met him inside the stable. Robert, the clan chieftain, stepped forward. "We want to ride with you, m'lord. This menace has been a thorn in our sides. We aim to see him finished."

Colin eyed him. "Lady Margaret said you suspected Walter MacCorkodale. Is that true?"

"Aye, but we had no proof. I would not point a finger at my lord's factor unless I could come to you with unshakable evidence."

"Very well." Colin surveyed his army. "Tonight we ride against our enemies and solve this mystery once and for all."

***

Margaret awoke in the cottage bed without a stitch of clothing. The fire had gone out during the night. She pulled the bedclothes up over her shoulders. The fragrance of cloves and spice, decidedly male, washed over her. She'd caught Colin's scent as soon as she'd walked into the cottage last night.

He'd been so angry, she'd nearly backed down. Mercy, his massive size intimidated her. However, for all that was holy, she owed it to Mevan to stand her ground. Margaret cringed. Mother would have been mortified. She'd actually slapped the beast. But she had to do something to make her pigheaded husband listen. Goodness, she nearly thought he'd put her back on her horse and point her toward Dunstaffnage in the dead of night in a rainstorm.

He could forget her heading there now. She was back in Glen Orchy, and she aimed to uncover a few things before she left. With no time to stay abed, she pulled the plaid from the footboard and wrapped it around her body.

Last night she'd hung her clothes to dry in front of the fire, and thanked her stars Colin hadn't returned to find her stark naked in bed. She fanned herself at the thought, praying he'd swiftly bring the plunderers to justice and confront his double-crossing factor. Oh how Margaret would like to be there when he did.

She pulled the dry linen shift over her head. Today, however, Mevan would be her first priority. She'd prayed for his rescue until she succumbed to sleep. She closed her eyes and prayed again.

A light rap sounded at the door. "M'lady?" A woman's voice. "I've some porridge for you."

Margaret quickly covered her shift by slinging the plaid around her shoulders. "Come in."

The round-faced woman walked through the door carrying a tray. "After your ordeal last eve, I thought you'd need some oats to warm your insides."

"That is very kind of you…ah…"

"Alana."

"Such a lovely name."

"Thank you." Alana set the tray on the table. "'Tis cold in here."

"Aye, I was just about to light the fire."

"I'll do it." She gestured to the chair. "Sit and break your fast, m'lady."

"'Tis ever so kind." Margaret sat and lifted the wooden spoon. Worry squeezed her stomach. She had to know... "Did they find Mevan?"

"Two guards brought him in before dawn. The rest of the men are still out there chasing the brigands."

Margaret swallowed. She didn't want to ask. "Is he...?"

"He's alive. Barely. The women are tending him."

Margaret pushed back the chair and stood. "I must see him. His heroism cannot go unrewarded."

Alana struck the flint. "Very well, I'll take you after you eat your porridge. But you'll have to be quick. An escort to Dunstaffnage is waiting."

"I shan't be going back there. Mevan is my responsibility. I will not ride away and leave him."

"Aye?" Alana questioned over her shoulder. "I think Lord Campbell gave clear instructions for the guard to take you back to the castle."

"He may very well have, but I *am* staying. My husband is not here to counter otherwise." She sliced her hand through the air. "That's the end of it."

Alana rose from lighting the fire and brushed her hands on her apron. "I do like your spirit, m'lady."

Margaret discarded her plaid and reached for her gown. "I'll see to Mevan's care and tend to a few things first. When I was here last, you told me the building project needs management."

Alana's eyebrows arched with surprise. "That I did."

"I want to meet Tom Elliot and speak to the laborers, among other things." Margaret turned for Alana to tie her laces. "Colin's son is well cared for at Dunstaffnage and shan't need anything from me for quite some time. I'm absolutely positive a few days here would be far more productive than at the castle."

"If you should need anything, mine is the first cottage up the hill." The MacGregor woman patted her shoulder. "Thank you for listening back at the river. I'd been wondering if anything would come of it."

"I only wish I could have acted sooner." Margaret turned. "You've been ever so kind. I should like to come calling if it wouldn't be any trouble."

Alana's cheeks shone bright red. "It would be an honor."

Margaret quickly ate a few bites of porridge then followed Alana to Mevan's cot, situated in a small room at the back of the stable.

"This is a hospital of sorts—where men are stitched up and that type of thing, since there's no abbey nearby."

Another thing to add to Margaret's growing list. "Once the tower house is completed I'll ensure a grand-sized chapel will follow."

"That would be a blessing indeed, m'lady."

A woman tended Mevan, cleansing his wounds. He lay on his back with linens pulled up to his waist. Margaret stepped to the bed to better inspect him. His shoulder was bandaged, with blood seeping through it. His face was bruised and swollen, his nose at an awkward angle, a nasty gash on one side. His eyes were closed, purple puffiness surrounding them.

This was her fault. Margaret wrung her hands. "Is he awake?"

He opened one eye to a mere slit. "Aye, m'lady," he managed through puffy lips.

Margaret dropped to her knees and reached for his hand, the only thing she could touch without causing more pain. "Thank you, thank you, dear Mevan. You fought like a lion."

He smiled, then grimaced.

She bent forward and kissed his fingers. "No need to say a word. We shall take you back to your family as soon as you are able to ride. I will see to it you are compensated for your gallantry."

Mevan licked his lips. "M'lady."

She stood and pressed a kiss to his forehead. "Heal well, for there's no one I'd rather have guarding my person than you, sir." Turning, she placed a hand on the attendant's shoulder. "See to it he receives uninterrupted care. If he should want for *anything*, notify me straight away."

She curtseyed. "Aye, m'lady."

***

It didn't take much convincing to dismiss her escort and put them back to work on the castle. However, they made it clear all would face the lord's ire when he returned. Margaret knew that well enough. She'd already faced Colin's ire more than she cared, but she wasn't afraid of him like the others seemed to be. He could affect a mean expression and bellow, but if he was going to raise a hand to her, he would have done it last night for certain.

She still couldn't believe she'd slapped him. What was she thinking? Perhaps they simply were not compatible. She huffed. Now was not the time to dwell on her misshapen marriage.

Tom Elliot was working under a lean-to with his shirtsleeves rolled up, chiseling out a stone buttress for the kitchen ceiling. He proved all too happy to tell her about the problems he'd encountered on this project. He appeared so wound up about losing his job, Margaret needed to say something to appease him. "If Lord Glenorchy finds the plunderer, you'll not be forced to continually make repairs. My guess is the supply will keep pace, as well."

"I certainly hope so. I order timber and tools, and God only knows when or *if* they'll arrive."

"Have you not a blacksmith on site?" she asked.

He spread his palms in a woeful gesture. "No, m'lady. We use the smithy at Dunstaffnage."

"Heavens, that is restrictive. Is there anyone in Glen Orchy who can work a bellows and an anvil?"

"Tormond Campbell is apprenticing at the castle now."

"How long has he been there?"

"Longer than I've been building Kilchurn."

"Hmm. It seems there's something we could do about that." She walked beside Tom and studied the foundation site. "I'd like to see this completed before Lord Colin returns."

Tom scratched his head. "That's unlikely."

"What do you need?"

He kicked a stone. "A steady stream of supplies and a great deal of prayers."

"I'll see to that." Margaret patted his shoulder. "Tell the men there will be extra rations if their goals are met."

Two men lumbered past, each carrying a yoke with buckets of water tethered to the ends. Margaret stared. "What's that?"

Tom clapped his chest with pride. "Water for the mortar, m'lady."

"You must be jesting."

"No." He eyed her as if she were daft. "We need water to mix mortar."

She sighed. "I helped my father build the west tower at Dunalasdair, and I assure you, men were not carrying water on their backs. That takes far too long."

Tom's face turned scarlet. "It works…"

Margaret pointed toward the loch. "Build a trough. One man simply stands beside it and pours in buckets of water. Gravity moves the water to your site. Simple. Have it done by the end of the day. Now, if you'll excuse me, I've a blacksmith to hail."

Drop-jawed, Tom stared after her as she turned and strode away. She would have this building project moving. Colin would see some improvement before he returned—providing he didn't arrive too quickly.

After sending a messenger to Dunstaffnage to fetch Tormond Campbell, Margaret sat down with Tom's ledgers. She would understand the problems behind this project, and find ways to solve them one by one. If Lord Glenorchy didn't want her meddling, he could go sit in a meadow of stinging nettles.

Chapter Thirteen

The Highlands, 15ᵗʰ October, 1455

If only this blasted drizzle would stop. At least the
trail hadn't been difficult to follow. Water filled the hoof
prints. The only problem was that it seemed to be leading
them nowhere. Colin had spent three damp and bloody
miserable days in the saddle, watching the tracks of three
horses pass beneath him until his eyes crossed.

He'd sent Robert MacGregor and his men to ensure
the shipment of sand arrived in the Firth of Lorn without
incident, and then to see it safely delivered to Kilchurn.
But that was only one shipment of many. Though Robert
had vowed an oath of fealty and demanded vengeance,
Colin waffled. He dearly wanted to trust the clan chieftain,
but trusting anyone outside his inner circle had become
nigh impossible.

Too many things needled at his mind during this
unholy, wretched chase. Margaret had risked her life to
warn him about Walter MacCorkodale. *For Christ's sake,
the woman is incorrigible.* She should have sent a messenger.
Perhaps an annulment would be necessary after all…and
it appeared he needed to find another factor quickly.

Ballocks.

Walter had been a trusted servant for years. He
collected the rents, bought and sold cattle and other

livestock, paid for shipments of sand, among other things. Had he been skimming coin from Colin, as well as supplies? A raging fire burned in his chest. No one stole from a Campbell and lived.

Moreover, no one attacked Colin's family. However, he held on to a thread of hope for Walter's innocence. It was unlikely a learned man like he would play outlaw and attack a noblewoman and her guard—especially his *lord's* wife. Surely, Walter wouldn't be bold enough to act with such incredible stupidity.

Colin would dig to the bottom of this, and it had better be soon, lest his armor *and* his limbs turn to rust. His inner circle of six trusted men who always traveled with him looked as bedraggled as he felt. Yes, these were Highlanders of rugged stock. Each of his loyal men would follow Colin into the fiercest battle and lay down his life without question. But no man was impervious to constant rain and bone-chilling wind. Winter stopped entire armies in Scotland, and sure as he breathed, winter was coming early this year.

"They're leading us into the Mamore Forest," Maxwell said, pulling Colin from his thoughts.

"Aye, this is becoming a mockery," Fionn agreed. "We go up there, and we'll end up atop Ben Nevis, neck deep in snow."

Colin quickly surveyed their surroundings. He'd been through this land before—so had his men, and not all that long ago, chasing after the Douglas traitor. "How far ahead do you reckon they are?"

Hugh, the best tracker in the Highlands, scratched his shaggy beard. "We've gained on them, 'tis certain. I'd say a half-day, mayhap less."

Colin pulled up his horse and drew the men into a circle. "You want out of this rain and into some dry braies?"

"Aye," the six warriors chorused.

"This isn't going to be easy, but we'll end this nonsense by nightfall." Every man nodded, eyes fierce. "Fionn and William, come with me. We'll head up the outcropping and cut them off."

Hugh shook the droplets of water from his helm. "Are ye bloody daft? One misstep on those cliffs and you'll meet your end."

"Do you want to chase these mongrels up the mountain—see us caught in a blizzard or worse?"

Hugh shut his mouth and glared.

Colin pointed a gauntleted finger at him. "Take the others and continue to follow the mongrel's tracks. We'll cut them off and drive them back toward you. If they make it that far."

Maxwell chuckled. "There's only three of them. I ought to be able to take them with one hand."

Close enough to reach, Colin clamped the young squire's arm and squeezed. "Never underestimate a foe you've not faced. The first time you do could be your last."

Colin split the men and took the treacherous pass. He probably hated heights more than any warrior in his company, but he would never ask a one to do something he wouldn't attempt himself. Fionn and William were the most skilled horsemen, and they'd both taken this route before. Colin couldn't consider taking the others across the slippery, wet narrow ridge.

They followed the game trail straight up through the forest until the foliage opened onto a rugged outcropping—mountain, in all truth. Colin stopped for a moment and scanned the forest below, looking for movement.

William pointed. "There."

Sure enough, riders flickered through the trees. Colin rested a hand on his pommel and leaned forward. "Why the blazes are they heading to nowhere?"

"Trying to keep us away from Kilchurn?" Fionn guessed.

Colin's fist tightened around his reins. "Bloody bastards. They're leading us away from a great many things." He met the eyes of each man. "Are you ready for this?"

Fionn nodded. "Aye."

William did too. "Aye. I'll lead."

Colin let him pass. William's horse could pick his way over a crossing no wider than three hands. The other horses would follow without spooking—he prayed.

When they stepped onto the stony shelf, Colin's stomach clenched into a hard ball. His sweaty fingers slipped inside his doeskin gloves. He glanced down and perspiration streamed into his eyes. He could face an entire army, but putting his faith in a horse to safely carry him across a treacherous path pushed his limits.

He clenched his teeth and focused his gaze on William's horse. The bay walked slowly, hooves clicking the stone. The sky above darkened.

Could we bloody go faster?

A sloppy drop hit his helm's nose guard. Colin's grip again slipped inside his gloves. A bolt of lightning flashed overhead. Colin jolted in his seat. His horse stutter-stepped.

Colin grimaced and prepared for death, every muscle taut.

The horse steadied.

Taking in a quick breath, he willed his bum cheeks to ease, sending a soothing message to his steed. It took every bit of self-control he had to maintain a relaxed posture.

Rain poured down in sheets. Within two strides, Colin could scarcely see the horse's rump in front of him. He resisted the urge to pull up and stop. There was nowhere to go but forward.

His big warhorse stumbled. Rocks broke away and hit the cliff hundreds of feet below. Colin's body jerked downward. Thunder rumbled like the deafening bellow of twelve cannons. With a grunt, Colin closed his eyes and tried to swallow.

Margaret's beautiful smile filled his chest, lightened it as if he were floating in midair. Her chestnut locks shimmered with sunlight. Her hypnotic green eyes focused on him, filled him with strength. Colin gathered his reins and pushed his heels down in the stirrups. "Stay with it, lad."

With his next breath, the warhorse found his footing. Colin tried to relax. "Good boy," he cooed. "Keep up, we're nearly there, lad."

The shelf opened to a rocky plateau. Colin shook his head. Every time he blinked, Margaret smiled at him. What the devil was that about? He squeezed his eyes and conjured a picture of Jonet. At first her face was clear, and then it faded.

"Are you all right, m'lord?"

Colin snapped his eyes open. Both Fionn and William had stopped their mounts beside him. Their expressions were filled with concern.

"What the bloody hell are we stopping for?" Colin barked.

William spread his palms to his sides. "You're the one who pulled up, m'lord."

Colin straightened and looked down the steep gorge. Waterfalls gushed with the newly fallen rain. "Have you spotted them?"

"They'd be behind us yet."

Colin clicked his heels and took the lead. "Good. Let's move off this mountain before the rain washes us down."

Colin led the way, hoping he'd never have to take that crossing again in his life. Lord, it did unholy, irrational things to his mind. The further down the slope his horse trod, the more his heartbeat returned to a normal rhythm. Never would he admit how much that crossing bothered him—especially in the driving rain.

Before dropping down to the path, Colin stopped. "We'll wait here."

Fionn pulled his bow from his shoulder. "I'll take care of them from the bluff."

"I want MacCorkodale alive—if he's with them." Colin held up his palm. "But aye, Fionn, set up here and cover our backs. William and I shall go down and meet them head-on."

William grinned. "They won't know what hit them."

"We'll tie our horses here and lie in wait upon the outcropping below."

***

Colin had begun to think the slippery bastards had turned back. When faced with driving rain and the promise of heavy snow higher up, he certainly would have. At least the men he left on the trail would intercept them if they did.

Lying on their bellies on a slab of rock, wearing armor was none too comfortable. But they did have an advantageous position above the path.

When hoof beats sloshed the muddy turf, the hair on his nape stood on end. At last he would have vengeance. Colin nodded to William, who slowly drew his sword. The first man came into view, hunched over, clutching his cloak closed at his chest—the dog had no idea he was about to lose his life.

A few more paces. Colin reached for his dirk and raised his chin. "Now."

Bellowing his war cry, he launched himself off the rock and hurled his body down the twenty-foot drop— right onto the back of the leader's horse.

The man jolted and flailed for his weapon. The horse sprung into a gallop. Holding the man's torso against his body, Colin pressed his knife to the blackguard's neck. "Pull up or the next log your horse jumps will be your last."

When the steed slowed to a trot, Colin yanked the bastard from his horse. Together, they crashed to the ground. Colin jumped to his feet. Chuckling, he sheathed his weapon. "Come at me, thief." He held up his fists. "There's nothing I'd like more this day than thrashing a beater of women."

The man's eyes darted side to side. He rose to his knees, then barreled straight for Colin, striking him just below the breastplate.

Balling both fists, Colin threw an undercut into the man's unprotected gut. Two punches to the face. The varlet bled from the nose, and backed away. Colin took two steps and slung his fist back for another blow. The man tried to block with his hands, but Colin's fist slammed into his face. Bone crunched beneath his gauntleted knuckles. The blow lifted the coward off his feet, sending him crashing to his back. He rolled to his side and wheezed.

Colin drew his dirk and dropped to his knees beside the pathetic cur. "I will have answers."

"Go to hell."

"Not before I send you there." Colin pressed his dirk harder. Blood oozed down the man's stubbled throat. "Who sent you after Lady Margaret?"

"No one. W-we wanted to rob her, 'tis all."

Colin pushed the blade harder. Blood streamed. "You expect me to believe you?"

"Believe what you like. I'm a dead man one way or the other." His teeth chattered. "You weren't supposed to follow us up the mountain."

Colin could no longer feel the rain or the cold. "I'll ask you one more time. Who's behind this?"

He pursed his lips.

Fionn led the horses beside them. "All dead, m'lord."

"Good. Build a fire. We're going to have to burn the truth out of this one."

The man's eyes popped.

Colin chuckled. "What did you think? I'd kill you without causing a wee bit of pain?" He tied the outlaw's hands behind his back.

No fire would start in the open, and the men resorted to lighting a small flame under a rock shelf where they'd found a few dry twigs. It was enough. Colin heated the tip of his dagger in the blue part of the flame. When the iron glowed red, he held it to the bastard's face. "If you tell me now, we can end this swiftly."

Shaking, the cur turned away. Colin grasped the man's bloodied chin and forced him to look him in the eye. "I'm not an uncompassionate man, but I give no quarter to those who cross me." Grinding his teeth, he held the scorching blade to the man's face and drew a slow line down to his chin.

The bastard howled like a castrated calf, his arms and legs shaking spastically. "Frigging bloody hell."

Colin handed the dagger to William. "Heat this up and make sure it glows red."

"Wait," the man pleaded.

Colin eyed him. "Who?"

"MacCorkodale wanted her dead."

"Why? She's an innocent woman."

The man spat blood. "Said she overheard something not meant for her ears."

William passed the red-hot knife to Colin.

The outlaw shook, his eyes wide with terror. "That's all I know. I swear." His legs squirmed. "*God's oath.*"

Colin wanted to torture him more—make him pay for touching Margaret. He eyed the sweltering metal and swallowed down his ire. Always true to his word whether he liked it or not, he doused his dagger in a puddle and sheathed it in his boot. "Very well. You shall suffer no more."

Standing, he pulled William aside. "Finish him."

Chapter Fourteen

Kilchurn Building Site, 23rd October, 1455

During her time at Kilchurn, Margaret spent her mornings reading to Mevan. The guard was sitting up and getting antsy to return to his duties. She urged him to rest, however, until Alana pronounced him fit enough to return home to his wife and wee bairns.

After leaving the surgery, Margaret found Tom Elliot. With All Hallows only ten days away, she wanted to discuss plans to prepare Kilchurn for winter. "Once you've mudded the walls, is there anything else to do until spring?"

Though lacking organizational skills, the stonemason proved to be quite knowledgeable about building a lasting structure. "We'll need to secure thatch over the foundation to prevent water from seeping in."

She started calculating a timeline in her head. "How long will that take?"

"Only a couple of days. Mudding takes the longest."

She eyed the workmen, absorbing Tom's every word. "When will we be able to start again in spring?"

He removed his bonnet and scratched his head. "Supplies should start delivering in March. We can clear off the mud then, too."

"How about building?"

"When the pre-work is over, we can commence as soon as weather permits."

Margaret cast her gaze to the clouds above. "March seems so far away."

"Aye, but it'll come quick enough." Tom pointed to the trough the men had built, now delivering water directly to the site. "Your idea has paid dividends already. Things will go much faster, especially if Lord Glenorchy stops the vandals."

Clutching her hands against her chest, she'd thought Colin would have returned with news by now. She'd also sent a missive to Dunstaffnage advising of her decision to stay on at Kilchurn. Surely he'd come soon. Not that she wanted to see *him*. She rather worried about his men. She and Mevan prayed every morning for their safe return.

The sentry upon the wall-walk blew his ram's horn and waved his arms. Margaret looked to the path through the void that would become Kilchurn's gate. Highlanders approached, leading a wagon.

Tom chuckled. "That would be Robert MacGregor and our sand."

"We are blessed indeed." Margaret craned her neck, searching for Colin or his men. The entire escort was MacGregors, with red plaids draped over their heads and shoulders to keep out the drizzle. Margaret stood on her future threshold and watched the procession gradually approach. A team of oxen lumbered, heads swinging from side to side, pulling the heavy load.

Laird Robert trotted ahead. "I'm happy to report we secured the sand, m'lady."

She clasped her gloved hands. "Did you come upon any outlaws on your journey?"

"Not with the MacGregor arms at the ready. No one in these parts would dare challenge me and my men."

She patted his steed's sturdy neck. "Mayhap we'll need such an impressive contingent of men to accompany all future deliveries."

"Could be a good idea." He glanced to Tom. "Though most of my guardsmen also work with the mason."

She considered Robert's words then held up a finger. "Surely we can recruit laborers more easily than soldiers."

"True."

Margaret again looked down the path. "Do you have news of Lord Glenorchy?"

"Forgive me. I should have mentioned it directly." Robert bowed his head. "The lord set out after the men who attacked your ladyship and Mevan—sent me and my men to escort the shipment."

Her tongue went dry, her chest tight. "Have you not seen them since?"

"No, m'lady. They rode north, up into the mountains."

Margaret covered her mouth with a gloved hand. The mountains could be treacherous in this foul weather.

"Have no fear. If anyone can track the bast…er…outlaws down, 'tis Colin Campbell and his band of fighting men. There's a reason he's returned home from two crusades—and a reason he's known as Black Colin. He puts fear in the hearts of all who face him."

Margaret studied the admiration in the chieftain's eyes. Truly, Robert MacGregor respected her husband. If only he would return, Colin might find it in his black heart to respect her.

***

Colin pushed inside the alehouse doors and beheld his backstabbing factor, collecting rents as if all was right with the world. Walter's eyes popped wide only for a moment, then shifted.

Guilty.

The double-crosser reached for his quill and made a notation.

The alehouse buzzed with crofters who came to Glen Orchy to pay their rents on the first Tuesday of every month. Colin's men filed in behind him. Walter pretended not to notice Colin, accepting payment from the next in the queue.

Colin's hackles burned as he marched toward his conniving factor. Walter snapped his gaze up and met Colin's stare. The stocky man floundered for his tankard. In his haste, the pewter vessel flew from the table, spewing ale across thresh-covered floorboards.

Walter watched while Colin's fingers wrapped around the hilt of his claymore. "I think you ken why I'm here, MacCorkodale."

The voices in the alehouse dwindled into utter silence.

"Whatever do you mean, m'lord?" The swindler's Adam's apple bobbed.

"You're a pathetic liar for a thief."

Walter held up two trembling palms. "I…I think you must be mistaken."

"There's no mistaking anything. The Lady Glenorchy overheard you talking about intercepting a load of my sand." Colin leaned down and placed his lips beside Walter's ear. "Worse, you sent a mob of incompetent thugs to silence her. That you have the ballocks to sit here and handle my coin as if nothing had happened proves your arrogance surpasses your cleverness by a league."

A bead of sweat trickled from Walter's temple. He stank of fear. The man's lips trembled, but he uttered not a word.

Colin tapped the tip of his sword against the floorboards. "I'll give you two options. You can fight me and die like a man, or hang from the gallows come dawn."

Walter shook in his pool of sweat and stared at his hands.

"I am not a patient man, MacCorkodale. What will it be?"

Sneering, the stocky man shoved his chair back and drew his sword.

Barmaids screamed and wooden benches scraped the floorboards.

Colin had his mammoth claymore raised before Water assumed his stance. He blocked the factor's feeble attack with a downward thrust. The flabby bastard reeled backward and tangled with his chair. Colin waited until Walter regained his footing. He hated fighting a weak opponent. Walter could give him no sport. But quarter could not be given. This leech had cut him in every way. He was not fit to take another breath on this earth. Rage burned a fire in Colin's breast. He wanted MacCorkodale to suffer. He lunged in with a cutting strike. Walter blocked.

Colin spun, eyed his target. In one swift downward hack, he sliced off the bastard's fighting arm.

Shrieking like a woman, Walter fell to his knees. Blood spewed from the wound. Colin snatched his dirk with his left hand and slashed it across the factor's exposed neck.

Eyes stunned, Walter dropped face first.

Colin watched the blackguard's lifeblood pool on the floor then turned to the astonished faces. "Let this be a lesson to the lot of you. If anyone crosses me, they will pay in blood." A hum of mumbles filled the room. Colin held up his hand. "All honest men will receive fair treatment by my hand. I wish this on no man."

He turned to William and Fionn. "Take his body to his clan chieftain and tell him of Walter's treachery. I'll not start a feud with a neighboring clan over blatant thievery."

***

Margaret clapped her hands, thrilled with the progress on the kitchen hearth. The bread oven was complete, and Tom Elliot had installed an entry shoot for water and an exit for slops. "Brilliant," she said, smiling broadly. "This will be the finest tower house in the Highlands."

The carpenters stopped hammering only for a moment to listen to her praise. After his arrival, Tormond had gladly set up a blacksmith station in the courtyard near the site where his shop would be built. It rang with the clang of a hammer on anvil as he pounded out iron nails.

Even Margaret could not believe their headway, and only in a sennight. Mevan had returned to the care of his wife. The Campbells and the MacGregors worked side by side and proved to be skilled laborers, with drive that matched her own.

She picked up a shovel to help mix the mortar.

"M'lady, your hands will be full of calluses if you keep working like that," Tom said.

"Rough hands are proof of a day well spent."

She'd been working beside the men for days, mostly directing their efforts, but when all were set to task, she reached for the nearest tool and pitched in.

She'd ruined her apron and borrowed another from Alana, but she didn't care. It was important to her to show the men she wasn't afraid of hard labor. The water trough fed a continual stream. Mixing at a steady tempo for a good deal of time, Margaret's arms began to burn. She pushed the shovel harder.

A man cleared his throat behind her. Margaret turned, but the bright sun kept her from seeing the face of the tall, broad figure.

"I told you to take an escort back to Dunstaffnage."

Margaret's heart jolted. She skirted aside to see his face. "Colin, you're back! I cannot wait to show you all we've—"

His eyes were dark, like a man bent on murder. "You should not be here."

Why on earth had she garnered hope he'd see her as useful? "I beg to differ, m'lord. Someone needed to see to Kilchurn."

He fisted his hips. "That would not be you. Duncan…"

"Is being well cared for by Effie." To hell with his arrogant, pigheaded balderdash. "Besides, the work will cease in a fortnight when we mud up for winter."

"I gave you an order and—"

She mirrored his stance, and fisted her hips with infuriated gusto. "I will attend Duncan throughout the duration of the winter, my lord."

"Ah, Lord Campbell." Tom Elliot walked around the corner of the kitchen walls. "You've married yourself a fine woman, if I may be so bold to say."

Colin glared at the master mason, who spread his arms and grinned. "You see, the kitchen would not have been started without Lady Margaret." He beckoned them. "Come and allow me to show you what I mean."

Thank the good Lord Master Elliot appeared when he did. Margaret could have again slapped Colin across the face, he maddened her so. God forbid she ever try that again. He'd lock her in the iron branks for certain. Elliot showed Colin the water trough and the blacksmith's station, while Margaret followed at a safe distance and kept her mouth closed. The mason did a fine job of extolling her virtues—far better than if she'd attempted to convince Colin of her own worth.

Elliot held forth as if he were giving the tour to King James himself. "Your wife knows her way around a building site, for certain."

Colin's beard had grown in while he was away, and he ran his fingers down it and pulled. "God's teeth. This is most unexpected."

Margaret smiled and stepped beside him. "And from the bills of lading, I've figured out how Walter MacCorkodale was cheating you."

"You have?"

"He was overpaying. That gave Walter the opportunity to skim a percentage before making payment. He's a slithering snake, that one."

"Was."

Margaret pressed a hand to her lips. "Did you?"

Colin's jaw twitched. "He's in hell with the devil."

"Oh my." She grimaced. "You should also know Robert arrived unscathed with the sand shipment, and Mevan is back at Dunstaffnage in the care of his wife until he can become my personal guard."

"*Your* guard?"

"I request him. He risked his life, nearly lost it so I might escape."

"I suppose he did." Colin's lips twisted. He wasn't half as overbearing as he'd appeared when he first arrived.

Margaret didn't give him a chance to rebut. "I say this calls for a celebration. I shall speak to Alana about it straight away. We'll kill a steer and tap a barrel of wine." Margaret started away and stopped. "You will be dining with us this eve?"

"Och." He pulled off his helm and shook his head. "Aye." How his hair could look so ravishing after wearing a helmet throughout the day, she had no idea.

Margaret dashed away before Colin could say another word. She'd listened to the MacGregor's music every night since Robert returned with his men. Oh, how she longed to take part in their country dances and sing.

Her insides fluttered. Best of all, somehow she'd managed to make Colin agree with her, as well as avoid his tirade. She'd have to remember to have Tom Elliot on hand should ever again Colin approach her looking like he could slam his fist into a stone wall without feeling pain.

Chapter Fifteen

Kilchurn building site, 30ᵗʰ October, 1455

Margaret dashed up the hill to Alana's cottage. Her friend would be thrilled at the prospect of feasting with Lord Glenorchy. Finally, the MacGregors and the Campbells would shed unease and become fast allies, just as both clans desired.

Out of breath, Margaret knocked on the rickety wooden door.

When Alana opened, her round face stretched with concern. "M'lady? Whatever is wrong?"

"Good…news." Margaret placed her hand on her chest and caught her breath. "The traitor has been brought to justice."

"They caught Walter?"

"With his hands filled with Campbell coin." Margaret couldn't allow herself to show untoward exuberance for the death of another, even an enemy. She crossed herself. "He's no longer of this world."

Alana mirrored Margaret's action. "'Tis for the best, m'lady."

Margaret smiled and grasped Alana's hands. "Agreed, and we shall celebrate with a gathering this eve."

Alana's eyes lit up. "And Lord Glenorchy has approved?"

"Aye." Margaret laughed. "Ask the men to kill a steer before he has a change of mind."

Alana clasped her hands over her heart. "Oh thank heavens. Our prayers are answered."

"It appears we're making progress, though there'll be much to accomplish once winter is over." Margaret rested a hand on her new friend's shoulder. "Besides, we need a great hall for our gatherings. We'll be lucky if the clouds stay at bay this eve after such a beautiful day."

"I shall pray they do. This could well be our last opportunity for a feast before the frosts move in."

"Can you spread the word?"

Alana pulled her cloak from a peg and draped it over her shoulders. "My oath, I will straight away."

"Excellent. I must bathe and find a way to soften these ugly calluses on my hands. If Lord Colin sees them, I'm afraid he'll tie me to a mare, send me back to Dunstaffnage and lock me away."

Alana studied Margaret's palms. "Blisters? My word, m'lady, what on earth have you been doing?"

Margaret bit her bottom lip. "A bit of labor to encourage the men."

"You're right, Lord Glenorchy won't like this a bit." She held up a finger. "I've just the thing." She pulled Margaret into her little cottage and lifted a small stoppered pot from the shelf. "This salve will fix you up in no time."

Margaret accepted the pot. "Aye? What's in it?"

"My own concoction—made from simple houseleek."

"Honestly? The weed that grows upon the thatch?"

"Aye—'twill take the sting away and your skin will be smooth as new. Just use it twice a day for a week."

Margaret offered a polite curtsey. "Thank you ever so much."

Alana walked her outside. "Leave the heavy work to the men. A highborn woman shouldn't be up to her elbows in mortar."

Chuckling, Margaret made her way back to the cottage almost as quickly as she'd ascended the hill to Alana's home. After working in the mud for days, she needed a bath and a clean gown. She couldn't help but skip. Oh to dance again. She could hardly contain her excitement.

***

Colin had walked the grounds with Tom Elliot, amazed at how much had been achieved during his absence. By the way the stonemason repeated her name, there was no doubt Margaret was the driving force behind the progress.

She'd attacked his sensibilities, trying to avert his anger. And he'd fallen into her ploy without a second thought.

When he arrived at Dunstaffnage and found she hadn't returned, he'd actually had annulment papers drawn. He'd made it eminently clear her main concern was Duncan, and she'd defied him.

But now, he second-guessed his actions. Had she been right to stay? Not that he agreed with her about Duncan. Perhaps he could let the issue rest for a fortnight or two. Regardless, he would have a serious conversation about her future priorities before the day ended, but quite obviously, Margaret possessed the ability to pull together and organize the men where others had failed. Still, he'd keep the annulment papers locked away. If she continued to defy him, her liability would outweigh her worth.

Colin looked the stonemason in the eye. "You've done well, Tom. I expect to see this level of progress come spring."

"Aye, m'lord." Elliot bowed his head. "If the shipments arrive on time, I reckon there'll be no further delays."

"I believe we've buried that problem for good." Colin glanced toward the cottage. "If you'll excuse me, I've something I must see to straight away."

He was quickly learning things were anything but dull when Margaret Robinson was around. She seemed giddy about the feast, which Colin honestly welcomed. However, he desperately needed a bath and a shave.

In the entry, Colin removed his cloak and armor, except his breastplate and hauberk underneath. Maxwell would be along shortly to provide assistance. Always a relief to shrug out of a cumbersome coat of arms, he sighed. He headed back to his rooms and hesitated. There was movement within. Drawing his sword, he pushed inside.

Colin's heart flew to his throat. His groin ignited into an almighty flame. Margaret stood in a washbasin without a stitch of clothing. Her arms quickly flew across her breasts and she sat in a rush, with water slopping over the barrel's sides.

Colin blinked and rested his sword beside the door. He should have averted his eyes, but he'd already seen her. Rounded breasts, full and ripe as sin, tipped with rosy buds, they defined succulent perfection. His fingers twitched. His palms could almost feel her soft flesh when his gaze had traveled to a slender waist. Then the shapely curve of her hips didn't disappoint. Before she splashed into the water, the dark chestnut brown triangle hiding her sex teased him, aroused his most base desires.

Wide-eyed, she stared at him. "A-are you planning to stare at me through my entire bath, m'lord?"

Colin licked his lips, and an unholy erection shot to rigid and jutted against his braies. Thank heavens the quilted codpiece beneath his hauberk covered it—barely. "Excuse me. I was not expecting to see you in my chamber."

She slipped her arms around her knees and pulled them tight to her body. "Where else would you have me stay?"

Of course she wouldn't sleep in the surgery, and she'd slept in this very chamber when they were traveling from Stirling. He crossed to the hearth and sat in an upholstered chair. "Apologies. I wasn't thinking."

"So…are…are you going to stay here?"

He turned his seat to face the fire. "I'll keep my back averted, if that makes you more comfortable." Why should he leave? This was *his* cottage and Margaret was *his* wife—at least until he signed the annulment papers.

"I'd be far more comfortable if you were not here at all." Her gaze seared into his back. "But if you must stay, I do appreciate your chivalry."

"A man should be able to gaze upon his wife without shame or embarrassment from either party."

"Is that so? I'm afraid I have little understanding of what you speak."

The water trickled. Colin's erection refused to ease. What was she doing? Could he catch a glimpse of her breasts if he turned his head slightly? He tried it. Blast. She'd shifted so she had her back to him—but silken, naked shoulders were delectable. His tongue shot out and tapped his top lip. If only he could taste her.

Colin clenched his fists. What was he doing, ogling Margaret? She must have known he'd come sooner or later. Was she trying to tempt him to her bed under the guise of innocence?

The smell of her soap wafted through the air. "What's that scent?"

"'Tis a lavender concoction from Loch Rannoch—my favorite."

"It is very nice—almost too nice."

"Why do you say that?"

Why does her voice have to make my heart thrum like a lovesick fool? "It does things to my insides it should not."

She emitted a nervous giggle. "You are funny. I doubt anything could affect you on the inside."

"Not much can." At least that was what he'd told himself over and over until he firmly believed it. "I'm pleased with your work here." Perhaps changing the subject would relive the painful ache beneath his braies.

The water stopped trickling. Colin took a chance and glimpsed. She regarded him over her shoulder. "Thank you, but you promised not to look."

"That I did." He faced the fire and watched the flames dance across the wood. "Things have not been easy these past months."

"I know." Her voice was but a whisper.

He waited for Margaret to continue, but the water started sloshing again. "I am very concerned for the welfare of my son."

"I assure you, m'lord"—a marked surety returned to her tone—"your son will be well cared for and educated. I give you my word I shall not abandon him during your indeterminate absence. As soon as he is able, I shall teach Duncan to pray, read and calculate sums." The water trickled. "But first of all, I do believe I will teach him how to love. That is the first and most important lesson for all infants."

Warmth spread through Colin's breast. "I daresay I agree."

"Truly?"

"Aye."

"I think the bairn will thrive here."

He sighed. "Glen Orchy is a magical place—so peaceful it always puts my mind at ease."

"That is a sign you're meant to be lord of these lands."

Colin stood. He walked toward her and reached out his hand. "Allow me to wash your hair." *What the bloody hell am I doing?*

She crossed her arms over her breasts and snapped her gaze to him. "You promised you'd keep your eyes averted."

He touched her tresses and ran his hand through them until his fingers met water. "I did, but I was wrong to do so." His voice deepened with his longing. He picked up a wooden bowl and knelt beside her.

Margaret's brows knitted when she met his gaze. Without removing her arms, she leaned forward and allowed him to ladle the water over her head. He took his time, massaging the water through her thick tresses. "May I have the soap?" he asked.

Margaret released one arm and fished through the barrel. Keeping her head down, she held up the soap. Colin wrapped his hand around her slender fingers. Tingles jittered up his hand, all the way to his shoulder. Reluctantly, he slid the cake from her grasp.

She took in a stuttering inhale. Unable to determine if his touch had affected her as it had him, or if she was merely cold, he wished he could see her face beneath her locks.

He lifted the cake to his nose and inhaled. As he closed his eyes, the fleeting picture of Margaret standing unaware and completely naked ravaged his mind. If only he were in heaven, he could gaze upon such beauty for an eternity.

Thoughts of the past would return to haunt him, but not in this moment.

Colin used circular, languid strokes to work the lather into her hair. Suds streamed down her flawless back, marked only by an adorable mole atop her shoulder blade. He squeezed the ends of her gloriously long tresses and watched the bubbles pop. His fingers trembled with his need to touch her.

"Mm."

Christ almighty, does she ken how sensual she sounds?

His erection lengthened with her blissful moan, so soft, he wondered if she'd actually been aware she'd uttered it. The fragrance floated around him, tempting him to nuzzle into her neck, push her arms away from her breasts and knead them. As soon as he saw her naked, he should have turned and walked out the door. Now she had him in her clutches and he was powerless to flee.

"Hold your hands over your eyes so I can rinse." His voice took on a deeper tenor, one he couldn't remember hearing…ever.

Margaret obeyed, keeping her arms tight over her breasts, though creamy flesh peeped through the crook of her arms.

When the soap completely washed away, leaving a wall of chestnut hair hiding her face, he sighed and set the bowl down. He pulled her locks to the side and peered at her face. Margaret slid her fingers to her chin and blinked at him. "Thank you, m'lord."

"I hope these big hands weren't too rough." His voice was still husky.

"You were as gentle as a chambermaid."

He stared into her pools of green, his heart thundering in his ears, the almighty strain beneath his braies relentless. He could think of nothing else but this moment and the exquisite, wet woman whose eyes captivated his soul. Her tongue shot out and moistened her bottom lip. Rosy as a pink bloom in spring, her mouth begged him to kiss it. Before his mind could trigger a rational thought, he covered her delectable lips, unleashing the passion coiled deep in his groin.

Closing his eyes, he parted her mouth with his tongue and showed his wife how to kiss a man. He slipped his hand to the back of her neck, frustrated he could not move closer, could not press his manhood against her body and show her the extent of his desire. His tongue plied hers until a gentle moan erupted from her throat. Her posture softened and she responded, her mouth becoming more impassioned.

With a deep breath, Colin eased away. Margaret's hands remained tight across her chest. He covered them with his much larger palms. "You are a beautiful woman."

She blinked. "But I thought…"

He grinned. "You thought what?"

Her gaze dropped in opposition to the blush crawling up her cheeks. "You didn't find me attractive."

He tugged her hands. She resisted. "Let me look at you."

Margaret nodded and dipped her chin. As he gently pulled her arms to the side, the ball of fire in his groin spread through his chest. "Holy Mary, Mother of God," he croaked. Beneath all her clothing, Colin never imagined she'd be so—so exquisite. On their wedding night, he'd taken her in her shift. In his haste, he hadn't paid a lick of attention to her beauty.

Margaret tried to pull away, but he held her fast. "You should never be ashamed to bare your flesh in front of me."

Her chin ticked up. "I should dress for supper, m'lord."

He released her hands, and she flinched. She blew on her palm and cradled it to her chest. "Are you injured?"

Wide-eyed, she shook her head. "No, m'lord."

He chuckled. She'd never be one for cards. "Show me."

"'Tis nothing, really." She held out her palm. Scabs crusted across it.

"What did you do? Build the water trough on your own?"

She hid her hand against her body again. "Not exactly."

"Tell me."

"When the sand came in, I got so excited, I picked up a shovel and…" She showed him both maimed palms. "I'll be fine in a day or two. Alana gave me a salve."

He should admonish her, but she looked like a downtrodden puppy—except for the satin breasts teasing him just above the water. He resisted his urge to drop to his knees and kiss her again.

Then his gaze flashed to the bed. No, he'd not give in to his desires. She'd driven him to the point of drawing annulment papers. It would take more than a passionate kiss to change his mind.

"Very well—but I don't want to hear of you doing hard labor ever again." He used his "commander" voice to ensure she understood the gravity of his warning. "I'll bring a plaid to sit upon, and see you at the gathering."

***

Margaret stayed in the water until it became uncomfortably cool. Her lips still tingled. She raised her fingers to them and closed her eyes. At first his mouth had been forceful, though not overbearingly so. When his tongue entered her mouth, it startled her. She thought to pull away, and then recalled how much she longed for Colin to kiss her on their wedding night. Her curiosity needled. With shallow breaths, she gave in. His gentle hand slid to the back of her neck and held her lips against his. Beard hair tickled a bit, but Margaret was far more distracted by everything else, like her hammering heart and the unexplained melting of her insides.

His mouth demanded she taste him. *Mmm. Fresh rain and spice.* With trepidation, she probed with her tongue and met his. Gently, the warrior swirled with such passion, the knot in her shoulders released and liquefied. Tight, warm desire spread between her hips, like it did when she used to think about Lord Forbes in a short doublet and matching hose. No. This kiss embodied a far greater intensity.

When Colin deepened the kiss, her breasts ached to press against him and rub. In that moment, it was all she could do to keep her arms crossed and not launch her wet body out of the bath. What on earth would spur her to such unbridled passion? Colin Campbell, the fierce Black Knight, was a quandary at best.

Everything turned cold when he pulled away. Did she catch a flicker of regret in his eyes? She pondered, trying to recall his expression. Then he had to keep touching her hands until he ran his thumbs over her blisters. Goodness, he looked cross. She thought he'd burst into a tirade for certain. But he didn't raise his voice—a wee bit stern, perhaps.

When she held up her hands, her nudity shamed her, especially when he studied her breasts. Then he turned away and left her to dress. She'd almost wanted him to stay. *Almost.* He'd looked toward the bed before he took his leave. If he'd stayed they could have ended up wrapped in the bedclothes rather than at the gathering.

She shuddered and reached for the drying cloth. Colin might come to her bed again one day. She clung to the hope he would not.

He doesn't even like me. Not really. A lonely void gripped her heart. Was this her lot in life? She might have an unhappy marriage, but she'd made friends here in Glen

Orchy. She'd established her place as lady of the keep. Colin couldn't take *that* away from her.

After Margaret dressed and rubbed in Alana's soothing salve, she did her best to dry her hair by the fire. She braided it and covered her head with a rose veil, secured in place with a green velvet band encircled with gold cord. Since leaving most her things at Dunstaffnage, she hadn't much to be creative with.

The cottage empty, she wrapped her cloak around her shoulders and headed to the growing crowd. The sun had set, and though the breeze blew in from the west, the clouds overhead were sparse. Huge logs crackled loudly in the fire pit, while men worked a fine-looking side of beef on a spit. The smoke-laced air smelled of char and roasted meat. Children laughed and chased each other around the fire.

Colin stood beside Robert MacGregor, deep in conversation. Margaret's heart fluttered. Her husband had shaved. His jaw was so smooth, it reflected the firelight. He'd removed his breastplate and wore a black doublet, fashionably short, with a mantle of fur draped over one shoulder. His hose hugged his powerful thighs. She fanned herself. He did have a physique to be admired— though she'd not admit it to a soul.

"Margaret." He pulled a folded plaid from under his arm. "We'll sit beside Robert and Alana."

Gooseflesh tingled across her skin. Would he steal another kiss this night? Kissing seemed so much more natural, so much more enjoyable.

The gathering hummed with laughter and talk. Colin spread the plaid over the mossy ground and offered Margaret his hand. "'Tis not a great hall, but these are our lands blessed by God."

She sat with her legs tucked to the side. "I do believe God's cathedral is the grandest."

Colin sat and reclined on his elbow. "It pleases me you can find enjoyment through hardship."

Margaret smiled. "'Tis a lovely autumn night. Why spend it indoors?" Fortunately, clouds hadn't rolled in as Alana had predicted. Moonbeams reflected white on the glassy loch.

Serving maids came around with flagons of ale. Margaret watched the others drink straight from them. "I suppose 'tis too much bother to bring out stacks of tankards."

Colin held the flagon out to her. "Aye, it is."

She drank heartily and dabbed her mouth with the back of her sleeve. "'Tis good."

Gold flecks in Colin's eyes sparkled with the firelight, and they crinkled a bit in the corners. He reached for the flagon and tipped it up, his gaze not leaving hers. "This batch is especially good." He turned to Robert. "Hats off to the brew master."

"Aye, there's none better than a MacGregor ale."

Trenchers filled with meat and breads arrived. Colin and Margaret helped themselves and passed the food along. Tonight no one needed to hoard—there would be plenty for all.

She swallowed a bite of succulently marbled beef. "'Tis nice to be in a circle where there's no high table or low."

Colin chuckled. "Or no table at all."

Robert's belly shook with laughter. "You're right there, m'lord. Nothing like breaking bread with the clan, drinking good ale and a roaring fire to warm you."

Alana looped her arm through her husband's and leaned forward. "How is Duncan, m'lord?"

"Well. Robust as a boy should be. The nursemaid tells me he's already eating gruel."

"Well done. We're all anxious to see him," Alana said. "Lady Margaret, are you looking forward to a bairn of your own?"

"Ah." Good Lord, Margaret's cheeks burned. "Duncan is my son now—should God grace us with more children, it will be a blessing."

Colin's eyes met hers with an unspoken question. She shook her head once, letting him know her courses had come. She swallowed hard. Gooseflesh spread across her skin. Did he want to see her with child? Her gaze dipped to his crotch and snapped back up.

He chuckled.

Oh queen's knees, he'd seen her look. She turned her face away. She mustn't *ever* allow herself to look at him there.

Across the fire, pipers filled their bladders with air. Margaret clapped. Among the musicians were a wooden flute, a lute and a drum. There most certainly would be dancing this night, and no one would keep her from it.

As soon as the instruments were tuned, the players launched into a country reel. Margaret tapped her foot while couples sashayed across the grass. "Who needs a dance floor this eve? The lea is fine." She grasped Colin's hand. "Dance with me for the next tune."

He pulled his hand away and rubbed it. "I'm not fond of dancing, lass."

Margaret pressed her fist to her lips. *Just when I thought the grouch was softening, he jerks away.* "But you dance so well."

His face went dark, as if the thought of dancing brought on a painful memory. Most likely it did.

Tormond, the blacksmith, stopped by their plaid. "Would ye care to dance, m'lady?"

Margaret gave Colin a hopeful look. He waved her away. "Go on, then."

Thank heavens. She would have died if she'd been forced to sit on the plaid all night without dancing.

***

Colin lifted the flagon to his lips and watched Margaret throw her head back and laugh while Tormond Campbell locked elbows and spun her around. Colin had been a sought-out dance partner at court, but the last time he enjoyed swinging a partner in his arms, it was Jonet's face smiling up at him. He no longer yenned for such frivolity. If only Margaret could fathom the pain that still spread like a chasm in his chest. True, he'd had moments when it didn't hurt so badly—mostly when he lost himself in Margaret's unholy, seductive gaze, but as soon as he departed her company, the remorse and the guilt returned with the vengeance of the grim reaper wielding a scythe.

Margaret smiled at him from across the flames. Her face lit up, aglow with exertion and happiness. She seemed happier here in Glen Orchy, as he was. Of course, there was nothing wrong with Dunstaffnage, where they would winter—hopefully for the last time. *Winter.* Could he justify holding off his return to Rome until spring? He must make a decision soon—both about the annulment and the date of his departure.

Tormond placed his hand on Margaret's waist and led her around the circle. The blacksmith was getting a fair bit too familiar. Colin sat forward. She smiled at her partner and spun away, then back. Blast it all, those bloody smithy hands were on her waist again.

"Is everything to your liking, Colin? From the scowl on your face I'd wager something didn't sit well with you," Robert said.

Och, something didn't sit well with him. *That fat-kidneyed codpiece spinning Margaret on the floor like he's a strutting pheasant.* "Nay. I just need another tot of ale, is all." Colin tipped back his flagon and guzzled it.

Robert pointed to a group of young bucks huddled at the sidelines. "I'll say everyone wants a turn with that pretty wife of yours. She's got all the laddies drooling in their cups."

Alana smoothed a hand over her skirts. "She's a beauty, that's for certain. 'Tis a wonder she's nay on *your* arm."

The music ended. Margaret laughed and clapped her hands, heading back to the plaid. A pimple-faced laddie had the gall to tap her on the shoulder. She looked so bloody innocent, clapping her chest in surprise, mouthing "me?" Colin wanted to stomp over there and admonish her... *You are a flirtatious tart, dancing and laughing like you're at court.* He rocked back on his haunches. Now he'd have to watch her take another turn with a slavering pup.

Colin stood and sauntered around the fire. No one would partner with his wife for the next dance. In the shadows, he patiently waited for the pipers to end their reel, then walked straight toward her. A gawky lad grasped her hand, but he reached for the other. "Lady Margaret promised this dance to me."

"M'lord?" Margaret gaped. "I thought you hated dancing."

He placed his fingers in the curve of her waist and pulled her closer to him. "Mayhap I've a feel for the music this night."

The bagpipes started in low. Colin led Margaret into the circle as the drum rolled a snare. He'd done this dance so many times, the steps came without thought.

Margaret moved with him, a step, a hop, a skip. Gracefully, she molded into him as if she were an extension of his very own body. He faced her and offered his hands. Aglow in the firelight, her cheeks shone like beacons calling to his heart. She placed her small palms in his and he wrapped his fingers around them.

Time slowed.

Watching her smile, his every heartbeat pounded against his chest. She was so much smaller than Jon...He blinked—Margaret was so small, his desire to protect her filled the hollow cavity in his chest. He led her into a spin. Her laughter uplifted him. Her gaze alive, tempting him to give in to her joy.

He focused on her lips. His breath caught. Rosy, bow shaped, petite, he wanted to kiss them again, wanted to taste her as he'd done in the chamber. He'd possessed her, naked by the fire, innocent. He'd wanted her then—just as he wanted her now.

Margaret's skirts brushed his calves, ever so lightly. His manhood stirred to life. Mayhap he could win her heart. But did he want to try? What about the papers?

The music ended and Margaret applauded. "They're wonderful."

"Aye." He kept his eyes focused on her. "Magnificent."

"MacCorkodale," someone yelled.

Colin's mind snapped to the present. He peered through the dark shadows in the direction of approaching hoof beats. Blast. He'd left his sword on his plaid. He ran his fingers over the hilt of his dirk and glanced at his men. They'd already armed themselves. Thank God the guard still had their heads.

Ewen MacCorkodale, chieftain of the neighboring clan, rode into the fray, mail-clad and outfitted for battle. His small army of mounted men encircled the gathering.

Colin pulled Margaret behind him, praying for a peaceful parley, though the death of Ewen's cousin had most likely sparked the chieftain's ire. Colin should have expected retaliation. He quickly surveyed the scene. All of the MacGregor men drew their arms—dirks, swords, poleaxes. No one had come to the gathering without a weapon. Aside from his sword, Colin had his dirk in his belt, an eating knife in his sleeve and a dagger bound to each ankle. Behind him, Fionn aimed his crossbow at Ewen's heart.

The errant chieftain was far outnumbered. Colin girded his loins and marched forward without drawing a weapon. He'd rather end this peacefully, for once in his life.

Ewen's beady eyes peered from under his helm. The man chose not to dismount—a sign of disrespect, though he kept his hands on his reins and away from his weapons. "Are you the man who killed my cousin?"

"Aye." Colin moved his fists to his hips, fingers brushing his dirk's hilt. "Walter promised fealty, yet he ordered his men to attack Lady Glenorchy after she uncovered his plot of thievery."

"You lie. My cousin was an honest man."

Colin smoothed his palm over his dirk's pommel. He'd killed men for less. One more accusation and this would become bloody. "How quickly you jump to Walter's defense. I've witnesses."

"And written proof," Margaret said behind him.

Ewen leaned around Colin and made a show of studying Margaret from head to toe. A lecherous smile spread across his lips. "You've a woman speaking for you now?"

Colin stepped in and latched his fingers around the big horse's bridle. "No one speaks in my stead, but if 'tis proof of treachery you seek, I've plenty—else you best prepare to join your cousin this night."

MacCorkodale glanced down to Colin's hand and then slid his gaze back to Margaret. He shifted in his saddle. "Word has it you're off to Rome soon."

"In time, perhaps." Distrust clamped Colin's gut. "I've a great many accountabilities to see to here first—especially tending the mess left by *your* cousin."

"Unfortunate," Ewen said, absently rubbing his chin. "'Tis not wise to leave such a fine woman alone."

Colin itched to pull the bastard from his horse and lay him flat. "Lady Margaret to you, sir. And *if* I sail for the Crusades, she will be well guarded. On that you have my word."

"I would expect no less." Ewen tipped his head to Margaret. "Apologies, m'lady. I meant no disrespect."

With a kick of his heels, Ewen spun his horse from Colin's grasp. "Come, men. I am satisfied with Lord Glenorchy's account...for now."

Chapter Sixteen

The Cottage at Glen Orchy, 30th October, 1455

Colin grasped Margaret's elbow far too firmly. "Come."

She wrenched her arm against steely fingers. "I'll follow, but I will not be muscled into the cottage by an angry knight." She detested the way Colin could change from charming to overbearing within the blink of an eye.

He glared and moved his hand to the small of her back. That wasn't much better, but at least it didn't hurt. Queen's knees, the man didn't know his own strength. After ushering her into the cottage, he slammed the door. "When a threatening chieftain rides into camp hellbent on revenge, I bid you hold your tongue."

"Me?" He was mad at *her*—not at the blackguard who'd spoilt the gathering? "But I spoke the truth."

"It matters not. He could have drawn his sword and commanded his men to fight with women and children underfoot. 'Tis my duty to protect you and the others in my care."

"You believe *I* put the entire clan in peril?"

"Aye, lady, you did." Colin paced and smacked his fist against the wall. "Did you see the way he looked at you? The bastard clearly undressed you from head to toe."

So now he was jealous? Margaret started her own pacing. "Oh please…"

Colin grasped her shoulders. "Do you have any idea how appealing you are? Must I keep you tethered?"

For heaven's sakes, he's completely nonsensical. "You, sir, are overreacting. He took his leave. What more do you want?"

His fingers clamped into her flesh. "Obedience. Respect."

Before Margaret could blink, he backed her against the wall and jammed his masculine frame against hers, pinning her there. She raised her chin to speak, but he crushed his mouth over hers. This was nothing like the kiss in the bath. His tooth scraped her lip. His tongue thrust with wicked force.

Her mind raged, conflicted between the hot cravings pooling in her loins and the sparks of fear firing across her skin. Margaret forced her fists between their bodies. She pounded on his chest and pushed away. Shaking uncontrollably, she wiped her mouth with the back of her hand. Blood.

She inched toward the chamber door. "Y-you would do well to learn something of respect, especially if you care to receive it." Her trembling hand grasped the latch. "You will not touch me like that again."

The last thing she saw was his horror-stricken face. She slipped inside, jammed her shoulder against the door and turned the lock as fast as she could.

"Apologies." Colin's voice leached through the wood. "I didn't mean to cause you pain."

In no way would she allow him margin to make amends. "Go away."

Margaret crossed her arms and hugged herself. Black Colin was an overbearing tyrant.

***

Colin could have taken his dagger and scored his palm for forcing his kiss upon her so brutally. He'd only intended to demonstrate his position as husband and Lord of Glenorchy. His actions had been far more brutish than he'd intended. He stared at the closed door. It was late and she was madder than a cook with no fire.

Now he'd done it. He didn't want a wife, and he'd forced himself upon her like a common scoundrel. Blast her to hell anyway. Ever since the day they were wed, his mind had been rife with conflict. Could she not leave him to his mourning? She wasn't even supposed to be at Kilchurn. Her place was at Dunstaffnage with Duncan. Ballocks to her meddling.

Margaret didn't want him to touch her? Fine. That was exactly how he'd planned this whole wretched marriage in the first place. After the mudding, they'd return to Dunstaffnage. He'd sign the annulment papers and prepare his men to set sail forthwith.

Effie could tend Duncan's needs for a few years, and then Colin would appoint a tutor.

He combed his hands through his hair and turned full circle. The lord of the manor would have to bed down in the fore chamber. With a table and four wooden chairs, he'd be more comfortable in the stable with the guard.

God would strike him dead before he showed his face to his men—it might have been acceptable when they were traveling from Stirling, but now they'd laugh him off his own lands.

No matter. Colin had slept in more miserable places than this. A knight could spend months sleeping in the dirt or upon a stone floor. On the morrow, he'd make a pallet of straw. Events of this night only brought back to full force the need to end this misshapen marriage and return to Rome.

He spread a plaid and stretched out before the hearth. *Jonet, why did you leave me, lass?* Closing his eyes, he willed himself to picture her raven hair, but in his dreams it turned chestnut, framing green eyes and a smile that could melt his icy heart.

***

Ewen MacCorkodale sat in the solar and tossed back a tot of whisky. It was too early to drink, but he needed something to ebb the fire in his chest. The only problem was the spirit made it burn more fiercely.

At least he'd faced his enemy—caught him dallying with the women. Ewen chuckled. Colin Campbell had bested him one too many times when they were lads. Though it had taught him a valuable lesson. Brute strength rarely ever solved anything, and a man could lose a great deal if he brazenly engaged in battle.

Ewen's henchman, Ragnar, pushed into the room. "Will you spar this morning?"

"Nay." Ewen gestured to the chair. "Sit. Drink with me." He reached for another cup and poured one for himself and another for Ragnar. "I could have killed that bloody arrogant bastard last eve."

The big man lifted the cup to his lips. "Why didn't we? I could've taken them."

Ewen sniggered at the henchman's overzealous bravado. "Because Campbell's man had a crossbow aimed at my heart. Besides, we were outnumbered."

Ragnar wiped his mouth on his sleeve. "The milk-livered Black Knight of Rome. I'd like to meet him man to man, without his army behind him."

"He's a snake, that one—and black suits the color of his heart." Ewen batted the air. "Attacking him directly has never been an option. He's got the king's ear. That's why it was so fortuitous to have Walter gain his trust—damn that miserable wench for overhearing him."

"I don't know. I prefer to fight a man rather than swindle him." Ragnar reached for the flagon. "I reckon the Black Knight was within his rights."

"What say you?" Ewen slapped the flagon from Ragnar's grasp, sending it crashing to the floor in a mess of shards and potent whisky. "Have you lost your mind? You were there when the king granted him lands. We risked every bit as much as that bastard—rode beside him—and yet were not recognized for our part in quashing the Douglas uprising."

The big man held up his palms. "Don't take me wrong. I'm no' saying I like the cur…"

"Walter was one of ours, my closest cousin. Do not ever say Campbell had a *right*." Ewen shoved the tip of his finger onto the table. "No one crosses me."

Ragnar folded his arms, chin jutting up. "So what will you do about it?"

Ewen stood and sauntered to the window. "He'll be off to Rome soon. Mayhap thievery isn't the best way to cut him down."

Ragnar emitted an ugly chuckle. The henchman knew what he meant. Ewen would bide his time, but one day, Colin Campbell would pay—right where it would hurt him most.

Chapter Seventeen

Dunstaffnage Castle, 10th November, 1455

Now the Kilchurn mudding had begun, Margaret sat in a rocker by the hearth, cradling Duncan on her lap. "What an adorable smile."

"He smiled?" Effie dropped the blanket she was folding and hurried across the room. "It's his first."

Margaret giggled and made a kissing sound. "Do it again for Mistress Effie."

The little bundle blinked and delighted them with a gummy grin.

Effie clasped her hands over her heart. "Oh my, he is a cherub—as beautiful as his father."

Margaret's brow furrowed at the mention of her husband, but the dark circles under the nursemaid's eyes concerned her more. "You look tired. How many times did Duncan wake you last eve?"

"Only once, but after his feeding, he decided it was time to tug on my wimple—right after he spat up on it."

"Oh heavens, the late nights are taking their toll."

Effie spread her palms to her sides. "Bah. 'Tis what I was born to do. He'll be sleeping through the night in no time, then crawling, feeding himself, walking." She let out a loud sigh. "And one day he'll no longer need me."

Margaret tapped her lips to Duncan's wee forehead. Effie clearly had a great deal of experience raising little ones. "That must be difficult for you."

"'Tis the hardest thing a nursemaid must do."

"Much like letting go of your own children, I'd imagine."

"Aye, very much the same."

Margaret rocked Duncan and hummed a lilting madrigal, watching his eyelids grow heavy.

Effie resumed her folding. "Your voice soothes him."

Margaret looked up with a sad smile. At least she could be of use to someone in this castle. Since the gathering at Glen Orchy, Colin had returned to his reclusive self, rarely taking meals with her, answering her questions with monosyllabic responses. He'd been working hard with his men, preparing them for their return to Rome. They sparred for hours in their heavy hauberks and armor. Colin said it made them stronger. *If a man practiced in his full kit, he could outlast any adversary.* That had been the longest string of words he'd uttered in the past ten days.

The bairn in her arms drifted off to sleep. Margaret stood and placed him in his cradle. "I could stay with him if you'd like to take a turn around the courtyard. The rain's finally stopped."

Effie reclined in a chair and picked up her needlework. "No, you go on. Find that husband of yours and tell him Duncan smiled."

Margaret wrung her hands. "If I can pull him away from his men."

The nursemaid offered a consoling pat. "If anyone can, 'tis you with your bonny smile. He'd best set to making another bairn before he sets sail."

Heat burned Margaret's ears. "You are incorrigible, mistress."

Effie shook her finger. "Someone needs to pull that man's head out of his arse, and you're the one to do it."

The old woman meant well, but she badgered almost as much as Margaret's mother. Heaven's stars, she hadn't mentioned a word about her lack of "marital relations" with Colin, but Effie had sniffed it out all the same.

"I'll return before supper." Margaret hurried out the door and toward the tower steps before Effie could further embarrass her.

Make a bairn? The woman must be daft. Colin no sooner wanted to visit her chamber than she his. Honestly, this was the worst marriage she could have imagined. At least if she'd married Lord Forbes, he would have been thoughtful of her, caring, respectful, tender…perhaps he'd kiss her frequently with the desire Colin had shown when she was in the bath. She shook her fists. One passionate kiss did not a husband make.

Who was that knight who'd kissed her all those days ago? He certainly was not the man who'd returned with her to Dunstaffnage. That man was an ogre, a bombastic, self-absorbed knight who cared naught for his wife or his bairn. The blackguard had only visited Duncan once since their return.

Margaret groaned and descended the stone steps. At least Colin allowed her to pour over Walter's ledgers. Since returning to Dunstaffnage, she'd spent most of her time either with Duncan or in the solar trying to make sense of the factor's entries. One thing was for certain—the man had been given too much freedom with Colin's coffers. Fortunately, Lord Glenorchy's holdings were vast. Going forward, Margaret might not collect the rents herself, but she would be present often and would audit the entries regularly. If Colin didn't seem happy with her involvement, at least he'd appeared resigned to accept it.

Fine. At least she had a great deal of work to attend to and occupy her mind. However, today the sun made an appearance after several consecutive days of drizzling rain. She pulled her cloak tight across her shoulders, then marched through the great hall and out into the courtyard. The scene resounded with a familiar clang from the smithy, horses trotting on cobblestones, voices grunting, swords clanging. *Swords?* That turned her head.

Naked torsos gleamed with well-muscled flesh.

She nearly tripped over her gown gawking at the sight before her. Merciful Lord of lords, her knees turned to boneless pegs. Though a crisp autumn day, half the men wore no shirts at all.

Had she been at Dunalasdair Castle, she would have thought it fortuitous to be so close to a mob of men, sweat glistening on their chests whilst they swung their practice swords. But in the center of the throng, Colin Campbell fought two at once—William and Fionn. His back muscles rippled with every thrust, every block— indeed, every single little twitch.

Margaret inhaled sharply. Unable to look away, she stood motionless. She'd been married to the man for weeks and yet had never seen him this naked. Colin wasn't wearing chausses, only a plaid belted low around his hips in the Highland style.

His arms bulged like fierce badgers, powerful and deadly. *Why, they must be as thick around as my thigh.*

Colin didn't let up. He advanced on his foes with relentless and brutal skill, driving them backward across the courtyard. Never had Margaret seen a warrior as fierce. *Black Colin of Rome.* A knight feared throughout Christendom, and now she knew why.

Her eyes glued to Colin's magnificent form, desire claimed her mind. She could not drag her gaze away, nor could she stay her thundering heart. Oh how she longed to smooth her fingertips over a warrior's muscular flesh. Heat coiled between her hips.

If only.

No man could possibly want to face Colin in battle. The other guards stopped to watch as he continued to beat his tiring companions. William thrust. Colin blocked with a downward strike. The sword flew from Willy's hand. Colin spun and took on Fionn. Lunging, Colin knocked him to the ground with his pommel. With a roar, the lord advanced.

William came from behind with his shield.

Margaret's hand flew over her mouth. "No!"

Her husband lowered his sword and turned. William slammed his targe against Colin's temple. Eyes rolling to the back of his head, Colin crashed to the ground.

"Merciful father!" Margaret dashed to his side. Blood pooled on the stone beneath. Colin didn't move. She dropped to her knees and held her cheek to his nose. Praise God, his breath warmed her skin.

Margaret jostled his shoulder. "Colin. Wake up."

But the big warrior lay unconscious.

She eyed William. The younger man spread his palms. "He dropped his guard."

"What were you thinking, hitting your lord in the head? He's not even wearing his helm."

William looked stunned. "He usually drives us until we can no longer stand."

Margaret wouldn't listen to excuses. Not now. She pointed. "You four, carry him to his chamber. Fionn, bring a ewer of hot water—and I mean hot, not tepid, do you understand?"

"I'll call for the physician," Hugh offered.

Margaret nodded and shooed him away. She hated physicians, but if she couldn't bring Colin around herself, it was best to have one on hand. "I'll fetch my medicine bundle and meet you there momentarily."

She lifted her skirts and dashed up the tower steps to her chamber. Fortunately, her mother had insisted she learn something about the healing arts. She now wished more. But as a dutiful wife, she'd packed a supply of herbs and remedies to accompany her to her new home.

Margaret arrived at Colin's chamber before the men lumbered up with him in their arms. She held the door. "Put him on the bed."

They did as asked. William paused. "What else do you need, m'lady?"

"Tend the fire. There must be no chill in this room." She glared at William, well aware Colin's enemies could seize an opportunity to attack a weak defense. "Keep this quiet. I want you to personally speak with each man who saw him fall. Tell them Lord Campbell is resting and will be sparring forthwith." She eyed him directly. "Do you understand?"

"Aye, m'lady. I'll do it now. Maxwell, you see to the fire."

Margaret set her bundle on the bed and regarded the men over her shoulder. "Thank you."

When Maxwell left to fetch an armload of peat, Margaret studied the jagged gash at Colin's temple. "Why did you take your eyes off William if you kent he would attack?" She knew the answer. It had been her voice calling out "no" that snapped him from his concentration. But why? He seemed impervious to every other sound erupting in the noisy courtyard.

She used a cloth to wipe away the blood now caked in Colin's hair. It still seeped, though he'd lost most outside. *So much blood in such little time.*

"'Tis best to stitch it before you wake." Margaret spoke to him as if he could hear. After bathing his wound with St. John's wort, she threaded a fine bone needle. Her fingers trembled a bit. She'd never stitched anyone before.

A knock resounded from the door.

"Enter."

Effie hobbled inside, wringing her hands. "I just heard."

Margaret held up the needle, managing to keep it steady. "He needs to be stitched."

The nursemaid glanced at Colin, wariness darkening her eyes. "Do you know what you're doing?"

"Snip off one suture at time?"

"Aye. Let me help."

Margaret gripped the needle tighter. "I'd like to do it."

"Of course. I'll attend you with the shears."

Margaret swallowed. She should allow Effie to stitch. The nursemaid had probably made countless sutures. Margaret had once practiced on a leg of pork. It was fleshy, unlike Colin's temple, which was ridged with bone. But he was her husband, and hers to care for. He mightn't want much to do with her, but by God, she'd prove herself useful to him. She made the first stitch, pushing the needle straight down, then pulled the thread through the jagged opposing edge.

She bore down to stop her stomach from convulsing.

"Good," Effie said. "Now make the knots firm, but not so tight they tear through."

Margaret bit her lip and prayed Colin's skin was as tough as pork. If pigheadedness had anything to do with it, he'd be fine. Winding the thread around the needle, she pulled the knot snug against his flesh and looked at Effie. The nursemaid snipped and nodded her approval.

With a deep inhale, Margaret tied off three more sutures.

Effie snipped the last threads and examined the wound. It didn't look half as bad now it had been closed.

Located at the side of his temple, his hair would cover most of the scar. "I couldn't have done better myself."

"Really?" The tension in Margaret's shoulders eased. "Thank you—that means a lot coming from you."

William and Fionn strode in with the physician. Black robed, with a black coif framing a gaunt face, he looked more like an effigy of death. He shouldered Margaret toward the wall and examined her work. "I daresay there won't be much of a scar." He looked back at the men. "How long has he been unconscious?"

Margaret stepped in and placed a protective palm on Colin's crown. "In the time it took for the men to carry him above stairs and for me to stitch his wounds—no more than two turns of the hourglass."

The physician frowned. "'Tis grave indeed. You did right by sending for me." He placed his black leather kit on the edge of the bed, untied and unrolled it. He picked up a tarnished lancet and a tin cup. "I believe a healthy bleeding will do him good."

Is he mad? Margaret forced her body between the physician and the bed. "You must be jesting. Lord Campbell lost at least a pint of blood in the courtyard—he hardly has any to spare. I'm quite certain."

The older man puffed out his chest, turning a brilliant shade of scarlet. "M'lady, you dare question a learned physician? Why, I've the king's charter—"

"I care not if His Eminence the Pope sanctioned your abilities, you will *not* stick that knife in one of my husband's veins. Not when he has already been bled."

The pompous man grumbled something about useless women under his breath, then stared Margaret in the eye. "Madam, if you do not move aside, I cannot attend the patient, and I assure you I am far more qualified than you."

Margaret's gaze slipped to the wooden-shafted blade in his hand. Her resolve strengthened straight up her spine. "I think not. I will see to Lord Glenorchy's care myself."

Effie clasped her hands over her heart. "M'lady?"

"That's my final decision on the matter." Margaret turned to William. "I want a sentry outside this door day and night. Effie, return to Duncan. I shall send for you should there be any change."

The assortment of tarnished lancets and picks made Margaret shudder to her toes. She rolled up the physician's kit and handed it to him. "I believe this is yours." With an air of confidence, she turned to the sentry. "Fionn, please escort Master Hume to his horse."

Margaret stood, arms crossed, guarding Colin's bed like a mother hawk while she watched everyone file out the chamber. When the door closed, she allowed herself to exhale. Shoving an errant strand of hair under her veil, she turned to Colin's peaceful form. Her stomach turned upside down. She had no idea if she'd done right by sending the physician away. Her gut told her yes, but looking at her trembling hands gave her doubt. She now held Colin's life in those palms, and if his situation declined, it would be her fault.

Margaret clenched her fists. "I will see you wake and rise from this bed Lord Colin Campbell of Glenorchy— even if 'tis the last thing I do on this earth."

***

Margaret dipped the cloth in the basin and wrung it out. After folding it lengthwise in quarters, she replaced it on Colin's head. Morning had turned to late afternoon, followed by dusk. The sun had set long ago. She'd refused to eat—couldn't, really. Not with Colin lying abed, still unconscious.

The priest had come and gone, making the sign of the cross and praying for Colin's recovery. The holy man started reciting last rites, and Margaret had abruptly stopped him. Colin would not die in her care.

But pray for him she did. She prayed for God's mercy and swift healing. She asked forgiveness for her errant thoughts. Her mother had been right. Margaret could be headstrong to a fault. She'd not given Colin a chance, even after Effie had explained how much he mourned Jonet's death. Margaret had lost her grandparents and remembered the lingering pain. How much more difficult would it be to lose a spouse, someone you lived with and cared deeply about as Colin so obviously had cared for Jonet?

Margaret's insides shredded. She'd been selfish, wanting and expecting Colin to shower her with attention, calling him a blackguard and feigning disgust and hate for him.

Colin's chest rose and fell beneath the bedclothes. Her heart crumbled. The great man seemed so peaceful. Margaret studied his face. His eyebrows were darker than his hair, arched boldly above his eyes, masculine yet not too thick. Due to the lateness of the hour, a dark shadow deepened the angular contour of his jaw, surrounding his perfectly formed lips. Oh how she remembered kissing those lips. Not brutally, but softly, reverently, with passion. What could she do to entice him to kiss her again?

His prominent Adam's apple bobbed, his lips parted slightly and he inhaled, his tongue clicking as if his mouth were dry. Margaret lifted a tankard of mead from the bedside table and used a spoon to ladle in a few drops. His Adam's apple moved again. Closing his lips, Colin moaned.

"Would you like some more?" she asked.

Colin opened his mouth ever so slightly. Margaret's heart thundered in her ears as she spooned in a somewhat larger portion. Colin swallowed and seemed content. She set the tankard down, and he shivered. The bedclothes had slipped down, completely exposing his chest, smooth and hard as a sheet of steel. Margaret brushed her fingers across his flesh. Tingles jittered up her arm. Her breathing shallow, labored. If only he could find it in his heart to love her.

Colin was so exquisitely firm, a far cry from her soft breasts. He moaned at her touch. "Margaret."

She snatched her hand away, her gaze darting to his face. But his eyes remained closed. "Colin? Can you hear me?"

He uttered not a word. Margaret pulled up the bedclothes and tucked them around his shoulders. She too felt a chill, and added some peat to the fire. She moved to the window and pulled the fur aside. The moon sat low on the western horizon, clouds sailing beneath it. Could the moon see Dunalasdair right now? So much had changed since she'd left her home. Were her parents well?

"Margaret...I...so..."

She whipped around and dashed to the bed. Colin's cloth had fallen from his head, but he was still unconscious. She dipped the linen in the basin, and he thrashed his head from side to side. "Margaret." His voice was louder.

"I am here." Margaret touched the cloth to his head. "Easy now. Lie still." She kept her voice as soft and soothing as possible. His face glowed amber in the candlelight—so gentle in slumber. Licking her lips, she leaned over him and kissed his cheek. She lingered there, the scent of spice filling her every breath. Swallowing, she studied his lips, then kissed them—warm, ever so soft, disappointingly unresponsive.

"I want to kiss you. Only you, husband. Will you ever let me in?" she whispered.

His breathing resumed a slow cadence. Wherever his mind was, he had spoken her name. What did that mean?

Margaret pulled her chair closer to the bed and rested her hand on his shoulder. Her eyelids hung heavily over her eyes, but she fought her urge to sleep. Colin's steady inhales became hypnotic. She finally gave in and rested her head on the mattress. She'd only close her eyes for a moment to regain her strength. But oh, that mattress had to be the most luxurious collection of goose down she'd ever placed her head upon.

Chapter Eighteen

Dunstaffnage Castle, 11ᵗʰ November, 1455

Sugared lavender. Colin awoke to a fragrance so heavenly, he thought he'd died and was attended by angels. However, there was only one person on earth who could smell as sweet—the woman he'd vowed never to allow entwine her lacy ribbons around his heart.

But she had.

The devil claim his soul, somehow the green-eyed vixen had inched her talons under his skin. Colin rolled to his side. His head pounded with a fury that churned his gut. Someone pushed into the length of his body and sighed. Headache be damned. He opened his eyes.

Margaret's soft bottom nestled against him, brushing his cock oh so suggestively. Colin nuzzled into her mane of chestnut locks and moaned. Somewhere in the recesses of his mind, a voice mumbled something disagreeable, but with one more deep inhale of Margaret's sweet fragrance, the inkling was completely suppressed.

He slid his hand around the dip in her waist and tugged her closer to his body. The shaft of his cock cradled between her buttocks. Blessed merciful mercy, heaven sent him a gift. If it weren't for the incredible pounding in his head, he'd swear he was dreaming. Margaret in his bed? How had that happened?

His cock throbbed and he rocked his hips. He cared not how she ended up beside him. A stone-hard erection consumed his mind. He'd suppressed his desires for so long, it was as if insatiable lust permeated his body. Colin slid his hand to Margaret's breast, full, round and utterly unbound.

"*Mo leannan*," he whispered the Gaelic endearment only reserved for someone very cherished.

He lingered, kneading lightly before he teased her nipple through her woolen gown, making it jut proudly against the fabric. A long sigh skimmed through her lips. Colin rose up on his elbow. Still asleep, she shifted her buttocks into him. Christ, her mere friction could make him come.

Slowly, he slipped his hand down and swirled his fingers around her mons. Margaret moaned louder and arched her back. Colin clenched his bum cheeks and held his cock against her bottom. He closed his eyes, and his head thundered like he'd been bludgeoned. *Is that why she's here?* He cast his mind back. The last thing he remembered was Margaret's startled eyes, her hands clasping over her mouth. *William—the overzealous warrior slammed me in the head.*

Margaret moved again. Colin's balls tightened with a renewed rush of heat. He didn't care if he'd vowed not to love another. Margaret had no right to be lying beside him rubbing her buttocks along his manhood. Any red-blooded man would lose his mind, attacked by her ungodly, alluring scent and heart-shaped hips that begged to be in his hands.

Colin grasped her skirts and tugged them up little by little, until his fingers threaded through the downy soft curls at her apex. His cods ached, his cock at the brink of losing his seed.

He strained for a glimpse of her womanhood, but settled for the smooth porcelain arc of her hip. He closed his eyes and slid a finger between her parting. Blessed be the saints, steamy moisture pooled there, as if she were waiting for him to enter her.

Margaret moaned and rocked her hips like a seductress. Colin wished he could slip himself between her legs and take her from behind. If it weren't for the blasted bedclothes separating them, he'd caress her with his sex rather than his finger.

He circled his hand around the nub of women's pleasure. Margaret pushed into him and spread her legs slightly. A drop of his seed spilled into the linens. "Margaret?"

Her leg jerked closed, and Colin ran his arm up across her shoulders to keep her from leaping off the bed. "Let me touch you, wife," he said with a low growl.

"You're awake?" Her voice cracked, and she tried to shrug out of his grasp and tug down her skirts. "I should…"

He held her tight to his chest. "No, *mo leannan*," he purred. "I want you here."

She relaxed a bit. "How did I end up on the bed?"

He brushed his lips along her neck. "Did you not lie beside me?"

"Nay, the last thing I remember, I was in the chair, allowing my eyes to close for a moment."

"Perhaps you climbed up in your sleep."

"Perhaps you pulled me."

He slid his hand to her flat belly and nibbled at her nape. "It matters not."

Margaret again tried to tug out of his arms. "Oh no, you mustn't. You've had a severe blow to your head."

He held her fast. "But this makes me feel better."

She hesitated. "I would think you'd have a miserable headache."

"Smelling your delicious hair, I hardly notice it."

She chuckled, a soft, womanly sound that made her entire body vibrate. Colin's aching cock reminded him of his dire need. But he would do this right or he wouldn't do it at all.

"Margaret." His voice but a whisper. "Relax and let me touch you."

***

Heaven help her. She'd awakened, legs exposed all the way up to her…her most sacred folds, the place where he'd callously shoved himself on their wedding night. For some unfathomable reason, she was now ablaze with an inexplicable longing, as if her legs had grown a mind of themselves—they wanted to spread for *him*.

Every fiber of her being told her to jump off the bed, but each time she tried, Colin pulled her into his hard, warm and very comforting chest. He slid his hand down and smoothed his fingers across her mons. If she were standing, she'd swoon. Then a chill ran through her blood. Did he intend to make her do *that* again?

Margaret bolted from his grasp and sat upright. "My lord. I may not be well schooled in these things, but I believe the proper way to make love to a woman is to kiss her, not…ah…what you were just doing."

A devilish grin stretched Colin's lips, and his eyes grew dark. "You want me to kiss you, wife?" He reached for her hand and tugged. "Come here."

Margaret hesitated. He didn't release his grip, but didn't force her, either. "You won't hurt me?"

With his free hand, he pushed away the bedclothes and bared his chest. "I promise I shall never hurt you again."

Her eyes drank in the banded muscles across his chest. A swarm of fluttering butterflies blossomed in her breast. How much she'd wanted him to show her tenderness. Oh yes, yes, yes, she wanted another kiss, just like the one in the bath. She hovered over him and gazed into his brown eyes. No longer reflecting the hard, coarse Highlander, they sparkled with a kindness she'd never seen before. Had the blow to his head knocked some sensibilities into him?

He licked his full lips and slid his hand around the back of her neck, enticing her to his mouth. Masculine lips met hers softly. She inhaled. He smelled of rugged male and sweetness combined. *Delicious.*

His tongue flicked out and tapped her lips. With one more gentle tug, he covered her mouth and closed his eyes, his deep groan filling her as if she could breathe in his desire. Margaret's heartbeat raced. She couldn't understand why the deep flame inside her body burned for him with unbridled passion, but if he turned tail right now, she'd die.

He inched his rough warrior hands down her spine. Her entire body trembled.

Without pulling her lips away, she kneeled astride him and smoothed her hands across his naked, rock-hard chest. His nipples grew erect to her touch, increasing the heavy longing in her own breasts. She pushed up and studied each rosy bud, tickling them with her fingers. "The tips are like mine."

A deep chuckle rumbled from Colin's throat. He moved his hands to her hips and guided her back a bit, atop his thick column of flesh. He was hard as a bedpost. Something clamped deep inside her loins with a driving, almost painful need for him to touch her. Beneath the bedclothes, he moved against her in a long, deliberate rocking motion. Margaret's eyes rolled back as her womanhood desperately craved for more.

This was nothing like their wedding night. His hands smoothed up the front of her bodice and kneaded her breasts, ripe and swollen with their desire for his touch. Oh yes. Heaven help her, this was sinfully magical.

He tugged up her skirts.

Margaret froze. Her eyes flashed open. She crossed her arms over her chest. Everything was so heavenly with the barrier of cloth between them. She didn't want the sensual passion to end.

"Lift your arms for me." His deep voice resonated and flowed like sweet cream.

She bit her lip. Oh how she desired more of his touch. Yes. He'd already seen her naked and hadn't hurt her then.

She met his gaze, filled with longing. Her breath stuttered. Slowly she raised her arms and let him remove her gown and then her shift. Completely bare, she continued to straddle him. Through the bedclothes, his manhood filled her crux. Driven by need, she thrust her hips and rode him until her body screamed "more."

Somehow, this wasn't enough. She must dare to be bold. "Now you." She moved aside.

Colin chuckled and pulled the bedclothes away. He slid his hand down and unclasped his belt. Casting it aside, he lifted his hips slightly and tugged the plaid off, dropping it to the floor. She stared at him. Tight heat pooled in her womb—her longing so intense, it hurt. Margaret could no longer remember the pain caused when he entered her on their wedding night. She craved to try it again. A flicker in the back of her mind reminded her of a fleeting moment of pleasure. Could she grasp the stirring again and make it last?

Colin wrapped his fingers around his member and stroked. "It cannot hurt you again. Never like the first time."

Alas, he understood her fears. Mouth parted, she watched him stroke himself, her own longing torturing until the insides of her thighs quavered.

Colin placed his palm between her shoulder blades and gently laid her down. Hovering over her, his lips moved intoxicatingly closer until they caressed hers. Licking her lips open, his tongue filled her mouth and kissed her fully. Prone, she allowed him to trail his deft fingers down her naked body. His mouth covered her heaving breast. Margaret arched her back and cried out as his fingers slipped into her womanhood. Every fiber of her being ached for more. She moved against his blessed touch, the tension mounting, her drive pushing her to some unknown brink of insane bliss.

Colin moved between her legs and kneeled. His eyes flashed with his rapturous grin. "I want to take you to a place you've never been." He dipped his chin, staring at her womanhood, his face only inches from her sex.

Was he going to kiss her *there*? She tried to close her legs, but met with hard shoulders. "Colin. You mustn't." She could scarcely utter the words, her body so inexplicably aroused.

"Close your eyes and give into the most erotic kiss of all."

Margaret dropped her head to the pillow and tried to breathe.

When his warm tongue caressed her flesh, a high-pitched gasp came from the depths of her soul. He licked again and turned everything molten. He claimed her mind—sensations curled through her body with a wave of unbridled, searing heat.

Powerless to flee, Margaret circled her hips in rhythm with his deftly relentless tongue. Every sinew in her body went rigid, driven by her insatiable need for more. She bucked harder—strange whimpers erupted from her throat. Suddenly, the crest of the wave unfolded like surmounting the top of the highest peak in the Highlands. With a cry, her insides burst into pulsing euphoria.

When Margaret finally opened her eyes, Colin smiled at her with the most devilish grin she'd ever seen in her life. "I want you to come again."

"Come?"

"Reach your woman's pleasure."

She chuckled. She could do that again? But this time when he ran the pad of his thumb across her sensitive spot, he showered her skin with kisses until her hips again rocked with desire. He rose to his knees and handled his erect member. "I want to make love to you."

Margaret didn't understand it, but her loins craved to have him insert his manhood inside her. She wanted to feel him fill her and slide in and out, as he'd done with his fingers. She nodded.

Colin guided it toward her. Margaret gritted her teeth and tensed, ready for the pinch. But he held the head just inside. "Am I hurting you?"

"Nay." Her voice breathlessly trembled.

Staring into her eyes, he slowly inched inside until he hit a spot that made her moan.

"I've filled you, m'lady."

Margaret moved her hips, straining to rub that spot again. He withdrew, then slid back with more ease— pleasuring her more than she'd ever dreamed possible. She grasped his back, then boldly slid her hands to his buttocks and showed him she wanted more friction. Colin thrust faster. "That's it, lass, you command the tempo."

He let her take the lead until she sank her nails into him, trying to force him deeper and deeper. The driving longing came again. If he stopped, she'd shatter. She cried out and whimpered, reaching her peak. Colin sped, sliding his manhood in and out. His entire body tensed and shook with a deep, bellowing roar.

He collapsed over her, breathing deeply as if he'd just returned from a rousing spar. Taking his weight on his elbows, he nuzzled through her hair and peppered her neck with kisses. "*Mo leannan.* You are sweeter than honey to a black-hearted knight."

Margaret closed her eyes and ran her fingers along the hardened flesh of his back. If only this moment would never end.

"I've been so unbelievably wrong, wrapped up in the agony of grief." He brushed his lips over her mouth. Closing his eyes, he tasted her again, their tongues dancing in glorious harmony. Colin tapped his forehead to hers. "You are the most amazing woman I have ever met." He kissed her cheek and then the other. "Was it good for you, wife?"

"Aye." A single syllable was all Margaret could utter as she savored him, all of him. She held him close, filled with euphoria. At last, they had truly become man and wife.

After kissing her temple, he rolled to his side and clasped his hand to his crown. "Och, my head hurts."

She gasped. How on earth had she allowed him to be so vigorous? *I'm such a muttonhead.* Margaret sat upright. "My stars, Colin. You could have torn your stitches with all that *liveliness*, or worse."

She stood and pulled her shift over her head. "Do you need some poppy juice? Some willow bark tea? You must be famished."

Colin reached for her hand and pulled her back onto the bed. "We'll worry about breaking our fast later. Rest beside me for a moment. 'Tis far more comfort than a bowl of porridge and a cup of mead."

***

Colin never cared to lie abed, but this day it had become a pleasant enjoyment watching Margaret take charge and dutifully dispatch everyone who happened by. Effie and every single one of Colin's inner circle of loyal men paid their respects. *Astonishing.* Margaret set each person to task. She worded her orders with such fineness, everyone willingly acquiesced to her wishes. The first being William, who was instructed to ensure every man, woman and child on the castle grounds was aware Lord Glenorchy was well, eating and spending the day at his leisure—Colin would hear supplications in the great hall on the morrow.

She'd set Maxwell to task, asking him to send a missive to the MacGregors inviting them to Duncan's christening, which she'd abruptly decided would take place in three sennights time. Ah yes, she dispatched Fionn to notify the priest.

Margaret turned and grinned at Colin with Duncan in her arms—Effie had been directed to enjoy some fresh air while Margaret cared for the babe. She missed not a step, carrying him around on her hip, setting things to rights. How could he have been so wrong about her?

Finally, she returned to the bed and sat. She held Duncan out. "I think this should be a family day, since you're abed and yesterday was the bairn's first smile."

"You don't say?" Colin smoothed his hand over Duncan's black locks. "Do you have a smile for your da, laddie?"

The babe scrunched up his face and launched into an earsplitting wail. For a moment it reminded him of the horrible night he spent wallowing in the depths of despair, listening to Duncan's cries echo down the passageway.

But Margaret swept him from Colin's arms and put her little finger in the babe's mouth.

Instantly, Duncan started suckling, quite content to be held to her breast. She smiled down at the bairn and slowly withdrew her finger. "There, there. Have you got a smile for me?" She emitted the cutest high-pitched laugh Colin had ever heard. Duncan gave her a huge, gummy grin. She giggled again and tickled his tummy. "You smiled, yes you did, you sweet little laddie." Margaret shifted her gaze to Colin. "Did you see him?"

"Aye. He's going to be a lassie killer, with dimples like that."

"I daresay he will—just like his da."

Colin gazed into Margaret's fathomless green eyes. She was attracted to him. He thought she'd been when they first met in the market, though since he'd behaved like such an arse, he scarcely gave her a chance know him. That she hadn't decided to hate him for all eternity completely boggled his mind.

He grasped her free hand and held it to his heart. "Can we start anew?"

"Pardon?"

Of course she wouldn't make it easy for him. "I'm afraid I've been despondent, withdrawn since we married."

"Aye. You've been grieving."

"I was that obvious? You didn't deem me indifferent?"

She bit her bottom lip and lowered her lashes. "At first I thought you hated me, but Effie explained how much you loved Jonet, how hard it was to lose her."

Colin grew quiet at the mention of his former wife's name. His lips quivered when he tried to smile. He tightened his grip on Margaret's hand. "Aye, her death tore out my heart. I never thought I could…" He swallowed back the words.

"Could?" she probed.

Colin almost said "love again," but stopped himself. Was he in love with Margaret? Her very presence picked up his senses, as if he were a predator and she the prey. Lately, when she was near, he could think of nothing else but to say he loved her. That would be irresponsible so early in their marriage—especially with the annulment papers still locked away. "I never thought I could ever *feel* again," he corrected. Thank heavens he hadn't signed them yet. He wouldn't be needing them after all.

Margaret chuckled and raised his hand to her lips. "Mayhap that knock on the head did you some good."

Chapter Nineteen

Dunstaffnage Castle, 12ᵗʰ November, 1455

Colin's head didn't feel much better the next day, but he refused Margaret's tincture to soothe the throbbing pain. They agreed he should sit in the great hall and hear supplications. If he stayed abed too long, rumors could spread and embolden his enemies.

Margaret clasped the Campbell plaid across his shoulder and fastened it with a bronze brooch. "I'd like to sit beside you this day."

He brushed her cheek with his finger. "Aye, but 'tis not a woman's place."

"Then I shall bring my lute and provide entertainment for your lordship."

He eyed her. "I suppose no one will think the better of it. And your music shall calm my aching skull."

"My thought exactly." She patted the brooch and smoothed the wool. "It will also give me an opportunity to observe without anyone the wiser."

"You shouldn't become accustomed to it," he warned.

"Oh? And who will be hearing supplications when you're gone?"

Colin clamped his mouth shut. He'd not thought of his journey to Rome in days, and after realizing how much he needed to make up to Margaret, he hoped Jacques de

Milly could do without him this crusade. Surely if the Hospitallers were in dire need, the grand master would dispatch another missive. No matter what Colin did, he'd feel guilty. He either must leave his new wife behind or turn his back on the brothers of the order. Neither choice was palatable. He preferred to put it off as long as possible.

Lute in hand, Margaret followed him down the winding stairs to the great hall. An assortment of crofters and other poorly dressed men were already assembled around the tables near the door. Colin preferred to have the commoners sit at the low tables, where they wouldn't be able to hear him on the dais. There was little privacy, but he tried to limit embarrassment for all parties.

William manned the door and kept their weapons. No one approached Colin armed, though he was sufficiently fortified with a dirk in his belt and daggers in the flashes of his hose. Maxwell always stood behind Colin, fully armed with claymore and an assortment of weapons. The lad knew well any confidence he heard on the dais must never be repeated.

The benches scraped over the floor while people stood and bowed. Colin nodded and bade them to sit.

Margaret perched upon a stool across from Colin, a respectable distance away. She strummed. The pounding in his head ebbed. She was right to keep the atmosphere light. Colin nodded to Maxwell. The lad was never late.

The first crofter climbed the steps, bonnet in hand, a bold plaid draped around his waist and shoulders, fastened with a thick leather belt.

Margaret's strumming grew a tad softer.

Colin nodded. "Good morrow, Hamish."

"Good morrow." The crofter's timeworn face frowned woefully before he bowed.

"What brings you to Dunstaffnage so early this morn?" Supplications always started slowly.

"Malcolm is stealing my sheep. Three gone in a week, I say."

Colin picked a speck of dirt from under his thumbnail. "And have you proof?"

The old fella spread his arms wide. "Me sheep are grazing in his paddock."

"Is Malcolm here to defend himself?" Colin scanned the faces in the hall.

"Nay, that milk-livered barnacle wouldna show his face."

Colin had heard the same tale a hundred times before. One man's word against another's, most likely. "Are your animals firebranded?"

"Aye, an X on the right hip of every lamb and ewe."

"Very original of you." Colin looked to the rafters. "Sheep stealing? Bloody oath, you'd think we were on the borders."

Margaret strummed faster and knitted her brows. Evidently, she thought Colin should do something to retrieve Hamish's sheep. That was exactly why women were omitted from supplications. Colin cleared his throat. "Hugh," he hollered. "Go with Hamish and inspect Malcolm's sheep. If any are firebranded with an X, they should be returned."

Hugh looked up from his morning meal. "Aye? But nearly everyone uses an X to firebrand their sheep."

Colin rapped his fist on the table. "Hamish shall lay claim to no more than three."

Margaret smiled. Hamish too, and he bowed obsequiously. "Thank you, m'lord. I'll nay forget this."

Colin rolled his hand impatiently. He could wager Malcolm would present before him on the morrow.

The next subject who climbed upon the dais blurted out he wanted an annulment.

Margaret launched into a woeful ballad of lost love. Colin could scarcely keep a straight face. In hindsight, having her serenade him was not the best idea he'd ever had. He squared his jaw and regarded the older man with consternation. "Why on earth do you want an annulment, Jamie? Has Morag not provided you with three bairns?"

"Four, m'lord, but she refuses to stop badgering me."

"Good God, man. Have you no cods? If a woman is nagging you, 'tis because you've allowed it."

Margaret's lovely voice slid down a dreary scale.

Jamie shook his shaggy, greying curls and stepped in closer. "I can no longer bear the sight of her."

Colin scratched his chin. Jamie looked a tad long in the tooth as well, fat belly and all. "Has your wife the means to support herself if you abandon her?"

Margaret's tune became suddenly cheerful.

"Nay."

"Do you think so little of Morag that you are willing to let her starve? What of your offspring?"

Jamie hung his head and clenched his fists.

Ah ha, the old blighter. "You have been unfaithful, have you not?"

He nodded.

"Find ye a priest. Confess, and do not come back here seeking ruination of the woman who birthed ye four healthy Campbells and lived to tell about it. Women are to be respected for their pains. Mayhap 'tis why she's nagging you—you haven't shown her proper respect."

Margaret's strumming became so invigorated, she might as well have stood and applauded. Though Jamie scowled, Margaret's smile put Colin's mind at ease. It wasn't easy to settle disputes of the marriage bed.

Colin's head pounded. He should have taken Margaret up on her tincture.

The day progressed with a barrage of petty woes, all of which were dispatched with little effort, until a man ascended the stairs, his haircut in the shape of a bowl, his hose dual colored—one leg green and the other red.

Colin would have thought him a court jester if his doublet had matched his chausses. "'Tis a bit early for Yule, what say you?"

"Yule? Nay. 'Tis the latest fashion." The lad removed his feathered cap and bowed. "Donald MacLean, at your service. I'm told you are in need of a factor, m'lord."

"Have you now?" Colin stood and walked around the odd fellow. "And where do you hail from, Donald MacLean?"

"Taynilt, the other side of Loch Etive."

Colin focused on the man's ridiculous hose. "I'm well aware of where Taynilt is, but not of you. Why haven't I seen your face around these parts?"

"I know not. I've lived here all me life."

"And what do you know about factoring?"

"I'm good with numbers, m'lord."

"I see."

Margaret strummed a minor chord, launching into another of her sad ballads. Colin resumed his seat.

"Tell me, Mr. MacLean, have you ever had dealings with the MacCorkodale clan?"

Colin caught the slight shift in the man's eyes. His knuckles whitened as he gripped his bonnet tighter. "Ah, no, m'lord."

Margaret stopped strumming and locked eyes with Colin. He nodded, appreciating the silent delivery of her opinion. He felt the same. *Never trust a man in two-toned tights.* Colin scratched his chin. "I'm sorry, but you are a little late. I'm afraid I've already appointed someone to the job—someone from the *Campbell* clan."

"But—"

"That is all, sir. Good day."

Margaret climbed down from her stool and sat beside Colin. "You're looking a bit pale. Shall I send for some willow bark tea?"

Colin pressed the heel of his hand over the sore spot. "I need something a bit stronger. Perhaps a tot of good whisky."

"That can be arranged." Margaret stood, but hesitated. "I didn't know you'd appointed a factor."

"I haven't, but the next man will be my kin."

"What about me? I supervised my father's factor." She kept her eyes averted.

Colin couldn't consider allowing his wife to perform the job of a hired hand. "'Tis too much for a noble lady with a keep to run and bairns to look after."

She frowned and started away. Colin caught her hand with the tips of his fingers. "I'll expect you to oversee the man I appoint. He won't take or spend a farthing without your knowing about it first."

Her grin lit up the room. She threw her arms around his neck and squeezed. "Thank you. Your trust means more to me than you know."

***

A sennight later, Margaret hummed while she embroidered the silk christening gown to match the skullcap she'd made.

Effie rocked Duncan beside the hearth. "You seem happy today, m'lady."

"Aye. I removed Colin's stitches this morning."

A distant look filled Effie's eyes. "I take it things with the lord have improved. I've noticed he's not quite so melancholy."

Margaret bubbled inside. "'Tis as if the blow to his head is what Colin needed to set himself to rights."

Effie laughed. "I wish it were that way with every man. Then all we women would need do is carry around a wooden club."

"You are terrible." Margaret chuckled, tying off her thread. "But I do think he's come to realize life continues on for the living."

"That it does."

Duncan made a cooing sound and stretched his little arms. Margaret had developed a fondness for her tiny stepson, with his crown of wispy black locks. "He's growing every day."

"Aye. I hope he'll not be too fat for that lovely gown you're making."

Margaret held it up. "'Twill be perfect. Besides, I've invited all the shire—the MacGregors as well."

"My heavens, surely the great hall will not be able to hold them all at once."

Margaret tossed the gown into her sewing basket. "We must. 'Tis important to me to see everyone fed and recognized, no matter their station. I shan't turn a soul away."

"You are generous, I'll say."

"I learned a thing or two helping my father collect rents from the crofters. There's no one who works harder or suffers more."

Effie nodded. "I daresay you're right."

"And why has the king appointed lords and ladies if not to show consideration to their subjects? The crofters till our land, the shepherds care for our livestock and the warriors fight to defend what is ours."

"It would be virtuous if all the gentry saw it like that. I'm afraid you're in the minority, m'lady."

Margaret looked away. Unfortunately, she was well aware charity was not important to all nobles. Her own mother had been too tight-fisted.

Effie rocked a tad slower. "Have you given more thought to redecorating your chamber?"

"I ordered a new comforter and pillows made. That should do for now. I'll ensure everything else is to my taste when we move into Kilchurn."

"But that could take years."

Margaret shook her finger. "Not if I'm overseeing the work, I assure you."

The nursery door opened, and Colin stepped inside. "Are you ready for your nooning, Lady Margaret?"

"Aye." She stood and stretched. "I'm famished."

Effie placed Duncan in Colin's arms. "Did you know your wife has invited all the Campbells and MacGregors to the christening?"

He gave the bairn a wide-eyed look. "Aye, we agreed 'tis the right thing to do." Duncan kicked his legs and cooed.

Effie snorted. "What on earth are you planning to feed them?"

Margaret lifted the babe from Colin's arms and placed him in his cradle. "Venison would be nice. We should plan a hunt."

Colin stepped in beside her, still enraptured with his son. "Do you hunt, Lady Margaret?"

She rolled her eyes at him. "If you think Lord Struan's daughter doesn't know how to handle a bow, then everything they say about the western Highlands being completely backward is true."

Colin looked to Effie. "'Tis settled, then—we shall plan a hunt."

"Ye need an entire herd," the old woman mumbled as Colin grasped Margaret's hand and led her out the door.

Margaret's heart fluttered. Would she ever tire of Colin's rough hands and his rugged touch? She hoped not. She loved the way he made her heart leap with every look and every caress. Marriage to the Black Knight had become perfect in the past fortnight. She never asked him why he had been so incorrigible when they first married. Besides, she knew he'd been in mourning. She still caught him distant at times. He even admitted he couldn't spend time in her chamber because of the memories there.

"Will you promise me something?" she asked, surprising herself at her boldness.

Colin stopped before they stepped down the stairs. "What is that, *mo leannan*?" Lowering his gaze, he bowed his head and fluttered kisses along her neck.

It tickled, but she didn't want to play, not quite yet. She placed her hand on his chest and sought his gaze. "Promise you will never behave like a tyrant again."

His face fell, and for an instant she feared the overbearing, feared knight would return and bite her ear clean off. "On my oath, I will never behave so badly." He then clasped her hands to his chest. "You didn't deserve my callousness. Forgive me?"

"Aye." She pushed up on her toes and kissed his cheek. "Now I ken the real Black Knight. He's locked away in a special place in my heart."

Colin emitted a low growl. Cupping her face in his powerful palms, he claimed her completely with his mouth. His kiss ignited a bone-melting fire that spread through her blood. He gradually edged her toward his chamber door.

Margaret paused and drew a ragged breath. "I do believe we should eat first, m'lord. I need my strength before we do *that* again."

Colin threw his head back with a rolling laugh. "You do have a way with words, wife. Come sup then, before I change my mind."

Chapter Twenty

Dunstaffnage, 30th November, 1455

Colin picked some late-blooming heather and walked down the tree-lined path to the graveyard beside the chapel. He hadn't visited Jonet's grave since the day they interred her into the ground. The dirt had settled. Moss and grass covered the plot, marked with a headstone that read: *Lady Jonet Campbell, Loving wife of Colin, Born 1432, Delivered into the arms of our Lord 1455.* The raven-haired lass had been only sixteen when they married.

A cold wind whirled its way under his cloak. He stared at the headstone—a lovely piece of granite, though as lifeless as Mariot's beside it. Emptiness surrounded him. The only sound was dried leaves on the forest floor crackling as gusts of wind swirled them on the air. Colin knelt and placed the clump of heather on her grave. "I'm sorry I haven't a rose for you, but there are none to be found."

Chilled, he glanced behind him as if Jonet's spirit might appear, but the wind just blew harder. "Duncan is growing. You'd be proud.

"But that's not why I came." Colin swiped a hand across his brow. "I need to release you, my beloved. I've found a mother for Duncan, someone I ken you'd like. I thought I could keep her at arm's length, but I cannot—and 'tis not fair to her if I continue to do so."

His nose started to run. He pulled a kerchief from his sleeve and blew. "'Tis best I get this over with. Goodbye, Lady Jonet. I shall nay forget you."

Colin stood and stared at the inscription on the headstone. He bowed once and proceeded back to Dunstaffnage. With each step, weight lifted from his shoulders.

***

Margaret wore her new fur-lined cloak pinned tightly around her neck. With matching gloves and hood, she'd surely be warm enough for today's deer hunt. She patted her mare's nose. "Where are the lads? Leave it to a woman to be the first to show."

"Ah, Margaret." Argyll's breath puffed in the chilly November air. "Ready for some excitement, are you?"

"Aye, but where are the others?" She glanced over her shoulder

"Fetching the dogs, I presume."

She patted the horse's neck. "I'm ever so glad Colin and I thought of it. Roasted venison will be perfect for the christening."

"Expecting a large crowd, are you?"

"Aye, and we shall need more than one beast to feed them all."

Argyll thumbed the string on his bow. "We shall do our best to see you satiated, m'lady."

"I'm so glad you've managed to slip away from court long enough to attend Duncan's christening."

"What kind of godfather would I be if I were not in attendance?"

Margaret chuckled. "And how are things at court?"

"Dull as always."

"Oh? Any interesting ladies about?"

"Of course, one would be completely blind not to appreciate the alluring courtiers in their finery."

Margaret arched her brows. "Any who've struck your fancy?"

His horse stuck his nose over the stall door, and he patted it. "Alas, no."

"Sooner or later you'll find a woman whom you want to wed, and she'll bear you many children."

"I'm in no hurry." Argyll removed a bridle from a peg on the wall. "And how are things here?"

She knew what he meant. The last time they'd talked, she and Colin were hardly speaking. Margaret clasped her palms to her burning cheeks. "You once told me your uncle was a good man."

"Aye, that I did."

She looked down at her boots. "You were right."

"'Tis good to hear. Colin cannot pretend to be an ogre for long. 'Tis not in his nature." Grinning, he slid the stall's deadbolt open. "Are you settling in?"

"Set in a routine for winter, anyway. Come spring, I'll move the household to the cottage at Kilchurn."

"You are a brave woman, venturing out beyond the fortress walls."

"One must be adventuresome if one wants a castle of her own."

"Touché." Argyll stepped into the stall, slipped the snaffle bit into his horse's mouth and fastened the bridle leathers. "Has Colin received further word from Rome?"

"Nay, he's heard nothing since he wrote explaining his circumstances." Margaret shuddered. She hated to think of Colin's inevitable departure, especially now they were finally growing close. Neither one of them had spoken about the Crusades. Honestly, she'd put it out of her mind. Surely Colin wouldn't consider leaving until after winter. She rubbed her abdomen. Perhaps, if luck was

with her, Colin would stay for the birth of their first
bairn—if she was indeed with child. She'd missed her
courses by a sennight, but needed to be certain before she
mentioned it to anyone.

Argyll patted her shoulder. "It seems to weigh heavily
on your mind."

"Aye."

He led the horse out of the stall. "Perhaps the grand
master has moved on to a knight with far less
responsibility than Lord Colin."

She bit her bottom lip. "If only your words rang true."

"There you are," Colin's voice boomed from the far
end of the stable. "I've had the guard swarming the castle
trying to find your whereabouts."

She dipped in a hasty curtsey. "Apologies, m'lord.
When I couldn't find *you*, I opted to look here."

Wearing a sealskin cloak and belted plaid, he appeared
every bit a powerful Highland lord. "Argyll." Colin
clapped his nephew on the shoulder. "Are we ready,
then?"

"Aye, spotters report a herd three miles northeast,"
Argyll said.

Colin rubbed his hands together. "It should be a
fruitful hunt."

Once mounted, the contingent set out with a half-
dozen hunting dogs flanking them. Margaret didn't need
to ask. Both Colin and Argyll never took to the trail
without being surrounded by highly trained warriors. At
least this was a happy hunting party, with hauberks and
heavy armor left behind.

Colin's shoulders were broader than any other's. He
was as formidable a knight in a fur-lined cloak as he was
in his shiny coat of blackened armor. Margaret rode in
beside him and studied his profile. She liked him better
with the breeze picking up his dun hair—it was far more

moving to watch him without a helm shoved atop his head, a nosepiece blocking the view of his handsome face. His helm made him look dangerous, unfamiliar. It even made his eyes darker, more fearsome.

Colin glanced her way and smiled. "What are you thinking, m'lady?"

Margaret waggled her eyebrows. "How a glass of mulled wine in front of the hearth will warm our bellies when we return."

"Mmm. Mulled wine and cheese."

"And pillows."

His grin spread and one eyebrow arched. "I like the way you're thinking, m'lady."

Evenings in the past fortnight had become her favorite. Since Colin had hit his head, his whole demeanor toward her had changed. He'd opened her eyes to the glories of lovemaking between a man and a woman. Never in all her days did Margaret think she would enjoy being naked with a man, but neither she nor Colin could manage to keep their clothes on once alone in his chamber. She giggled.

"What?"

"Thinking about you, is all."

He grinned, his eyes dark.

With yelps and excited barks, the lead dogs launched into a run. The hunt was on. Excitement racing through her blood, Margaret used her crop and spurred her mare to a gallop. Riding a stallion, Colin could have easily barreled ahead, but he remained beside her.

Yonder, a large herd of deer fanned out through the forest. Colin beckoned her down a narrow path. "Come."

Margaret followed, the mare breathing in rhythm with her hoof beats, straining to keep up with the big stallion. Colin pulled his bow from his shoulder and snatched an arrow. Margaret couldn't see past him. But with a turn of his head, she saw him shove his reins into his teeth. Colin loaded the bow and took aim. His horse missed not a step. Releasing the arrow, Colin bellowed a frustrated growl and pulled his horse to a stop. "Bloody missed by a hair."

Close behind, Margaret reined her mare too late. Her mount skidded headlong into the stallion's rump. He neighed and reared. The mare's hindquarters kicked up. Propelled forward by the sudden jolt, Margaret lost her seat and flew over the horse's head.

Shrieking, she curled into a ball and prepared to land hard. The ground approaching, she squeezed her eyes shut.

"Ma-r-gar-eeeee-t," Colin yelled, as if time slowed.

Feet slamming into the ground, followed by her bum, she hit a patch of moss. She plopped to her side in a heap. Was anything broken? She waited for the familiar throb of pain.

Colin leapt from his horse, raced to her and dropped to his knees. "God's teeth, are you all right?" He gathered her in his arms before she could speak. "Tell me you're unhurt."

Stars cleared from her vision. "I think I'm well."

He brushed her cheek with the tips of his fingers. "My heart stopped when I saw you flying through the air as if you'd been launched by a catapult."

Margaret chuckled, the effort causing a sharp pain her side. She winced. Why on earth would her ribs hurt? Had the fall jostled her insides?

Colin's eyes filled with a pained expression. "You *are* hurt."

She twisted her shoulders and took in a deep breath. "That feels better."

"Are you certain?"

"Aye."

Colin sat back and cradled her in his lap. "I never want to see you flung from a horse again. For a moment I through I'd lost you."

Margaret cupped his face with her hand. Though he shaved near every morning, his stubble prickled her fingers. She liked the ruggedness of it—so different from her own skin.

His brown eyes glistened, and his lids lowered as his gaze slipped to her lips. "Mulled wine, cheese and pillows for m'lady?"

A familiar pull of desire coiled deep inside. She emitted a sultry chuckle. Threading her fingers behind his neck, she drew his lips to hers. Something about kissing Colin in the forest with a cold breeze tickling her skin heightened her need for him. He must have felt it too, because his hand deftly slipped under her hem.

Ignoring an intense flutter between her hips, she tried to push it away. "Colin, your men are everywhere."

He took a cursory glance over his shoulder. "I see no one."

"But 'tis cold."

His relentless fingers found her womanhood. She gasped, and Colin muted the sound with his mouth. He slid his finger inside her, and Margaret mewled like a cat. Beneath her bottom, he grew hard. "If only we were in front of the hearth now," she managed in a breathless voice.

Colin used her moisture to tease that spot which could drive her mad. Since they'd become intimate, the man knew no bounds. The Black Knight could bend her to his will with a look.

Between them, he tugged his plaid up and exposed his shaft—as big around as her wrist. Margaret marveled at how he could fit it inside her, but God she wanted it now. If only.

"Colin, we mustn't."

"Straddle me."

Oh how that wicked glint in his eye attacked her sensibilities. With a hitch to her breath she stared at him, mouth open.

"Come, lass. No one will see, and we'll circle your skirts around us for modesty."

Her inner core squeezed with naughty anticipation. "I think you've done this before."

"Perhaps, but never with you, and never has my yearning run so deep."

She ran her tongue across her lips, and Colin groaned. Effortlessly, he lifted her by the waist and coaxed her legs astride him. He lowered her with her knees either side of his lap.

She gasped. "Can we do it like this?"

"Aye," he growled.

He lifted her up so her apex skimmed him, spreading moisture over the tip of his cock. The floral scent of her womanhood wafted up to their faces, so hot it took the cold away. The wind tickled her skin, heightening her need in concert with Colin's hands. The naughtiness of touching his sex to hers in the forest ignited a ravenous yearning so deep, she could scarcely contain the urgency.

Colin claimed her mouth with his tongue, and she plied his with equal force, boldly reaching down and guiding his cock inside her. Such a vulgar word, *cock*, but it felt so erotic embedded inside her body.

He smoothed his hands to her hips. "Look at me, Margaret."

With languid strokes, she used her knees to control the rhythm. She not only rocked up and down, she arched her back so the base of his shaft tickled her most sensitive nub. Her breathing sped. Colin's too. His eyes did not leave her face, his lips parted. His breath came in short gasps. So erotic his expression, her breasts swelled. The pressure built. Colin squeezed her buttocks and forced the tempo faster. A cry caught in the back of Margaret's throat. Colin bared his teeth and held in his urge to bellow. Together they reached the peak of passion, their bodies quivering in unison.

Collapsing against him, Margaret ran kisses along Colin's neck. "You've turned me into a wanton woman."

He chuckled. "All the better for me, wife." He ran his fingers up her sides. "How are your ribs?"

She pressed her hands against his. Aside from a little pain upon inhaling, she felt fine. "A tad bruised, nothing more."

He refastened his kilt, then helped her up, smoothing his hands over her skirts. "I think you'd best ride with me, just to be certain."

"Are you jesting?" She arched a brow at the big warhorse. "Ride double on your stallion?"

"Pegasus? He's harmless."

"Aye? Have you noticed how harmless he is biting a mare's back when breeding? I'll say he's quite the boorish beast, if you ask me."

"Is your mare in heat?"

Margaret shook her head on a laugh. "Nay, else you'd have been the one sailing through the air, not me."

As usual, Colin got his way in the end. Together they rode back to Dunstaffnage, Lord Glenorchy cradling his bride across his saddle, pulling the mare beside them. The hunting party beat them back, and they were met at the gate by a worried Lord Argyll. "I was about to send out a search party."

Colin gave him a wink. "Margaret had a bit of a fall."

She waved her hand. "Not to worry. I'm quite all right. Lord Colin is simply being overcautious."

However, when Colin carefully lowered her from the saddle, she was indeed stiff. "I daresay a glass of mulled wine will be welcomed." She rubbed her backside and stretched her back.

***

Colin felt like celebrating. Margaret had the most astonishing way of blotting out all his cares. In her arms, he could think of nothing but his love for her. How had it happened? Never would he have believed he could love again.

Watching her flit about his chamber, removing every pillow and cushion and stacking them around the hearth, filled him with contentment. She skipped to the bed. "Come, help me pull off this huge comforter."

"Do you think we shall need it?"

"We need every comfort known to man."

With a tap at the door, a servant brought in a selection of breads and cheese, and the most coveted warm mulled wine.

Colin waved the servant inside. "Set it on the table and that will be all, thank you."

Colin and Margaret had supped in his chamber nearly every evening in the past fortnight. Honestly, they should be dining in the hall with Lord Argyll this eve, but Colin couldn't bring himself to do so—not with all their talk about wine and cheese. By the time he got Margaret back to the castle, he was ready for another round with her. God she was remarkable, hiking up her skirts in the wild. How on earth the king convinced her to marry him was a quandary. Lady Margaret could have any man in Scotland—and blessed be the stars, he was her lucky suitor.

Colin took Margaret's hand and walked her in front of the crackling hearth. "Since the room is warm and we have multiple plaids *and* my comforter to wrap around us, I think we should dine disrobed."

Margaret's eyes flashed wide. "You cannot be serious. What if a servant finds us?"

"We can cover up, just as we would if we were in bed."

She clapped a hand over her mouth and giggled. "You're simply scandalous."

"Aye, but isn't it so much more fun?" An adorable blush crawled up her cheeks. How could she be bashful after a fortnight of swiving like rabbits? Colin made quick work of loosening her laces and slipped the wide-necked gown from her shoulders.

Margaret crossed her arms over her shift.

Colin stepped in and ran his fingers through her hair. "Why shy all the sudden?"

She lowered her arms. "I am not."

His eyes dipped to her bow-shaped mouth and he was overcome with an urge to kiss it. Licking his lips, he lowered his head and showed her the depth of his love for her. By the time he pulled away, they were both completely unclothed, his cock pointed directly at her. Colin held her at arm's length and drank in her beauty. He must never compare her to his previous wives. From here on, he'd be content to fill his eyes only with the sight of her beauty. Margaret's flesh was alive, supple and his to worship. In this moment, she filled his mind completely.

She sat first and pulled him beside her, tugging the plaid across her lap.

He fingered the wool. "Are you chilled?"

"A little…not really."

Colin brushed the plaid aside. "Then allow me to feast my eyes upon you." He kissed her hand and ran his lips up her arm.

She sighed. "Are you hungry?"

"Mmm. Famished." He forced himself to pull away and place the tray in front of them. He reached for a slice of bread and held it to her lips. "Well-earned sustenance, *mo leannan*."

Together they reclined against the pillows, ate and sipped the warm wine. Colin eyed her lute resting beside the hearth. "Will you play for me?"

She arched a brow with her sidewise glance. "A strumming naked strumpet?"

Margaret's little innuendos could make him laugh like no woman he'd ever met, and he did so from his gut. "Exactly. Last night you played for me fully clothed. Why not an erotic concert this night?"

Crawling toward her lute, she giggled. Oh how he loved her willingness to indulge his fantasies. Admiring her heart-shaped bottom, prone to him, he could make love to her right there, but the prize would be all the sweeter if he waited.

Grasping the instrument, she situated herself atop a cushion and smiled. Her eyes drifted to his crotch. Colin liked her boldness and he lengthened for her. Her eyes grew dark and she sucked in a breath, pulling the lute across her lap.

She strummed a chord, blissful notes vibrating between the chamber walls. Colin's heart swelled. She opened her mouth and sang a happy madrigal, so light and airy, Colin could swear the music was alive. It floated and swirled around him almost as if he could grasp it.

He reclined against the cushions and watched. Margaret's plush breasts jostled slightly with her movement, the pearly buds pointed at him, begged him to suckle them. He licked his bottom lip. They would be the first stop on tonight's journey to heaven.

She watched him with a heavy-lidded gaze, yet her sultry voice missed not a note. Colin smoothed his fingers along a silk cushion, imagining her skin smoldering beneath. Longing clamped around his manhood. His reaction hadn't gone unnoticed. Margaret's voice softened. Colin spread his legs and let her feast her eyes on what he was about to give her.

When she strummed the last chord, Colin could resist her no more.

Chapter Twenty-One

MacCorkodale lands, 30th November, 1455

Mounted on his steed, Ewen circled his bullwhip over his head and cracked it midair. "Get up, ye wee beasties." It had been a good year for his heifers. He'd left it a bit late for firebranding the calves, but today it wasn't raining and the task needed to be done with.

He and his men had rounded up the herd of red shaggy cattle and were driving them toward the yard just outside the keep's walls. In front of him, a steer bucked and gallivanted, until he stopped at a clump of grass. Digging in his spurs, Ewen galloped after the stray. With a flick of his whip, he lashed the beast's hindquarters.

The steer brayed, his eyes rolling back. Zigzagging, Ewen drove the blighter back to the herd with quick snaps of his whip.

Ragnar rode in beside him. "That's a fine-looking piece of beef. I'd be careful with that lash."

Ewen chuckled. "Makes the bastards more tender."

The lead man hopped off his horse and opened the yard's gate. "There's a Glenorchy firebrand on this one," he hollered.

Ewen waved him on. It wouldn't be difficult to alter the brand.

Ragnar chuckled. "Thieving cattle, are we now?"

"Wheesht. Don't tell me you're getting soft on me. Besides, it wouldn't be the first time."

The big henchman shrugged and leered with a sideways look. "Was at the alehouse yesterday. Word has it Glenorchy has invited all of Argyllshire to his son's christening two days hence."

Ewen pulled up his horse. "You don't say?"

Ragnar smirked. "Ye aim to pay the bastard a visit?"

"Why not?" Ewen tugged the whip through his fist. "I think we've left his coffers alone far too long. There's an open invitation, you say?"

"Aye."

How can I ignore an opportunity to pry? "Mayhap I'll poke around a bit, find Glenorchy's latest weakness. That should be easy enough."

Ragnar dug in his spurs and chuckled. "'Tis a good thing, m'laird. Things around here have been rather dull."

***

Two days after the hunt, Margaret and Colin processed to the chapel. Effie walked behind them, carrying baby Duncan. It was a blustery day, spitting with rain, and Margaret had ensured Effie wrapped the bairn snuggly in furs before they set out. It was fitting the babe's christening would be his first foray outside the castle walls.

Colin had donned his ceremonial armor. Margaret would have preferred he wore a doublet with matching hose and fashionably pointed shoes, but it mattered not. Their garments were covered with heavy fur cloaks. Besides, her husband looked like a king in his impressive blackened armor.

The priest waited as the procession neared the chapel's threshold. Everyone invited had come—the Campbells of Argyll and Glenorchy, as well as the MacGregors. Most attendees would be forced to wait outside the small chapel's walls as the mass was said, but Margaret had discussed with the priest that all who approached God's table would receive holy bread and wine. The five deer felled on their hunting expedition would be the main fare at the feast—thank the good Lord for providing such abundance.

Margaret only hoped they wouldn't be hit by a torrential downpour until after mass. She worried about her guests, especially the MacGregors, with whom she'd become so attached in the short time she'd stayed in Glen Orchy.

Alana stood beside Robert near the chapel door. Margaret held out her hands and kissed her friend on each cheek. "Why are you not inside?"

"'Tis packed to the walls."

"Surely there's a place for the MacGregor chieftain and his wife in the front."

Alana clapped her hand over her heart. "But those chairs are reserved for family."

Margaret took her hand. "And that's exactly why we've reserved them for you." Honestly, her parents were not in attendance and Colin's had passed. What better way to strengthen the relationship between the clans?

Colin smiled and bowed to Robert. "Aye, of course, please join us."

He then winked at Margaret, an appreciative gesture that spoke a thousand words.

It was a lovely service, and the priest followed Colin's wishes to keep it short, with so many people attending outside in the cold. Duncan behaved amiably, with scarcely a whimper when the water was ladled over his head. Colin gazed upon Margaret through the entire mass, his reverence so palpable, Margaret felt as if the bairn had been born of her body. Her heart filled with warmth. Colin had finally accepted her as wife and mother. Now if only she could add to their brood and survive in the process.

***

Before the feast, Colin swapped his ceremonial armor for the more comfortable dress of a Highland lord—a plaid belted around his waist and a linen shirt with the Campbell colors draped from his left shoulder to his right hip. So many people crowded the tapestry-lined walls, there was nary a need for the roaring log fire in the grand hearth. Guests sat elbow to elbow at the long wooden tables, and yet some remained standing. Colin had never seen Dunstaffnage's great hall so fully packed with people. "Remind me to review Kilchurn's floor plans. The great hall must be larger than this by half."

Margaret raised her goblet. "I like the way you think, m'lord. Never turn away a guest, for one small kindness could lead to a lifetime of fealty."

"You're a generous woman. I like that." She'd even added more chairs to their table on the dais and invited people to sit along the platform edge.

At Colin's opposing side, Argyll elbowed him in the arm. "What the devil is Ewen MacCorkodale doing here? Surely you didn't invite him."

Colin planted his feet square on the floor. A rush of heat shot through his fingers and toes. "I did not, and would never invite the cousin of the man who nearly ran me into ruin."

Argyll frowned. "I could ask him to leave."

"And cause a stir?" Colin took a healthy swig of wine. "'Tis a celebration. If he behaves, there is no reason to sour the gaiety for Lady Margaret."

"I shall keep an eye on him."

"My thanks, nephew."

Argyll signaled for his henchman. "You'd do the same for me. Enjoy the evening. My men will see to order."

The big henchman moved to Argyll's side, and they spoke in hushed tones.

Eyeing them, Margaret clasped Colin's arm. "Is everything all right?"

"Aye." He patted her hand. "Just taking a few wise precautions to ensure it stays as such."

With a clap of his hands, servants poured into the hall laden with trenchers of roasted venison, fresh bread and scrumptious honey-baked apples. Colin's stomach rumbled when the succulent smells wafted from the kitchen doors. He stood and raised his cup. Benches scraped across the hall floor as every guest followed his lead. "My friends, I thank you for celebrating my son's christening with me and his stepmother. Duncan is well on his way to becoming a just and diplomatic man. Welcome to my table. I wish you all good health."

"Good health!" The hall resounded with the cheer.

Colin held his cup and eyed every person at the high table. Robert MacGregor and his wife, the priest, his adoring Margaret on one side. Argyll sat beside powerful clan cousins with whom they were both allied.

As dinner ended, Colin touched his lips to Margaret's ear. "Are you ready to play for us, *mo leannan*?"

"Are you sure? We could just bring the musicians in now."

"I want to show you off to the clan. 'Tis not often I hold a gathering as large as this."

"Very well." Margaret picked up her lute from behind a tapestry and moved to a stool Colin had placed there that morning. Aside from the day he heard petitions, she'd mostly serenaded him in his chamber—at least when he wasn't ravishing her.

He pulled his dirk from its scabbard and pounded the hilt on the table. The noise in the hall gradually abated.

When finally the lower tables quieted, he gestured to his wife.

Her faced turned as scarlet as the red tapestry behind her—so endearing. She strummed the introduction of the ballad she'd practiced for him, then her voice sang out clear as a crystal bell.

Jaws dropped across the crowd and Colin's heart swelled with pride—until his gaze settled on Ewen MacCorkodale. Colin could not mistake the deep desire reflected in the man's eyes. One male predator could sniff out another from fifty paces or more, and MacCorkodale sat a mere twenty paces away. The man leaned his elbow against the board and spread his legs, a long-toed shoe pointing directly at Margaret. The dipped tilt to his chin, the wolfish grin and the tongue that slipped out and moistened his bottom lip made the hair on Colin's nape stand on end. He slid his fingers over the round pommel of his sword. One wrong move and Ewen would be a dead man.

Margaret strummed her final chord. The hall erupted in applause. Colin clapped loudly, drowning out all others on the dais.

"Ewen's applauding nearly as loudly as you." Argyll nudged him. "Shall I escort him out?"

"Nay. Let the bastard step out of line. It would be my pleasure to introduce him to my claymore."

The musicians took their places on the balcony. Servants quickly folded tables and lined the walls with benches to create enough space for dancing. At once, Ewen MacCorkodale approached the dais and bowed. "Lovely ballad, m'lady." He gestured to the crowd. "It touched the hearts of all."

"Thank you," she replied with genuine grace, dipping her head respectfully.

"May I have the honor of this dance?"

Colin stood. "The first dance should be with the lady's husband."

He didn't miss the lesser laird's fleeting sneer. Ewen bared his teeth ever so slightly before he bowed. "Forgive my impertinence." Then he had the gall to reach for Margaret's hand. "You will then reserve the second dance for a poor chieftain, m'lady?"

Margaret smiled graciously. How she could be so damned amiable given the present company was beyond Colin's imagination. "Of course. It would be my pleasure."

Colin grasped his lady's hand and led her to the floor. "You needn't dance with him."

"Aye, but it may help smooth the tainted blood between our clans."

"After Walter's skullduggery, I doubt our alliance will ever be more than tolerant, and barely that."

"But it was Walter who erred, not his cousin or his entire clan."

"Lady wife, you are wise beyond your years. But blood runs thick in the Highlands. Ewen must prove himself ten times over before I forgive Walter's crimes against my house."

The dance ended quickly, and blasted MacCorkodale moved toward Margaret as if he had some sort of claim. Colin clenched his fist and leaned his lips to her ear. "Save every other dance for me this night. I am not disposed to sharing you with anyone."

Returning to the dais, Colin scowled. Ewen's looks didn't lighten his mood. Tall, with auburn hair and dark eyes, the neighboring chieftain had always had a way of turning the ladies' heads.

Margaret seemed to be enjoying herself, smiling. But then, she loved to dance. She'd certainly reminded Colin of that fact enough. Often, in fact, she had Colin up dancing in his chamber while she hummed the latest court tunes. A slow grin crossed his lips. The dancing always ended well—with him on top, usually, though he might even enjoy the endings with Margaret on top more. And he would have her in his arms again this very night. Ewen MacCorkodale could take his thick, wavy locks and shave his head. Damn him to hell.

A messenger approached through the side door. "Apologies for the interruption, m'lord, but I've been sent from Rome…"

Chapter Twenty-Two

Dunstaffnage Castle, 2ⁿᵈ December, 1455

The missive bore the seal of His Holiness, the Pope. Colin resisted his urge to slide his finger beneath the red wax and read. Argyll glanced over Colin's shoulder and raised his eyebrow.

Shoving the missive into the folds of his plaid, Lord Glenorchy turned to the messenger. "Please, go to the kitchens and eat your fill. I shall pen my reply on the morrow."

The man bowed and took his leave. Argyll refilled both their goblets. "Are you not going to read it?"

"After the celebration." Colin's shoulder ticked up. "Besides, I ken what it contains."

Argyll held up his goblet. "I was wondering when His Holiness would become involved. Word in Edinburgh is the Turks are gaining the upper hand in the East."

Margaret returned to the high table flushed and breathing deeply. "I say, the minstrels are splendid. I do hope they'll be frequent visitors."

Colin forced a smile. "They're well practiced indeed."

"Whatever is wrong?"

God's teeth, was every woman a mind reader? Colin cleared his throat and stood. Bowing, he offered his hand.

"I cannot bear to watch you dance with any other than me."

That must have satisfied her curiosity, because she giggled and grasped his hand. "I care not to dance with any other than you...if you can manage to keep up with me."

"Are you questioning *my* stamina?" Oh how her wit could blot out all trepidation. Colin blocked the missive from his thoughts and led Margaret to the floor.

***

Colin appeared distracted as they climbed the tower stairs to their apartments. Perhaps he was uncomfortable with so many people bedding down in the hall, or mayhap the late hour and ample drink had affected him. Margaret was tired, too. Her slippers pinched her swollen feet. She'd danced and danced all night, just as she'd dreamed she would.

"I've never in my life enjoyed myself as much as I did this night."

Colin threaded his fingers through hers. "I'm glad of it." He led her into his chamber and closed the door. "I received a missive I must read."

She stopped short. "Oh? Who is it from?"

He pulled the folded vellum from inside his doublet. "It bears the seal of His Holiness."

A lead ball sank to the pit of Margaret's stomach. "Pope Callixtus?"

"Aye, the man himself." There was no humor in Colin's chuckle. He gestured for her to sit by the hearth then took the seat opposite.

Margaret folded her hands in her lap, her nerves jumping across her skin. Colin slid his finger under the seal and read. Watching him, it seemed to take forever. "What does it say?"

Colin stroked his fingers down his chin. "Things have become dire. The Ottoman sultan, Mehmed, demanded tribute from the Order of St. John. When Jacques de Milly refused to pay, the infidel retaliated with raids." Colin looked up, his expression so grave, he could have aged five years within the snap of her fingers. "The islands of Symi, Nisyros and Kos have been sacked. The Pope is summoning all Knights Hospitaller and their ships."

"A sea battle?"

"Aye. An all-out war." He combed his fingers through his hair. "It never ends."

"But we're heading into winter. Surely the troops will stand down through the season."

Colin smirked. "Not in the Mediterranean Sea. Winter is but a blustery spring day on the Isle of Rhodes."

"Isn't it dangerous to sail across the Atlantic with Grandfather Frost so near?"

"Not as dangerous now as it will become. I must make haste. The longer I wait, the more perilous the crossing will be."

Margaret stood and paced, pressing her hands against her midriff. The room spun. She knew this day would come, but had put it out of her mind. *Dear God in heaven, why now? Sailing into winter? That is madness. How could the Pope summon a call to arms before Yule? How many other knights would put their lives on the line crossing the wide ocean to take up the cross for Christendom?*

"How soon?" she asked, clinging to the possibility for delay.

"As quickly as supplies can be gathered and loaded on my galley."

Please God no. "Are you taking the fleet?" she asked weakly.

"Only one, given the weather and our need to continue trade in Scotland."

The room spun faster. This couldn't be happening. Not when things between them had become so blessedly perfect. Margaret's stomach convulsed with a wave of nausea. She'd only had a touch of queasiness in the mornings for the past sennight, but the bouts had passed as soon as she broke her fast. She swallowed hard. Her stomach heaved. She clapped her hand over her mouth and raced to the privy closet.

Bending over, she couldn't contain the horrible noises escaping her throat. Over and over she retched. Her body purged everything she'd consumed that night until yellow bile burned with one last heave.

Colin placed his hand on her back and rubbed. "There, there, *mo leannan*, 'tis not as bad as all that. I know the news is grave, but all will be well. You mustn't fret. I've lived through two crusades. I swear on my name I'll live through another."

Margaret wiped her mouth with a cloth, cringing at the bitter taste in her mouth. "I need watered wine and mint."

"Of course. Come." He grasped her elbow. "Sit and I'll bring it to you."

Trembling, Margaret allowed him to lead her to the chair. She could keep the news to herself no longer. After taking a long draw of the watered wine and a few chews on the mint leaves, she set the cup down with a shaky hand. "You'd best sit as well, for I have something I must say."

Colin brushed his fingers along her cheek. "You should—"

"Sit. Please." She again pressed her palms to her abdomen and rubbed. "'Tis early yet, and I didn't want to say anything until I was absolutely certain, but I believe my sickness confirms it."

Colin stared with knitted brows. Heaven's stars, the man had been through this before. Must she utter it? The concern in his eyes deepened.

She covered her face with her hands. This had to be the absolute worst time to make such an announcement. "I'm with child."

Colin didn't move.

Margaret spread her fingers to better see him.

His face grew dark, then his brows arched and eyes popped wide. He formed an O with his lips. "You mean…you're… When?"

"I missed my courses a fortnight past and they still haven't shown. I could be wrong, but I think not."

He tapped his fingers to mouth. "Late summer, then?"

She cringed. "Aye, most likely."

"A year younger than Duncan." Grinning, Colin bounded out of his chair. He lifted and cradled her with ease, spinning her in a circle. "'Tis the best gift you could have given me. It will make returning home all the more sweet."

"You are not angry?"

"Why would I be?" He rested her on the bed and clasped her hands. "The only folly is I will not be here for his birth." Biting his lip, Colin glanced away.

She understood his pause only too well. With every breath, a shred tore from her heartstrings. Soon he would be sailing away to fulfill his knightly duty. She mustn't show him the depth of her despair. Pushing up, Margaret sat straight and squared her shoulders. "I do not want you to worry, husband. My father says I am stronger than any woman he's ever met. I will bear you a healthy child and live to hold you in my arms again."

He sat beside her. "I must make arrangements."

Dear Lord, if only I could cling to him and plead for him not to go. "I shall manage. Besides, I have Effie."

"That you do." Colin reached for her hand and smoothed his palm across it thoughtfully. "I do not think I could survive if I lost you."

"Nor I you." She held his palm to her lips and kissed. Closing her eyes, she inhaled deeply. Could she capture his scent and keep it in a stoppered vial? "Let us think on it no more this night. I want to hold you in my arms and feel our bodies join. It is a memory I'll need to lock away and cherish until your return."

With a deep chuckle, he lifted her silver circlet and tugged the wimple from her head. "Then we shall make this a night to remember through all eternity." Casting the headpiece aside, he led her to the hearth and flung cushions to the floor. "First I want to watch the flames dance across your skin."

He grasped her shoulders. "Stand perfectly still. I can touch you, but you cannot touch me."

Heat tightened her loins. "Is it a game you wish to play?"

"Aye. I want to strip you bare."

Moving behind her, he first unbraided her hair and ran his fingers through it all the way down past her bottom. His hand slid up her hips and unlaced the back of her gown. She took in a deep breath as the wooden slats inside her bodice eased their constricting hold. He slid it from her shoulders and ran his hands down over her breasts. Closing her eyes, Margaret moaned and circled her head back until it rested on his chest.

"You mustn't touch me, wife."

She liked it when he made up new games. With a tug, he unlaced her shift and pulled it over her head. In just a few flicks of his fingers, she was completely naked, excepting her hose and slippers. Colin stepped around and gazed at her front. Margaret reached out her arms, but he held up a finger. "Only I may touch."

She smiled. "When will it be my turn?"

"After you have been completely and utterly ravished."

Margaret laughed. "And who's to determine that, me or you?"

He knelt. "I think I'll allow you that honor." *My, he is confident*. He removed her slippers. His fingers tickled as he untied her ribbons and languidly slid her hose down each leg. By the time he pulled the last one from her toes, her inner thighs were already quavering.

Colin reached for her hand. "Recline on the pillows."

She did as told, watching his manhood respond beneath his kilt. She rested comfortably on the rug with a pile of cushions behind. It was nearly impossible to resist her urge to tear his clothes from his body and pull him atop her. Completely naked, she was at his mercy. Oh yes, she undoubtedly would do to him every succulent thing he tried with her.

Kneeling at her side, he kissed each eye and kept his hands to his sides. His lips caressed her cheeks and found her mouth. He allowed Margaret to return his kiss, and she plunged her tongue into him, sucking with ignited fervor.

Colin continued to tickle her with feathery kisses down her neck and each arm, licking each finger as his dark, sultry eyes watched her. When he at last reached her breasts, they ached for his touch. His swirling mouth lingered, teasing her nipples, suckling them until she cried out.

He nipped down to her navel and entered it with his tongue, giving her an erotic preview of his cock entering her core. Margaret prayed he would part her legs and lick her there, but he slid his mouth down and up each leg.

When he kissed her arches, she thought to grasp herself and come to her own touch, but she resisted committing such a sin.

"Colin. Pleeeease."

Without a word, his eyes grew even darker with his wicked smile, and he pushed her legs open with his shoulders. He slid down onto his belly, keeping her legs apart. He'd never held them this wide, but she nearly convulsed with the ecstasy of being completely prone to him. He stared at her womanhood and inhaled. "God, you are divine."

He licked her fully. Margaret whimpered as her sensitive flesh quivered.

"Again," she demanded, so close to release, he could not possibly stop. Colin slid his tongue in and out of her and then sealed his mouth over her flesh and suckled. Blinded by the intensity of the flame coiled at her apex, she cried out, thrusting her hips, circling them around his merciless kisses.

Stars crossed her vision as her body exploded into a sea of shuddering joy. When she finally recovered her senses, she pulled him into her arms. "You were right. Every time is better than the last."

He rested his head on the pillow beside her. "I love you."

She stared into his eyes, filled with intense rapture—something far greater than passion or desire. He did love her, and Margaret returned his love with every fiber of her being. "And I you."

***

Colin had nearly fallen to sleep in Margaret's arms when she moved. "Now you." Still naked, she stood and tugged his arm. "You must stand."

Immediately awake, he chuckled. This would be fun. His wife was never one to buck a challenge. God bless her.

She was so much smaller than he. Margaret nearly had to stretch her arms and rise to her toes to remove the plaid over his head. Taking her time, she slid his dirk from his belt, his eating knife from his sleeve, and unlashed his daggers from his calves. Her small fingers tickled him as she unfastened his belt and sent his kilt falling to the floor.

His linen shirt tented above the hem. Unlacing the bow under his chin, she tried to pull it over his head, but couldn't reach. Willingly, he kneeled and she tugged it slowly, drawing out his torture.

"Up," Margaret commanded.

Colin raised a brow her way but obeyed, his cock jutting from his loins like a tree limb. Her breasts swayed while she walked around him, her eyes appraising him as she would a fine stallion. He wanted to throw her down and make love to her right there, but it was Margaret's turn to take the reins.

As they were now both naked, his boots and knee-length hose tied with black flashes were out of place, but that did nothing to detract from his yearning. She picked up his hand and licked his finger, then stretched out at arm's length and curtseyed. "May I have this dance?"

He chuckled and reached for her, but she stepped back.

"A volta, but you cannot touch me…only I you."

That would be difficult during the lifts, but Colin played along.

Her swaying breasts enticed him as she danced, swinging her hips, naked—her bottom was more suggestive than he'd ever dreamed. No woman had ever danced for him without a stitch of clothing. He could scarcely recall the steps.

For the lift, she circled her leg around his hips and ground her mons into his manhood. Colin swallowed. All he had to do was back her into the wall and slip inside. Twirling away, she bent over the chair, her lovely bottom teasing him. He groaned and moved swiftly, his cock aching to enter her from behind. But Margaret spun from her pose and curtseyed deeply. Rising, she panned her eyes from his boots, stopping at his swollen member, then collided with his gaze, the lust darkening her deep pools of green, sending him into madness.

She inclined her head to the rug. "'Tis your turn to recline."

If she touched his cock right now, he'd spill across the carpet. His ballocks burned with fire as he sat against the cushions. She stood over him, hands on her voluptuous hips, as if deciding where to start. She gave him reprieve by removing his boots and hose—not really *reprieve*. She kept her exquisite body just out of hand's reach. Fingers twitching, he forced himself not to lean forward and trace his hand along the curve of her hips. Obey the rules of the game he must, lest he lose. He regained a semblance of control until she kneeled and straddled his legs.

For everything holy, her hands did not slide to his flesh, but cupped her breasts and pushed them together. Colin's tongue flicked out and tapped his top lip. If only he could bury his face in her plush velvet valley.

"Do you like to see me touch myself?" she whispered.

"Aye," he growled hoarsely.

Her gaze dipped to his loins. "I like to watch you stroke it."

He moved his hand, his fingers aching to give him release.

"No. Not this time." She smiled like a devil cat.

Margaret kept her hips in the air as she leaned down and kissed his thighs. Blessed be the saints, would she be so bold as to take him into her mouth? How charmed was he to have a wife so brazen? Her tongue flicked kisses around his manhood, but didn't touch it.

"Open." She slid down and forced her shoulders between his legs. One gnash of her teeth and his breeding days would be over. But straddling her made a bead of seed leak from his cock. She tickled his balls with her tongue and then suckled them. Never in his life had any woman turned his cods into tight, raging fireballs. His cock tapped his abdomen, rigid as the blade of his sword.

Margaret fluttered kisses up along the shaft without grasping it.

God save me. "Pleeeease," he groaned.

She gripped the base of his manhood with her small fingers and slid her mouth over it. Moaning, Colin's eyes rolled to the back of his head. He clenched his bum cheeks, and gnashed his teeth. "My God, I can take this no longer."

In one move, he pulled her over him and impaled her onto his aching member, her sheath so tight and slick, he wouldn't last but a few strokes. He grasped her hips and slid her up and down. She arched her back, finding that spot she craved to have rubbed.

Colin's heart raced and his lips trembled as he worked her hips faster. Margaret gasped, and he exploded, his seed shooting into her as she cried out and shuddered with her own release.

When his breathing finally slowed, he wrapped his arms around her and kissed her forehead. "How in God's name will I survive without you?"

Chapter Twenty-Three

Dunstaffnage Castle, 5ᵗʰ December, 1455

Colin opened the door to Margaret's chamber. She sat
on a stool while the chambermaid brushed his lady's long
tresses. Like spun silk, her hair glistened with amber
highlights reflecting off the fire. He stepped inside and
cleared his throat.

Margaret looked up and her face brightened with the
smile he'd grown to love. "My lord. Is all well?"

"Aye." He shifted his gaze to the maid. "Please leave
us."

He watched the woman exit and then bolted the door
behind her. "I need to speak to you without prying ears."
He returned to Margaret and clasped her hands between
his. "Before I take my leave, I must give you a token in
utmost secrecy."

He reached in his leather purse and pulled out two
silver rings, one large, one small, both encircled with the
same Celtic design that had no beginning and no end. He
took her right hand and slid the smaller ring over her
index finger. "I had two identical bands forged. And then
I had the mold destroyed so never again will a ring be cast
thus." He slid the larger one onto his finger. "We will
wear these as a silent reminder of our bond."

Margaret held her hand up and examined the polished silver band in the candlelight. She then grasped his hand and compared hers to his. He admired the workmanship, too. The rings indeed were identical, with a woven pattern encircling both. A gasp caught in the back of her throat. "Oh my, Colin, they're beautiful—so intricate." An errant tear streaked down her cheek.

Colin dabbed her eyes with his sleeve. "If you should receive my ring from afar, you will know I have fallen. Tell no one of our pact—henceforth, the rings shall be referred to as our token signs."

"Tokens," she repeated. "How clever of you, how utterly thoughtful."

He grasped her palms in his. "I cannot express enough the importance of keeping this pact secret. Tell no one what our tokens are."

"'Tis like a cipher."

"Of sorts," he agreed.

Margaret glanced aside. "And if I should perish, I will have this ring sent to you in the Holy Land."

Colin pulled her into his embrace. "You will not fall, nor shall I. These tokens are to be an ever-present reminder of the depth of our love."

Sadness reflected in her lovely eyes. "I vow I shall never remove mine."

"Nor shall I."

Margaret squeezed his arms and then stepped back. "I also have a gift for you."

She went to the board and opened the velvet-lined box she kept there. "My mother gave me this on our wedding day. It was passed down through the male heirs of her family for countless generations, but since there was no male heir in her time, her father gave it to her upon marriage to my da." Margaret pulled out the large crystal stone she'd worn at their wedding and cradled it in her hands. "Legend has it the man who wears this charmstone in battle will live to vanquish his enemies, and anyone who drinks the water into which it has been dipped will have good health and a safe journey home."

Colin didn't know what to say. The gem was a priceless heirloom—part of her dowry. "Are you sure?"

"What good are its charms to me whilst you're risking your life in battle?" She held up the necklace. "Kneel."

Colin did as she commanded. "You honor me."

Margaret fastened the chain and stood back to admire the stone. "The bold setting suits you far more than it does me."

She opened her arms. Colin needed no more encouragement. He embraced her, his heart near bursting. Why, when love reached its pinnacle, did something always happen to shatter his happiness? Why had he been so pigheaded when they'd first wed? If he'd given in to his heart, they would have shared many more nights in each other's arms.

He nuzzled into her hair. "I wish I could be here for you when your time comes."

"God willing, I shall be fine." Margaret's voice had a slight tremor.

He dipped his chin and kissed her, showing the passion and pain that filled his soul. If only he could devour her and take her spirit with him, he might find solace in his destiny. He held her tightly and showered her with kisses. "I swear to you I will not take a blade to my beard until I return to you."

"Make haste, husband, for I like you best with your face smooth. It will be such a shame to cover your beauty with unkempt whiskers."

Colin's heart twisted into a hundred knots. Damn it all, he knew this was coming. Why did Margaret have to look at him with soulful eyes and pretend this was all right?

He hugged her tightly. "Do not worry about Kilchurn. Focus on the babe growing inside you, for he will be a testament to our love."

"If only you could stay long enough for the birth."

"I wish it could be so."

She cast her gaze downward. "If you must go, I shall deliver you a healthy bairn and then see to it your castle presides over Glen Orchy for your return."

He cupped her lovely face in his hands, torn between two loyalties. "If it's a boy, name him John for my order, and if it's a girl, name her Margaret after the love of my life."

**

Margaret thought her heart would burst as she walked down to the pier beside Colin. She held her chin high and clenched her teeth to fight back her tears. Lord Glenorchy wanted her to show a strong front and be supportive of his men. But every fiber of her being wanted to scream and wail, plead with him not to go.

She clutched his hand with all her strength, walking alongside him as if she were heading to her own execution. Behind them, Mevan stood guard from a respectable distance to ensure Margaret made it back to the castle safely after Colin's galley sailed.

Once they arrived on the pier, he wrenched his fingers free and grasped her shoulders. "I promise I will write to you upon every available chance."

Not trusting herself to speak, she nodded.

He pulled her into his embrace and pressed his lips to her ear. "I love you."

"Don't go," she whispered.

He held her at arm's length. "I will make haste to return to your arms."

"I will hold you to that, my lord."

He dipped his chin and gave her a much-too-fleeting kiss on the lips. "Until then, you will be at the forefront of my every thought." With that, he turned his broad shoulders and proceeded up the gangway and onto the ship.

Margaret touched her fingers to her trembling lips. When would he kiss her again? With a stuttered breath, a tear slipped from her eye and streamed down her cheek.

"Cast off," Colin boomed.

Maxwell offered her a quick salute before he pulled the ropes over the hull. At the bow, the black Portuguese cannon sat upon the deck like an invitation to death. The cast iron gun was big and ugly. It embodied the frightful dread roiling on her insides.

Gradually, the galley ebbed away. Clutching her arms to her body, Margaret stood alone and watched Colin sail out the Firth of Lorn. Dark clouds loomed above and a cold breeze picked up her veil. It cut through her cloak like knives, but she remained. On the pier she stood until the galley became a speck on the horizon, and then disappeared, swallowed by dark blue waters.

Blinking, she realized tears had been streaming down her face. Her throat raw, Margaret hung her head and made her way back to the castle. *How in God's name will I cope without him?*

Chapter Twenty-Four

Dunstaffnage, 25th December, 1455

Colin had been gone twenty days—nearly three sennights of emptiness. She'd locked his chamber and slept alone in her drafty room, bundled beneath the comforter, shivering in the winter cold. Margaret had forced herself to green the castle in preparation for Yule, but her longing for Colin hung around her neck with the weight of an anchor.

After spending the morning vomiting her porridge, she'd dropped to her knees and prayed her misery would be short-lived. On Christmas day, Margaret would usually attend mass with her parents in Dunalasdair's chapel, but the snow on the ground was impassable. She couldn't even ride to chapel beyond the Dunstaffnage gates, let alone travel to Loch Rannoch with a four-month-old infant.

Afternoons were always easier on her insides, and she sat on the floor in the nursery beside Duncan. He could now hold his head up and roll over. Margaret strummed her lute and the bairn smiled. "You're fond of music, are you, little fella?"

Margaret strummed again—a minor chord. Closing her eyes, she sang a woeful ballad. Duncan didn't seem to mind. He kicked his feet and grabbed them with his little fingers, cooing all the while.

A tear streamed down her face. This Yule, the babe was the only family she could share the holiday with. Given the snow, she couldn't expect her parents to show up at the castle gates—or even Argyll. He was at court celebrating with the king and queen. Christmas at court must be an extravagant affair, with mysteries and plays each of the twelve days.

This was so different from every other Yule she'd experienced with her parents, brothers and cousins. One could never feel lonely at Loch Rannoch.

Alas, Colin was gone. Only God knew when he'd return to her.

Margaret shuddered and pulled the plaid tighter around her shoulders. No matter how much wood she piled on the fire, the cold north wind blew in from every window and crevice in this drafty old castle. With winter came the dregs of an icy and dead season.

Effie stepped inside, her arms filled with wood. She dropped the pile beside the hearth. "Thank you for allowing me to spend the morning with my son, m'lady."

Margaret set her lute aside. "Of course. Is he well?"

"Aye. Looking forward to the feast this eve."

Margaret glanced to the fire. "Mevan and his men assured me we'd have pheasant to spare."

"'Tis grand you are so generous, m'lady."

"'Tis my duty as matron of the keep." She forced herself to smile. "I want every soul in my care to be well fed and in good cheer."

Effie sat on a stool beside Duncan and pulled him onto her lap. "'Tis time you indulged in some cheer of your own."

"Colin said no one could fool you." Margaret sniffed. "But I'm afraid a bout of melancholy has consumed my heart. Yule without Colin or family…"

"What say you? Your family is the entire clan." Effie gave her a sideways look. "And ye'd best raise that chin of yours if you want your bairn to be healthy."

Margaret reached for a stick of wood and tossed it on the fire. "I cannot pretend all is well. My heart cannot bear to have Colin away, fighting in the Crusades, not knowing whether…"

Effie arched a brow. "Would Colin want you to pine for him as you do?"

"Nay," Margaret said, staring into the rising flames.

"Then I suggest you go to your chamber, don a festive gown, go down to the great hall and dance."

Margaret glared at the old woman. Effie smiled like a child caught pinching a piece of apple tart. Queen's knees, she could not chastise the nursemaid—especially when she was right.

Effie smoothed her hand over Margaret's shoulder. "Ye've arranged for minstrels, have you not?"

"Aye."

"Then you should dance."

Margaret tapped her hand to her chest. "Without Colin?"

"Yes, without Lord Glenorchy. The entire clan now looks to you for leadership—you said yourself you want them in good cheer." The nursemaid shook her finger. "You alone set the tone for their peace of mind. Do you think for a minute the entire castle hasn't been in mourning with you these past sennights?"

Margaret clapped her hands to her cheeks. "It has been that obvious?"

"Aye. It has." Effie regarded Duncan in her arms. "Even this wee bairn senses your sadness, as does the one you're carrying."

Margaret rubbed her palm over her stomach. If anything, she'd lost a quarter-stone with the sickness, and she knew that wasn't good. "Do you honestly believe the bairn inside me feels unhappiness as I do?"

"I have no doubt. And you'd best listen to the likes of me. I've been nursemaid to over a dozen babes. I ken what I say."

Margaret had no idea how much her mood had been affecting others. Neither Duncan nor her unborn child could suffer because of her selfishness. "Well then, I shall begin today. 'Tis the birthday of our Lord—what better time to start anew?"

"Aye, m'lady. I can think of no better time than now." Effie flicked her fingers through the air. "Now off with ye."

With a renewed sense of purpose, Margaret dressed in a green velvet gown, trimmed with ermine. Aside from the dress she'd worn at her wedding, it was the finest gown she owned. Everyone stood when she arrived in the great hall.

She clapped and called for silence, smiling broadly. "I thank you for sharing my table for this, our Yule feast. Though the wind whistles outside, we will be warm within. Eat and make merry, dance and laugh, for I ever so want to share joy with each one of you. Happy Yule."

"Happy Yule!" every voice boomed in unison.

The resounding and cheerful noise made the bairn inside her flutter with excitement. It may be the dead of winter, but to Margaret's heart, spring had come early. There was much to do, and Margaret would prove to the world she could manage in Colin's stead. She would ensure the Campbell Clan thrived and prospered.

Her husband would return home to flourishing and wealthy lands. She vowed it.

Chapter Twenty-Five

The Vatican, January, 1456

A cardinal ushered Colin into the starkly decorated papal apartment's anteroom. Pope Callixtus III sat in a high-backed mahogany chair upholstered in red velvet. Dressed in white robes, the old man's skin withered beneath his coif.

Hearing his name announced, Colin strode up to His Holiness and knelt, swallowing his grimace at the pain of kneeling in his battle armor. Though he had jointed knee-guards, the metal cut against bone. The Pope held out his hand. Colin took it and kissed the ruby ring he had once kissed when it adorned the hand of the late Pope Nicholas. "It grieves me to attend you under such dire circumstances, Your Holiness."

"Rise, sir knight." Callixtus pulled his gnarled hand away. "How was your journey?"

"Difficult. Three men perished. Winter seas always take their toll. My small galley was forced to cross at the channel and hug the shore all the way from Northern France."

"It is a tragedy to lose those who fight for right. But their deaths will not be in vain."

"I pray not." Colin bowed. "I have a sound ship armed with the latest six-foot Portuguese cannon. I am yours to command."

The Pope clapped, and a Cardinal stepped forward. "You will take Peter, the Archbishop of Tarragona, to Rhodes. With him you will command a fleet of sixteen ships and drive the Turks from our stronghold islands."

Colin nodded to the cardinal. There was always a holy man assigned to every crusade—monks in the order also fought, though Colin could not take an oath of celibacy because he was married.

Peter bowed politely. "How many man your galley?"

"Twenty well-trained fighting Highlanders."

"We sail at dawn."

"Very well. That should give me time to gather provisions." Colin deeply bowed to the Pope. "With your blessing, we shall prevail."

After His Holiness made the sign of the cross, Colin took his leave and headed to the pier. From experience, he anticipated many months of fighting ahead. The sooner he sailed into hell with his men, the sooner he could return to his beloved Scotland and Margaret.

He'd written several letters during the journey to Rome, all of which he dispatched before climbing the hill to meet the Pope. Margaret would receive all at once. He'd numbered them so she would open each in the order written. If only he could watch her face when she did.

***

During winter, Margaret met with tailors and weavers, selecting patterns for tapestries and bedding for the new castle. She'd ordered a fabulous landscape tapestry of Loch Awe for Colin, with Ben Chruachan in the background. His canopy and comforter would be a rich emerald-green silk. She'd spent more coin on his chamber than any other. But her husband's rooms should be the grandest of them all.

March arrived at Dunstaffnage with blustery wind and driving rain. That didn't slow Margaret. She ushered grooms bearing trunks into the nursery. "Effie, we're moving to the cottage at Kilchurn as soon as weather permits. I want everything packed and ready to be loaded onto the wagons."

The old woman planted fists on her hips. "You're serious? 'Tis miserable out there. We should wait until spring has taken root."

"In no way will I sit in this drafty castle for another two months."

Gurgling, Duncan rolled over and rocked on his hands and knees. He'd be crawling soon. Margaret swooped the bairn into her arms. "I've sent for Tom Elliot. Last November, he promised me work would begin in March."

"Och, the men can start without ye getting in their way."

"Perish the thought. What they need is leadership." Margaret set Duncan on the blanket. "Now set to packing, and I shall do the same."

"But what of your condition?" Effie wrung her hands. "The cottage will be cramped with the three of us."

Margaret rolled her eyes to the ceiling. "I've already planned to build on a nursery. That will be Tom's first task." She smoothed her hand over the small bump in her belly. "This bairn won't be cosseted. Besides, Alana is the best midwife in all of Argyll. 'Tis better for the bairn to be born in Glen Orchy than here."

Effie frowned at the trunks. Margaret patted the old nursemaid's shoulder. "It will be fine. You'll see. The three of us will be cozy in the cottage."

"Soon there'll be four."

Margaret grinned. "Aye, so start your packing."

Margaret had the household necessities stowed in trunks within two days. By a stroke of luck, the weather cleared. With Mevan in the lead, she set out with a handful of servants and a dozen Campbell guards.

When she arrived at the building site, Tom Elliot was there to greet her. He already had the laborers working with shovels and barrowing away the mud and thresh. Margaret grasped his hand warmly. "How fared your winter, Master Elliot?"

"Well. Glad to be back on the job. My coffers are wearing a bit thin."

"We shall see what can be done about that. I want this keep thriving before Lord Glenorchy returns." She glanced toward the cottage. "But first you must build on a nursery to the cottage."

His beetle brows pinched together. "Is that necessary? It will slow our progress."

"I've brought healthy guardsmen from Dunstaffnage to help. It should take no additional time. Put them to work forthwith. I want it done in a fortnight."

"A fortnight, m'lady?"

"Aye." She spread her arms wide. "Complete with hearth."

"But—"

"You'd best make haste, else your purse will remain empty." Margaret inhaled the fresh air as she strode away. It enlivened her to be back at Kilchurn. The dead of winter gone, she could face the coming months with renewed purpose.

***

It was early August when Margaret waddled through the portcullis of her tower house with Tom Elliot. She was proud of her belly, now so large, no amount of fabric could hide it. Her only sorrow was that Colin would not be there to share in the birth. He'd promised to send a missive once he reached Rome, yet it had been almost eight months since he set sail and she'd received not a word.

"The first floor is complete, and the great hall above will be finished before winter sets in."

"You've done a fine job." She pulled a torch off the wall and walked to the dungeon. Droplets of water splashed on the stone floor. "This room is aptly dank."

"Aye, but necessary for keeping the peace." He reached for the torch and led her through the guardhouse into a sturdy passageway. "The cellars are dry and will keep the food cool. I've fashioned a grand hearth for the kitchen."

Margaret stood inside the immense fireplace, which had been started last autumn. "Many a feast will be prepared here." To her right, the bread oven recessed into the now completed thick stone walls. "I can practically smell the loaves baking already."

"And it's only a few paces from the great hall for easy access."

The baby kicked with Margaret's excitement. A bit lightheaded, she leaned against the wall. "This child is ever so anxious to come out and see the progress on the new keep."

Tom grasped her arm. "Are you all right, m'lady?"

"Aye, just a passing pang."

"Your time will be upon us soon. A building site is no place for a woman in your condition."

"So repeats Mistress Effie. Do not fear. I shall be confined soon enough." Margaret smoothed her hands over her wimple. "I detest the thought of it."

"Can I escort you back to the cottage, m'lady?"

"No, you have much more important work to do, Tom. I'm pleased with your progress. Give the men an extra ration of bread and ale for their efforts, and after the babe is born, we shall kill a steer and have a grand feast."

"I'll look forward to that, m'lady."

Alone, Margaret walked the short path through the trees to the cottage. Though Colin had insisted she remain at Dunstaffnage for her confinement, she would hear none of it. The nursery had been completed on schedule, Effie and Duncan had settled into the cottage, and Alana was on hand as her midwife. Margaret trusted the MacGregor woman far more than Master Hume, the old physician. Besides, birthing a bairn was women's work.

A pain clamped around her womb so hard she fell to her knees. Her head spun. She gritted her teeth to bear it. A rush of hot liquid flushed down her legs. *'Tis time.* Panting, Margaret waited until the pain subsided. She could see the cottage through the trees ahead. Surely she'd make it before the next pain came.

She rushed as quickly as she could, trying not to jostle the baby. Pregnancy was alien to her. Being the youngest, she'd never seen a woman actually give birth, though Alana and Effie did their best to explain what to expect. At first the pains would come far apart and grow closer and closer until the baby was ready to slide out.

Breathing heavily, she pushed through the door. "Effie! Fetch Alana. I've lost my water and the pains have begun."

Effie blanched. "Your water has shown already?"

Nodding, Margaret supported herself on the chair with one hand and held her swollen abdomen with the other.

"Haste ye to the bed." Effie signaled to the serving maid to run for Alana and tugged on Margaret's elbow. "Come, m'lady."

Another pain hit her like someone had wrapped a noose around her belly and tied it to a team of oxen, drawing the rope tighter with every breath. Margaret clamped her hands around her stomach and panted. "Merciful heavens, it hurts."

Effie rubbed the small of her back. "Breathe through it. Do not rush. We'll move to the bed soon enough."

"If I can manage to stay on my feet." As the gripping pain began to ease, Margaret took a step. "I think I can make it."

Effie supported Margaret's elbow and aided her into the chamber. "Hold on to the bedpost while I layer the old linens atop the mattress."

The old matron worked quickly and helped Margaret change into a clean shift. "Rest against the pillows. Try not to push. 'Tis too early in your labor."

Margaret nestled her shoulders into the pillows. "Thank you." She swiped a hand across her brow, moist with sweat.

"I'm here, m'lady." Alana strode into the room attended by three other women. "Where is Duncan?"

Effie pointed. "He's napping."

"Mistress Lorna will care for the bairn." She eyed Margaret. "You lost your water?"

"Aye."

"How far apart are your contractions?"

Margaret convulsed with another.

Effie smoothed a hand over her hair. "Far enough apart to walk to the bed and allow me to spread the linens."

Margaret panted through the blinding pain. She clenched her teeth and started to bear down.

"Boil a cauldron of water," Alana ordered. "Where are the swaddling cloths? Is the ewer full? Come on, ladies, we have a bairn on the way."

She grasped Margaret's hand and rubbed it gently. "'Tis not time to push yet. Try to ease yourself."

Margaret could have strangled her. "Are you completely mad?" She gasped for air, a bead of sweat rolling into her eye. "My entire being is screaming for me to push."

Alana's gaze softened. "I know. But I've birthed five of me own and assisted at least twenty other women. I ken what I'm saying. Listen to me and you might survive to hold your bairn in your arms."

An icy shudder coursed over Margaret's skin. Not once had she allowed herself to consider she might die giving birth to her first babe, but now the reality of her potential death struck her with a crashing wave of trembling and nausea.

The afternoon turned into dusk. Margaret writhed in a pool of her own sweat, struggling to hang on, completely at her wits end.

Alana ordered the candles lit. Effie, at eight and seventy, excused herself and retired. Night filled the chamber, dimly lit with candles. The pains were coming frequently. Margaret's hair stuck to her face. Alana held a cool cloth to her forehead, but that didn't help.

With each contraction, she pushed with every shred of remaining strength. Her eyes strained in their sockets as she clenched her teeth and bore down. Her arms shook of their own volition.

Alana held up the linens. "I can see his head. It won't be long now."

"It better not be." The entire bed shook with Margaret's effort. She hissed through her teeth. "Why isn't Colin here? He did this to me then left me alone— *curses* to the Pope as well."

"Aye, m'lady." Alana's voice was ridiculously soothing.

Margaret didn't want to be soothed. She pushed the midwife's hand away from her forehead. "Take that cloth from me and make this insufferable pain stop."

Alana stepped back. "Breathe."

How could that woman be so placid at a time like this? "I can't take it anymore!" Margaret screamed. Her insides felt like they were being ripped out.

"He's coming, m'lady. Push…push…*push*!"

Margaret bore down with everything she had, exhaustion making her lose control. Her fingers shook as she splayed them beside her on the bed. Pushing, her body stretching, she thought it would never end. Then suddenly, the pain subsided, the stretching eased. Margaret's eyes blinked open, blurred through her sweat.

A tiny voice cried. It sounded more holy than church bells.

Alana walked to her, holding a beautiful bundle. "'Tis a boy."

Margaret laughed out loud, her heart soaring to her throat. He was the most beautiful tomato-red bairn she'd ever gazed upon. "John." Margaret reached out her arms. "Colin asked me to name him John." The babe yawned adorably. He had a smattering of brown fuzz pasted atop his damp head. He smelled as fresh as apple blossoms.

"'Tis a fine name." Alana untied the bow on Margaret's shift. "You must make the bond. It burns a wee bit when the babe starts to suckle, but the pain doesn't last."

Margaret held the tiny bundle to her breast. John turned his head as if he could smell her milk. Latching on to her nipple, he suckled. It did sting a little at first, but watching the angelic face of her son feeding from her body made her heart swell. "Dear boy, you will remind me of your father until the day I take my last breath."

***

The third day after John's birth, Margaret felt well enough to take a brief stroll through the cottage gardens. A messenger approached with a parcel. Margaret could scarcely breathe. Had Colin's letters finally arrived?

The man hopped down from his mount and bowed. "M'lady. I've a gift from my esteemed chieftain, Ewen MacCorkodale of Loch Tromlee."

Margaret's spirits sank to her toes. How desperately she wanted news of her husband. She forced a polite smile. "It was kind of your laird to think of us."

She read the missive congratulating her on the birth of her son, though it mentioned nothing about Colin, not even well wishes for his safe return. Inside the parcel was a lovely tatted woolen receiving blanket. Margaret smiled at the messenger. "Please offer my deepest thanks to your laird. His gift was very thoughtful indeed."

Margaret carried the blanket into the cottage and held it to her nose. It smelled fresh, like newly fallen rain. Though she was disappointed she'd not received news from Colin, the neighboring laird had been quite considerate. Most likely, Ewen MacCorkodale was nothing like his cousin, Walter. Mayhap it was time to put Walter's dishonesty behind them. They should become allies. If Margaret developed good relations with the MacCorkodales, together with the MacGregors, the Campbells of Glen Orchy would be an unstoppable and formidable Scottish force.

Chapter Twenty-Six

The Mediterranean Sea, August, 1457

Colin dispatched another packet of letters to Margaret before sailing from Rhodes. Last August, they'd been successful in driving the Turks out of the isles of Imbros and Limni, but now reports flooded in with news of Mehmed's decimation of the Holy Land. The sultan's fleet of Ottoman ships was again on the advance.

Colin's galley wasn't the smallest of the Hospitallers' ships, but it was far from the largest. The order had acquired a newly designed Portuguese carrack with nine gun ports on each side. Its impressive design and immense size changed sea battle strategy for good.

It was with pride Colin stood at the helm of his Scottish *Birlinn*, flying the pennant of the Order of St. John. His cannon had fired the blast that sank two Ottoman ships at Imbros, a significant win for his men, earning them respect among the French faction to which the Scots had been annexed.

Only a fool wore armor when fighting at sea. It bore too great a risk for death by drowning. Colin and his men wore reinforced quilted doublets under their red Hospitaller tunics, adorned with white crosses and edged with gold fringe.

He squinted into the mid-morning sun. "Where are the bastards?"

Now one and twenty, Maxwell attained his majority a month ago. The breadth of the young man's chest had filled out considerably. "Spies reported plans to sail at dawn. It should be any moment now, m'lord." He stood on a rowing bench, shaded his eyes and pointed. "There."

Colin strained in the direction of Maxwell's finger. He didn't see anything at first, but gradually enemy ships dotted the horizon like chess pieces. His stomach churned, as it always did in anticipation of a battle. He watched the fleet near, its numbers of oared longboats continuing to grow. "Holy bloody hell. We must be outnumbered five to one."

The galley slowed in the water as rowing men stood to gape at the approaching fleet.

Colin snapped around. "Man your oars. Full speed ahead. Ramming tempo."

"Ramming, m'lord?" Maxwell had not yet mastered the art of hiding his emotions. A grimace of terror stretched his features.

No one must doubt him. Colin needed to bolster his men's confidence and focus on winning the battle. "Man the cannon. We'll blast the first ship in range out of the water." He clapped his hands in rapid succession. "Send the infidel to hell in the name of St. John!"

"Deus vult!" the men bellowed, the Hospitallers' war cry.

Closer and closer the enemy ships sailed. "Archers, at the ready," Colin commanded as he raised his arm to signal the cannon. If he timed it right, the big gun would blast a lead ball precisely when they passed the first longboat.

"Fire!"

With a touch of the torch, the cannon boomed and recoiled. The shot whistled through the air. With no time to watch, Colin addressed the archers. "Fire at will and hit your mark. I want not an arrow wasted."

The cannon ball slammed into the enemy ship's hull. A crash of splintering wood sailed across the open sea. "Pull the rudder hard starboard!"

Boom.

A cannon from the enemy ship blasted so loudly, Colin could hear only a high-pitched tone. William's mouth moved, but Colin couldn't make out a word. He waved his arms and pointed ahead. "Fire another round and sink that ship."

Sink it they did, and the next, but as far as the eye could see, an endless mass of Ottoman ships bore down on them. The air bit the back of his throat, thick with smoke and the pungent odor of sulfur. Colin's eyes watered with the sting. Surrounding cannons blasted an endless barrage of lead balls. In the mayhem, Colin's cannon shot depleted—his cache of arrows would be next.

"Ramming straight ahead," Colin commanded, and his men set a course for the next approaching ship.

Flames raged on the vessels around them. Colin could no longer spot the carrack or the other allied ships. They were heading into the bowels of hell, and he would fight to the death to keep the Turks from the Isle of Limni. *By God, I drove them away once. I'll do it again.*

When he regained a fraction of hearing, a familiar high-pitched whistle sailed overhead. Colin held his breath and waited for the splash. But the lead ball crashed into the center of his galley's hull. Something sharp sliced open his cheek. Oarsmen flew over the side. Another fell with a lance-sized splinter spearing his gut.

The galley immediately took on water. Colin swiped the blood from his face as the sea rose to his knees. He gave the only order that might save the lives of his remaining men. "Abandon ship!"

Ignoring the gash on his cheek, Colin worked frantically to help his men plunge into the sea. He didn't see the boom when it broke from the mast, but he heard it snap…right before it crashed into his skull.

***

The unbearable pressure encroaching inside Colin's head was so intense, his teeth throbbed. His eyes wouldn't open. He tried to swallow, but only stringy goo clung to his gums. His throat grated as if someone had plunged a rasp down it.

Trying to move, he inhaled. A weak cough produced sickly phlegm, but no fouler than the pungent surrounding odor. Stale piss stung his nose—filth like rats, too. He moved his fingers. Damp straw, musty. Something hard jutted into his back.

Am I in hell?

Colin forced himself to open his eyes. Dim light surrounded him. *It must be night.* But a ray of brilliant light shone in from an opening in the wall above. Groaning, he squeezed his eyes shut against the excruciating pressure. He turned his face away from the unforgiving light.

"Colin? Are you awake, m'lord?"

He recognized the voice, but couldn't place the name. Colin tried to open his eyes again. A young face was bent over him. *Maxwell?* He wasn't sure. "Water," he croaked.

"Aye, m'lord. I'll fetch it straight away."

Colin closed his lids, tapping his swollen tongue to the roof of his mouth.

A hand slipped to the back of his neck. "I'll raise you up a wee bit."

Colin hissed at the driving pain. A cup touched his lips. He swallowed greedily until he tasted. Coughing, he spewed the foul water across his chest.

Maxwell kept him up. "Come, m'lord. You need to drink some more."

"K…killing…me?"

"'Tis all we have. I drink it myself."

Colin gazed at Maxwell's face, and his vision cleared. He raised his chin for the squire to tip the cup again. This time he drank down the sulfur-smelling liquid. After Maxwell pulled the cup away, he tried his voice again. "Where are we?"

"In a Turkish pit."

Someone moved behind him. "Left to rot I'd wager." Colin didn't recognize the voice.

He tried to remember—they were in a sea battle. All seemed lost. "What happened?"

Maxwell sat on the musty hay beside him. "The boom snapped—knocked you unconscious. The ship went down so fast, there wasn't time to think. I slung my arm around you and grabbed the nearest floating piece of timber."

Colin tried to concentrate on the lad's words, but his head throbbed. "The crew?"

"Who knows? Some dead for certain. Willy's here. Don't know what happened to the others."

"Are we on an island?"

"No one knows. They pulled us out of the water and stuck us in the bilges. Before we went ashore, they blindfolded us and shoved us down those stairs." Maxwell pointed to a narrow case of steps leading to a black door.

"How long?"

"Two days."

No wonder Colin's tongue had turned to scored leather. "Why didn't they let us drown?"

Maxwell scratched his arm, black dirt beneath his fingernails. "Wish we knew—planning something hideous, no doubt."

"Bargaining chips, I'd wager." William's deep voice came from behind.

Colin blinked. "So they just dumped us down here to rot?"

"Aye, with a few other brethren." Maxwell lowered his voice and leaned closer. "Italian, French, even a bloody Englishman."

The agonizing pain in Colin's head made it difficult for him to think. He found the lad's hand and gave it a feeble squeeze. "Thank you."

Everything mercifully faded into blackness.

***

Enjoying an afternoon in the cottage garden, Margaret balanced John on her lap and watched Duncan use a child-size barrow and shovel to move dirt from one heap to another. Effie was able to spend less time in the nursery due to worsening rheumatism, and Margaret had naturally taken on more of the daily supervision after John's birth a year and one month ago.

Thus far, John looked more like his father than Duncan did. The babe had dun-colored hair and brown, soulful eyes. Every time Margaret looked at him, her heart squeezed. Nearly two years had passed with no word from Colin. She closed her eyes. *Dear God in heaven, protect your servant, Colin, and bring him home to his family soon…* Words she repeated countless times.

Hammering came from the tower. The roof would be finished soon. That lifted her spirits. She'd already had the carpenters build the tables for the great hall, and the tapestries had arrived from Edinburgh. Soon she'd have wagons bring their beds and furniture from Dunstaffnage.

It was all so exciting. If only Colin were here to be a part of it.

Margaret had acquired more cattle and sheep—even invested in Galloway ponies. Since she'd taken the helm, the Campbell wealth had grown exponentially. Things were almost perfect…aside from a wee problem with missing cattle. It didn't happen often, but had occurred enough for Margaret to realize someone was thieving a beast now and again. The culprit was smart about it, too. Only one cow would disappear. The shepherds would search the Glen Orchy lands without so much as a trace, not even a carcass.

Margaret suspected the thief was of the two-legged variety, possibly building his own herd, pinching but a cow per month. Mevan had the guard on it, however. She had every faith he would eventually uncover the guilty party.

Effie appeared from around the corner and took a seat on the garden bench beside Margaret. "Are you still planning to go to the Michaelmas Feast at Tromlee Castle?"

"Aye. Robert and Alana have agreed to accompany me, with Sir Mevan as our guard."

Effie harrumphed.

What did she expect Margaret to do? Lock herself in the cottage and refrain from showing graciousness toward their neighbors? *Surely not.*

As Lady Glenorchy, she had a responsibility to encourage kindly relations between neighboring clans. Laird MacCorkodale had been ever so kind in the past year, sending several gifts. It was past time to thank him properly.

The following day, the early autumn ride to Tromlee was invigorating. It was the first time she'd ventured away from John, but it would only be for one night. Soon she'd be back at the cottage with the boys, listening to the construction efforts, debating the final touches with Tom Elliot.

But today she would enjoy herself. They'd only been riding for two quarters of a sun's traverse when Tromlee Castle came into view. It was a tall, narrow tower, surrounded by a curtain wall—almost a miniature of the castle Margaret and Colin were building in Glen Orchy.

She tapped her heels against her mount. "I do hope there will be plenty of dancing, and some charitable soul takes pity on a lonely matron."

"I'll dance with you, m'lady," Robert said.

"Then I shall hold you to it." Margaret cued her mare to a fast trot. "Come along. I can hear the pipers filling their hide bags already."

***

Ewen MacCorkodale could scarcely contain his excitement when Margaret Campbell walked through his door. Ever so subtly he'd been keeping an eye on her, plying her with gifts, planning each move with the careful stealth of a landowning laird who got what he wanted.

With her husband off fighting in his third crusade, there was little chance of Glenorchy's return to Scotland…and if he did, Ewen would know about it long before the man reached Kilchurn. As laird, he may not be as powerful a baron as Lord Glenorchy or his nephew, now titled the wretched Earl of Argyll, but Ewen was more cunning. An alliance built between neighboring clans would build his family's wealth *and* augment his standing at court. But he must tread very carefully, bide his time. One wrong move would not only incite a feud he couldn't win, it would lose him the grand prize.

Lady Margaret only need glance his way to stir the fire in his loins. He wanted her almost as much as he wanted Colin Campbell's land. Almost.

He held out his hands. "M'lady. How kind of you to come to my humble gathering."

Her sad face blossomed into a beautiful smile. "Thank you, m'laird. You have been most generous by inviting us."

"Please. Call me Ewen."

Watching the cautious arch of her brow, he admonished himself. *Do not push her.* He gestured toward the high table. "Please, do dine beside me."

Margaret turned to her guests—the milk-livered chieftain Robert MacGregor and his wench. "Thank you for your generosity, but I must keep company with my escort."

Blast her damned propriety. He forced his most genuine smile. "Yes, of course. I shall make room for all three."

"Splendid." Margaret clapped. "You are truly a most accommodating host."

Her smile did something to his insides. He wasn't quite certain what it was, but being close to her, smelling the light bouquet of her perfume, instilled a lightheartedness he couldn't recall experiencing in the past.

He must guard against her charms. Allowing himself to be smitten was most certainly not a part of his plan. He was in charge. Not she.

He held the chair for her. "Have you news of Lord Glenorchy?"

She sighed deeply. "Alas, no."

"How dreadful." Ewen had difficulty keeping sarcasm out of his voice. He motioned toward two vacant seats at far end of the table, where Robert MacGregor and his wife could sit out of earshot.

He reached for the ewer of his best wine—a costly vintage reserved for the most special occasions. "May I?"

"Yes, please."

He poured for her and then himself, and raised his glass. "Cheers for a pleasant evening where we can forget our trials, if only for a brief interval."

"Agreed." Margaret sipped. "Mmm. Your wine is delicious."

Ewen swallowed against the flutter in his chest. "And how is the progress on Kilchurn?"

"Ahead of schedule this season. I'm looking forward to moving the boys into the new nursery."

"And your chamber?"

"That too, though I daresay the cottage has been more than comfortable."

He held the goblet to his lips. "Though a woman of your stature deserves grander comfort."

Something flashed in her eyes. His comment hadn't sat well with her. Perhaps she was not as prideful as most of the other highborn women he'd met. Interesting. A woman with her beauty should be pampered endlessly. Had Lord Campbell been lax in his attentions? *I'm sure the beef-witted knight is far too arrogant to give a woman her due.*

It had been two years since she'd last seen her husband. Ewen knew. He'd counted every last day.

He spared no expense, at least for the high table. His best wine, nutmeats and fruits shipped all the way from the Caribbean. Cook entered the hall carrying a masterpiece. Atop a trencher, the exact likeness of a peacock perched, its brilliant tail feathers flowing in waves to the floor.

Margaret clasped her hands under her chin. "Oh my, your efforts exceed that of the king's table."

She exaggerated. His idea for the peacock came directly from Stirling, but still, Ewen's chest swelled. "I thought you'd like it."

Cook made a show of placing the trencher on the table and arranging the feathers so Lady Margaret could admire them.

"Well done," she bubbled.

The cook bowed. "Thank you, m'lady." Then he lifted the peacock's breast slightly. "The surprise is beneath."

She closed her eyes and inhaled the aroma of the sweet meat. "My, 'tis too beautiful to eat."

Ewen brushed his fingers across the back of her hand. "Nothing is too beautiful for you, Lady Margaret."

Her smile waned and she pulled her hand away, turning the silver ring around her finger. It seemed a nervous gesture he'd noticed before. Ewen wasn't dissuaded, confident he'd made a lasting impression. "I've killed a steer for the meal as well." His insides fluttered at his ruse.

"Did you now?" She arched her delicate brow. "Tell me, laird. Have you noticed dwindling numbers in your herd?"

"Nay. Are you saying you have, m'lady?"

"Aye. Not too often, but every now and again, a beast turns up missing."

Under the table, his foot began to twitch. "Thieves?"

"I believe so, someone trying to increase his own holdings."

This conversation couldn't have continued more to his liking if he'd written the script. "Or take advantage of a lady whose husband is away."

Margaret frowned and sipped her wine. "Perhaps."

Ewen pounded his fist on the table for added theatrics. "I will not stand for such a wrongdoing against a delicate lady such as yourself. Please allow me to intervene on your behalf."

She tapped a finger to her lips. "Do you have an idea who is stealing my cattle, laird?"

Shaking his head, he held up his palms. "It shouldn't take me long to find the culprit. My henchman can sniff out a thief in the next burgh. I'll set him to task at first light."

Margaret placed her hand over his and squeezed. "My thanks for your gracious kindness. My man, Mevan, would be more than happy to accompany your men."

Ewen couldn't help the sly grin spreading across his face. "That most likely won't be necessary, m'lady."

After the feast, the minstrels clambered onto the balcony. Margaret let out a little gasp. "Why, I believe those are the same musicians who played at Duncan's christening."

"Aye, the same."

"Oh my. I daresay they are the best in the Highlands." Her eyes flashed with excitement. "You shan't keep me from dancing this evening."

He stood and bowed. "I do hope you will do me the honor."

She grasped his hand. "I'd love to."

Ewen chuckled to himself. The last time he'd seen Margaret dance, her face made the entire room glow, and tonight was no different. When she'd arrived she could have even looked a tad melancholy, but swinging her around to the music made her laugh and clap, appropriate for a woman of her age.

She danced tirelessly, though rarely cast her gaze his way. She watched the other dancers or kept her eyes downcast. If he asked a question, she'd offer a guarded response at best. Did she not know the wine, the minstrels, the fact that he was dancing with her through the night were all for her? Bloody hell, this was the first time in his life he'd held a St. Michaelmas Feast.

Patience. Earn her trust.

When the music ended, Ewen offered his elbow. "Allow me to escort you to your chamber."

She bit her bottom lip. Her gaze darted around the hall. Ewen smiled inwardly. Laird Robert and his wife had retired long before the music ended. "Surely there is a serving maid who can show me the way."

"I wouldn't hear of it. Come, m'lady. You are my esteemed guest." He led her up the tower stairs. "I know not how you're managing alone."

"I say, you do underestimate me. Lord Glenorchy has been gone two years, and his estate has prospered. Forgive my pride in saying so."

"Not at all." He led her down a passage on the third floor. "But I was referring to more delicate matters."

He stopped outside the guest chamber and lifted her chin with the crook of his pointer finger. Her green eyes were so penetrating, he swore she could read his mind. Her beauty emboldened him. "Your bed must be cold at night."

She snatched her arm from his and stepped back. "I am quite certain I do not care for the direction of your conversation, m'laird."

Blast. He'd warned himself over and over, yet meeting her gaze had turned him into a lecherous cur. "E-excuse me, m'lady. I meant no disrespect."

"I'd thank you to remember my station. I dearly hope that we can remain friends, but I will always and forever be faithful to my husband." She opened the door and gave a curtsey. "My gratitude for a lovely evening."

He bowed. "M'lady."

The lock clicked. Ewen turned on his heel and bounded down the passageway to the laird's chamber. He'd spent the entire evening gaining her trust, plying her with his *wealth*, and then he had to push her in the last hour. He strode to the sideboard and poured himself a tot of whisky.

He would coax Lady Margaret into his bed, but he must do so short of a scandal—and with the promise of her hand. Without her lands, the alluring woman was useless to him.

Chapter Twenty-Seven

The Island of Symi, February, 1458

The piss-soaked straw still burned Colin's eyes. He'd been in the Ottoman pit for six months now. The only thing keeping him alive was his memories. Had Margaret birthed a son or a daughter? Of course she'd have survived the birth. He knew it in his soul. A woman with her grit could bring a brawny lad into the world. Another son would be nice—but a daughter would also be a blessing. Regardless, the child would be healthy and loved. When he closed his eyes he could see Margaret smiling, chatting, naked. Thoughts of his *leannan* gave him strength in his darkest hours.

No other prisoners had been interned. He, Maxwell, William and a handful of other knights rotted in the bowels of a fortress. He'd been on the brink of death the first three months of his tenure. Thank God for Maxwell. The squire had tended Colin and nursed him back to some semblance of health.

He reached up and rubbed the knot at the back of his head. It still brought on vicious headaches, but Colin's vision and memory had returned. At least for the most part. Not a man in the pit knew where in God's name they were.

Getting information out of the guards was a useless effort. They spat and spoke in an indecipherable tongue.

The iron gate above creaked open. A man tumbled down the stone steps, his back bleeding from welts of the lash. Colin scurried over to him. Dark hair and dark skin. He looked as if he could be one of the infidels. "Maxwell, bring a cup of water." Colin levered up the man's shoulders. "Who are you?"

He wailed and shook his head.

"*Que êtes-vous?*" Colin asked in French, the language of the order. He made the sign of the cross known only to the Hospitallers.

The man drew a cross on his chest in a weak reply. "Pierre Laurent."

"*Français?*"

"*Oui.*"

"But you look like a Turk."

"'Tis why I'm here."

"A spy?"

Pierre took a moment to catch his breath. "*Oui.*"

"Where are we?"

"Symi."

Colin balled his fist. They were close enough to Rhodes that they could swim. Maxwell arrived with the water. Colin held the dirty, communal wooden cup to Pierre's lips. "Drink."

The man guzzled and sputtered. "*Merci.*"

"What are our chances for escape?"

The man laughed. "From here? We're in a pit, if you hadn't noticed. There's only one way out."

"How many guards above?"

"Too many to count."

"Guess," Colin demanded.

"A dozen."

"How many paces from the gaol to the sea?"

Pierre hung his head, as if all was lost. "How should I know?"

"We cannot be far. I can smell it when the wind comes through the window." Colin glanced at the small hole at least fifteen feet above them.

He pulled the knight to the wall and piled the somewhat clean hay he used for his pallet behind him. "Rest here. I wish I had something to cleanse your wounds, brother."

"*Merci*. Your kindness will not be forgotten."

Colin frowned. "Do you know why they're keeping us here?"

"No. There's been some talk of using Christians for human shields when they march on Jerusalem."

"Or public hanging," William said.

"*Oui*." Pierre swallowed with effort. "Or worse."

Colin stood. Restlessness jittered through his limbs for the first time since he awoke in this dank dungeon. He scanned the defeated faces of the men around him. "Who wants to break out of here?"

A few laughed. "As if there's a remote possibility of that," said the Englishman. "We'll all rot if they don't hang us first."

"You're right," Colin agreed. "If we do nothing, eventually the Turks will tire of feeding us and we'll be led to the gallows or the stake."

Every single man shuddered at the thought of being burned like their brothers, the Templars, over a century before.

"I pose a challenge." Colin stood erect and strode across the line of bedraggled prisoners. "We tone our bodies day and night—become fit beyond anything we've ever imagined."

"Then what? Muscle our way out of here?"

"Exactly." Colin eyed the narrow flight of stone steps. "When they open the gate to toss our bread, we push forward and overtake them. The strongest man first."

They all brayed like bleating sheep and dismissed his idea with waves of their hands. All except the big Scot on the end—his man, William. Willy's eyes blazed. He shoved himself to his feet and stood beside Colin. "I'd rather die fighting for freedom than let them put my neck in a noose."

Colin eyed the others. "Who else is with me?"

A Frenchman stood. "Death or freedom."

Colin jammed his fists into his hips. "That's right. We're close enough to Rhodes to swim."

"I'm in," said the Englishman.

"We start tonight." The miserable Turks would keep him from Margaret's side no more.

***

Another year passed. Fortunately, as Laird Ewen had promised, he'd caught the cattle thief straight away. Though he didn't say exactly how the culprit met his end, he assured Lady Margaret the problem had been snuffed for good. No more cattle had gone missing and her herd prospered. She owed the neighboring laird a debt of gratitude.

John was now two and Duncan, three. Margaret watched the boys trot across the nursery with hobby horses between their legs. John's legs were stubby like a toddler, though Duncan had become leaner and longer. He led his younger brother in a circle. "To Rome, to Rome."

John shook his fist in the air. "To Woam!"

Margaret laughed and clapped her hands. "Good knights, save me."

They both dropped their toy horses and barreled to their mother's side.

"Story," John said.

Duncan pushed for a place on Mama's lap. As far as the lad was aware, Margaret was his flesh-and-blood mother. "Tell us about Da."

He asked about his father several times per day. She only wished she'd had years of happiness with Colin rather than a few short months. Margaret tugged John up so each child shared a knee.

"Of course you know he's a fierce knight."

"Black Colin." Duncan thumped his chest proudly.

John threw his head back and squealed.

Margaret sat straight with pride. "Aye, and he puts fear in the hearts of all who face him. No one can wield a fiercer sword than he."

"How tall is he, Mummy?"

"So tall you have to stack two Duncans and two Johns right on top of each other." They were growing so fast, the measurement was probably off, but she didn't want to favor one lad over the other. In Margaret's mind they were both her boys. Goodness, she was the only parent either lad knew.

"When will he come home?" Duncan asked for the ten thousandth time.

"Home," John echoed.

Margaret's heart twisted into a knot. "Soon. We must pray every night that he returns to us soon."

The door opened and a serving maid popped her head inside. "Lord MacCorkodale has come to call, m'lady."

Margaret sighed. True, Ewen's company was better than spending the afternoon alone, but the neighboring laird had been calling a bit too frequently for her taste. However, she would never forget his kindness. She kissed her boys. "Be good for Miss Lena." Effie had retired to her son's cottage a few months back. Margaret missed the old nursemaid.

"Och, but we want to hear more about Da," Duncan complained.

Margaret tapped his nose. "I'll tell you about the day we met when I come to tuck you in tonight."

John clapped. "Da, come home." He was cute as a button, and still looked so much like Colin.

Margaret straightened her wimple and headed to the stables. She and Ewen had planned to go riding to check on her cattle. Now that her herd had grown, she needed to ensure the shepherds weren't overgrazing. Business was prospering. *At least when Colin returns, he'll not have to worry about the family coffers.*

Ewen had her mare saddled. "Looking lovely as always, m'lady."

She took the reins and allowed him to give her a leg-up. "Thank you. I do appreciate your taking the time to ride with me, though I could have had Mevan do it. 'Tis his duty, after all."

"Aye, but I couldn't resist riding on such a lovely day, and with such pleasant company."

Margaret chuckled. "As of late, you've wasted far too much time frittering away your afternoons with me."

He mounted his steed. "'Tis no bother."

"It should be. You ought to be at court looking for a woman to marry and bear your heirs."

"Alas, I have no interest in court."

"Oh? And to whom do you plan to pass your estate if you die without issue?"

He shrugged and looked her way. Margaret had seen that look in his eye more than once, and it gave her pause. If she weren't a married woman, she'd think he wanted to court *her*.

"Margaret."

She laced her reins through her fingers. "Hmm?"

"I've stopped asking if you've received word."

Three years. She was grateful he hadn't asked in some time. She cued her horse to a fast trot.

Ewen pulled beside her. "Have you considered that perhaps he hasn't written because—"

A fire ignited in the pit of her stomach. "No." She shook her finger. "And I pray you would not think it." Margaret leaned forward and thrashed her mare with her crop, spurring her to a fast gallop. What in God's name was Ewen alluding to? How on earth could he make assumptions? Until she received Colin's token, she would *never* believe him dead.

Chapter Twenty-Eight

Simi, the Mediterranean, March, 1459

Colin watched the sun pass through the gap above. He used it as a sundial. One more quarter and the sun would set. A quarter after that, food would come. The prisoners got the slops, which contained very little meat. But at last, after months of training and watching, the men were ready to mount their escape.

"What is the first thing you'll do when we arrive back on Rhodes?" Maxwell whispered.

"I shall pen a missive to Margaret. God's teeth. The poor woman probably thinks me dead after living in this hell for the greater part of two years." Colin glanced at the young man's filthy face. "And you?"

"I shall eat an entire steer all by myself."

"Meat?" Colin rested his head against the stone wall and swallowed. "The word makes my mouth water."

Darkness slowly cast a shadow across the cell. Colin climbed the stairs and took his position. If his plan didn't work, they'd never be free. The men crept into the shadows below, out of sight of the gate. The hinges of a heavy door screeched in the distance. Colin recognized the guards' greeting, giving praise to Allah—the same one the Turks bellowed when they attacked.

Footsteps echoed down the passage. His heart thundered in his ears. He wiped his sweaty palms on his ragged tunic and sucked in a deep breath. When the guard rounded the corner, Colin hunched over and grabbed his gut. "H-help me," he groaned, watching the enemy from beneath his stringy hair.

The guard stared at him and growled something in his foreign tongue.

"Oh, oh, oh, oh…my innards." Colin curled down a little further, eyeing the placement of the man's sword and the dagger bound to his ankle.

The guard grumbled in a threatening tone. Colin planted his feet and wedged his bum against the stone wall. The Turk jerked the door open and lunged in to shove him away. Colin snatched the dagger and plunged it into the guard's gut while yanking the sword from his scabbard. He pushed the stunned sentry over the steps to the dungeon floor below. The men crowded behind him.

Colin slipped the dagger to Maxwell and swiftly led the charge through the passageway. Chairs scraped across the stone floor as Colin rushed into the chamber. The first man wasn't fast enough to grasp his blade before Colin slashed his throat. The second didn't make it either. Maxwell upended the table, knocking four off balance, while Colin engaged the remaining pair. God help him, it felt good to wield a sword.

His muscles taut from hour upon hour of relentless toning, he quickly regained his fighting edge against the enemy guards. He lunged and drove his blade into the man on his right. The battleaxe from the left came with ferocious speed. Colin hopped aside. Not far enough. The blade sliced across his unprotected chest. With a raging bellow, Colin spun and lopped the head off the man who'd cut him.

Roaring their battle cry, another wave of guards flooded through the narrow passage. Single file, Colin faced each one, the sword in his hand becoming an extension of his arm. He fought with the fury and hatred that had built up after two years of wallowing with rats in the dank pit of hell.

"Freedom or die!" he roared.

With no time to check his wound, he fought like a raging madman until they were all dead. Colin turned to assess the carnage. One Hospitaller down, twelve Turks dead. The crusaders armed themselves with swords, daggers and battleaxes. Colin motioned to Pierre. "Lead the way."

The Frenchman crept ahead, keeping to the shadows. They were only about one hundred paces from the water. Mooring rings gaped at them, with not a single boat in sight.

Colin could have killed another hundred Turks. "God on the cross, give us strength."

"What do we do now?" Maxwell asked, his eyes dipping to Colin's blood-soaked shirt. "Bloody hell, you're cut."

"'Tisn't bad. You can stitch me up in Rhodes." Colin eyed a stack of wooden pilings. "Two men to a pole. If we can't row home, we'll float. Quickly."

A bellow came from the direction of the gaol. Colin yanked Maxwell's arm and raced to the stack of wood. He'd be damned if he was going to spend another night in the dungeon.

Arrows flew overhead. Hit through the chest, the Englishman screamed as he plunged into the white-capped sea below.

"Hurry!" Colin shouted.

Together the men pushed an entire heap of pilings into the water.

Another round of arrows hissed above them.

The shouting grew closer. Footsteps clapped the cobblestones.

An arrow skimmed Colin's ear.

"Jump!"

His voice was silenced by a rush of seawater flooding his mouth.

***

It was a snowy March day. Ewen had a gut-full of winter, and this late storm brewed up a foul mood. His henchman pushed into the solar with muddy boots. Ewen was about to launch into a tirade when Ragnar tossed a satchel onto the table. "A batch of missives from Glenorchy."

"You're serious?" Ewen untied the drawstring and pulled out a folded piece of vellum. "I'll be the son of a toothless whore."

"Too right." Ragnar sauntered to the sideboard, helped himself to a cup of Ewen's best whisky and tossed it back. "'Tis grizzly cold out there. The flakes are coming down in sloppy wet drops."

Ewen ignored him and filed through the missives. Would the bastard not die? Even Ewen had thought Glenorchy had met his end. Sure enough, the blasted things bore Campbell's seal. "We've been so long without word, I was sure the rutting rat was dead." He glared at Ragnar. "Did you kill the messenger?"

The henchman sniggered and poured himself another tot. "Of course. Tied a rock around his belly and dumped him in the loch. Just like all the others."

Ewen stood, shoving the table into the rogue's backside. "If you're going to be so freehanded with my whisky, you'd best pour me a cup, else I'll slice off your cods, ye insolent lout."

Ragnar turned as red as the tapestry on the wall. "Apologies, m'laird. I didn't think you'd mind given the cold." He ran his fingers across his dirk. "And me confidence."

Ewen narrowed his eyes. He didn't like Ragnar's tone, even if he was kin. Mayhap he'd need a stone in his belly and a permanent dip in an icy loch—if he didn't curb his arrogance.

Ewen would have killed a lesser man for helping himself to his best whisky. God's damnation, Colin Campbell was back to sending missives to his poor, forlorn wife. Ewen sank into his seat. At least Ragnar had been vigilant. Two years without a missive and he'd caught the courier before he handed the satchel of vomitous love letters to Margaret. The henchman was good for something.

Ewen ran his thumb under each seal and read every wretched missive, hoping there'd be mention of that damned token Margaret insisted she'd receive. If he could replicate it, she'd be his for certain. The past year had taken quite a toll on her and her little brats. Ewen was wearing her down. If it weren't for that blasted token, she would have agreed to a swift marriage by now.

***

Margaret took the boys to Dunstaffnage for Eastertide. Met with sloppy snow and mud, she hesitated when they passed the turn for Effie's cottage. "Mevan, we shall stop here with the lads. Send the guard ahead and come inside. We'll wait out the storm with Mistress Effie."

They were so near the fortress, the guardsman, clad in a cold and uncomfortable hauberk, nodded his helmeted head.

Besides, Margaret had intended to invite the boy's old nursemaid to the feast. A detour would serve two purposes.

John and Duncan huddled together under a woolen plaid on a nag that was too old to spook. At five and four, both lads had started riding lessons, but Margaret didn't care for the idea of them handling a mount for such a long distance. Though Duncan had complained the loudest, Mevan tugged them beside him on a short lead. Duncan only stopped complaining after the guardsman attached a set of reins to the horse's halter and handed it to the lad. Content he had some semblance of control, Duncan rode, pretending he was a knight, while John shivered behind him.

"Come, lads—I'll bet Mistress Effie has a warm drink and something tasty to eat," Margaret said, following Mevan at the turn.

"Och aye, I'm freezing." Duncan had dropped the knight play several miles back, and now shivered as much as his younger brother.

When she spotted smoke puffing from the chimney, Margaret breathed a sigh of relief. Once they dismounted, she grasped the boy's mitten-covered hands and led them up the path to the stone cottage. With a thatched roof, it wasn't much different than the cottage at Glen Orchy— quaint, homey.

Mevan knocked on the door and stepped aside.

"Who is it?" a frail voice called from within.

"Lady Margaret." She grinned down at the boys, their noses red as apples.

"My heavens." Footsteps shuffled and the door opened. "What on earth are you doing out in this miserable weather?"

Margaret looked up, only to be splattered by sloppy flakes. "The sky didn't appear half as bad when we left Kilchurn."

Effie stepped aside. "Well, what are you standing there for? Slip yourselves inside and shrug out of those wet woolens." Ever the nursemaid, she started removing caps, mittens and damp surcoats. "My, both of you boys have grown a hand's-breadth since I last saw you. And Lady Margaret, you've been away for too long."

Margaret unfastened her cloak and hung it on a peg. "*I've* been away? I wish you'd take my offer and move into Kilchurn. We'd love to have you."

"Aye, but my son needs me now he's lost his wife."

Dry enough, Margaret pulled Effie into an embrace. "And how have you been?"

"Well, aside from my aching back. No one ever said growing old was easy." Effie bundled up the boys' woolens. "Have a seat at the table and I'll spread these things over the hearth."

The room was warm, smelled of delicious spices, and Margaret rubbed her hands to bring back the feeling. "Thank you ever so much, Mistress Effie."

John climbed onto the bench. "Do you have any oatcakes?"

"And Mummy said you'd have something warm to drink," Duncan said.

Margaret shook a finger. "You must wait until Mistress Effie offers. 'Tis impolite to ask."

Effie turned with her hands on her hips. "Excuse my impertinence, the lot of you must be chilled to the bone. Would you lads like some hot mulled cider and a bowl of plum pottage?"

Duncan licked his lips. "Aye."

"Please," Margaret corrected.

John rubbed his belly. "That sounds delicious, *please*."

She sat on the bench beside Mevan and sighed. "Thank you ever so much. We stopped not only for refuge from the snow, but to invite you to the Eastertide celebration. Players are coming from Edinburgh to perform the mystery plays for the Crucifixion and Resurrection—feasts both on Good Friday and Easter Monday."

Effie set five tankards on the table. "Sounds like a grand celebration. I'm surprised you're not having it at Kilchurn." She passed a kettle of warm cider to Mevan.

Margaret watched the guard fill her cup, the tart whiff making her mouth water. "Thought about Kilchurn, but I haven't been to Dunstaffnage in so long, I owe a grand feast to our subjects here and I hoped Argyll might pass through for the holiday."

"Argyll?" Effie picked up the ladle. "Since he was granted the title of earl, word is he's become indispensable to the king. I doubt we'll see him in these parts for a year or more."

Margaret's shoulders drooped and she heaved a sigh. "Unfortunate."

Effie stopped ladling pottage from the cast iron kettle on the hearth. "And what business have you with the earl?"

Margaret stood to help serve the wooden bowls filled with spiced fruit and meat. "Spending so much time at court, I was hoping he may have heard something about Colin or the Crusades."

The old woman eyed her. "Still no word?" She glanced at the boys, concern etching her brow. "Four years, is it?"

"Aye." Margaret hated to admit it had been that long. Colin had never even set eyes on John.

Effie sat across the table and covered Margaret's hand with a warm palm. "The boys will need a father soon."

Margaret's gaze shifted to the angelic faces of her sons. Eating like starved cats, they paid no notice to Effie's remark, though Margaret's worry grew each day. "I do not even want to think about it." She shrugged. "Ewen has been showing some interest in their welfare." He'd made remarks at the least, though hadn't become endeared to the boys yet.

"Ewen?"

"MacCorkodale," Mevan said, reaching for his tankard with a snort.

Margaret clapped her hands to her cheeks. Why on earth should the mention of the neighboring laird make her blush? Her feelings for the man ran no deeper than friendship.

Nonetheless, Effie gave her a concerned glare. "You cannot be serious."

Margaret stirred her potage. Effie had a knack for overstepping her bounds, but then her eyes would sparkle with an apologetic smile. Margaret rarely chastised her. "I believe I mentioned I was hoping to run into Lord Argyll, did I not? Aside from that, the laird has been nothing but kind and very concerned for my welfare."

"I'm certain he is." The old woman made no attempt to hide her sarcasm.

"He stopped the cattle thieves when I was building the herd."

Effie rolled her eyes. "Did he, now?"

Lady Margaret sipped her cider. Warmth slid all the way through the tips of her fingers. "Will you please attend Eastertide with us? I'd love you to join us at the high table with the lads."

Effie placed her palm on her chest. "Me? To be an honored guest?" She winked at the boys. "How could I resist?"

Margaret sighed. It would be a good holiday. Still, disappointment settled heavily upon her shoulders. If only she could meet with Argyll, the earl might help her garner news of Colin. Presently, she clung to hope. His token hadn't come back to her. She turned the matching ring on her finger. A small treasure, it bore witness to their undying love.

Chapter Twenty-Nine

The Isle of Rhodes, April, 1460

The monk ushered Colin into Jacques de Milly's private rooms. Behind the grand master's embroidered chair, a rich tapestry of blue and gold hung down from a canopy suspended from the ceiling. This was where the great man received supplications. Having aligned himself and Scotland with the French sector of the Rhodes fortress, Colin had dined with the grand master many times, but rarely had he been to his private rooms. These were mostly frequented by knighted priests and monks—pure men who had taken up the oath of chastity.

Colin wore a long black tunic with a white cross of St. John embroidered on his chest, and a black skullcap, similar to that of the monks—a nice reprieve from roasting in his armor. He strode up the aisle and kneeled, bowing his head.

"Rise, Sir Colin." Jacques rubbed his thumb over a brass disc in his rosary. "You look troubled."

"Aye, 'tis with a heavy conscience I come to you."

"Have out with it." Jacques sat forward. "A knight cannot do battle with a troubled mind."

"My lord, I have been on crusade for five long years. A fact reflected in my beard." He gestured to the neatly groomed facial hair, which now touched mid-chest. "I left my wife great with child, my son only a babe in arms. My affairs have been without my governance, and I fear what will happen to my lands should I not return soon."

The grand master stroked his own beard thoughtfully. "These are the problems of married men and those who maintain property. I took the oath of chastity to avoid such conflicts."

Lead sank to the bottom of Colin's gut. With the endless fighting, he feared he'd never be released.

Jacques held his hands up and addressed the monks who lined the room. "Jesus told Peter to leave all behind and follow him. Peter left his lands, his wife and his family to be a disciple."

"As did I, my lord. But Peter returned to his kin."

"Eventually, though God was always his first concern."

Colin's throat tightened. Was he wrong to covet Margaret's arms? "As it should be," he forced out.

The grand master stood and stepped down from his chair, placing his hand on Colin's shoulder. "Help me take back the city of Archangelos. You were bred for battle, Black Colin. I cannot lose you until Rhodes is once again completely under the order's rule."

***

It was with a heavy heart that Margaret rode beside Ewen. In a few days, her entire world had crumbled. She'd clad herself in a stoic front for so long, but the things most dear continued to be stripped away. How much longer could she go on without the world falling apart around her feet?

Three days past, the king's guard rode into Kilchurn announcing the death of James II, killed by an exploding cannon called the Lion. The king unwittingly stood beside the cannon during a demonstration. Hells bells, Scotland was at relative peace—aside from the Crusades. Fought on foreign soil, it wasn't a war against the homeland, but one waged for all of Christendom.

Margaret hated war.

In the courtyard, they'd shouted long live the king. James III, at the age of nine, was still only a lad. The king's mother, Mary of Guelders, had already been appointed regent to reign in his stead. The same woman who'd suggested Margaret be matched with Colin.

It seemed nothing was right in Scotland. Two days later, another sentry rode through Kilchurn's gate. This one announced the death of Lord Struan. Margaret hadn't seen her father since her wedding day.

Remorse clamped her gut.

Though the Campbell guard accompanied her, the MacCorkodale laird insisted on providing escort to her father's funeral. They departed early that August morning to make the long journey to Loch Rannoch in one day.

The sun hung low in the western sky, and Margaret's behind ached from hours of relentless riding. At last, Dunalasdair Castle came into view, intensifying her yoke of sorrow.

All seemed surreal, as if she were in a dream. Numbed by the news of two great men dead, she drove her horse forward, yet tears refused to come. Had the years hardened her, surviving without Colin, putting her fears behind, feigning good humor?

She'd been away from Dunalasdair for so long, wound up in her own affairs, taking care of the children, building the castle, dealing with the supplications from crofters and everyone else who traded with the vast Campbell estates. She'd lost any chance to see Da again.

The chains of the portcullis creaked under the gate's weight as it rose to allow her into the old familiar bailey. A groom helped her dismount. She rushed into the castle and straight to her mother's chamber.

In the past five years, Lady Robinson's hair had taken on a silver hue. She sat staring into the fire and paid no mind to the sound of the door. Margaret dashed to her mother's side. "I came as quickly as I could."

"Margaret?" Mother's tear-streaked face brightened. "You came."

"Of course I did. We left as soon as the messenger arrived."

Mother pulled her into a tight embrace. The fragrance of pure Highland air and lavender swept through her being. *Home.* Too much time had passed since Margaret had held Ma in her arms. The stress of the past five years constricted her throat and threatened to burst in a flood of tears—but now was the time to be strong. She clenched her fists to regain her strength. "How are you holding together?"

Mother wiped her eyes with a kerchief. "Well enough, I suppose." She grasped Margaret's hand. "He didn't suffer long."

She clutched her fingers around her constricting throat. "The fever took him in the night?"

"Aye." Mother clasped her fists to her chest and released an anguished wail. "What am I to do without him?"

Margaret's heart squeezed. Must everything end in pain? "There, there, Ma, everything will be all right," she cooed. "Robert is lord now. He will see to your comfort."

"I know." She flailed her hands. "But I am alone."

Margaret sat beside her mother and cradled her until the weeping subsided, while knives of her own pain stabbed at her heart. Too well she knew what it was like to sit alone night after enduring night. At least she could cling to the hope Colin would eventually return. Could she not?

***

Before the funeral, Margaret paid her respects in the chapel's vestibule. Seeing her father's lifeless body laid out on the board hit her in the stomach. Her head swooned. She covered her mouth. *Life is but a fleeting moment in time, and suddenly you are no more.*

The day drudged on. Completely dazed, Margaret sat through the service. Though she tried to be strong, a voice in her head repeated, *Where is Colin? Is he with Da?*

Everything proceeded in a blur to the tune of her mother's sobbing. Ewen MacCorkodale remained beside her like a wall of strength.

Margaret had retired to her chamber to dress for the evening meal when Mother tapped on the door and entered. She'd washed her face and appeared stoic. "Dear child, you must forgive me."

Margaret crossed to her. "Whatever for?"

"Alas, you have come home, and I've spent the entire time wallowing in my own sorrow."

She gave her mother an affectionate hug. "You need to grieve. 'Tis unhealthy to hold it in."

Mother took in a deep breath and sighed. "I do not think I have any tears left." She grasped Margaret's hand and pulled her to the embrasure in the window and bade her to sit on the embroidered cushions. "We must talk. It has been too long since I last visited you and the lads. Tell me. What news of Colin?"

Margaret bit her bottom lip and looked at her hands.

"Still nothing?"

This time it was her turn to well with tears. Her fingers trembled. "It's been over five years." A tear spilled from her eye and dropped onto her hand. "I even sent a missive to the Pope, with no response."

"And what is your relationship with Laird MacCorkodale? He didn't leave your side all day."

Margaret drew in a heavy sigh, fully aware Ewen's presence must appear untoward. "He's a friend. I asked him to remain behind in Glen Orchy, but he insisted upon accompanying me."

"By the way he looks at you, his feelings run far deeper than friendship."

She buried her face in her palms. "I cannot even think of it."

Mother smoothed her hand over her daughter's back. "You must consider the fact Colin may never return."

Margaret splayed her fingers and cast her gaze toward the ceiling. Could no one understand how much Colin meant to her?

Mother folded her hands. "Your boys need a father."

"But I have not received Colin's token. He swore I would know he had fallen if a messenger arrived bearing only the...symbol." She turned the matching ring around on her finger. She would *never* tell a soul about their pact. They'd sworn an everlasting vow to each other. It was the only concrete covenant she could hold on to.

"You've not received his token, nor have you received a single letter. As you've said, it has been five years." Mother stood. "You may never see either. At some point you must come to grips with that."

When Mother left, Margaret dashed to the bed and buried her face in a pillow. She'd held in her emotions for so long, five years of pent-up worry burst forth. Rocking herself, she wept into the satin. A gut-wrenching, torturous bout of melancholy swept over her. Colin had yet to lay eyes on John. He couldn't be dead. She prayed to God to show her a sign.

The ram's horn sounded, announcing the evening meal. Tears still streaming from her eyes, Margaret poured some water into the bowl and used a cloth to wash her face. It shamed her not that she'd been weeping. After all, this was a day of great mourning. Her father dead, her husband missing—who wouldn't succumb to a bout of uncontrollable tears?

After supper, Ewen offered Margaret his hand. "Will you take a walk with me in the garden? 'Tis a fine summer's eve, which must be enjoyed."

With a nod she accepted, praying her eyes were no longer swollen. The fresh air invigorated her. With the azaleas in full bloom, the garden was alive with reds and brilliant pinks.

Ewen's strides were long compared to hers. "Is it nice to be home?"

"Aye, though sad. It will never be the same now Father's gone."

"True, but 'tis peaceful here."

A willow warbler called. "It seems a world away from Kilchurn."

He gestured to a bench. "Would you sit, m'lady?"

Margaret would have preferred to walk, but something in his pinched brow made her bite her tongue and do as asked.

He kneeled in front of her, taking both of her hands between his large palms. They weren't as big or as rough as Colin's, but then Ewen wasn't a warrior like Colin.

"Margaret, I have stood beside you all these years...watched you suffer in silence as you waited for Lord Glenorchy to return home."

"Aye, you've been a good friend." She tried to pull her hand away to pat his cheek, but he held her fast.

"I must ask you to reconsider my proposal of marriage." He cleared his throat. "I love you."

Margaret gaped, staring into Ewen's pale blue eyes. Yes, he'd said the words, but why did she feel nothing?

His eyes pleaded. "You must know combining our houses will build the strength of our families."

She bit her bottom lip. "Duncan is the rightful heir to the Lordship of Glenorchy."

"Of course he is—will always be, but you are the lady. Join with me and we shall continue to build the dynasty."

She paused a moment and measured his words, her heart heavy as a stone. "But I do not love you. I-I'm married to Colin. I've not received his token." How many times must she repeat herself?

"Margaret. At some point you need to realize he's not coming back. Your *token* is lost. Perhaps you should choose a date—decide upon a time when you will relinquish hope."

He was a good man and would be a good role model for the boys. As much as she wanted to resist, Ewen's words must be considered.

"You owe it to your own sanity, my love."

No word in five long years.

What other option did she have? The boys needed a father—but she also needed more time. She sighed, with a nod of her head. "If Colin has not returned by the time the Kilchurn chapel is completed, I shall accept your proposal."

Ewen held her hands to his lips and kissed them. Margaret's heart fluttered with the image of another man doing the same. A man now lost to her.

Chapter Thirty

The Isle of Rhodes, January, 1461

The fighting continued nonstop for nine grueling months. Every living soul on the Isle of Rhodes had been driven behind the walls of the great Hospitaller fortress. Colin couldn't remember the last time he'd slept a full night. The tension in the air was palpable, and the stench of unclean humanity and sewage sweltering in the hot sun pervaded his nostrils.

Having given up his tiny cell to a homeless family, he lay on his pallet, watching the sky. The firmament above changed from midnight blue to cobalt at the mere blink of his eye.

Dawn.

Colin rose and woke Maxwell. "'Tis time."

Full battle armor today. The squire had gone through the ritual of helping Colin suit up so many times, the once tedious task had become nearly as easy as putting on chausses and a surcoat. Fortunately, a cool breeze blew in from the Mediterranean. It would make the fighting easier.

Colin spun the ring on his finger. Then he pulled it off for the first time since he'd put it on whilst Margaret watched. The Celtic pattern had worn in the past six years. He held it up to Maxwell. "Today you will not fight."

"But I—"

"Hear me." Colin placed the ring on a thong and tied it around Maxwell's neck. "You will hide in the church catacombs. If I should die this day, take my ring back to Lady Margaret and tell her I love her. Tell her I did not witness a single sunrise without thinking of her." He grasped the young man's shoulders and shook. "Promise me you will do this."

Maxwell's jaw twitched, then he nodded once. "I swear my oath."

By the time the squire buckled Colin's last finger gauntlet, the courtyard was astir with fighting men, all in various stages of dress. No one spoke. The only sounds were of iron scraping against mail and leather slipping though buckles.

"William, bring me a tankard of water." Colin's voice cut through the silence.

The knight did as requested. Colin unclasped the charmstone from around his neck and dipped it in the water three times. "Lady Margaret gave this stone to me. Its charms have kept me alive all these years. Legend is anyone who drinks the water into which it has been dipped will have good health and a safe journey home." He refastened the stone around his neck and took the first sip. "Drink, all of you. We need the stone's special powers against the Turks this day more than ever before."

Colin passed the cup to Maxwell and watched each man sip. He hadn't given a second thought about the reputed magic of the stone. But it had survived with him all this time. He should have died when the boom hit his head—or in the Turkish prison, or in any of the battles he'd led in the past year. The stone hadn't failed him, nor had it been lost. Its charms were genuine—Margaret's charms.

Colin inspected his weapons—dirk on his right hip, sword on his left, a dagger lashed to each leg iron. He picked up his targe and pike, and headed to the stables. The groom already had Colin's warhorse fitted with armor and saddled. He climbed up the mounting block and took the reins. Nodding his thanks, he rode back to the courtyard at a slow trot.

He glanced at the grim faces of the men—some his, others serving knights from every corner of Christendom. One thing reflected in each man's eyes.

Fear.

That was no way to start a battle. Colin spurred his horse to a canter and rode back and forth in front of the gates until all eyes focused on him.

"Are we going to let the Ottoman Empire drive us out of Christendom?"

"No," someone hollered from the crowd.

"One person says no? That does not sound like an army ready to face the fiercest battle of their lives." He slammed his pike into the ground. "I ask you again. Will you allow the *rutting* Turks to take *our* lands?"

"No," a unanimous roar boomed from the crowd.

"Will you return home a coward and a failure?"

"No!"

"Are you ready to fight for your God and your freedom?"

"Yes!"

Colin gave the signal for the heavy gates to open. "Who are you fighting for?"

"God!"

"What are you fighting for?"

"Freedom!"

"We will not let them win…"

"Deus vult, Deus vult, Deus vult!"

Leading the ancient crusader's cry "God wills it," Colin led the charge out the gate to face the Ottoman army.

Joined by the cavalry, Colin steadied his pike against his steed's shoulder as they approached the enemy at breakneck speed. His fearless horse breathed a steady, but labored rhythm beneath his heavy plate armor. Colin glared into the eyes of his opponent, riding head-on, the bastard's sword held high, ready to strike.

One step before impact, Colin raised his pike and launched it into the heart of the man who aimed to chop off his head. The Turk's stunned eyes bulged before he fell from his horse, trampled by his own men.

Colin snatched his sword and swung, fighting the onslaught right and left, spinning his horse in the fray, heads and arms flying, men shrieking in pain, thudding to the ground. Hour after hour he fought, swinging, thrusting, hacking. There was no time to check his men. A sea of Turks washed over them. Cannons blasted from the battlements. Arrows hissed overhead, and though Colin's muscles burned with the weight of his armor and the relentless fighting, he could not stop.

His battle lust grew until something blunt struck him from behind. Bellowing, Colin spun and swung his blade. Out of the corner of his eye, a battle hammer flung through the air, straight for his temple. The weighty weapon connected with bone-jarring force. Flung from his saddle, his eyes rolled back.

He'd never see home.

Goodbye, my Margaret. My token will release your heart.

Colin's body thudded to the ground. Blackness took him to a place with no pain.

Chapter Thirty-One

Kilchurn Castle, 1st May, 1461

As they grew, Duncan and John became more similar—almost like twins. It was the Beltane Festival, and Margaret shared her plaid with Ewen near the big bonfire. All the children, Campbell and MacGregor skipped around the maypole, weaving their ribbons as they laughed and danced to the piper's tune.

Ewen sipped from his flask while Margaret clapped and laughed with the children. She glanced at Ewen's face. A quirky smile crossed his lips, and he took another swig, keeping his gaze fixed across the courtyard.

Margaret followed his line of sight. Alana's eldest had just come of age, and she wore a gown that revealed far too much of her young flesh. Margaret grimaced, but leaned in so only Ewen could hear. "Morag just turned five and ten. She's a sweet lass."

He snapped his gaze away and chuckled. "A lassie such as her won't stay a maiden for long."

"Pardon me? Please excuse your vulgar tongue."

Ewen took a long draw from his flask. "Apologies, m'lady. I meant nothing untoward—just making an observation."

"I don't care for that train of thought, especially coming from a leader of men."

"Aye, but all men think with their cods. We cannot help it."

"I think you may have indulged in a wee bit too much spirit this eve." Margaret scooted away by a hand's breadth.

He held the flask upside down and belched. "'Tis empty. I suppose I'll have to switch to ale."

"Mayhap you should seek your bed."

Ewen shrugged.

Margaret pursed her lips and looked away. The laird usually wasn't so uncouth. She hated the way Beltane and spirit brought out people's unsavory side. Ewen was no different. Thank heavens she'd not seen him inebriated before—drunkenness didn't become him.

The bagpipes stopped, and the children all fell to the ground in a heap of laughter. Margaret stood and clapped. "Duncan, John. 'Tis time to turn in."

John's bottom lip jutted out. "Och, Mummy, we're having so much fun."

Mistress Lena stood, but Margaret held up a hand. "I'm ready to retire. I'll take them up." She dipped a quick curtsey to Ewen. "Goodnight."

She grasped the boys' hands and led them into the tower before Ewen could protest.

"I wanted to dance some more," Duncan complained. "You always make us go to bed when everything starts to become fun."

Margaret strengthened her grip. She would have allowed them to stay up a bit longer had Ewen kept out of his cups. One thing she hated was watching a man overindulge in spirit. They became loose with their tongues, as well as their hands.

Amongst the courtyard filled with people, a black chasm filled Margaret's chest, as if she were completely alone. If only Colin would return home. Alas, hope was running out.

She put the boys to bed and read them a passage from *The Manual of Good Conduct for Children.* Though it contained valuable and important material, it never failed to put them to sleep.

She shut the nursery door quietly and headed down the passage to her chamber. Footsteps echoed up the tower stairwell. Margaret listened for a moment. They were heavy steps, like a man's. She darted to her door— Beltane was renowned for its ill effect on people. They lost their sense of propriety, became emboldened.

She grasped the latch.

"There you are." Ewen slid between her and the door, smiling broadly.

She frowned at the sour whisky odor wafting around him. "Laird, whatever are you doing up here?" She'd never invited Ewen above stairs, and his presence here now sent prickles along her nape.

He brushed an errant lock of hair away from her face. "Do you not think 'tis time we took another step? I've resisted you for so long. 'Tis Beltane." His voice grew husky. "The night when women choose their bed partner." He placed a hand on her waist.

Margaret's entire body shuddered. Ewen's warm hand upon her body was nearly more than she could bear. She gazed into his pale eyes. Filled with lust, they stared at her. Her traitorous insides fluttered. No, Ewen wasn't as handsome or brawny as Colin, but he was a flesh-and-blood man. Too many years had passed since a man placed hands on her with an unmistakable intent to ravish.

But she couldn't.

Groaning, Ewen tugged her body against his. He crushed his mouth over her lips. Knees turning to mush, Margaret clenched her fists against her deep, base urge for passion. Heat swirled inside her loins, and her breasts ached from the friction of Ewen's chest colliding with hers.

He thrust his tongue into her mouth. Margaret responded, sucking, swirling. Oh God, she wanted to feel a man make love to her, wanted to be caressed and dig her fingers into powerful shoulders.

But not with the fleshy man who had her backed against her chamber door. Margaret's mind took control of her reckless senses and screamed *no*. She closed her eyes and pictured Colin in her arms. She must, she absolutely *must* remain faithful to her husband—at least until hope had run its course.

"Mummy," a tiny voice called from down the darkened corridor.

Trembling, Margaret pushed away and swiped a hand across her mouth. "Yes, John?" Her voice shook in time with her trembling fingers.

"I had a bad dream. Can I sleep with you?"

"Of course you can, darling." Thank God for little angels.

Ewen grasped her arm. "But we…"

Steeling her resolve, she shoved her finger in Ewen's sternum. "You shan't tempt me like that again. Either you wait until we are wed or you can head back to Tromlee and remain there."

***

The next morning, Margaret awoke to John's tiny fingers playing with her hair. Toasty warm beneath the coverlet, she smiled at her youngest son, and the chasm in her heart stretched. The image of Colin brought tears to her eyes.

He clasped her face between his tiny palms. "Are you all right?"

She dabbed her eyes with the linens. "Och aye. Just missing your father, is all. Your bonny face reminds me of him."

"It does?"

"Aye." She mussed his hair. "And we'd best rise afore the master-at-arms comes and breaks down the door."

John squirmed. "And skewer me with his dirk."

Margaret took pause. "Where did you learn that?"

"Duncan always says it."

Margaret sighed. She'd have to have a word with Mevan to ensure the boys weren't learning to be heathens. But first she had something more pressing to attend. After breaking her fast with the lads, she set out across the courtyard and surveyed the construction of the chapel.

"M'lady. You're up early," said Tom Elliot. He gestured to the foundation. "The mortar's nearly set. We can start on the walls in a sennight."

"No." She tapped the foundation with her toe. "I want you to take your time on this project. Think on it as your masterpiece. Leave nothing for granted, spare no expense."

His face lit up. "Honestly?"

"Yes." She flung her arms wide. "I want this chapel to be your legacy, your greatest feat of architecture."

He rubbed his hands. "Yes, m'lady. I'll need to revise the drawings."

"Then I suggest you set to it, Master Elliot. Make the nave as grand as Melrose Abbey."

Smiling, Margaret proceeded to the solitude of the gardens. This would be a very long engagement indeed.

Please, Colin. If you are alive, I anxiously await your sign.

Chapter Thirty-Two

Dunstaffnage Castle, March, 1462

Lord Argyll, now titled the venerated *Earl* of Argyll, stopped at Dunstaffnage on the king's business. His life had been a whirlwind of madness since the death of King James II, followed by the crowning of his son, a child, now James III. The king's mother, Mary de Guelders, had assumed the position of regent. The posturing and feuding throughout Scotland gave Argyll not a moment's rest. This particular morning, he broke his fast in the solar and reviewed the ledgers of accounts on behalf of the king.

His groom stepped inside and bowed. "Lord Argyll, the matron Effie wishes an audience with you."

"Colin's old nursemaid?" He pinched his brows. "Whatever would she want with me?"

"She didn't say, m'lord. Shall I send her away?"

"No, ask her in. I'm sure it will be a trivial matter—one easy to appease."

Effie, bent over a cane, hobbled through the door. "Thank you for seeing me, m'lord."

"'Tis my pleasure." Argyll hopped up and pulled out a chair. "Mistress Effie, what news?"

She shook her head sorrowfully. "'Tis very grave indeed."

He took the seat beside her. "Tell me."

"You are aware Lady Margaret has agreed to marry Ewen MacCorkodale after the Kilchurn chapel is built?"

Argyll swiped his hand over his chin. He wasn't aware. What else had changed while he'd been at court? "I'm sorry, I've been away so long, I'm afraid that information has slipped past me." He leaned forward. "When is the chapel scheduled to be completed?"

"Midsummer." She grasped his hands and squeezed. "I know in my heart Colin is still alive. But he's written not a word. Lady Margaret has put Laird Ewen off for years, and now time has run its course."

"This is serious indeed." He drummed his fingers on the table. "I've received no word of Uncle's death. Yet it's been…seven years with no word?" My, how time had slipped away. But it wasn't like Colin Campbell to abandon his affairs. The lead in Argyll's gut did not mirror Effie's feelings. *Has Glenorchy been killed?*

"Aye. What is Lady Margaret to do with two boys and no husband? They're now approaching critical years."

Argyll sat back in the chair. "And what makes you think he still lives?"

Though her skin was wrinkled, her blue eyes sparkled with an intelligent flicker. "First of all, he gave my lady a token and vowed if she received it, she would know he was dead. She has *not* received a single thing. Secondly, I know Colin as well as you do, m'lord. He's alive. I can feel it in these old bones." She pushed a gnarled finger into his sternum. "You must fetch him and bring him back before that onion-eyed varlet sneaks his way into Lady Margaret's bed. Once Ewen MacCorkodale gets his hands on Campbell lands, you can bet the boys will be booted out and new deeds drawn."

"Dear God." His mind raced. What were the options? Whom else could he send? The body should be retrieved. Above all, family lands and titles must be protected.

Effie boldly poked him again. "You must leave at once."

Argyll blinked. "I cannot just pick up and sail across the high seas." He was an *earl*, for God's sake.

"You're Colin's only able kin. You've been to Rome. You know where to look. Who else could find him as fast as you?" She stood and fingered the bold medal of the Earl of Argyll, which hung on a heavy chain across his chest. "You must surely ken you owe all your success to him. Dunna be an arse and pretend he didn't foster you and turn you into the great earl you've become today." She spat on the floor. "You'd be a sniveling, bull-witted measle if it weren't for Colin Campbell."

Effie dropped to her chair, panting and fanning herself from her exuberant discourse. Argyll ran his palm over his mouth. The old nursemaid was always one to speak her mind—no matter whom she addressed.

Argyll didn't care to be ordered about by a bent old woman who looked not a day younger than eighty, but she was right. Blood ran thick between the Campbells, and the Lord of Glenorchy had had more to do with making Argyll an earl than his own father. He could not sit idle while another man claimed Colin's wife and lands—and Effie spoke true. Argyll had been to Christendom as his uncle's squire. He probably knew more about the Order of St. John than any man in Scotland.

Could he afford the time?

Who else can I trust?

***

Another year's Mayday festival behind them, Margaret walked through the garden with Ewen. He held her hand firmly. She tolerated his affection. After all, it had been nearly seven years since Colin left. She had no other marriage prospects, no other suitors.

Margaret studied her betrothed. His face wasn't spectacular. He had a noble hook to his nose, his chin bold, not effeminate in the least. But there was something about his eyes she couldn't quite put her finger on. A dark shade of blue, they shifted—never really focused on her for long. She really shouldn't let that bother her. He was a laird with many responsibilities, and a myriad of thoughts must course through his mind at any given time. Even his conversation hopped from one topic to the next—except when he pressured her.

Today he appeared to be in good humor. "When we are wed, you shall not have to worry about anything except the latest fashions and dances."

She chuckled. "I do love to dance, but I rather enjoy keeping a finger on the pulse of the castle."

"'Tis a man's job." He gestured toward the roofless chapel. "That building should have been completed last summer. I'm surprised you haven't fired Tom Elliot by now."

If he only knew she'd been the one to slow the mason's progress. "Not to worry. The chapel will be complete soon."

"Yes it will, and you shall not be faced with such daunting tasks ever again." He stopped and pulled her around to face him. "The chapel's completion is why I asked you to walk with me. We must set the date."

Margaret chewed her lip, a weight pressing on her chest. She could put it off no longer. She must face the fact Colin was gone for good. The boys needed a father. Keeping Ewen at bay only hurt their future prospects. She wasn't about to petition the queen and marry someone unknown to her. Ewen was a laird and had been kind and patient. "I've given it a great deal of thought."

His eyes brightened. "Oh?"

"We'll have a big gathering for the Lammas Day Feast."

"Aye, the harvest looks promising already. The day of the feast, then?"

"I was thinking the morning after—August third. It has a nice ring to it."

Ewen held his fists in the air as if he'd just won the grand prize in the Highland games. "At last we will be wed. We shall be the talk of Argyllshire the entire summer."

Margaret tried to smile. So she was his conquest? A prize he'd won? She didn't honestly want a tender, earth-shattering communion of emotion. Did she?

He grasped her shoulders and planted a slobbery kiss on her lips. "You'll not regret this."

She took in a deep breath and smiled broadly. That did feel better. After all, what did she expect? She was now nine and twenty. Her days of fluttering hearts and breasts swelling with desire were long gone. She must now make decisions for the good of her children and her kin.

Ewen stepped back, holding Margaret's hand out at arm's length. "I must away to court. The regent has summoned me to parliament."

"Very well." Margaret dipped in a curtsey. "Haste ye back, my...friend." She could think of nothing more endearing. She certainly would not refer to him as dear, love or sweetheart. Those worlds refused to form upon her lips. She would never utter those words again.

Margaret watched Ewen's bold stride as he left her standing in the midst of her herb garden. Basil and rosemary scented the air. She sighed. She'd finally agreed to a date. At least Ewen was happy and would stop pressuring her.

She proceeded down the path to the daffodils in full bloom. She kneeled and examined the brilliant yellow petals. Rubbing a finger across one, the wonder of God's creation flowed through her like living breath. A soft breeze caressed the back of her neck and her skin grew alive, tingling.

Dear God in heaven. I am begging you for answers. Was Colin lost at sea? Did he even reach Rome? Was he upset with me? Did I misinterpret his love? Help me to understand what went wrong. Above all my questions and all my desires, if there is the slightest chance he lives, I beg of you, please, please, please show me a sign.

Chapter Thirty-Three

Edinburgh Castle, 17th June, 1462

Aside from Mevan, Margaret told not a soul the real reason for her trip to Edinburgh, where Queen Mary had moved court for midsummer. As far as anyone knew, she'd journeyed out to find the perfect fabric for her wedding dress, and as such could not be accompanied by her future groom. Ewen had traveled north to attend Highland games in Inverness, and thus hadn't objected to her departure. He didn't even know of it. *Thank the stars for small mercies.*

Though she'd written countless letters and given them to her faithful courier, Ewen's youngest brother, she'd never received a word from Colin or His Holiness. Her last hope was to gain an audience with the queen. The regent should always be the first to receive word if one of their nobles was killed abroad.

Margaret's skin twitched while she waited in the queen's hot outer hall. A large wooden table sat in the center of the big room, filled with smelly courtiers waiting for an opportunity to present their petitions to the queen.

Margaret had a good chance of being seen today, the second day spent sitting on one of the hard wooden benches lining the wall. She'd slipped the queen's page a silver sovereign and stressed the importance of her business.

Two days of nervously drumming her fingers did nothing to bolster confidence. Yes, she was nobility, a wife of one of the most powerful barons in Scotland...though he hadn't set foot there in seven years. A fact that would quickly see his good deeds forgotten, especially after the death of James II.

Hundreds of errant thoughts whirred through her head. Why had there been no news of the Crusade? Would the queen think her a fool or ask her to be a lady in waiting, God forbid? Surely with two boys at home, she could plead a case against that.

The door opened. The smug page stuck his nose in the air. "Lady Margaret Campbell of Glen Orchy."

Her hammering heart flew to her throat. Swallowing, Margaret stood as quickly as proper decorum would allow and pressed her hand to her chest to quash her rapid heart. "Thank you," she whispered, carefully planting each foot as she entered the queen's inner chamber.

The room exuded wealth. Oozed it. From the richly painted friezes on the ceilings to the purple and gold tapestries on the walls, no expense had been spared. The queen sat in a well-padded throne, covered in red velvet. She wore a velvet gown with a black skirt and red bodice, lined with ermine. Adorning her head was a matching hennin, which only revealed a hint of her auburn hair.

The queen placed her palms together and inclined her fingers toward Margaret. "Well, come forward, Lady Glenorchy. I haven't all day."

Cheeks burning, Margaret briskly walked ahead and performed a deep curtsey—the same one she'd dipped into on her wedding day.

"Rise," Queen Mary said, sounding like she'd rather be someplace else entirely.

Margaret wiped her sweaty palms on her skirts. "I've a matter of utmost urgency and am in grave need of your assistance, your highness."

The queen nodded impatiently. Margaret clutched her palms together and launched into a quick explanation of Colin's disappearance. "You see, Lord Glenorchy did not send me his token. I've received no formal word of his death, only rumors."

The queen gestured to the dignitary, who continuously scrawled with his quill. "Lord Chancellor, have you record of Colin Campbell's death?"

"None, your highness."

The queen frowned. "Seven years and no word, you say?"

"Aye, your highness."

"It does rather sound as if he's met his end. Have you word from anyone else in his retinue?"

"No, your highness."

"Then the evidence most certainly speaks of dread." The queen's gaze darted to her clerk then back to Margaret. "Shall we record his death? He has issue, no?"

"No…I mean, yes, Colin has two sons, but I'd prefer to wait to declare him dead." She clapped a hand over her mouth. "Not yet, anyway."

"Very well." The queen dismissed Margaret with a flick of her wrist.

"Please…have you news of the Crusade?" Margaret stammered. She still had so many questions to ask. "Any word from the Pope?"

Shaking her head, the queen looked away with disinterested eyes.

"Come." In a blur, the page grasped Margaret's elbow and ushered her to the outer chamber.

The hum of voices buzzed around her, eyes slanted her way, the room spinning. So that was it? A few words with the queen only to walk away with no news whatsoever?

Her trip to Edinburgh had been a complete and utter waste of time. She stumbled toward the door, pushing people out of her path. She couldn't breathe. Not a soul had heard from Colin or his men.

He'd vanished.

Staggering to the courtyard, she found Mevan. "I must purchase some fabric and we'll be on our way."

He knitted his bushy brows. "Did you see the queen?"

She nodded, casting her eyes downward. "No news."

"I'm sorry, m'lady."

Pressing her hands to her face, she choked back tears. "It was worth a try."

She could no longer hope.

After the noon meal, Margaret rode out with her cohort of twelve men, including Mevan. The path from Edinburgh to Kilchurn was long and arduous, but she didn't regret her decision to go. At least now she had her own proof and wasn't relying on anyone else's word. Colin and his men disappeared somewhere between Dunstaffnage and Rome, never to be heard from again.

***

The third day after leaving Edinburgh, Margaret and her guard rode into the dense forest along Loch na Bi. She'd traveled this trail several times in the past, even camped here once. Surrounded by steep sloping hills, there was only one narrow path in and out.

A chill rippled across her skin, almost like a warning. She couldn't put her finger on it. She wanted to stop and listen, but that would be silly. There was no place to gather. Force them all to pull up single file while she listened? For what? Definitely inane and pointless. The sooner they passed through the thick wood, the closer they'd be to Loch Awe. They'd reach Kilchurn before nightfall.

Halfway, her skin again prickled. The hair on her nape stood on end. Eyes scanning the dense forest, she fingered the dagger in her pocket.

Bellowing shrieks echoed from behind the trees. Before Margaret could blink, a man raced toward her, a thick iron hammer in his hand. His eyes were wide and wild. Roaring like a madman, he bared his teeth and groped for her arm.

No time to think. Margaret pitched to the side and swiped her knife across his face.

Blood streamed down his cheek. Snarling, he tried to yank her from her mount. "Ye bitch, ye cut me."

She held tight to the pommel. In a lightning-fast move, he clutched his fingers around her throat. She tried to wrench away, but his hands clamped like a vise. She couldn't breathe. Her voice box croaked with choking sounds. The world spun.

Margaret clawed at his hands, gasping for life-giving air.

Blood running cold, she thrashed, trying to free herself from the man's brutal grasp. Her fingers tightened around her dagger. Clenching her teeth, she drew upon her remaining strength and plunged the blade into his shoulder. Wailing, he released his hold, brutally swinging his weapon. The weighty hammer slammed into her arm.

Bone crunched. Margaret screamed, digging her heels into her mare's barrel. Searing pain radiated up her arm. Was the bone shattered?

The mare leapt over a mass of fighting men. Her arm jostled with mind-numbing pain. Mevan appeared from nowhere and latched on to her bridle. Galloping at full speed, he led Margaret from the mayhem.

She clutched her arm against her body. Warm blood oozed through her sleeve and dripped to her skirts. She dared glance down and push her sleeve back. The skin was broken, and a large knot swelled under the throbbing pain.

"Are you all right, m'lady?" Mevan hollered.

"My arm is broken," she managed a high-pitched reply.

"Hold on. I'll have you to the castle in no time."

Mevan drove the horses hard, the steady grunt of air forced through their nostrils with every pounding step. White froth bubbled on the mare's neck. Margaret's arm jostled. She gritted her teeth against the jarring, and focused her mind on the trail, on getting home to her boys—anything but the fearsome face of the barbarian who attacked her.

The forest opened.

Kilchurn loomed ahead.

"Open the gate," Mevan boomed.

He rode straight into the courtyard and gingerly pulled Margaret from her horse, cradling her in his arms. "Summon the healer at once."

Margaret placed a shaking hand on his mailed chest. "Thank you. I can walk." Her head spun.

"I wouldn't hear of it, m'lady. I'll see you to your chamber."

He carried her up the winding stairwell, straight to the comfort of her bed. Again she thanked him. "Do you know who attacked us?"

Mevan's brow creased. "Never seen them before— outlaws, for certain."

"What about the other men?"

"We should know soon. Any survivors won't be far behind."

Alana dashed into the chamber. "What on earth happened?" She took one look at Margaret's arm and slapped her hand over her mouth with a gasp.

Mevan stepped beside her. "We were set upon by outlaws. Lady Margaret was struck by a hammer."

"Heavens, no!" Horror flashed in Alana's eyes. "Who did this?"

"A band of twenty or more." Mevan tapped Margaret's shoulder. "I'll gather an army and leave at once. I'll find these brigands and ensure they're brought to justice."

Margaret nodded and cast a grim frown at Alana. "There will be more men to tend."

"My heavens. But first I need to set your arm. The sooner I do it, the cleaner it will heal."

A clammy sweat covered Margaret's skin. She'd seen bones set before, and undoubtedly the cure hurt far worse than the initial blow.

Alana worked quickly. She gathered two flat pieces of wood, a stick and rolled bandages, then ushered in two sentries to hold Margaret's shoulders down. "I'll not lie to you, m'lady. This will hurt."

Alana held up the stick and Margaret opened her mouth, willing back her urge to vomit as she bit down on it. Her heart thundered, her body trembled and she nearly wet herself. Margaret clenched her abdominal muscles taut. She couldn't lose complete control. When Alana stretched Margaret's arm to the side, she jolted and hissed.

Panting, she stared at the canopy above the bed and ground her teeth into the stick. In one quick move, Alana jerked the bone into place. Bucking, Margaret screamed bloody murder through her teeth. Stars flashed through her eyes. Her throat burned. Her body convulsed beneath the steely hands holding her to the mattress.

Blinking once, all went black.

***

Margaret had no idea how much time had passed when consciousness returned. Her arm throbbed. She splayed her fingers, met with a sharp jolt of pain that traveled up her shoulder and rattled in her skull. She licked her parched lips and cracked her eyes open.

Ewen jumped up from a chair beside the bed. "Margaret?"

She feigned a smile. Why did her heart not flutter at the sight of him? "How long have you been here?"

"A day. You've been asleep for two."

She tried to push herself up and grimaced. *My stars, that hurt.* Margaret used her good elbow and scooted her hips beneath her. Resting awkwardly against the pillows, she raised her gaze to Ewen's face. "And my guard? Did they all make it back? Has Mevan found the outlaws?"

Ewen placed his hand on her shoulder. "Och, you've been unconscious for two days and you're worried about the guard?"

She shrugged away from his touch. "I most certainly am."

"Kirk dead, three with minor injuries—they'll live." He sat back in his chair. "Mevan and my man, Ragnar, brought in four outlaws this morn. They'll hang on the morrow."

Margaret hated to hang any living soul, but outlaws had no place on this earth. She swiped her hand across her forehead. "Why?"

"Thievery. What else?"

"I cannot believe it." She shook the cobwebs out of her head. She must visit Kirk's kin straight away and pay them alms. "Would you please call the chambermaid? I'd like to dress."

"I think you should stay abed for another day at least." He crossed his arms and made no attempt to assist her—not one fluff of a pillow. "What on earth were you thinking?"

Margaret's arm ached. "Pardon?"

"You went to Edinburgh without me."

So that was what had his braies in a twist? "I needed to purchase some fabric for my wedding gown." She softened her voice. "I wanted to surprise you."

His lips formed a thin line. "This is exactly why we should be married straight away."

He knelt beside the bed and clasped Margaret's hand between his palms. "When I received word you'd been hurt, I nearly died." His eyes shifted sideways, and then he kissed her fingers. "Do you know how worried I was?"

She sighed. Of course he would be worried. Her trip to Edinburgh was reckless, but now she'd returned with no news of Colin, she could accept her lot. Surely she could not repeat that to Ewen. He'd never understand. "I apologize. Though I'd assumed a guard of twelve men was sufficient, I was clearly wrong." But they would have been attacked whether Ewen was with them or not. What if he'd been killed? Where would she be then?

"Once we are wed, you shall never again be out of my sight." He raised his chin and brushed his lips across hers. A flicker sparked deep inside. Yes, Ewen cared for her deeply, and she would find it in her heart to return his feelings. She owed him that.

Chapter Thirty-Four

The Isle of Rhodes, 19th June, 1462

Colin stepped off the transport onto the pier. He still couldn't remember anything from the two weeks after the battle on Rhodes—couldn't believe he had survived. After he'd recovered from his bludgeoning, the fighting continued endlessly. The days blurred together. A black hole stretched his heart. He'd stopped writing to Margaret. He'd die in this hell. No question. He would die, just like all the others.

Of the fifty men who accompanied him, only a handful remained—Maxwell, Hugh, William and a few more. His armor hung heavily from his limbs, as if the weight of the entire fortress rested on his shoulders alone.

He turned to Maxwell. "Come. If I don't remove this armor soon, my blood will boil and I'll be as dead as a roasted pheasant." Sweat saturated his doublet and braies beneath—dampness mixed with dirt, salt and blood. His skin chafed.

In his cell, Maxwell quickly untied and unbuckled Colin's walking "oven." The squire had reached his majority five years ago, and yet he continued to serve the Black Knight without a word to request his own promotion. Colin took a deep breath as his breastplate was removed. "'Tis time you became a knight."

Maxwell stopped mid-motion. "M'lord?"

"You're of noble birth. You have proved yourself in battle ten times over. 'Tis time I made it official before we're all cut down."

He looked as if the thought had never dawned on him…or he figured he'd be dead before the opportunity arose. "But who will be your squire?"

"How about the Earl of Argyll?" A voice boomed from the passageway. "He squired for old Lord Glenorchy once before."

Colin's gaze darted to the door. It couldn't be… "*Earl?*"

"Aye, a lot has changed in seven years, uncle." Argyll stepped inside Colin's cell and fanned his nose. "Good God, you smell like gas from a privy."

Colin passed a hand across his unbelieving eyes. "Have you become so soft you've forgotten the stench of battle?" *Is this a hallucination? Argyll? Here?*

"Soft? I'll say things are anything but soft in Scotland."

Blessed be the Virgin Mary. It is he. Colin's knees grew weak at the mention of his homeland. He staggered forward and pulled Argyll into his embrace. "My God. 'Tis good to see you."

The younger man gave him a firm clap on the back and coughed. "What the devil happened to you, and why have we not heard one word from you in seven long years?"

Colin stepped back. "What? Aside from the two years I spent in a Turkish dungeon, I wrote once a week, sometimes twice."

"Prison? Really?" Argyll scratched his head. "Word in Scotland is you were killed."

"Nearly was—more than once." Colin grabbed two drying cloths and tossed one to Argyll. "Come. We can continue in the bathhouse. Not a single missive has reached Lady Margaret, you say?"

"Not a one." Argyll followed him out the door and down the passage. "Worse, she's engaged to marry Ewen MacCorkodale."

Colin jolted as if he'd been dealt a blow to the gut. "God's teeth." His throat closed. He leaned against the cloister wall. "I…I've only survived each day knowing she was waiting for me."

"We must hurry. According to Effie, your lady has put off his advances until the completion of Kilchurn's chapel. But time's running out. It's due to be completed this summer."

"The chapel's nearly finished?" A million thoughts flooded his mind. Margaret must have completed the tower house. *Margaret*. "Did she? Is she? How is? What about?"

"Slow down." Argyll shook his head. "I must admit, my affairs at court have kept me away from Kilchurn *and* Inverary. I haven't been to see Margaret since John was christened near six years ago."

"John?"

"Aye, your son."

"A son?" Colin ran his fingers down his long beard. "I knew she was with child, but never allowed myself to dream…"

Argyll beckoned him forward. "I've arranged a transport for the morrow. After you bathe, you must pack your belongings. I shall tell you all on the journey home."

Colin pushed off from the wall. The news had dealt such a blow, his legs could barely hold his own weight.

He'd beg an audience with the grand master this night and gain a pardon. Surely he wouldn't balk. No knight could be expected to remain in Rhodes while a snake slithered between the linens of his bed.

Colin nearly vomited before he climbed into the steamy washtub. He made quick work of cleansing the stench from his body. Argyll did the same in the basin beside him. Colin ran a rag over his face. God in heaven, he needed a healthy tot of good whisky. He clenched his fists. He had to ask. "Does she love him?"

Argyll lowered his cloth and frowned. "I left before I could speak to your lady. But what do you expect? She has two boys to raise, your dynasty to supervise."

"But does she love him?"

"I know not. Rumors spread of your death. What other choice has she whether she loves him or not?"

Colin threw his head back and roared, releasing years of pent-up anguish. How could this have happened? Never once had she left the forefront of his mind. Had someone schemed against him? He could not allow MacCorkodale to move into his castle, change the deeds on his land, claim Colin's property as his own.

But Margaret, his dear, sweet, beautiful Margaret. Why had she given up hope? He still wore the ring on his finger. He hadn't sent her the token.

Did she still wear hers?

He froze.

What if she no longer loved him?

Chapter Thirty-Five

Kilchurn Castle, 15th July, 1462

Alana insisted Margaret wear the splint and sling for two months. One more grueling month to endure. The MacGregor woman wouldn't even allow her to remove it for the wedding.

But that was the only thing Margaret could fault her for. Alana had shown herself as a God-given angel so many times, even from the first day they'd met. She'd known it was a risk, yet she stood her ground and spoke true about Walter MacCorkodale. That seemed ever so long ago.

Margaret used a key she'd found hidden in Colin's sideboard and slid it into a keyhole of his chest. She and Alana nearly had his things packed, and this was the last. Since he'd left it locked, she'd respected his privacy and kept the chest that way. In fact, his whole room remained locked after she'd moved everything to Kilchurn.

Soon another man would occupy this chamber. Margaret's heart twisted, weighing heavily in her chest with a familiar pang. Alas, Colin hadn't spent one minute within its walls. He'd never see the landscape tapestries she'd ordered, nor would he lie beneath the forest-green silk comforter she'd once thought suited him. Honestly, her memory was fading and she could scarcely remember the contours of his face.

The hinges squeaked when Alana shut the lid of a trunk. "What will you do with all this?"

Margaret released the key and surveyed the three large trunks. "Perhaps I shall stow them in the tower. The boys will most likely want to search through Colin's effects when they come of age."

"Good thinking, m'lady."

Margaret turned the key and opened the small chest's lid. It was filled with neatly stacked parchment and missives. She reached in and grasped the top document. The penmanship scrolled with lavish strokes, and she moved to the candle to better read.

By royal charter, Colin Campbell, Lord of Glenorchy, hereby submits petition for the annulment of his marriage to Margaret Campbell, Lady of Glenorchy…

Margaret froze. Prickling heat fired across her skin. *God strike me dead where I stand.*

The parchment fell from her trembling fingers. Gasping for breath, she clutched her broken arm to her stomach and bent forward. Bitter bile stung her throat. Head spinning, she staggered forward and rested a hand on the sideboard.

"Lady Margaret." Alana rushed across the floor. "Are you unwell? Goodness, your face has drained of all color."

Margaret covered her mouth with her palm, trying to swallow. "He was…" She couldn't say it.

"What?"

"He…he…" She met her friend's concerned gaze. "Colin was planning an annulment."

"No." Alana picked up the paper and studied it. "I do not believe it. Lord Colin was completely, utterly in love with you when he set sail. Of that I am absolutely certain."

Margaret stared at the document like it was a missive from hell. "Th-things didn't start well for us. I feared he was going to send me back to Loch Rannoch more than once." Tears stung her eyes. She shook her finger at the parchment. "An-and I was right."

Alana studied the document. "I cannot read much, but it doesn't look like it is signed."

Margaret reached out then snapped her hand back. "On what date was it drawn?"

Alana looked at it blankly and shrugged. "Not certain, m'lady."

"Oh heavens." Margaret paced. She must know when he'd drawn the papers. If it was after he'd been knocked out by William, he would have deceived her for certain.

Oh Mother Mary, help. I'm not sure I want to know.

Margaret cast her mind back. She'd been married on the eighth of October, 1455. Colin's accident had been a month or two later. Palms perspiring, she grasped the document. Trying to hold it steady, again she read the first line. She choked back an involuntary heave.

Have I been played for a fool all these years?

Scanning to the end, she found no date. Stunned, she let out a slow, ragged breath. Annulment papers were the last thing she thought she'd find in Colin's secret chest.

Alana's feet shuffled. "Anything?"

Margaret glanced up. "'Tis not dated."

"Is it signed?"

Margaret shook her head and dropped her arm. "Nay."

Alana slapped a hand to her chest. "Then he acted out of anger and didn't follow through."

Margaret tore the parchment down the middle and shoved it back in the chest. "I've no idea what to think." She slammed the lid and buried her face in her hand. "What if he never did intend to return?"

The words attacked her heart like knives. She wanted to race up to the battlements with his vile wooden box and hurl it into the depths of Loch Awe. Though she tried to hold her torment in, sobs boiled up from the depths of her gut and racked her shoulders. How could he have deceived her?

She'd waited seven long years—built his keep—raised his children. And he was going to *ruin* her?

"My lady, of course he planned to come back. If I know Colin Campbell, he would have done anything to return to you and the boys." Alana pulled Margaret into a matronly embrace and smoothed a hand over her shoulder. "There, there. Lord Colin loved you. I remember how he gazed upon you at Duncan's christening. His eyes were filled with adoration as if you were the only woman in the chapel."

Margaret closed her eyes and forced out a staccato breath. *If only I could believe it*. Through her tears, the silver ring flickered with the candlelight. *And what of his token?*

***

She'd been wearing the brace for six sennights. The miserable arm ached and itched and kept her awake half the night. Margaret flexed her fingers and made a fist. The pain was getting easier to bear.

"Does it still hurt, Mummy?" asked John.

She glanced up from her bench in the garden. "'Tis coming good. I'll be happy when I can remove this sling. The wretched thing drives me mad."

"Throw down your sword, we have you surrounded," Duncan hollered, pointing his wooden weapon at John.

The younger boy whipped around with a challenging stance. "I'm protecting her ladyship. I will die defending her honor."

Where did he learn such chivalry? Margaret chuckled and mussed John's hair. "My knight in shining armor, come to rescue me."

Duncan lowered his sword. "I want to be the good knight."

Margaret beckoned him to sit beside her. "You can both be good knights, for a man is not truly a knight unless there is goodness in his heart."

She looked at their angelic faces—both reminding her so much of Colin. But their father had been a fantasy to them, a knight in blackened armor who existed only in bedtime stories. "Three days hence, you shall have a new stepfather." Her insides cringed.

John scrunched up his face. "You mean Laird Mac...Cor...dale?"

"Aye. He'll see to your training as you become men." She'd made the right choice for her boys.

Duncan pushed out his bottom lip. "But Laird Ewen's always so serious."

"I don't think he likes us," John said.

Margaret tapped John's nose. "Why?"

"He frowns a lot and tells us to be quiet." John affected a scowl. "'Wheesht,' he says all the time."

"He never plays with us." Duncan rapped his wooden sword on the bench.

True, Ewen was serious, and he didn't have children of his own. But he'd promised to become more involved with the boys after he moved to Kilchurn. "He'll love you as his own once he resides in the lord's chamber."

Duncan planted his feet with a look of defiance. "But that's Father's chamber."

Margaret's heart wanted to burst. She still hadn't recovered from finding the annulment papers. It was as if she and the boys had been living a lie. "Do you even remember your father?"

His lips quivered. Margaret reached out and pulled the boy to her breast. "Laird Ewen will help you lads become knights and teach you the rules of court."

John rested his head against her shoulder. "I don't want to fight or go on a crusade and be killed."

"You can become whatever you want, John."

Duncan pushed away. "But I want my real father to come home. I don't need a stepfather who looks at me like he hates me. He won't be nice. I know it." He turned and ran.

"Duncan!" Margaret watched him race through the garden path and into the castle. She wasn't the only person who needed to become accustomed to the changes. And change things would...in three days, to be exact.

Chapter Thirty-Six

The Firth of Lorn, 2ⁿᵈ August, 1462

Early morning, Colin alighted from the galley with Argyll and his men. Without his ship, the journey took far too long, changing transports in port cities until they chartered a galley in London. Colin touched Maxwell's shoulder. "Take the men and ready the horses. Arrange for a wagon to haul our gear. Meet us at Effie's cottage. We'll ride from there."

Though he could use a bath, Colin took Argyll and headed toward Effie's home. They walked past the chapel where Duncan was christened, and also where Jonet and Mariot were buried. So much time had passed. Everything looked the same, yet different, almost odd.

Argyll stood behind Colin while he rapped on the wooden door.

"A moment," Effie's brittle voice came from within.

The door creaked open. Colin gasped. She'd aged so much, bent over a cane, her hair completely white.

She gaped at him. "Lord Jesus almighty, you look like you fought with the devil and lost. If it weren't for your eyes, I never would have recognized you." She had uncouth spirit. Some things hadn't changed.

Colin ran his hand down the beard that now reached his navel. "We stepped off the ship and came straight here."

She gaped at him. "With not a moment to spare. Where have you been? Why were you gone so long? You're a stranger to your children." Yes, this was the outspoken Effie he'd always known.

Colin glanced at Argyll and sighed. If only she knew he'd been fighting against Satan for seven long years. "May we come in?"

She stepped aside and held the door wide. "Yes, apologies. I must be losing my manners in me old age. Sit at the table and I'll fetch some bread and cheese."

Though Colin was starving, there wasn't time. "No need, mistress." He pulled out the bench for her. "I bid you sit."

Effie hobbled over, a puff of flatulence tooting from her backside. She ignored her impropriety and lowered herself onto the seat. "You are aware today is the Lammas Day Feast?"

"Is it?"

Her black gaze darted to Argyll. "He doesn't know?"

Argyll straddled the bench across from her. "What?"

She rolled her eyes to the ceiling. "Lady Margaret told Laird Ewen she would marry him the day after Lammas Feast unless she received word Colin lived." She shook a gnarled finger. "How could you be away such a long time without nary a word?"

He plopped on the bench beside her and cradled his head in his hand. "I sent parcels of letters near every sennight. Argyll said not a one reached her."

Effie slammed her cane into the floor. "That milk-livered swine. I smell a rat as large as Dunstaffnage Castle."

"MacCorkodale?" The name flowed bitter on his tongue.

"Aye, who else?"

"Does she…" Colin wanted to be sick, but he had to ask. "Is she in love with him?"

The old woman's face pruned when she pursed her lips, but her eyes were fierce. "Would she have put him off all this time?"

Colin grasped her hand. "I must know."

"I've been retired for ages—all is hearsay brought from Kilchurn. I've not seen Lady Margaret since Eastertide three years ago."

He slumped. How ridiculous he would look if she shunned him.

A tattered surcoat by the door caught his eye. "May I borrow that?"

Her face twisted in question. "The old coat my son wears to tend the pigs?"

"Aye, you said I look like shite. I may as well dress like it too."

"What the devil?" Argyll said.

Colin grinned for the first time in—well, probably in seven years. "I have a plan."

***

They drove the horses hard the twenty miles to the mouth of Loch Awe, the site of Kilchurn Castle—Colin's castle. Before the trees gave way to grassy lea, Colin signaled for the men to stop. In the distance, the keep grandly towered above the loch. Kilchurn stood paramount, ruling over the pomp and beauty of the scene. Verdant mountains, torrents, lakes and wood united to pay it homage. Indeed, his castle had become a magnificent and formidable fortress—more modern and grander than Dunstaffnage, and peaceful in its mighty setting. *Ah, Lady Margaret. How much she has accomplished.*

"Colin?" Argyll said. "What *is* this plan of yours?"

Colin waffled between drawing his sword and leading his men on a charge to take the castle, and his original scheme. He ground his back molars and pointed. "Take the men to the old stable and wait. I do not want anyone to recognize us."

He dismounted and handed his reins to Maxwell. He removed his cloak and claymore as well, passing them to the young knight who still acted as squire. After hiding his dirk in his belt, beneath the peasant's surcoat, Colin pushed a tarnished helm over his head and traipsed through the mud. Kilchurn's gates were open wide, welcoming all to the feast. Passing through the portcullis, he stopped and stared at the capstone above the heavy wooden gate. His initials were carved into the sandstone beside the Campbell crest. Next to that were etched Margaret's initials. *How long ago had she commissioned this work?*

Laughing, people pushed past, paying him no mind. He recognized one. *Mevan, Margaret's guard.*

With gooseflesh rising on his arms and along his nape, he walked inside the gatehouse—a vaulted ceiling of stone—a dungeon on his left—unoccupied. Smells from the kitchen wafted—freshly baked bread for the Lammas Feast, roasted pork and something sweet. *Apple tart.* He salivated.

A stranger in his own castle, stepping into the busy courtyard, Colin drifted as if he were not inside his body. Music filled the air. Children laughed and played a game of tag. A boy ploughed straight into him. Craning his neck, the lad's brown eyes looked stunned. "Sorry, sir. I...I wasn't looking."

The corner of Colin's mouth ticked up, and he placed his hand on the boy's shoulder. It was almost as if he were looking into a mirror that took him back in time. "Are you John?" His voice quavered.

The boy stepped away, his eyes wary. "Yes, sir."

A young lass skipped up to John and slapped him on the back. "You're tagged."

Colin's son turned and ran toward the mob of scattering children.

His heart in his throat, Colin's gaze darted from one young face to the next. Which one was Duncan? Darker hair, slightly taller than John—it had to be his eldest son using a smaller boy to shield himself from getting tagged. Colin laughed aloud.

No one spoke to him. No one even looked his way.

The ram's horn blared, announcing the feast. Everyone headed into the tower. *The Great Hall.* Colin knew exactly where it was—at least on the drawings. He waited for the guests to pass, watching John and Duncan shove each other through the door. It was all he could do not to pull them into his embrace and tell them who he was.

Ascending the stairs, his breath stuttered. Everything was exactly as he'd planned it and more. Lined with richly embroidered and colorful tapestries, the hall could rival any other in the kingdom. Tables filled with people circumvented the walls. Immediately, his gaze snapped to the dais at the far end. His breath whooshed from his lungs. Far more beautiful than his memory, Margaret sat at the head table, wearing a crimson gown, her hair held back by a conical hennin. The styles had changed a bit. Lord have mercy, she was a vision.

His gaze shifting downward, he gasped. Every muscle in his body tensed.

Her left arm hung in a sling. Oh God, what happened? Had she fallen? Had she other injuries? Colin should have been on hand to protect her. He drew upon the last remaining ounces of self-restraint and resisted rushing to the dais and groveling before her. What had he done? Why had he stayed away for *seven* years?

Alas, she looked like a queen. His heart twisted and yearned for her touch, until Ewen MacCorkodale stepped beside her and kissed her cheek. Colin clenched his fists. Margaret gave Ewen a nod and reached for her goblet. The rogue took the seat beside her, his eyes not leaving her lovely face.

She glanced up.

Colin snapped his gaze away and sat on a bench at the lowest table. His gut churned. Seeing his enemy plying his wife with a kiss ignited a fire burning so hot, his fingers itched to pull the dirk hidden beneath his costume.

The kitchen door opened, and servants filed to the high tables. Their trenchers laden with fresh breads and roasted pork, Colin's mouth watered. He could practically taste the meat.

The hall rumbled with excited voices, laughing and recounting stories. Behind him, a Campbell man had helped birth a calf that morning. Beside him, an old man tapped Colin on the shoulder. "Mind if we sit with you, mate?"

Colin tilted his helm so it partially covered his eyes, and gestured to the bench. "Please do."

"Hopefully there'll be a few scraps left by the time the trenchers make it this far."

Colin could have broken his nose with one blow. "I'm sure Lady Margaret has planned enough for all," he grumbled, his voice far gruffer than he would have liked.

The man's wife climbed onto the bench across from them. "Aye, she's a generous woman. I'll say."

Colin tried to converse with the couple, while continually glancing over his shoulder. Margaret talked and laughed, but not once did she touch the man beside her.

A servant stopped and offered Colin the quaich—the communal cup, filled with Scottish whisky passed to every soul at a Highland feast. Colin held up his palm and shook his head. "I'll not be served by any hand but that of Lady Margaret."

The servant eyed him from head to toe, his mouth forming an O. "My heavens, a proud beggar? You should be eating the scraps off the floor."

Colin fingered his dirk. He'd not soon forget this servant's hospitality. Clenching his gut against the urge to teach the moron a lesson, he firmly struck the table with his fist and eyed the man with inarguable intensity. "Go fetch your lady."

With a sarcastic grunt, the servant stuck his nose in the air and traipsed to the dais.

When he whispered in Margaret's ear, her gaze snapped up. Colin's heart stopped. She smiled at him pleasantly, but no familiarity crossed her face. Next to her, Ewen shook his head. She placed a calming hand on the bastard's shoulder and then, with that same hand, plucked the quaich from the servant's fingers.

***

The large man sitting at the lowest table stared from under his old helm like a starved wolf. The wide nose guard almost completely hid his face. He appeared to have a strong back, and Margaret wondered what tragedy had transpired to turn him into a beggar. With an unkempt and outrageously long beard, he'd certainly never been to Kilchurn before. *All guests must be honored.*

She poured the contents of the two-handled quaich in a tankard, placed it on the table and filled it with her finest whisky. Blast her one-armed immobility.

Ewen pushed his chair back. "You cannot be serious? I should throw the old beggar out."

"You'll do no such thing. This is Lammas. Our doors are open to everyone."

Ewen grumbled under his breath, but stood and bowed. Margaret was honestly relieved he didn't accompany her to the far end of the hall. If he preferred not to show charity, he could remain on the dais.

The indigent man had intense posture. He watched her approach. The full beard hid the exposed part of his face—so long, it almost rested in his lap. With ragged clothes, Margaret assumed he'd smell foul. When she neared, only the faint musk of a man who perhaps had journeyed a long distance reached her nose. Gooseflesh rose across her skin. *Odd.*

She offered her most amiable smile. "Thank you for sharing our table, sir."

He did not meet her gaze, but bent his bearded head toward the pewter quaich in her hand. His helm prevented her from seeing his eyes. Her skin again tingled. Had she met this man before?

She held out the cup.

His tongue slipped through his lips and moistened them. Large hands moved slowly to accept the pewter vessel. "My thanks for your gracious kindness."

The rough pad of his pointer finger brushed hers. Burning heat radiated from the spot he'd touched, and she rubbed it against her skirts. Surely she must have seen this man somewhere. Her mind raced. He didn't speak like a beggar.

Raising the quaich to his lips, his hands quavered slightly.

Margaret's heart twisted. *He must be starving.*

The helm cast a shadow across his face while he drank. A satisfied rumble rolled from his chest. He lowered the cup and bowed his chin. "You have generously served me your finest. I am in your debt, m'lady." His voice was gruff, and he kept his eyes downcast, passing her the quaich.

Margaret reached for it. A tiny metallic sound tinkled inside.

She glanced down.

The token!

He removed his helm. Dark brown eyes met hers.

The quaich crashed to the floor. Gasping, her hand flew to her chest.

Colin.

"My God." Margaret's knees buckled. A cry erupted from the deepest recess of her heart. Her hand clasped his grizzly face. Falling, her fingers smoothed down rock-hard shoulders. Tears streamed from her eyes. Her entire body quaked. Downward she dropped until her knees hit the floor. "Husband. Forgive, forgive, forgive me."

The room spun.

She crouched over his feet, her tears splashing his leather boots. She cared not if they were covered with mud. Tenderly, she brushed shaking fingers over them and kissed each one. "Praise be to God. You have returned."

Chapter Thirty-Seven

Kilchurn Castle, 2nd August, 1462

Watching his wife grovel at his feet whilst her arm hung in a sling was more than Colin could bear. He gently grasped her shoulders. "*Mo Leannan*," he said in a low voice, helping her to stand. "You're hurt." He cupped her beautiful face in his hands. "Let me gaze upon you."

"Colin... What?" She leaned her cheek into his palm. "Why..."

Footsteps thundered from the dais. "Remove your hands from her, you ruttish, fly-bitten beggar," Ewen bellowed, bounding toward them, shoving tables while people scurried out of his path.

Snatching his dirk from its hiding place, Colin spun and faced the backstabber. MacCorkodale had been behind every thorn that had ever plagued him. With all the hatred built from years of fighting soulless men, this was his nemesis, his most loathed enemy.

Ewen stopped midstride. The bastard's face twisted with surprise. Guilt. Then horror. He sidestepped. His gaze shot to the door. Pushing a woman aside, he darted toward the courtyard.

With a roar, the Black Knight started after him.

Margaret wrapped her fingers around his wrist. "No." She stumbled with the force of Colin's retreat.

He stopped midstride. "I must avenge you."

Her green eyes softened his lust for blood. "He showed me kindness."

All guests' eyes were upon them. John and Duncan raced in and clung to their mother's skirts, confusion written on their faces.

Mevan followed, his sword drawn, his expression grave. "Lady Margaret, back away."

"Stop," she cried. "Can you not see? 'Tis Lord Glenorchy."

"My God." Mevan lowered his weapon.

Colin shoved the dirk in his belt and inclined his head toward Margaret's guard. "My men are in the old stable. Tell them MacCorkodale is on the run. They'll know what to do. Tell them to retrieve my letters first."

"Letters?" Margaret stepped beside him. "What letters?"

"I sent parcel upon parcel of missives to you. It became known to me you received not a one."

"Is all well, Mummy?" John asked.

Margaret didn't look at the lad right away. Her face blanked with a sharp gasp. Then, as if dazed by Colin's news, she looked between the angelic faces. "Lads. This is your father."

They regarded him, astonishment and wonder on each face.

Now was not the time to chase after vengeance. Colin removed the grungy surcoat and kneeled. "I've missed so much. Look how big you are." He mussed Duncan's hair. "You ran to your mother's side to protect her. You men have done well in my stead, and have made me proud." Somehow, he managed to keep his voice from quaking.

The boys' eyes grew round as silver sovereigns. They exchanged bewildered glances. Together they wrapped their arms around Colin's neck.

"Da!" John exclaimed.

Tears streaked down Duncan's face. "I knew you'd come. My da is the most fearless knight in all Christendom."

Colin shut his eyes and stood, holding, hugging the lads in his arms. Tears glistening upon her cheeks, Margaret wrapped one arm around them, her smile lighting up the hall.

The room erupted in applause. Even the rude servant clapped his hands and bowed. Mercy, how Colin wished they weren't surrounded by a hundred guests. He had seven years upon which to catch up, and he wanted to start now. With a lad on each hip, he inclined his head toward the dais. "I believe we have a feast to continue, m'lady."

Margaret's smile radiated through the hall. "That we do, m'lord."

While they walked, the pipers filled the hall with a resounding pibroch of the Campbells. Benches scraped across the floor. Every soul stood and sang with passion. For the first time, Colin climbed the steps to the Kilchurn dais and joined in, singing in his deep bass, complemented by the youthful voices of his children and Margaret's sultry alto.

***

It was very late when the guests bedded down or took their leave. Colin followed Margaret to the nursery to check on the boys. Both lads were bundled in their beds, sound asleep.

Colin couldn't stop looking at Margaret. How could she be so much more beautiful than he'd remembered? He'd put her on a pedestal, but seeing her in the flesh exceeded all expectation. And there he stood beside her, his beard unkempt, his body in need of a bath. How could she bear the sight of him?

He carried a candle in one hand and threaded her fingers through his other. She led him along the passageway of his castle. Everything was foreign, not familiar like a man's home ought. *Give it time.*

They passed a door on the right. "My chamber adjoins with yours."

Good. Then next would be his. Opening the door, Colin swallowed. The fire had been lit, as had the candles atop the hearth. Numb, he stood at the threshold. His bed had been moved from Dunstaffnage, as had his sideboard, upholstered chairs and settee. The plaid rug on the floor was new, as were the magnificent landscape tapestries and bedclothes. Yet nothing had a homey feel. Margaret must have transferred his things and locked the door, except for the occasional dusting and clearing of cobwebs.

"Is something amiss, m'lord?"

Colin jolted, then chuckled. "No. All is nicely appointed, thank you." Time had put an awkward distance between them.

She glanced sideways. "Would you prefer it if I left you alone, m'lord?"

"Colin." He grasped her shoulders and stepped close. "Call me Colin." Closing his eyes, he pressed his lips against her forehead. A warm heartbeat pulsed beneath his lips. Seven years of war melted from his icy heart.

She chuckled. "You kissed me like that on our wedding night."

He led her inside and shut the door. "Do not remind me. I'll carry the shame of my actions that night to my grave."

She shrugged. "You were in mourning. 'Tis to be forgiven."

"Mayhap by you." He walked her to the settee. "Shall we sit for a moment?"

Margaret complied, and smoothed her skirts with her one good hand. So many questions coursed through his mind. Had she fallen in love with MacCorkodale? He couldn't bring himself to ask. The hall had been too loud to hold any kind of conversation. They'd danced and laughed and stared at each other, but not much of anything had been said or understood.

"Tell me again. What happened to your arm?" If MacCorkodale had anything to do with it, he'd die the slowest, most painful death imaginable.

Margaret ran her hand over the sling. "'Tis nearly healed." She blushed adorably. "I spirited away to Edinburgh to gain an audience with the queen. Before I married Ewen, I had to know if she'd received word from you or the order as to your whereabouts."

Colin cringed when she uttered that bastard's name. "Why did you need to be secretive about your trip?"

She closed her eyes and pinched the bridge of her nose. "Ewen would have insisted on accompanying me."

"And you didn't want him to?"

"No." She plied him with a pleading gaze. "He'd convinced me you were dead, but I needed more proof."

Colin's heart squeezed. "I take it the queen couldn't give it to you?"

"Nay."

"Did MacCorkodale do anything to harm you?" He clenched his fists against the hate roiling in his gut.

"No. Mostly, he acted gentlemanly."

His back stiffened. "Mostly?"

"There was an occasion or two when I felt he wanted to push me too far, though he backed down when I made my wishes clear."

Colin knew exactly how the spineless vermin weaseled his way into her good graces. MacCorkodale would have pushed and taken advantage of her affable nature until she snapped. He ground his knuckles into the seat cushion.

She sighed. "I digress. A dozen Campbell sentries accompanied me. On the narrow path along Loch na Bi, we were besieged by outlaws. I was hit with a hammer before Mevan could spirit me away."

Och, twice attacked whilst traveling? Christ. Colin rubbed his forehead. "I never should have left you alone."

She splayed her palm. "What could you do? Go against the Pope and the edict of God?"

"Only man wages war, and when you are in the middle of it, 'tis hell on earth." He hated that it had consumed him. "I should have been here with you and the boys."

Margaret fell silent for a time. The crackling of the fire filled the chamber. Colin studied her profile—refined, regal, a goddess.

She caught him staring and smiled sadly. "What happened in Rome?"

"I was stationed in Rhodes, mostly." Colin swallowed, then groaned. "Too much killing. Mehmed and his Ottoman Empire are hellbent on claiming the Holy Land. Their ruthless, clandestine methods are slowly chipping away at our forces. A man cannot sleep at night for fear he'll never wake." He stared into the fire, the hellishness of it all seizing his heart again. "Too many nights I slept in my armor, ready for an attack."

Margaret threaded her fingers through his—gentle, feminine fingers, soft as pure silk. He never wanted to release them.

Colin blinked. "'Tis all in my letters. If they still exist, you can read them."

She scooted toward him. He closed his eyes and inhaled. Oh how he'd missed her sweet bouquet.

"Not one reached me. Who would…?" Her mouth dropped open. "Do you think…?"

"Aye. The bastard you were about to marry had something to do with it for certain."

Her brow furrowed. "But he always tried to protect me."

Colin smoothed his other hand over her fingers. "So he could lay his hands on Campbell lands."

She sat erect. Her eyes probed his, as if the realization of the ruse had sunk in. "I cannot fathom how he could be so deceptive, so dishonest. Why, I think Effie suspected he was the one who'd been stealing our cattle."

He squeezed her hand tightly. "Turned cattle thief, did he?"

"I'm not sure, but when I told Ewen about a problem we were having with the odd missing beast, he offered to set his man to the task of ferreting out the thief. Later, he only told me he'd found the culprit and that was the end of it." She drew in a stuttered inhale. "I thought him a champion."

All she had to do was say the word and Colin would barrel out into the night and kill the fly-bitten swine. "Blackguard," he growled.

But she held fast to Colin's hand, raising it to her chest. "Thank God you arrived before I went through with the wedding. I tried to put it off for years, but Ewen persisted." Her eyes rimmed red. "He tricked me and took advantage…" A tear slipped from the corner of her eye.

"There, there," Colin said, sliding his arm around her shoulder. "That cur will be caught and punished." *On my oath.*

She swiped her hand across her face. "'Tis all so overwhelming. Forgive me."

Colin nuzzled into the green silk at her temple that held her hennin in place. "There's nothing to forgive. With no word from me in seven years, I'm surprised you held out this long."

"I wanted to hold out forever…but the boys…and the keep." She bit her bottom lip as if to stop herself from saying more.

"I could not have built a finer castle myself."

He kissed her temple again. *Sugared lavender.* Only Margaret could smell as sweet. Lowering his gaze to her mouth, he bowed his head and caressed her lips ever so gently. 'Twas a simple kiss, but it sent a shiver across his skin.

Margaret smoothed her hand over her chin. "Do you think we could trim that awful beard?"

He threw his head back, a rolling laugh burst from his gut. "I've grown rather attached to it."

"Rather, it has grown attached to you."

"I would like nothing more than to be groomed by your capable hands, wife."

***

Colin here at last? She still could scarcely believe it—and none too soon. Praise God, her prayers had been answered. Why on earth was she so nervous? Her fingers hadn't stopped shaking since the moment she'd realized it was he. How crafty his disguise had been.

Aye, his grizzly appearance was a tad barbaric, but did nothing to allay his rugged good looks. Perhaps shaving him would put her jittery nerves at ease. Every night Margaret yearned for Colin's touch, and now she was like a virgin again, unsure what to do or how to show affection. Heaven help her, she'd nearly married a ruthless scoundrel.

The more she considered it, the tighter her chest became. With all her heart, she wanted to show Colin how much she loved him. The annulment papers came to mind. She shook her head. *No. Colin would not be here if he had intended to proceed. I will not think of those vile documents again.*

She took a step toward the adjoining door. "I'll fetch my shears."

When she pushed into her chamber, the heavy air lifted and her mind cleared. Margaret pressed her palm against her chest. Colin had come home. Again tears stung her eyes while she dug in her basket. Would he ever forgive her for trusting Ewen? She would do everything in her power to prove to Colin her loyalty and love.

Taking a deep breath, she pushed through the door. He'd moved to the chair and had his back to her. If possible, his shoulders had grown even broader in his absence. Perhaps fighting nonstop did that to a man. His dun locks had been trimmed to his nape, and they glistened blond in the firelight. The man's stature was so magnificent, Margaret would wager he could turn lead to gold.

When the door closed, he turned and smiled. *Colin's smile.*

Her knees wobbled like boneless limbs.

"I was afraid you might be feeling too tired," he said.

"How could I be tired on an eve like this?" She crossed the floor and slipped her arm out of its sling.

He tapped the splint ever so lightly. "You mustn't jostle it."

"'Tis splinted, and I only need to use my fingers. I'll do most of the work with my right."

"Are you sure you'll not do further damage?"

"Aye. A fortnight and Alana says it'll be as good as new." She held up the shears. "Are you ready?"

His eyes sparkled with a wee bit of humor. "I have only one request."

"Aye?"

"Remove that ridiculous headpiece."

She laughed, reaching back to pull the pin securing her constricting veil in place. "The new styles are rather garish." In one tug, the conical contraption fell to the floor. "Oh my. I am clumsy with one hand."

He pulled the snood from her head and her hair cascaded to her waist in a messy heap. He fingered a lock. "One-handed you are far more graceful than any swan."

"You embellish the truth, and I thank you." Again she held up her shears.

He raised his chin and gazed into her eyes. "Trim me close, my love."

Colin need say not another word. Her heart melted. His deep voice still vibrated within her breast. *My love. Can he truly forgive me?*

Margaret forced herself to steady her hands. As she stepped in, the alluring fragrance of musk and spice enveloped her. With each snip, Colin transformed until she trimmed the hair from his left cheek.

She gasped and lowered her hands. A deep, jagged scar had been hidden by his whiskers. "My word. What happened?"

"Bloody hell." He brushed his fingers across the mottled pink skin. "It has been concealed for so long, I'd nearly forgotten. This was caused by a splinter from my own ship—right before it sank."

"With each word, your crusade gets worse." Margaret knitted her brows and examined the deep scar. To think he'd been so close to death.

"Pardon my vulgar tongue. I've been too long away from the finer sex."

"'Tis not that." She trimmed the last bit of scraggly beard and smoothed her hands over the closely cropped beard that remained. "I...I never want to be separated from you again."

Colin grasped her waist with a firm hand. Margaret's blood rushed hot through her veins. She'd scarcely felt a thing when Ewen touched her, but all her husband had to do was focus his gaze upon her and she was enslaved.

His fingers clamped into her flesh. "I want to hold you in my arms forever."

She grasped his wrists and dropped to her knees. "Can you forgive me?"

"There is nothing to forgive." He tugged her up and gently set her on his lap. "I don't want to cause your arm pain."

"My body is tingling so, I doubt I could feel pain this night."

He placed a finger on her lips and slowly trailed it to her chin. When he reached her neck, gooseflesh coursed across her skin. He hesitated for a moment, his gaze dipping to her breasts. "During all my time away, I lived as a monk." He closed his eyes. "I feel as trepid as a virgin."

She shuddered. "As do I."

"You didn't?"

"Nay. Not once."

"God, I love you."

"Kiss me, Colin."

Dark, soulful eyes met hers, wounded with atrocities she could only imagine. The longing in them was physical, profound. He lowered his gaze to her lips and dipped his head. Margaret's womb inflamed with longing. His lips brushed hers lightly. His tongue slipped out, and she opened her mouth to receive him.

Tasting of whisky and male, his mouth crushed over hers. With a rumbling groan, his fingers sank into her back and kneaded. Margaret clamped her good hand around his neck, holding on for her life. His ardent kiss ignited a bone-melting fire that raged through her blood.

Against her buttock, he lengthened. Her body responded with desire. Her breasts ached for his touch. She ground her hips into him. Oh God, she could feel passion again.

Another deep rumble filled her mouth.

Utterly possessed by him, Margaret whispered, "Make love to me."

**

When her sultry voice expressed the words he'd dreamed of hearing, Colin forced himself not to rip the gown from Margaret's body and take her like a barbarian. He'd abstained for so long, he clenched his stomach muscles to restrain his base desires and mount her like a stallion rides a mare. Besides, he could cause no further injury to her arm.

"I want to do this right," he forced out.

She nodded and stood. Turning her back, she pulled her thick tresses around her shoulder in an unspoken request to unlace her gown. He rose. Thank heavens she had her back turned and couldn't see his trembling fingers fumble with the ribbon. Colin needed to cool his blood, act like a man of four and thirty.

With every tug of the laces, a little more of her scent ensnared him. She'd been bound so tight, he wondered how she could breathe. When at last he pulled the ribbon free, she inhaled deeply. Warmth from her body caressed his face. He ran his hands over her shoulders, her long neck prone to him. He inhaled her intoxicating scent and fluttered kisses along her nape.

Her billowing skirts brushed the tip of his cock. His eyes rolled back, but it wasn't enough. Colin pushed the gown from her shoulders, sending it to the floor with a whoosh.

He hesitated, but she uttered not a complaint. The gown's wide sleeves did not constrict her wounded limb.

He slid his hands down her narrow waist and pulled her hips against his. A luscious, soft woman's bottom teased him through her thin linen shift. He need only lift it up to slide into her from behind. He licked his lips and pressed harder.

Margaret seductively moved her hips. If she did that again, he'd spill in his braies. He eased away, and she turned, her green eyes dark, her lips red. Her mouth parted. She unlaced the front tie of her shift and slipped it from her shoulders.

He was afraid to move. Her beauty had Colin so entranced, if his cock met the slightest friction, it would erupt. Her breasts had enlarged since he'd left, her tummy more rounded from birthing John, no doubt. But the added curves made her even more alluring.

She looked wantonly, facing him wearing only her hose and slippers. Swallowing hard, Colin knelt to untie her garters. Holy Mary Mother of God. The floral bouquet of her sex hit him between the eyes. His cock strained, demanding to be set free. He worked quickly to untie the ribbons, remove her shoes and tug down her hose. Mouth completely dry, he regarded the triangle of chestnut locks that hid her treasure.

As if she could hear his thoughts, she opened for him. The air flooded with her scent. His tongue darted out and lapped her. Moaning, Margaret thrust her hips forward, opening her sex to him. He spread her wider with his fingers and swirled his tongue around her sensitive button. She rocked against him, and ran her fingers through his hair.

He slid a finger inside her slick, wet core. She mewled, her thighs quivering around his face.

"Don't stop." Her voice hoarse, incredibly erotic.

Colin took her cue. He slid his finger faster while his tongue relentlessly licked.

Margaret's breathing sped until she gasped. Her body stiffened, then her thighs convulsed with earth-shattering quivers. Crying out, she came undone in his mouth.

Clenching his gut against his urge to release his seed, he continued to lick until her breathing ebbed.

She tugged at his shirt. "Now you."

Chuckling, Colin stood. "I'll not have you using that arm."

"But…"

He scooped her up and carried her to the bed. Gently he rested her atop the pillows.

"I want to undress you," Margaret persisted. "Here I'm completely bare, whilst you remain clothed."

Colin tugged off his shirt. "I'll remedy that fast enough."

***

As she reclined on Colin's bed, Margaret's insides still pulsed. Her inhibitions and fears fled. She wanted Colin to see her naked, and more so, wanted to feast her eyes upon his flesh. When he discarded his shirt, she bolted upright. Another ugly pink scar slashed across his powerful frame.

"Goodness, what happened?"

"'Tis nothing."

"Did your armor not protect you from such a blow?"

"I had no armor."

Margaret traced her finger along the jagged wound— trailing from his right chest, it marred his well-toned flesh all the way to his left hip. "Why?"

"'Twas when I escaped from the filthy Turkish dungeon."

With every word, the atrocities he'd experienced unfolded. How long had he been imprisoned? What was it like? How did he escape? Margaret pushed these questions from her mind and kissed the puckered flesh. She ran her lips down every painful inch, her insides tearing, her heart bleeding for him. Reaching his hip, she pressed her cheek against his warm skin. "What can I do to take your pain away?"

He smoothed his hand over her head and grasped a lock of hair. Raising it to his nose, he inhaled and closed his eyes. "To hold you in my arms again is all I need, *mo leannan*."

She unbuckled his belt. He kicked off his shoes and removed his hose. Wearing nothing but his linen braies, Margaret stared at his manhood straining against the thin linen. She reached for them with her good arm and tugged, but she only managed to expose part of his hip.

Grinning, he helped her push the undergarment to the floor.

Margaret's breath stuttered. "It has been so long."

He crushed her in his arms and kissed like a man starved. His tongue danced with hers, his hard body plying her flesh. The thick column of his manhood jutted against her mons. The coil of hot desire filled her again. But this time she must have him inside her.

His kiss eased as he cradled her in his arm and pulled back the bedclothes. With one arm, he lifted her and set her atop the linens.

Colin crawled beside her, kneeling. Carefully, he placed her injured arm on a pillow. "Are you sure we should do this?"

"Aye." She panted. "I need you to join with me and become one. I cannot wait much longer."

He pushed between her legs and kissed her. Gradually, he lowered his body until his manhood caressed her hungry flesh. Sparks sizzled deep inside her womb.

"I'm dangerously close to spilling my seed."

"We have a lifetime ahead of us." She grasped his shaft and guided it to her entrance. His groan thrummed through her fevered womanhood. "I want a daughter this time."

He thrust deep and pulled back. His breathing sped with every plunge. He filled and stretched her, rubbing the spot that would send her to the stars. Margaret bucked against him, mewling uncontrollably. His scent enveloped her. His cock filled her. Every inch of skin craved more until she froze at the pinnacle of ecstasy. In one earth-shattering burst, she pulsed around him. "Colin, oh Colin. I will love you forever!"

With a roar, Colin thrust and exploded within her. His body shook with his violent release, his breath coming in staccato gusts.

After, Margaret rested in the crux of Colin's arm. She floated like in a dream, tickling her fingers over his powerful chest. She grasped the charmstone and rubbed its polished surface. "It looks untarnished after all you've been through."

He grasped it together with her fingers. "Aye, I daresay the legends are true. I could have died any number of times, but your charms remained with me."

"Then it truly is a precious heirloom which must continue to protect our family throughout all generations."

"We shall cherish it and see our kin does as well." Colin sighed and wrapped Margaret in his arms. "At long last, I can sleep soundly with you nestled by my side."

Chapter Thirty-Eight

Tromlee Castle, 3rd August, 1462

Colin hated to leave Kilchurn the next day, but he could no longer allow his men to act in his stead. Argyll had come to fetch him, and together they rode onto the neighboring lands. Tromlee was but an hour's ride—an ideal location from which to prey upon a grieving lady and her vast estate.

Colin had killed more men than he could count, but never did he have a yen for it. Today, however, he not only wanted Ewen MacCorkodale's blood, he wanted complete ruination of the man and his clan.

The Black Knight's men guarded the curtain wall and gates, weapons at the ready. No one said a word when he rode beneath the portcullis. Not a soul filled the cobbled courtyard. Even the blacksmith's hammer had been silenced.

Dismounting, Colin faced Maxwell. "Where is he?"

"Bound and under guard in the solar on the second floor. His men are all contained in the pit."

Colin nodded and marched into the dank, moss-covered keep, with Argyll on his heels. He clamped his hand around the hilt of his sword. One clean swing and he could behead the fobbing traitor.

He clenched his jaw so tight his molars ached. He'd force himself to adhere to Margaret's wishes. She'd borne the worst of it.

Arriving at the solar door, he nodded at the sentry to open it.

Ewen MacCorkodale's fear permeated the room like shite. Colin slowly slid his dirk from its scabbard and stepped up to the cur. He'd like to cut the bastard's bindings and face him down right there, man to man...but that was not what Margaret wanted.

Instead, Colin stood beside him and watched the sweat trickle from his brow. "Uncomfortable, are you?"

Ewen stared ahead. The coward jolted when Colin used his dirk to cut the gag from his mouth. Then Ewen had the gall to smirk and stretch his jaw.

Colin smoothed his blade along the swine's neck. "The pieces of the puzzle fall into place at last. You were the mind behind Walter's treachery. You have always tried to swindle me and take what's rightfully mine." Colin pushed the blade hard enough to break the skin. "Why?"

Ewen leaned his head away from the weapon. "Ye are arrogant. I fought alongside you to rid Scotland of the Douglas threat, and to whom did the king award lands?"

Colin smirked. MacCorkodale had brought up the rear and cleaned up the carnage whilst Campbell men fought the battle. *And he reckons he's entitled?* "Funny. I didn't see you beside me when I stormed the keep."

"You always were too proud to give a care for those who stood behind you."

"I beg to differ," Argyll said.

"'Tis the earl spewing off for you now, is it?"

Colin frowned at his nephew. He'd handle this. "You took advantage of a woman. Where are my letters?"

Ewen looked sideways. "Burned." He chuckled. "Every one of them."

Argyll stepped in. "What happened to the messengers?"

Ewen smirked. "I couldn't allow them to walk away, now could I?"

Colin slammed the bastard's face with the hilt of his dirk. "You murderous, milk-livered coward."

Blood streamed from the corner of Ewen's mouth. He lowered his gaze and licked.

Pacing the room, Colin worked to calm his boiling blood. When finally he'd regained his composure, he faced his quarry. "Lady Margaret requested leniency, though I cannot say I agree." He sheathed his dirk. "Out of respect for her wishes, Argyll will fit you with irons and drag you to Edinburgh. If you survive the journey, you will stand trial in his majesty's court."

Ewen blanched. Fitted with irons, once found guilty, it would be easy for the king's men to hang him from the battlements alive. It could take weeks for him to die while the crows pecked at his flesh. Colin could live with such a verdict.

Good.

"I will petition for your lands to be stripped and passed to the Campbell clan." Colin snatched his dirk and buried the blade into the table. "And then I shall think on you no more."

A stream of sweat bled from Ewen's temple. "You cannot do this to me. No respectable chieftain should be disgraced by irons—"

Argyll and the guard muscled the traitor out of the room.

Colin balled his fists against his urge to murder MacCorkodale here and now. "Aye, no *respectable* chieftain should."

Ewen's bellows echoed down the passage. Colin sat in a chair and rested his head on his hand.

"What shall we do with the others?" Maxwell asked, stepping inside.

"They're all murderers and backstabbers. Hang them." Colin stood and opened the cupboard. Had a single letter survived?

"Pardon, m'lord." A serving maid stepped in, holding a leather satchel. "Are ye looking for your missives?"

Colin snapped up his head. "You know about them?"

"Aye. I couldn't save them all, but I hid those he didn't burn straight away."

Colin strode forward and took the satchel from her hands. "Why did you not spirit these to Lady Margaret?"

"I hoped I could one day." She lowered her gaze. "He's my laird. I didn't know all he'd done until now." She hid her eyes with her hand. "I cannot read. I'm ever so sorry."

Colin placed a hand on her shoulder. "'Tis nay you who needs to be punished. It was brave to come to me. I thank you."

***

Sitting on the floor in Colin's chamber, Margaret held a kerchief to her face as she read Colin's letters. She could not make it through a whole missive without shedding tears, each passage more impassioned than the next. If she had but received one of these, she never would have allowed Ewen MacCorkodale to become so close.

She steadied her breath and read aloud. "...*Every night when I return to my cot, I think of you. Memories of your winsome smile, your tenacious spirit and the way our love grew deep roots during our short time together gives me solace. Without you, I would not be able to withstand the misery that surrounds my every waking moment...*"

Taking a deep breath, she fanned herself with her hand. "I cannot believe not one messenger made it to Kilchurn."

Colin sat beside her, twirling a lock of her hair around his finger. "Ewen intended to claim our lands and sell you out. Duncan and John would have ended up with no inheritance. He'd already had the deeds drawn. He only needed to marry you."

Margaret wanted to scream. "He promised he would recognize the boys' birthright." She wailed into her kerchief. "I cannot believe I was thus deceived."

Colin rested his hand on her shoulder. "At last 'tis over, and our boys are well protected."

With these missing letters combined with her horror of finding the annulment papers, Margaret could withhold her questions no longer. Through bleary eyes, she stared at the missive in her hand, the penmanship declaring undying love. "When I thought you dead, I unlocked your document box and found annulment papers." She dared glance at his face, his eyes expressing shock and the horror similar to how she'd felt on that day. *He truly does love me.*

Shaking his head, Colin held up his palms. "I must explain—"

She placed her hand in his. "There is no need."

"But you must know. I thought I'd destroyed those documents. I-I drew them up in haste shortly after we'd arrived in Dunstaffnage." He pulled her onto his lap and smoothed his hand over her hair. "Oh, Margaret, my love, I was so confused. Once I'd learned what a loving soul you are, and the enormous talents you possess, you would have had to move heaven and hell to make me sign them."

Margaret blinked, and a tear slid down her cheek. "After reading these letters you wrote, with all my heart I believe you."

He nuzzled into her hair. "Ah, lass. You are so fine to me."

She dabbed her eyes and reached for the next missive, filled with a tale of woeful pain and suffering. "Will the Turks never stop?"

"They are an evil force. The Arabs war with each other as much as they do with the Christians." He shook his head. "Their beliefs are as strong as ours."

"Will Christendom prevail?"

"The infidel may march into Jerusalem, and they may crush the Hospitallers, but no one can take down the power of Rome."

She folded the vellum in her hands. "Are you certain?"

"All of Europe will be at war if they try."

Margaret placed her hand on Colin's arm. "Please promise you will never go back."

"War is for a younger man." He kissed her cheek ever so tenderly. "Besides, I could nay again leave your side."

She returned his kiss. "Thank you."

The door opened and she scooted aside, beckoning the lads. Giggling, Duncan ran to Colin and John to Margaret.

"'Tis time for the evening meal," Duncan said.

John wiggled onto Margaret's lap. "I'm famished."

"What shall we eat?" Colin arched his brows with a devious glint in his eye. He pretended to bite Duncan's foot. "Laddie toes?"

Duncan squealed. "No!"

Laughing, John darted toward them. "We'll eat Da's nose."

"My nose?" Colin grasped both boys and wrestled them to the ground, gnashing his teeth with a huge grin. "I'd much prefer younger meat…bwahahahaha."

Margaret laughed, watching Colin roll on the plaid rug with his sons. *This is how it should be.* Finally a family again, their boys would grow into great men in the shadow of the honorable and powerful Black Knight of Rome.

The End

Author's Note

This work of fiction is loosely based on the legend of Colin Campbell, the First Lord of Glenorchy. I found a few different accounts of this legend during my research and tried to pull the most important facts from each. Per the Black Book of Taymouth, Colin Campbell, First of Glenorchy, was also known as the Black Knight of Rome (or Black Colin of Rome), and it is believed that he participated in three tours in the Crusades. Though he was married four times, I only mentioned three wives in this story. His last two wives were Margaret Robinson and Margaret Stirling, respectively, and I could not discern for certain which one was responsible for the building of Kilchurn Castle, thus I took literary license and chose Margaret Robinson.

After they were married, Colin was called away by the Pope for this third and final crusade. It is believed he spent most of the seven years away with the Knights Hospitallers (The Order of St. John) on the Isle of Rhodes fighting the Ottoman Empire. As legend has it, Ewen MacCorkodale did try to woo Margaret during the seven years Colin was on crusade. Ewen intercepted every missive from Colin to Margaret and killed the messengers. Margaret was unaware of Ewen's treachery and only agreed to marry him when it appeared there was no hope for Colin's return.

The tokens were mentioned in every version of the legend (though one represented a broken ring, and the other, two rings). The charmstone still exists today and is housed at the family estate at Taymouth.

When Colin was called away shortly after their marriage, Margaret was left to build the keep and raise Duncan. The genealogy charts I used aren't clear on the date of John's birth, but the lad did grow up to become the Bishop of the Isles.

Also, for those who might wonder, Glen Orchy is a glen in Argyllshire, and is two words. The title, Lord of Glenorchy is one word, thus the different spellings in this book.

Excerpt from Amy's Next Release:

A Highland Knight's Desire

Highland Dynasty Series ~ Book Two

Coming March, 2015

Chapter One

Melrose Abbey, January, 1478

Before she knelt, Meg stole a glance behind her. A silent sigh slipped through pursed lips. As he'd promised, her tenacious guard wasn't standing at the rear of the nave watching. She had a number of things she wanted to accomplish on this pilgrimage, most importantly, gaining an audience with the abbot. After pleading nearly the entire two-day journey from Tantallon Castle, she'd convinced the guard to allow her a modicum of freedom—at least within the walls of Melrose Abbey.

Out of the corner of her eye, a bronze cross flickered. It sat atop an altar in a quiet aisle chapel. Meg tiptoed over. She'd have complete solitude there.

Kneeling, she folded her hands and gazed at the cross. She'd prayed endlessly for guidance, but presently her mind blanked. She closed her eyes. Ah, yes...

Firstly, thank you for our safe passage, and thank you for all my blessings...aside from my unruly red hair and my claw of a hand, but we've discussed that hundreds of times. I'm well aware Arthur will be unable to find me a suitable husband. I must take matters into my own hands…Well, give them over to you, God. That's where I belong, serving you. Please help me gain an audience with his holiness, the abbot that I may make my wishes clear and take up the veil…

Someone tapped her shoulder. She glanced up. A pair of white-robed monks stood behind her.

"Come," one said.

Meg's heart fluttered. Had her prayers been answered so quickly? "Are you taking me to the abbot?"

They exchanged glances. "Aye," the tallest one clipped. A jagged scar etched the side of his cheek.

Meg eagerly stood and gestured for them to proceed. The corner of the shorter one's mouth smirked. They were an odd pair, indeed.

Single file, she walked between the two men. The tallest led her straight to the rood screen concealing the choir. Abruptly she stopped and clapped her hand to her chest.

The shorter one waved her forward with a flick of his wrist.

"I cannot." She kept her voice low. "I've not yet taken the veil."

The taller monk frowned, stretching his scar downward. He clamped his fingers around Meg's elbow, his grip a bit forceful for a monk. "You must pass this way to meet the abbot." He whispered so softly, Meg could hardly discern his words.

She drew her arm from his grasp and inclined her head toward the entry. If this was what God intended, then she'd proceed. Surely, she would commit no sin entering restricted holy ground for the purpose of declaring her wishes to become a novice.

Crossing through the ornately carved rood screen, Meg walked into the dim choir where only monks who had taken the vow of chastity, poverty and obedience were allowed to worship. The walls were lined with two tiers of choir stalls where each monk would pray from lauds to compline. Their footfalls loudly echoed up to the vaulted ceiling.

A poke in the back caught her attention. The leader had already moved through and held open a thick wooden door. Meg understood the impatient look on the man's face. She'd seen the same expression from her brother a hundred times before. She hastened her pace. Why was there never enough time to stop and admire her surroundings?

Stepping outside into the frigid air, she shielded her eyes from the sun. "I'm surprised the abbot is aware I'm here. I hadn't yet made a request to meet with him."

Neither man said a word. They'd spoken to her earlier, so they mustn't have taken a vow of silence. Was this an area of the abbey where no one was allowed to speak? Were they near the sacred tomb where Robert the Bruce's heart had been laid to rest—yet another thing to which Meg wanted to pay homage on this her first pilgrimage.

She quickly scanned the surrounding garden. There were no graves at all. The monks sped their pace yet again. Arriving at a doorway leading through the cloister wall, the shorter stepped beside Meg and grasped her arm. "We'll be taking a detour, miss." This was the first time the stout monk had spoken.

Miss? The daughter of a Scottish earl, Meg's respectful courtesy was "my lady".

Something was awry.

Meg's mind clicked.

Her blood turned to ice. *English*. No mistaking it, this man had an English accent.

"Release me." Meg dug in her heels and yanked her arm away. Her heart flying to her throat, she shuffled backward and raised her skirts with trembling hands.

"Help!"

Gasping in short bursts, Meg sprinted toward the abbey.

Footsteps slapped the mud behind her. "Bloody hell, Isaac…"

A hand clapped over her mouth and another around her waist. Meg struggled, kicked, scratched, anything to break free. In the blink of an eye, the stocky monk hauled her outside the abbey curtain walls. Not a soul in sight, three horses stood tethered at the tree-line edge.

Screaming through the brutal palm clamped over her lips, she kicked and thrashed her entire body until the imposter brutally slapped her across the face. Recoiling, Meg's feet touched ground. She shrieked and tried to run. Fingers of iron held her in place. A gag filled her mouth while unforgiving hands bound her wrists.

Scarred Monk grabbed Meg by the waist and hefted her onto the horse's back, belly first. Before she could right herself, the short one lashed another rope around her wrists and tied her hands to her legs under the horse's barrel.

Margaret cried out through the coarse cloth biting into her mouth. She jerked her arms, only to pull her legs under the horse. Her body slid sideways awkwardly. *God in heaven, why are they doing this?* Her gaze darted from side to side as she tried to scream louder, only to be muted by the foul-tasting gag.

The men mounted. One tugged her horse's lead and raced away at a gallop. Meg clamped onto the horse's short hair while her gut thumped into the unyielding gelding's back. Her heart raced faster than the hoof beats. Her chin slammed into the steed's barrel repeatedly— until stars crossed her vision.

End of Excerpt from A Highland Knight's Desire

Other Books by Amy Jarecki:

Scottish Historical Romances

Highland Force Series:

Captured by the Pirate Laird

The Highland Henchman

Beauty and the Barbarian

Return of the Highland Laird

Highland Dynasty romances coming in 2015:

A Highland Knight's Desire, March

A Highland Knight to Remember, May

Highland Knight of Rapture, July

Pict/Roman Romances

Rescued by the Celtic Warrior

Celtic Maid

Contemporary Romances

Virtue

Chihuahua Momma

Visit Amy's web site: www.amyjarecki.com

If you enjoyed *Knight in Highland Armor*, we would be

honored if you would consider leaving a review.

~Thank you!